MY LADY, THE SPY

BARBARA DEVLIN

Copyright © 2015 Barbara Devlin

Published by Barbara Devlin
The Brethren of the Coast Badge is a registered trademark ® of Barbara Devlin.
Cover & Interior art by Wicked Smart Designs
EBook ISBN: 978-0-9858548-4-3
Print ISBN: 978-1-945576-88-1

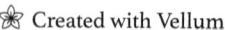 Created with Vellum

DEDICATION

This book is dedicated to my courageous little sister Tina Castillo. Thank you for always smiling patiently whenever I announce my next great endeavor. You cheered through the sleet and biting winds of an exceptionally cold January day while I ran a marathon. You stood proudly as I donned a uniform and entered law enforcement. You held my hand when that career ended abruptly due to a line-of-duty injury. You cried happy tears as I married the man of my dreams. No matter what I do, you're always there, and I'm so grateful for you. All my love, Hurley.

To my best friend Dee Rowell. You are the Ethel to my Lucy. You'd give the shirt off your back to help a friend. Your constant reassurance and endless strength has given me the confidence to look adversity in the face and offer it a crude hand gesture in return. Don't know what I'd do without you.

To Jeanne Adams and Leah Grant, talented writers and my Sultry Sisters. You were with me at the inception of this series, and your comments and criticism were priceless. We had more fun plotting and drinking, drinking and plotting. I owe you a debt I can never repay.

To Jax Crane, web designer extraordinaire, and Lyndsey Lewellen, amazing graphic artist, for bringing my vision to life. To Stacy Boyd, for giving me the best advice of my writing career. I am forever grateful. And to Cheryl Ferguson, for reminding me just how much I love to write.

Last but not least, to women in law enforcement, everywhere.

Can Dirk accept
that his Ladylove
and the Spy
exist as two sides
of the same coin?

PROLOGUE

The Ascendants
England
The Year of Our Lord, 1312

So much had changed in so little time, and in some ways his tiny stone cell had offered a measure of security he now lacked. In one minute, Arucard was locked in White Tower and a prisoner of the King, and there was no uncertainty in the four stone walls that defined his world, as well as his limitations. In the next instant, he wore the insignia of a knight of the realm, he enjoyed the Crown's favor, and he was betrothed, and there was naught certain about any of the accompanying responsibilities, as freedom could be a double-edged sword. It was the last aspect of his newfound status that gave him the most concern and left him wondering if it might have been easier to have burned at the stake, because he bore a specific stigma as a cross, and he knew not how to resolve the flaw in his character prior to his wedding.

Telling himself there was naught wrong with a thirty-two-year-old-virgin, Arucard decided he had no worries—unless, of course, he was the virgin in question. As a Templar Knight, he had no interest in or use for women. In fact, he had taken a vow of celibacy on the same day he joined the order, because only the most chaste knights could ascend to the glorious hereafter. But the Templars were no more, and his tenuous position in England necessitated a marriage to protect those for whom he was accountable and to prove his loyalty to King Edward.

And as he suspected, it had been five years since he fled the Continent with his fellow warriors of the Crusades. Five years since the Templars had been hunted, tortured, and killed during Philip the Fair's Inquisition. Of an estimated two thousand knights, only five persisted, as far as he knew. Five Templar mariners—all remained wanted men by the king of France.

The mantle in his grasp bore the familiar red cross centered on a field of white and matched the modest, unadorned cloak that was the standard attire of his once great knighthood. How he had worn the uniform with pride, how he had cared for the pristine fabric as though it were a second skin. In a sense, it had been a part of him, a part of his identity, every bit as much as his own flesh. Yet it could define him no longer. With a flick of his wrist, he sent the garb to join the other clothing that burned brightly in the fire.

After a healthy gulp of ale, which he needed, he studied the badge of the Brethren of the Coast, the fledgling order formed by his new master, a price paid to accommodate the fighting men without a home. The seal, fashioned of gold, featured a wind-star design, a large blue diamond at the center, and the Latin phrase *Nulli Secundus*, Second to None, as was their motto.

The bejeweled piece was similar to his current uniform in its splendor. His fur-lined cloak and rich blue mantle festooned, haphazardly, with gold braids violated the tenets by which he had long existed. As a Templar, he had been taught that unnecessary excess led to immorality. While he understood that his survival in a foreign land, his allegiance to a foreign king, and his union to a creature, who for all intents and purposes was foreign to him outside the maternal realm, required equally foreign customs, he kept his hair cut short and his face clean-shaven, true to his Templar ascendants. And despite the King's generosity, Arucard much preferred the simple, understated clothes.

"I found it," Demetrius stated proudly, as he pulled up a crude wooden stool and sat before the fire, whither the men gathered to toast—or rather roast Arucard's impending nuptials. "My grandsire wrote an oath when first he entered the military, and I am certain it is contained within these pages."

"What is so important about an old oath, brother?" Geoffrey shifted his weight, as he peered at the antiquated log.

"History," Morgan responded as he neared. "We are the last of our generation and the first of our kind. Never again will the Knights Templar sail as Templars, but neither will we sail quietly into the night, shrouded in deceit and disgrace. We shall live on as the Brethren of the Coast."

"Precisely." With a snicker, Aristide clutched a pitcher and refilled the goblets. "And we must never forget from whence we came."

"Especially as we face the future." Given fate posed a far more dangerous prospect than his past, Arucard lifted his chin and sighed. "And all of its uncertainties."

"When do you wed?" Morgan made a pitiful attempt at

concealing a smile, and Arucard had the sudden urge to punch him in the nose, as his brothers found sport in his predicament.

"Tomorrow," Arucard replied, as a chill settled in his chest, and he fought nausea. "In the morrow."

"So soon?" Geoffrey rolled his eyes and whistled in monotone. "Have you seen her?"

How had he known to expect that particular query? Arucard shook his head. "I have not."

"Thine is a precarious situation, brother." After flicking through the pages, Demetrius abandoned his search momentarily and raised his goblet. "Better you than I."

With a grin, Aristide ventured to ask, "Do you, perchance, know her name?"

"Isolde," Arucard replied with a shuffle of his feet. "She is the daughter of a nobleman, or some such."

"Oh, no. Not a pampered princess." Unaware that he had just voiced Arucard's chief concerns, Morgan frowned. "As it is safe to assume she has not seen you, let us hope she has a sense of humor."

"Let us hope she can cook," Geoffrey said, as he tore a piece of bread from a loaf. "As we are at your command, and Demetrius has quite the appetite."

"Let us hope she is fair," Arucard corrected. "Else all shall be for naught, for I will sail to the end of the Earth to escape her."

His response garnered a chorus of laughter, and, for a scarce second, Arucard's spirits lightened. Yet the fact remained he was trapped in an arranged marriage he neither wanted nor welcomed.

"How many babes do you intend to get on her?" Oblivious to the discord he had just wrought, Demetrius flipped through the torn pages of the mangled tome. "Five or six?"

"Babes?" And so Arucard returned to the plight foremost on his mind, as he swallowed hard. Before he could beget children, he had to learn how to copulate. While he was not ignorant of the physical requirements involved in the primitive act, he had no clue how to please a woman, and London was filled with dissatisfied ladies, as evidence by the unwanted attention he garnered during dinner at court. "I-I have given it no thought."

"Well, you had better think about it." With an arched brow, Demetrius cocked his head. "And what will you do should the damsel fall in love with you?"

Flames crackled, and Arucard gazed into the blaze.

Love?

A violent shudder rocked his frame, as he considered the daunting prospect. Although he was quite familiar with the brotherly love upon which his knighthood was founded, he was entirely unfamiliar with the emotion as defined by the relationship between a husband and a wife. Naught on the battlefield could have prepared him for such a predicament. He was a Templar Knight, a creature of habit, and a no-nonsense man who preferred an equally staid existence. In the end, he knew only one way to live.

Pray.

Eat.

Weapons practice.

Repeat.

Then retire.

And there was no vacancy for a woman.

"Brothers, I fear we have secured our freedom on very hard terms." With a terrible grimace, Morgan scratched his cheek. "Very hard terms."

"I fear we shall all be expected to wed," Geoffrey added.

"Not on your soul," Demetrius said with an air of cold determination.

"Never." Aristide pressed a clenched fist to his chest. "I should sooner end my own life than take a wife. Regardless of what the English believe, no one shall convince me, not even the King, that a matrimonial commitment is worth eternal damnation."

Perchance now was not an appropriate time to tell his brother knights that, indeed, the King had commanded just that, Arucard pondered in silence. The shock of his imminent nuptials had yet to wear thin, and the road ahead would be paved with similar hardship and resignation, he suspected. His marriage to Isolde was just the beginning.

"Found it!" Demetrius stood, clutching the tattered captain's log. "Gather round, brothers."

In desperate need of distraction, Arucard extended a hand, palm down, and his fellow Nautionnier Knights followed suit, one atop the other, forming a tight bond forged of blood, flesh, and bone. "Brothers, we have fought the good fight, but we have lost the first skirmish. Yet, despite those who would wish otherwise, we survive. Mighty England is now our home, and her King is now our commander, but our destinies belong to us, and we shall not sink into the annals of history, remembered only by our dishonor. From this day forward, let it be known that the Templars remain, though mayhap by another name. We are the Brethren of the Coast. As our Heavenly Father is my witness, in times of war and chaos, we will be revered and feared."

A roar of concurrence erupted, and from the surrounding woods the strident cry of some nocturnal beast echoed in agreement. Amid a crescent of oaks, beneath the stars, by the light of a fire, the Knights of the Brethren proclaimed their own oath. It was a promise written by men long dead but not forgotten.

Love, honor, and devotion were the beginning of our Order. Bonds of kinship and friendship, all-important. We uphold these principles embrace for embrace, desire for desire, for one, for all. For King and Country we stand, for love and comradeship we live.

CHAPTER ONE

The Descendants
France
April, 1811

*D*eath came in a matter of seconds, and it chose a beautiful, star-filled night. In the silver glow of moonlight, the blood staining the front of her peach silk gown, and oozing between her fingers, appeared black as soot from a chimney.

"Oh, Colin. I am so sorry." Voices echoed in the distance, and *L'araignee* peered into the darkness to check the vicinity. "I never should have left you alone."

Amid the blooming rose bushes heralding the advent of spring, the renewal of life, another life had ended. The head cradled in her lap had once sported a boyish expression that melted many a female heart. Now, with his face eerily devoid of emotion, she bent and kissed the only spot on Colin's forehead not covered with blood.

"I will avenge you, my sweet angel." Despair was a bitter

pill, and *L'araignee* clenched a fist and swallowed a sob. "I swear it on the graves of my parents."

A search party drew nigh, and she had to depart or risk a similar fate.

Yet it was so hard to let go.

Her partner would be buried in an unmarked grave, with no ceremony, prayer, or eulogy offered. And no mourner would shed a tear.

Because no one grieved the death of a spy.

"Over here. *There is someone over here!*"

"I will cry for you, and I shall carry your memory forever," she said in a whisper. For the last time, she caressed his cheek and eased his head from her lap. She pressed her fingers to her lips, and then touched his cold flesh. "Be at peace, my darling."

Rustling in the bushes brought her up short.

"You there, stand fast," an unknown male ordered.

"I think not," *L'araignee* stated softly below the interloper's earshot.

In a flash, she ran behind a tall hedge to a hailstorm of protestations. Ah, a garden was an excellent hiding place. After eluding her pursuers and gaining a measure of safety among the topiaries, she doffed her gown, slippers, and undergarments and rolled everything into a tight ball.

Quickly, she dropped to her knees and crawled beneath the thick canopy of a thorny shrub, which opened countless tiny cuts in her flesh. Ignoring the burning sensation, she smeared handfuls of damp earth on her skin as camouflage. When footsteps approached, she covered her mouth, because the slightest gasp could betray her location. Through the foliage, she counted five rows of buttons on a hussar-style waistcoat and bit her lip. The man was a member of General Bonaparte's *la Garde impériale*.

And *L'araignee* was in trouble.

If Bony wanted her, she had been well and truly compromised.

Fear shivered down her spine. She saluted the disconcerting reaction and set it aside, because now was not the time for hysterics. She had to get to a safe house. Had to make a run for the Belgian coast. If her communiqué had reached London, Colin's friend, a trusted ally, should be anchored offshore.

Dirk Randolph would take her home.

Information of utmost importance had to be delivered to the Ministry of Defense and the Counterintelligence Corps. What she possessed was vital to national security, and she could not fail in her duty.

Colin had died for what she knew.

There was a traitor to the Crown in their ranks.

The situation was urgent, and she had to move. With the stealth and skill of a seasoned agent, she slipped between row upon row of ornamental trees and bushes in the elegant garden. Conversation ahead halted her flight. With nary a sound, *L'araignee* shimmied on all fours and sheltered in the underside of a large holly. The pointed leaves snagged her hair and the bundled clothing.

"I thought I saw someone come this way."

From her vantage, several pairs of hussar boots appeared on the path.

"Well, there is no one here now." The guard kicked a small stone. "Get some privates from the infantry, and have them dig a hole for the body. I am returning to the ball."

L'araignee sat still for several minutes. Despite inclinations to the contrary, she remained calm and patient. An ambitious military man could be lurking in the vicinity, in hopes of making a name for himself at her expense. It was an old trick; one she knew well.

"You are so very sly," she whispered to herself. "But so am I."

She waited a tad longer.

Muffled footsteps caught her trained ear, and she shook her head and smiled.

They would not catch *L'araignee* that night.

STANDING on the quarterdeck of the *Gawain*, Dirk Randolph, third Viscount Wainsbrough, folded his arms and sighed in frustration. Thus far he and his crew had eluded enemy detection, but their luck could not hold out forever. For three nights, he had anchored off the Belgian coast, and still there was no sign of Colin or his partner in espionage, a notorious spy known as *L'araignee*, The Spider. Only Colin and a select group of high-ranking members within the covert Counterintelligence Corps knew the identity of one of the most accomplished operatives in British history. Dirk wondered if possession of that secret had put Colin's life in peril.

The urgent dispatch his friend had sent to London via emergency channels requested immediate extrication, regardless of exposure, for himself and *L'araignee*. Yet there had been no elaboration, no explanation. And for an agent of the Corps to risk discovery, something had to be dreadfully wrong.

A burst of light appeared on the beach.

Two quick flashes followed in succession.

"Captain?"

"I see it, Mr. Scott. Gather a small, armed accompani

ment." Dirk smiled as he pondered a reunion with his roommate from his years at Eton. "All hands about ship, off tacks and sheets, and prepare the jolly-boat. Bring our countrymen aboard safely."

The second in command dipped his chin. "Aye, sir."

As a knight of the Order of the Brethren of the Coast, an elite group of mariners descended from the Templars, Dirk had been born into power and privilege. With that power came awesome responsibility, which was never lost on him. A Nautionnier Knight, like his father before him, he served the Crown in silence, and there were never any accolades, no applause, for a job well done. As always, his mission was one of extreme danger and was pertinent to the national defense effort.

Dirk checked his timepiece and then navigated the companion ladder. On the main deck, he paced. Finally, the familiar sound of oars slicing water brought the crew to the larboard rail. His men assisted the returning sailors, and his first mate turned to help a cloaked figure.

A lone cloaked figure.

While the jolly-boat was secured, he studied the diminutive silhouette shrouded by a hooded black cape, the traditional uniform of the Counterintelligence Corps, and tried but failed to ignore the implications. Since Colin stood at a hearty six-foot-two, Dirk knew that person could not be his friend.

That was the enigmatic *L'araignee*.

"Welcome aboard the *Gawain*." He extended a hand. "I am Captain Randolph. My orders are to provide safe passage to England and deliver you directly into the custody of Sir Ross Logan at the Ministry of Defense."

The palm that settled in his was soft and delicate, decidedly feminine. "Are you Dirk Randolph?"

The voice matched the hand.

Despite his surprise, he nodded. "At your service."

"I have something for you."

She drew back the black hood, and a pair of velvety brown eyes met his gaze. Filled with soul-stirring sadness and raw vulnerability, her potent stare struck him as a punch to his belly, and he wondered just how much ugliness of war she had seen. He searched his mind for something to say, a bit of comfort to ease her worried expression, and opened his mouth.

"You are a woman."

And he was a blooming idiot.

At his clumsy exclamation, Dirk expected her to laugh, or at least smile, but she had done neither.

"Yes, Captain Randolph, I am a woman." Her brow furrowed. "Well, I was when last I checked."

Dirk chuckled, but she had not responded, in kind. "I was anticipating a man," he admitted however late.

"Yes, I am a rarity in my occupation." She whisked a stray tendril from her heart-shaped face. "My sex is an asset that is often underestimated or overlooked in my profession."

My God, was it truly possible? A lady spy? "May I assume you are the operative called *L'araignee*?"

"You are correct." She freed a gold chain from her neck and offered it to him. "Colin wanted you to have this. He told me I could trust you with my life."

"On my honor, I will not betray your confidence." He accepted the jewelry, recognized it in an instant, and frowned.

A miniature reproduction of a shako plate dangled from the chain, and Dirk had seen it many times. The embossed brass insignia of the 68th Light Infantry was similar to that worn on a military uniform hat and bore the rank of lieu-tenant, to which Colin had risen before transferring to the Counterintelligence Corps. Although he enjoyed the intrigue and excitement of the Corps, Colin had been a lobster, naval-speak for red coat, at heart and had, therefore, kept the miniature next to his.

Though suspicion nipped at his heels, and cold dread permeated his chest, Dirk had to ascertain his friend's fate for his report. "What of Colin?"

"He is gone." Her voice was bereft of emotion, as if she were commenting on something as droll as the weather.

His insides twisted at the prospect of never again seeing his old friend. "Are you sure?"

"Yes." She sighed. "I was with him when he passed."

"A pity that. He was a good man." Dirk studied the spy with sad eyes, but her ghostly demeanor belied no hint of her character.

She averted her gaze. "He was like a brother to me."

"Ship, sir." The call came from the tops. "Three points off starboard."

"All hands make sail." Drawing on years of seamanship, Dirk quickly assessed the situation. Given the primary objective of his mission, he could not expend the consider-able effort required to take the French vessel as prize.

"What are you going to do?" the operative inquired.

"Run like smoke'n oakum. Sharpshooters to the tunnels." Dirk sprang into action. "Kill the lanterns and ready the guns, but stand fast until she is close enough. Mr. Scott, escort our guest to my cabin. All quiet on deck."

The crewmen worked quickly to douse the lights and then assumed their stations. The only sounds heard were the raising of the lower deck ports and the guns being prepared to engage the enemy. A thunderous roar signaled the battle had commenced, and the first shot landed short of the starboard bow. Water sprayed over the rail, and the *Gawain* shuddered beneath his feet.

"Hell and be damned, her captain must be wet as a scrubber," Dirk cursed. "Mr. Scott, get to your post. Miss—"

"Rebecca."

"Right." He grabbed her by the wrist. "Rebecca, you are with me."

The beautiful agent in tow, Dirk stumbled his way to the quarterdeck. When the ship heeled hard a-larboard from an additional premature blast, evidencing an inexperienced foe, he hugged her close and shielded her from a rush of ocean water. She appeared frightened, and he guessed that she might never have endured a sea skirmish. To her credit, the spy remained in his wake as he took a position at the wheel and evaluated the tactics of his imbecilic opponent.

"Wonderful. The blasted greenhorn has her full and by." The French corvette approached, and he signaled a tar to hoist the colors. "Come up with the wind, Mr. Hanson. Have your men brace aback the mizzen topsail."

"Aye, sir." The boatswain conveyed the appropriate orders, and the middle watch scrambled into the rigging. Soon, a blustery gale filled the main topsail, and the *Gawain* soared atop the waves.

"Are you out of your mind?" At his side, Rebecca folded her arms, and then unfolded them. "We are headed straight for it."

"Do not worry." His fingertips itched, his muscles flexed, and the thrill of action burned in his loins. Dirk checked his bearing and chuckled. He was a Nautionnier Knight, and he was bloody well enjoying himself. "I know precisely what I am doing."

The enemy kept their topsails to the mast, which was

another fatal mistake indicative of an incompetent leader. Tension mounted, and a third adversarial barrage overshot the target. He glanced at his guest, and she inched closer. Dirk prayed she would not scream.

"Are you all right?"

Rebecca indicated the affirmative but said nothing.

"Good." They were coming into range, and his heart pounded in his chest. Nerves charged, and he shuddered. "Cover your ears."

"What?"

"Sharply, men. Aim for the main. *Fire!*"

As the volley sounded, the *Gawain* reverberated from the recoil, and the spy with sad eyes jumped. The roar of the guns was deafening, and he had intended to spare her the shock. When she stumbled forward and clung to the quarterdeck rail, she glanced at him, mouth agape, from over her shoulder. In any other circumstance, he would have offered comfort and support, but there was nothing he could do at the moment. Dirk held his palms to his ears, and she arched a brow then followed suit.

"Hold positions. *Fire!*"

The second assault scored a direct hit and toppled his opponent's mainmast.

"Stand fast, boys. *Fire!*"

A blaze burned in the lower ports and provided a fortuitous distraction, and his men continued to attack the French warship until they passed the stern.

"Mr. Hanson, lay all topsails aback and spring her luff."

"Aye, Cap'n." As before, the bosun repeated the order, and the middle watch made the necessary adjustments to the rigging.

The new tack brought them parallel with the enemy vessel, and Dirk clutched the helm. "Fire at will!"

Additional shots came in a rapid salvo, and the lethal broadside devastated his adversary's hull. If the foolish captain were lucky, he might be able to limp to France.

"Well done, lads. Cease fire. We have done enough damage, and she will not bother us again on this voyage—"

The spy with sad eyes flew into his arms and buried her face in his chest. Just as fast, she withdrew and checked herself. With a hand at her throat, and the other fisted at her bosom, Rebecca bit her lip.

"Forgive me, Captain Randolph." She was breathing heavily as if from overexertion. "I meant no offense."

"None taken." He took a single step forward, and she took a single step in retreat. "Are you injured?"

"N-no. I am fine." The agent hugged herself. "In my years of service, I have never observed a sea battle, as most of our transports tend to avoid the usual lanes. It is quite different from my work."

"I imagine so." Dirk turned and gathered his charts in an attempt to cool his blood and calm the curiously live cannon in his crotch. Hell and the Reaper, he had not suffered such an affliction since he was a giddy schoolboy at Eton. "Mr. Scott, an extra portion for every man."

"You hear that, boys?" The second in command smiled, as cheers erupted from the waist of the main deck.

After completing a few course corrections, he dispatched his first mate to prepare accommodations for his guest and relinquished the wheel to the helmsman. Standing as official escort, he ushered the spy to his quarters. As they passed the galley, he inquired if she were hungry and offered her food. To wit the operative politely declined his hospitality. At the entrance to his cabin, he opened the door and handed her over the threshold.

Lightning fast, she rotated on a heel. "Captain

Randolph, I am not here to entertain you while we sail to England."

"I beg your pardon?" She could have knocked him over with a feather.

Rebecca lifted her chin to impressive heights. "I have no intention of spending the night in your bunk."

"Is that so?" Her posture reminded Dirk of his mother, and he laughed. "Then we are in agreement, because I do not intend for you to spend the night in my bunk."

"Oh?" She appeared to relax, and it seemed that his statement had defused what was shaping up to be a prime temper. "Then why am I here?"

After securing the door, he leaned against the oak panel and set hands on hips. She was a veritable spitfire. "Because I was expecting a man."

"And that makes a difference?" Her eyes sparked.

"It does to me." No one, not even his first mate, had ever spoken to him with such fervent fortitude, especially aboard his ship, and he decided he liked it.

"Forgive me, Captain, but I have been on the receiving end of some rather salacious proposals from men tasked with my protection."

"So you leapt to unsupported conclusions woven from whole cloth?" Poor thing seemed so contrite that he could not resist teasing her, even though he would love to offer her a salacious proposal or two.

"I misjudged you." Rebecca walked to his dining table, pulled out a chair, and slid to the seat. "My sincerest apologies."

"None necessary. Normally, when I carry members of the Corps, they sleep in the fo'c'sle with the men, so as not to arouse suspicion." Wary of another outburst, Dirk strolled to his desk and retrieved a bottle and a couple of glasses from the bottom drawer. "I am certain that a woman of your intelligence understands why I cannot allow such an arrangement? At the very least, it could cost me a member of my crew. And I am equally positive Logan would not appreciate having his star employee treated as one of the boys. Care for a brandy?"

Rebecca yawned and rubbed her eyes. "Yes, thank you."

"You look tired," he said as he poured the amber intoxicant.

"I am positively spent." She accepted the glass he held for her and took a sip. "You see, I have been on the run for three days."

"Sorry to hear that. I thought to have you wait here while my men empty a cabin we currently use for storage." Dirk pulled out a chair and sat opposite his fascinating guest. "The prior owner of this ship often traveled with his family, and the room functioned as a nursery, or so I was told. It is not much but will afford you some privacy."

With something between a sigh and another yawn, the agent said, "I truly regret causing so much trouble, Captain."

"Again, no apologies required. Would it place my head in peril if I asked you to call me Dirk?" He studied her delicate frame that seemed to bear the weight of the world. "And what is your full name, if you are at liberty to tell me?"

"You make sport of my offense, and you forgive my poor manners. My, what a charming host." She tucked a wayward lock of hair behind her ear. "Since I have been exposed, and my life is currently in your hands, I cannot see the need for secrecy. It is Wentworth—Rebecca Wentworth."

Eyes narrowed, Dirk propped his elbows on the table and rested his chin in his hands. "Not Lord Calvert's sister!"

"One in the same," the spy declared haphazardly, as though she had just imparted a new sewing technique.

"Good God." Disbelief rang in his ears. "And Lucien approves of your chosen occupation?"

"My brother knows nothing of it."

He fell back in his chair and dropped his hands to his lap. "How could he not?"

"It is simple, really." Rebecca shrugged. "Lucien is a lieutenant in the Royal Navy and serves Captain Collingwood aboard the *Intrepid*. When in port, he busies himself with endeavors characteristic of a man his age, to which I am sure you can relate, and believes I am a lady of leisure."

"A lady of leisure?" Dirk choked on his brandy. "So, is your contribution to the war effort an attempt to avenge the deaths of your parents?"

The minute he asked the question, he wished he could take it back.

With an expression of unutterable sorrow, the spy simply said, "My reasons are my own."

A knock at the door preceded the first mate's entrance.

"Cap'n, the cabin is ready."

"Thank you, Mr. Scott. That will be all." Dirk stood and considered the unusual noblewoman. Dress her in the latest confection, coif her hair in the most recent fashion, and she could pass for a blushing debutante at Almack's.

But not tonight.

The liquor had worked on her in ways he had not intended, as she had deteriorated from weariness to unqualified exhaustion, wilting as the delicate petals of an exotic rose that had thirsted too long for water, and he had to help her up. "Come, my dear. You need rest."

"Walking me to my room, Captain?" She clutched his elbow. "Are you always so noble?"

"You may depend upon it."

Still no hint of humor.

"And here we are." His was no grand gesture, as her accommodations were next to his. "Do not feel as if you must take breakfast with the first watch. I would consider it a personal failure if you did not think yourself a guest aboard the *Gawain*."

"Thank you, Dirk." She crossed her arms in front of herself. "I bid you a pleasant rest."

"And I you." For some reason he could not fathom, he reached for her hand and pressed on her knuckles a chaste kiss. A subtle gasp, barely a whisper, passed her lips, and he smiled. "Goodnight, Rebecca."

Dirk returned to his quarters and stretched out in his bunk. Staring at the timbers, he envisioned the brown-haired spy with melancholy eyes sleeping in the adjacent chamber.

Lady Rebecca.

How well he knew her history, but never in his wildest dreams would he have placed her in her current predicament. Because her father had been a member of the peerage and a military man, the family tragedy still circulated in the smoking rooms at White's.

Rebecca was the youngest child and only daughter of Dawson Wentworth, fifth Earl of Calvert, and her mother had been a citizen of France. They were visiting relatives in the Loire Valley when fighting broke out in Nice, in 1796. In the riots of revolution, the earl and his wife had been murdered. Rebecca and her older brother Lucien, under the protection of their nanny, had escaped the mobs and fled to England.

Rolling on his side, Dirk pondered what might have

happened between the time her parents were killed and the present. Who guarded her, and why had she been allowed to join the Corps? Romantic illusions aside, she should never have been permitted to trade in espionage. It was not decent work for gently bred ladies of character, and he had not wanted to contemplate what she had seen and done in the process.

As a Knight of the Brethren, he had participated in a brief counterintelligence scheme. The mission was dirty, unglamorous, and dangerous, and the experience had left an indelible mark on his conscience and wounds that had yet to heal.

A strangled, feminine cry brought him alert.

Dirk leaped from the bunk, snatched a candlestick from the table, stormed into the hall, opened the door to her chamber, and charged forth. Prepared to confront a randy sailor, he was surprised to discover the room empty but for its female occupant.

"Colin, I am sorry." She sobbed in her sleep, tossed and turned in her bed.

The depth of her anguish, the intensity of her fear, sent a chill through his body.

"Shh." Quietly, he closed the door and placed the candle on a side table. Sitting on the edge of the mattress, Dirk stroked her hair and told himself not to look at the pair of lovely breasts bared when she kicked beneath the covers. Only a cad would ogle a defenseless woman. "You are safe, Rebecca. I will let no one harm you."

With his thumb, Dirk smoothed the lines that creased her forehead. When he could no longer resist temptation, he shifted and pulled the blanket to her chin. As he whispered reassurances, he studied her cute little nose and rosy lips. Arched brows matched her chestnut hair, and her skin was pure alabaster. Only the occasional soft mumble revealed an inner turmoil.

The lady was a contradiction.

THE SKIES COMPOSED A HEAVENLY collage of blue, pink, and yellow, and sunlight kissed the waves, glittering as countless stars on the ocean. A gentle breeze filled the sails and flapped the canvas, and wooden beams creaked and groaned like an angry giant as the mighty ship rode the water. Standing on the poop deck, Rebecca inhaled the signature scent of brine mixed with kelp.

The bad dreams had returned with a vengeance.

Often the underworld of espionage followed her in sleep. An incubus with many faces had haunted her slumber, and the boyishly sweet image of Colin had joined her cadre of tormentors. With unnaturally crimson eyes, the visage of her former partner had laughed at her, and the hideous squall penetrated her ears even now. In the dark hours, she had run from, but had never escaped, her spectral hunters. While most women her age conjured whimsical heroes bedecked in shining armor, riding to the rescue, Rebecca enjoyed no such fantasy.

Until last night.

"Good morning, Captain Randolph."

"Has anyone ever successfully startled you," he inquired as he joined her at the rail.

"Not unless I so choose." She glanced at her knight and appraised his appearance.

With austere features and amber-colored eyes, the naval man was exceedingly handsome. His thick brown hair was close cropped and neatly combed, his tall frame lean and muscular. Her initial assessment was that Dirk was not one given to excess. The ivory lawn shirt, fawn colored breeches, and polished top boots were as conservative as his lodgings.

In training, Rebecca had learned that private accommodations often mirrored the character of their occupant. The captain's lone nod to luxury was the wall covering of oak. His other intimate effects were decidedly utilitarian. Instead of a bed, a bunk bereft of silk and satin sat in a corner. Cotton linens and a mended quilt draped the mattress. The bathing area consisted of a large bath and a washstand, all sparkling clean. A mahogany desk held pride of place before the stern windows, and a log, maps, and charts were neatly arranged with nary a speck of dust.

Indeed, Dirk Randolph was a man of order. Rebecca surmised that in his life, as in his quarters, everything had its place.

"Is that coffee I smell?" She also detected a hint of soap and shaving foam.

"It is." With a grin, he offered his mug. "Do ladies not favor tea?"

"I would not know, as I have had little time to be a lady." A gull soared in the air, and she traced its path as she sipped the steaming brew and hummed her appreciation. "This is delicious."

"Do you never smile?"

Rebecca choked on the hot liquid.

"I have seen few things in my lifetime that made me want to smile. War is ugly business." She stared at the horizon and tried to ignore the misery of her situation. "Men commit heinous atrocities in their quest for freedom and democracy."

"There you have me, but the war will end some day."

Rebecca recalled Colin's violent demise, and a chill slithered over her flesh. "Perhaps, but a spy never plans beyond the present."

"I suppose I can understand your position. Is that why you expend so much effort admiring the landscape?"

She had misjudged Dirk's acumen. As she met his too insightful gaze, she suppressed her amazement at his correct assertion. "There is something special about the dawn hours. In some respects, sunrise is a rebirth."

"Is that what you are hoping for?" He leaned on the rail and pointed at another gull. "A rebirth?"

How could he read her so well?

"No. Not for me but for our country." The shoreline in the distance piqued her curiosity. "Tell me, Captain, why have we not docked in London?"

"Because I am avoiding the usual routes." Dirk stood upright. "I am carrying valuable cargo and am unwilling to chance another attack."

"Do you believe your mission has been compromised?" The helmsman ascended the companion ladder, and Rebecca lowered her voice. "Have I put you at risk?"

"Lady Rebecca, all of my missions involve risk." He chuckled. "But you are safe aboard the *Gawain*. I trust you slept well?"

"I did." In silence, Rebecca counted to three and lowered the boom. "After you came into my quarters."

A charming blush colored his cheeks, and Dirk shuffled his feet. With the look of a child caught with his fingers in the cherry compote, he said, "My intentions were honorable. You screamed, and I thought a member of my crew had disturbed you."

How chivalrous of him.

In that instant, Rebecca decided she liked Captain Randolph.

"And you sought to protect me?"

"Yes." He averted his gaze then stared into her eyes. "Wait a minute, you were dreaming. How did you know I was there?"

"The well-honed survival instincts of a spy." She shrugged and opted not to temper her response, because she guessed that, for her, with him, polite decorum was unnecessary. "Had I sensed a threat, I would have come fully awake."

Which is why she had not bothered to conceal her nakedness. She had wanted to know how the oh-so-noble mariner would react, and he had not disappointed her.

"And I am not a threat?" Dirk frowned, and his tone implied she might have insulted him.

"No."

"How can you be so sure?" he asked with obvious agitation.

Rebecca smoothed the folds of her black cape and realized she also enjoyed his verbal fencing. "Because I could take you in a fight."

"I beg your pardon?" Hands on hips, he added, "I am twice your size."

"That may be, but I suspect you fight fair."

"Of course." Righteous indignation invested his patrician features. "I am nothing if not a gentleman."

"There ends the lesson, Captain."

CHAPTER TWO

*L*ondon slept as the carriage rocked along the city streets. Cloaked in black wool, Rebecca inched to the edge of her seat and peered at the passing storefronts. How nice it was to be home. Even in the dead of night, with dark windows and empty sidewalks, the heart of the British Empire beat with an intensity that pervaded her flesh and quickened her pulse.

"The Ministry of Defense is closed at this hour." Swallowing her excitement, she eased into the squabs and stared at Dirk. "Where are you taking me?"

"Randolph House."

"Why?" Trepidation mingled with disappointment. Perhaps her gallant naval man was not so honorable, after all. "My brother maintains our family residence. I can stay there."

"Because my orders are to deliver you into the hands of Sir Ross Logan," he said with an air of superiority that grated her nerves. "Until such time, you are my responsibility."

"I see." His proprietary demeanor pricked her pride; she

was not a child. Had the man not realized she was better trained to defend herself than was he? "Tell me, Captain. What happened at Deptford?"

"I beg your pardon?" Though his question implied ignorance, a tick above his right eye betrayed comprehension of her query.

"When we docked." Inhaling deeply, Rebecca summoned her spy instincts. "There was a commotion in the rigging."

"Ah, that." Dirk compressed his lips. "I issued the wrong orders, which necessitated a reversal of my commands."

"Really?" Suppressing laughter, she plucked a speck of lint from her cloak. "Do you do that often?"

"No," he replied without hesitation. "I have not done anything quite so foolish since I was a midshipman."

Though Rebecca suspected he would rather cease her chosen topic of conversation, she asked, "And why did you err tonight?"

"Because my concentration was off." Her would-be-protector adopted a charming pout and vented a groan. "I was distracted."

"And what distracted you?" Had her decision to join him on the quarterdeck diverted his attention and caused his faux pas? Though she had tried not to disturb him, she could not help but stare as he barked directives. Had she been the source of his discomfit?

"Well—"

The carriage came to a halt.

And Dirk all but ran from the equipage.

"We are home," her temporary guardian said as he turned to hand her down.

Rebecca took a single step and froze. "The lanterns—

your servants have been alerted to our presence." She glanced left and then right. "We must leave."

"Relax." Dirk slipped an arm around her waist. "I dispatched my cabin boy with a missive informing my staff of our impending arrival. And my mother is in residence."

"Your mother?" She ascended the entrance stairs, and the front door opened. "You live with your mother?"

"Of course." He gave his attention to a servant. "Good evening, Hughes."

"Welcome home, my lord." A stodgy, very proper English butler bowed.

"Lady Rebecca is staying the night." He passed his great-coat and gloves to Hughes.

"Very good, my lord." The butler accepted her cloak. "I will wake the staff to prepare accommodations."

"Excellent." Dirk cupped her elbow. "We shall wait in my study."

The foyer of the stately Mayfair mansion boasted oak paneling and sumptuous leather wall coverings. And although the entryway had marble floors, the hall sported burgundy carpet, which lent the abode a decidedly mascu-line air. As aboard ship, the dwelling was not extravagant. The furnishings, devoid of flamboyant prints and garish trimmings, appeared of the highest quality, and she surmised that practicality must be a long-running trait in the Randolph family.

Bookshelves covered two walls, and the subtle smell of cigar smoke lingered in the spacious study. While Dirk flipped through a large stack of correspondence, Rebecca perused the titles and was nonplussed to find the discourses confined to sailing, hunting, and fishing tech-niques. Curiously enough, there were neither etchings nor erotic literature. She selected a volume touting the ultimate guide to club hauling and settled into a Hepplewhite chair.

"Did you find something of interest?" her host inquired and perched on the corner of his desk.

"I am not sure," she said while studying a picture of a ship. "Please, do not feel as though you must entertain me. I am capable of occupying my time."

"I am using you as an excuse." Dirk glanced at the mountain of envelopes. "They are invitations, you see. The Season will soon commence."

"And you are not a fan of stale teacakes and weak lemonade?" Rebecca closed the tome that may as well have been written in Greek and set it on a side table.

"I endure the monotony for the sake of my mother and the title." After opening each missive, he placed the engraved stationary in one of two piles. "And you?"

"I have never attended a ball in London, but Colin assured me I did not miss anything of significance." Rebecca slipped off her gloves and inspected the welts that remained from her duel with the thorny hedge. "My occupation requires a low profile, and the Corps does not follow the social calendar. How could I explain a sudden absence?"

"You must have fascinating tales to tell." Dirk pressed a finger to his chin in an affectation of thought that she found strangely endearing. "But, as a woman, would you not prefer to lead a normal life with a husband and children? Have you ever considered leaving the Corps?"

Bloody hell, he seemed so naïve and...so noble.

She would wager her dowry that she could teach him a few things about the world.

"What is normal?" A blaze crackled in the hearth, and she stared into the flames. "I fear my tenure as a spy might never afford me the freedom to marry, much less have babes."

"Has it been that bad?"

The quiet sincerity with which he broached his query struck a chord. It had not occurred to her that someone would deem her wifely material, especially if the same person were apprised of her true vocation. Had the man honestly thought her fit for such a role? Her chest tightened, Rebecca fought uncharacteristic tears and caught him in her sights.

"May I ask a personal question?"

He dipped his chin. "Indeed."

"Why did your butler automatically assume I would be sleeping in a guestroom?"

His mouth fell agape, and the room grew silent as a tomb.

Dirk blinked and tugged at his cravat. "Because I believe a viscount's bed should be saved for his viscountess. Neither would I insult my mother in such vulgar fashion." Dropping a portion of missives on the floor, he frowned. "When I keep a mistress, I lodge her elsewhere."

Good heavens, the captain was a veritable saint.

Shame and regret burned as a lead ball in her belly, and Rebecca struggled to form an apology. A knock at the door gave her pause, and relief washed over her when Hughes peeked inside.

Saved by the butler.

"The lady's chamber is prepared, my lord."

In a rush to escape the mess she had created, Rebecca stood. But her principled host claimed her hand, brought it to his lips, and pressed a chaste kiss to her knuckles. And her knees threatened to buckle.

"Hughes will show you to your room," he said as he

ushered her into the hall. "We shall meet Logan in the morning."

Like a dutiful child, Rebecca followed the butler. Surreptitiously, she studied the paintings adorning the walls of the gallery and noted many resemblances to her host. Once ensconced in her chambers, she blew out the candles, doffed her boots, dropped her cloak, stripped, and slipped between the soft cotton sheets of the large four-poster bed. Staring at nothing, she stretched her arms and crossed them beneath her head. With a yawn, she conjured a mental image of the handsome sea captain with a quiet, unflappable nature.

Dirk Randolph was the perfect English gentleman.

He bowed politely, held open the door, helped her into the carriage, and served as her escort. He treated her with dignity and respect; something she had little experienced from anyone other than Colin in her trade. Such courtesy was oddly refreshing. She felt almost human in Dirk's company.

Yet she seemed out of place in his world.

And in her attempt to fit in, she had resorted to childish teasing. Her question concerning her quarters had been a deliberate attempt to throw him off balance. Other than a momentary lapse of comportment, he had remained stalwart as ever. During her work for the Corps, Rebecca learned it was the quiet ones who usually had something to hide. She wondered what Captain Randolph kept hidden beneath his placid façade.

And then Rebecca wondered why she cared.

Perhaps it was because, like her, Dirk seemed lonely.

"Ho-hum." She patted her mouth, rolled onto her belly, and snuggled up to a cold pillow. A creak tickled her ear, and she came out of the bed in a second. Tiptoeing across the floor, she spied a sliver of yellow light at the foot of the entryway. Rebecca leaned close and listened for the slightest sound of an impending intrusion.

ON THE OPPOSITE side of the oak panel, Dirk held his breath and pressed his ear to the door. There were no shouts of alarm, no cries of horror, and nothing to indicate his enchanting guest was suffering another nightmare. Although he knew he could not stand guard for the remaining dark hours, he hoped only pleasant visions visited the alluring spy while she slept under his roof.

Why it mattered, Dirk could not discern.

Nothing about the intriguing operative, or his reaction to her, made any sense.

But what he steadfastly refused to admit, to himself or anyone else, was that he desperately wanted to turn the knob, enter her room, chase away her demons, and create sweet dreams in her arms.

"LADY REBECCA, it is good to see you again."

Sir Ross Logan, the mysterious head of the Counterintelligence Corps, lifted the beautiful spy's hands to his lips, and Dirk suddenly wanted to hit the man in the face.

"I am saddened by the loss of your partner." Logan escorted her to a chair. "I recruited Colin myself."

"As far as I am concerned, he can never be replaced." Rebecca drew back the hood of her black cloak and sat. "My only hope of avenging his death is to thwart our French counterparts."

"Colin's dispatch provided vague information." Largely ignored, Dirk took a position at her side and asked, "What can you tell us?"

She gazed at him and then directed her response to Logan. "There is a traitor among us."

His face betraying no hint of emotion, Sir Ross rose from his chair, walked to the front of his desk, and sat on the edge before her. "How do you know?"

"Someone slipped a note into Colin's pocket while we attended a house party in Paris. It was crowded, and he did not see the perpetrator who delivered the missive. But the message addressed him by his code name, Eagle. And it demanded that he reveal the identity of the spy known as *L'araignee* or risk assassination."

Perplexed by her contradiction, Dirk scratched his temple. "I thought you never attended the balls?"

With a half-hearted chuckle, Rebecca said, "Colin posed as French *nouveau riche*, and I portrayed his mistress. We circulated throughout the Parisian ballrooms to maintain our cover and gather national secrets. The French generals love to boast of their military prowess." She smiled and batted her eyelashes. "You would be amazed by what you can learn during a waltz, Captain."

At her admission, his mind filled with bawdy images of what she might have done, of salacious acts she could have performed, in the name of duty. How many life and death situations had she survived? What danger had she courted? And what sins had she committed in service to King and Country?

"You are very brave," Dirk replied with sincere admiration.

"When was your first contact?" Sir Ross inquired.

"Shortly after we discovered Massena is planning to attack Wellington at Fuentes de Oñoro."

"*What*?" Shock investing his expression, Sir Ross bounded to his feet. "Have you warned the Ministry of Defense?"

"Not directly. We sent an official communiqué last month, just after Graham's victory at Barrosa Hill, detailing Massena's plans for a counter attack to re-take Portugal," she explained. "Did you not receive it?"

"My God, someone must have intercepted your correspondence in transit. We must get word of this to Wellington and Beresford immediately." Sir Ross snatched a pen from an inkwell and a sheet of stationary from atop the blotter and wrote a few sentences. "Dirk, would you kindly summon Clarkson?"

"Of course." He walked to the door, opened it, and cleared his throat. "Sir Ross requires your presence."

"Aye, sir." The skinny young man in drab attire nodded and jumped from his seat.

"Sir Ross, are you saying you never received our letter?" Rebecca asked, as Dirk closed the distance between them.

Logan narrowed his stare. "This is the first news I have heard in regard to Massena's forthcoming assault."

When the secretary approached, she pulled the hood of her wool cape over her head and faced Dirk. He wondered if the agent feared for her safety even in the confines of the Corps' headquarters.

Clarkson clicked his heels. "You have need of my assistance, Sir Ross?"

"Deliver this at once—in person." After affixing his seal to the envelope, Sir Ross handed the note to his secretary.

"Yes, sir." Clarkson sketched a hasty bow and exited the room.

"Who would do such a thing?" Dirk fisted his hands and shook his head. "Who in our government would deliberately withhold vital war information from our generals?"

"I do not know." Sir Ross rubbed his chin and frowned. "Any number of persons could have seized that dispatch, but only a handful of operatives could have matched Colin with his code name. And another more disturbing and telling revelation is that even fewer agents know of the existence of *L'araignee*. Whoever the traitor is, he must be a high ranking member of the Ministry of Defense, which will make catching the blackguard a tricky affair."

"But I do not believe my true vocation has been discovered." Rebecca propped an elbow on the armrest. "Napoleon's guards did not come for me until Colin had been killed."

"That is a point of fact in our favor." On another sheet of stationary, Sir Ross began taking notes. "Were you able to ascertain the origin of Colin's assassins?"

"Yes, they were French." Her brow furrowed, and she gazed at Dirk. "I am positive they were from the Denis network."

"The Denis network?" Dirk leaned against the back of her chair.

"They are our French counterparts." Sir Ross returned the pen to the inkwell and steepled his hands atop the blotter. "Joachim Denis is ruthless and prefers primitive torture to conventional interrogation techniques. He is an animal with a real taste for the bloody business. We have never rescued a member of the Corps alive from his clutches. Consequently, we have no idea what he looks like."

Dirk shuddered and pinned Rebecca with his stare. "And this man is after you?"

"I believe so," she replied with polite acceptance, as though she had just been invited to tea.

"Bloody hell." He smacked a fist to an open palm and looked at Sir Ross. "What are we going to do about this?"

The head of the Corps reclined in his chair and studied Dirk, then Rebecca, and then Dirk again. "You know, whoever is behind this scheme must have an operative here —in London. And if we are to have any hope of capturing the villain, we shall have to lure him into the open."

Dirk crossed his arms and exhaled a sigh of frustration. "And how do you propose to go about it?"

"The person that identified Colin as a member of the Corps must believe that Rebecca was, in truth, his mistress. Suppose she were to appear in the ballrooms of the ton during the Season. Do you suspect the traitor would attempt to contact her?"

"You are not suggesting we use her as bait?" Dirk dropped his hands to his hips. "She would be in grave danger. She could be killed."

At that moment, the lady in question stood and clutched his elbow. "Dirk, it is all right. I have been a spy these past five years, and I am well aware of the risks. But I am not married and have no children. My parents are dead, and the responsibility of providing an heir lies with my brother, so I have no one else to consider. This is my duty."

"Logan, you cannot let her do this—" In that second, Dirk realized that he, not Rebecca, was the object of interest. Sir Ross smiled, and gooseflesh covered Dirk from top to toe. "What are you thinking?"

"I find your concern for my agent commendable." The head of the Corps chuckled. "Perhaps I have a solution that will serve both our purposes, but I shall require your full cooperation."

Dirk swallowed hard and wondered for what mission he had just volunteered. "I do not follow."

With an unholy grin, Sir Ross lowered his chin. "You know, you two make a lovely couple."

Were he a woman, Dirk was certain he would swoon.

"I beg your pardon?"

"You are a successful nobleman with an impeccable reputation and a sizeable fortune." Logan sounded like a marriage-minded mama on the hunt for a prospective son-in-law at Almack's. "What say you? Has any society miss caught your fancy? Made any promises to a bit o' muslin?"

"Not yet." Dirk shifted his weight and tugged at his cravat. "Why do you ask?"

All trace of amusement vanished as Sir Ross said, "Because I need to know if there is a kitten in your closet that will bare her claws if I send Rebecca on a tour of the *ton*'s ballrooms on your arm."

Dirk opened then closed his mouth. "There is no one."

"Sir Ross, you cannot be serious." Rebecca appeared just as perplexed by the suggestion. "Do you intend for Captain Randolph to court me?"

"In some respects, yes." The head of the Corps nodded. "But I only want him to *pretend* to court you."

Her eyes grew wide. "But—he is not an agent of the Corps."

"Do not be fooled by the elegant attire and polite decorum, *L'araignee*." Sir Ross made additional notations. "Viscount Wainsbrough is no babe in the woods."

Rebecca cast him a side-glance, and Dirk mustered a smile.

She blushed.

He checked the polish on his boots.

"Perfect." Sir Ross pounded the desk. "You have the

smitten lovers look down already. We can circulate a rumor and plant an item in the scandal sheets. Lady Wainsbrough and Lady Calvert were old friends." He stared at Dirk and arched a brow. "Since Rebecca is unmarried, your mother decided to bring her to London for a Season. You will form an attachment, thereby providing an acceptable excuse to remain at her side."

Dirk faced Rebecca. In unison, they blinked.

"Can you manage such a charade?" Sir Ross asked. "Speak now."

"Well—" Dirk choked on his words.

Rebecca clutched his hand. "I suppose—"

"It is possible—"

"We could—"

"Enough." Sir Ross silenced them with a dismissive wave. "I can see you shall get along famously, because neither of you seem capable of forming a single coherent sentence."

"Were my mother and Lady Wainsbrough friends?" Rebecca inquired.

"Does it matter?" Sir Ross shrugged. "So much time has passed since her death, I daresay no one will remember otherwise."

"But, I should think it highly improper for me to reside under the same roof as Viscount Wainsbrough." The charming spy pressed a palm to her bosom. "Will there be no scandal?"

"No," Dirk replied. "My mother will provide a suitable chaperone for the gossipmongers. No one would dare gainsay her or her friends, and her participation will reinforce the image we are attempting to project. Of course, I must enlist her aid and that of my comrades. And I would speak with Admiral Douglas."

"I concur." Sir Ross nodded and returned to his seat. "Admiral Douglas aside, you need to protect Rebecca's true occupation. Tell them she has been serving in the war effort as an interpreter for Wellington. We have used that front on numerous occasions, and it would explain why a traitor suspects she possesses vital information and thus be in grave danger."

"What about my past?" Rebecca asked in a melancholy tone.

"To what do you refer?" Dirk spied the dark shadows looming in her sad brown eyes and cursed his stupidity.

With her hands settled in her lap like the finest lady, she inclined her head. "As I mentioned earlier, I acted as Colin's courtesan while in France. If that aspect of my career becomes common knowledge, my brother and family name would be ruined."

"I dare anyone to cast aspersions on your character." Dirk dropped to a knee before her. "You have my solemn vow that such accuser would meet the end of my sword at dawn."

"You would defend my honor?" Rebecca rested a palm on his shoulder. "Truly?"

Had she so little faith in mankind?

The urge to protect her, to champion her cause, burned as an unquenchable flame, and he met her questioning stare. "With my life."

Her sad eyes brightened. "It would appear that I have a new partner, Dirk Randolph."

∼

THE BRETHREN of the Coast gathered for an impromptu meeting at the home of Admiral Mark Douglas. Dirk's life-

time friends and knights of the Order were in full atten-
dance save one. Blake Elliott, the duke of Rylan, and
Damian Seymour, the duke of Weston were there when he
arrived. Lance Prescott, the marquess of Raynesford, and
Dirk's younger brother, Dalton, followed shortly thereafter.
The noticeable standout was the most recent knight of the
Order, Trevor Marshall, earl of Lockwood, and newlywed
husband of Blake's sister, Caroline.

Whirling in like a waterspout, with a box of cigars
tucked under his arm and a smile stretching from ear to ear,
Trevor beamed with excitement. "Sorry I am late, but I had
to wait for Dr. Handley."

As Trevor closed the door, Blake leapt from his chair.
"Dr. Handley? What is it? Is my sister unwell?"

"I do not think it is bad news, brother." Damian, the
voice of reason, placed a hand on Blake's shoulder. "Nor do
I believe Caroline is sick."

"My wife most certainly is not ill." With a cat that ate
the canary expression, Trevor lifted his chin. "She is
increasing."

"Hear! Hear!"

"The devil you say."

"About bloody well time."

"Knew you had it in you, old boy."

"A little Lockwood."

"I am going to be an uncle."

"Caroline and I would be honored by your presence at
dinner, this evening." Trevor doled out cigars. "We want to
celebrate the impending arrival of a new member of the
Brethren."

"An excellent notion, Lockwood." Admiral Douglas
smiled and nodded at Dirk. "And since we have official

business that requires our attention, let us save our felicitations for tonight."

The mood turned serious, and the Brethren assumed their respective places.

"Now, to the matter foremost on our agenda," said the head of the Brethren.

As Admiral Douglas relayed the information from Sir Ross to the Nautionnier Knights, Dirk studied each face for any signs of doubt. Never had he lied to his family, but the circumstance necessitated desperate measures. He had to put Rebecca's welfare first.

"Wait a minute." Wide-eyed, Lance leaned back in his chair. "You are going to squire Lady Rebecca about as a love-struck suitor?"

"Oh, this I have to see," Dalton said as he held a hand to his belly and burst into laughter. "The poor lass has been saddled with the most boorish lover in the kingdom."

"I do not see any cause for such hilarity, brother," Dirk reproached his younger sibling, whose guffaws only increased. "And I resent your unflattering characterization of my courtship skills."

"So Wellington is employing female interpreters?" Damian furrowed his brow. "Strange, I have never heard that before."

Blast it all, Dirk could ill afford such pointed questions.

"Her mother was French, and she is fluent in the language. Also, I understand Rebecca traveled extensively throughout France and is familiar with their customs." Silently, Dirk prayed he was not visibly perspiring. "I think it highly progressive of Wellington to avail himself of her knowledge and talents without being blinded by her sex."

"Unless Wellington finds her sex an added bonus. The man's reputation precedes him." Dalton hung on the armrest of his chair and waggled his brows. "Do tell, what does our female compatriot look like?"

"Her face is fair, she comes from excellent stock, and her deportment and carriage are of the first rate." Dirk somehow managed not to punch him in the nose.

"Sure you are not describing the latest bit of horseflesh at Tattersall's, brother mine?" Dalton said as he repeatedly flipped a coin. "How are her teeth?"

"You know, any of us could pay court." Blake poured a brandy and offered it to Dirk. "You have already delivered the lady to London, and we would not want you to feel over-burdened. I should be too delighted to donate my services as escort."

"Not by a long chalk!" Dirk bit his tongue on a sharp retort.

Lance winked at Damian.

Trevor elbowed Blake in the ribs.

And Dirk realized he had just shown his hand.

He tried to recover his composure. "I mean...that is to say...Lady Rebecca is a very fine lady. She and I have already been introduced, and she is, at this moment, ensconced in a guestroom in my home. To change things now would only raise undue suspicion."

"Of course it would," Trevor said with unmasked conde-scension.

"Well then, I suppose we have covered everything." With a smirk, Admiral Douglas handed embossed documents to Lance and Dalton. "These are your orders, gentlemen. Due to some recent revelations procured by a member of the Corps, you two are to transport reinforcements and supplies to Wellington's position commencing tonight."

"What about Caroline's dinner?" Dalton asked,

"You will be leaving later," the admiral explained. "As that concludes our business, we are adjourned."

In search of a quick escape, Dirk headed for the door, but Damian blocked his exit. "So, where is your new ladylove now?"

"Shopping," Dirk said with a roll of his eyes. "With my mother."

CHAPTER THREE

*A*ctivity abounded in the merchant district that catered to the cream of London society. Graceful equipages of all makes and models streamed up and down the roadways, and the sidewalks were filled with elegantly dressed gentlemen and women. Like a child at the candy counter, Rebecca peered through the window of a quaint stationary store on Bond Street. Thus far, she had patronized the glovers, the linen drapers, and the milliners.

"So many treasures." She sighed and pressed her nose to the glass. "So little time."

After meeting with Sir Ross at the Ministry of Defense, Dirk had taken her to see the viscountess Wainsbrough. Lady Elizabeth, his mother, had immediately insisted Rebecca address her informally as Beth.

"Come along, dear." The viscountess gave her a gentle nudge. "There is much to be done if we are to get you ready for the start of the Season."

Because the gowns she had worn while working in France were still in Paris, she lacked suitable attire to engage in a courtship with Dirk in front of the *haut ton*. Of course, since she had been posing as a courtesan, her dresses were not what good society would consider appropriate for polite company. So, after a brief visit to Calvert House, during which Beth had declared Rebecca's old clothes too juvenile for a woman of her status, they embarked on a mission to purchase a new wardrobe.

Although she had often procured various accouterments in the line of duty, Rebecca had been forced to confine her choices to those deemed *de rigueur* for a mistress. How she enjoyed buying items that reflected her personal taste and style. And though Sir Ross would no doubt frown on such indulgences, she also acquired scented bath soaps and oils and an expensive bottle of perfume.

"Rebecca, stop dawdling." Beth tugged her wrist. "We must get to the hosiery before it closes for lunch."

"Did you see the engraved papers?" She bit her lip. "Should I not pick up some cards?"

"Why do we not use that as our excuse to shop another day?" The viscountess laughed and handed a package to the footman. "Then we might avoid one of my son's lectures on the merits of economy."

"Do you not share Dirk's...that is, he seems a bit—"

"The word is *cheap*, my dear. And I daresay he inherited his frugality from his father." Beth cast a sly smile as they strolled, arm in arm. "But I have an account of my own, money I stashed away over the years, which I use as I see fit."

Rebecca paused. "Really?"

"Yes." The viscountess ushered her inside the hosiery. "And if you are to succeed with my son, I suggest you do the same."

"But our courtship is temporary," she whispered.

"Sweet child." Beth cupped her chin. "You should let an old woman dream. Now, we must complete your ensemble."

Several shops and a few pokes and pulls later, Rebecca found herself tucked inside the Wainsbrough town carriage, which was loaded with a mountain of packages. Her heart was light, and her reticule was not so heavy. When she entered the foyer on the heels of Dirk's mother, the man foremost on her mind greeted them.

"Good heavens," he exclaimed. "Did you buy out the entire stock of women's finery?"

"We gave it our best effort," Beth said as she handed her gloves to the butler.

"Mama, you are a bad influence—"

"Do not take that tone with me, Dirk Henry Archibald Randolph." The viscountess patted his cheek. "Rebecca needed an entire wardrobe, and you did ask for my help. But I am for a nap."

He followed his mother and paused at the foot of the grand staircase. "When I requested your assistance, I did not intend for you to bankrupt the viscountcy."

"Fear not, my lord." Rebecca doffed her gloves and stepped forward. "I spent my money, not yours. It would have been inappropriate for you to assume the cost of clothing my body. Do you not agree?"

Flushing red to his cravat and, she was positive, beyond, Dirk tugged on his collar. "I-I-I...suppose."

"Wonderful, we concur." She drew nigh and lifted her chin. With their noses mere inches apart, Rebecca said, "Now, I think I shall take a *long...hot...bath*. I bid you a pleasant afternoon, my lord."

As she attempted to exit a splendid scene, he caught her wrist. She canted her head, and he arched a brow. Slowly, deliberately, he brought her hand to his lips and brushed a kiss across her bare knuckles. Inhaling a shaky breath, she swallowed her surprise when he turned her palm up and pressed his mouth to her damp flesh. Pulse points blazed to life, and desire shivered over her skin.

Rebecca feared she might swoon.

With a devastating smile, Dirk released her.

"Enjoy your bath."

The man was a fast learner.

She nodded once and traced the path taken by the small army of footmen that had carried her purchases to her guestroom. Upon entering her chambers, she noticed an envelope propped against her vanity mirror.

"What is this?"

Rebecca picked up the crisp white stationary bearing her name in very precise script. The viscount's seal revealed the author, but not the purpose, of the curious correspondence.

"Why would he write me a letter when we are living under the same roof?" she asked no one as she broke the wax and unfolded the missive.

My Dearest Lady Rebecca,

Please accept this modest proclamation as my formal statement of intent to pay court to your person. You have my word as a gentleman that I shall endeavor to preserve your virtue during our most noble mission for the Crown. I greatly esteem you and am committed to the success of our joint venture.

Your most humble servant,

Dirk, Viscount Wainsbrough

What began as a few giggles soon erupted into a full-blown belly laugh. How predictable, how sensible, how perfectly honorable was her captain?

"So he will endeavor to preserve my virtue, will he?" She wiped a stray tear from her cheek and snorted. "Darling Dirk, you are too good to be true. But I think your virtue is in greater peril than mine."

Rebecca crossed the room and rang for a bath.

While the footmen and maids made the necessary preparations, she rummaged through several boxes until she located a bottle of lavender water. After dismissing the servants, she poured a small amount of the scented concoction into the tub, disrobed, and sank into the fragrant warmth. A knock at the door had her inching lower.

"Come."

"Your pardon, my lady." A squatty-bodied maid with salt and pepper hair entered the chamber. "His lordship asked that I inform you of an invitation to dine with the Earl and Countess of Lockwood, this evening. And your dress was delivered."

The domestic walked to the armoire. "Shall I air it out proper for you?"

"Please, do so." Rebecca closed her eyes and sighed.

"Also, his lordship wanted you to know that he is in his study, should you care to join him."

"Thank you." Smiling, she rested her head on a bath cushion. "Tell Viscount Wainsbrough that I have decided to lie down and will see him when we depart for dinner."

Let the chivalrous knight wait.

"Yes, ma'am." With a quick curtsey, the maid quit the room.

In her mind, Rebecca envisioned Dirk's face and pondered his reaction to her new finery, which happened to be his favorite color, a fact his mother provided without prompt. The burgundy gown cost twice as much as the other selections, but she simply had to have it. The odd

Frenchwoman, who preferred a monocle to eyeglasses, had insisted it was part of another order, and she could not let Rebecca purchase the stunning creation. But she had made the designer an offer no sane person could refuse.

The dress signaled the opening round in a game her spy skills could not have predicted.

Because despite her best efforts, despite her heretofore-vaunted personal restraint, Dirk possessed a mysterious power to stir her blood, assail her senses, and charge her nerves whenever he neared. Her palms dampened, her pulse quickened, the world around her disappeared, and nothing else mattered.

In short, Rebecca liked him.

And it was obvious she affected him, too. The handsome viscount blushed and stammered at her suggestive remarks, which were all in good fun. Although her curiosity could be nothing more than an immature desire to flap the unflappable captain, her competitive nature demanded she enter the arena.

But there was another, more important, motive behind her actions. While she remained confused in regard to his questions concerning her future and prospects as a wife and mother, there was one fact of which she was absolutely certain.

Rebecca wanted Dirk Randolph.

But could he truly want her?

Most noblemen considered a woman with an occupation beneath them. They married ladies of leisure, not female spies. Still, Dirk had planted a seed, one that grew by the minute. And their mock courtship provided the perfect venue in which to explore the possibilities.

Could she forever doff her black wool cloak of the Corps in favor of an ermine collared pelisse?

Could she trade her pistol and dagger for an oriental fan and an opera glass?

Those were questions for which Rebecca had no answer, but she was more than willing to throw down the gauntlet. Thus her sights fixed squarely on the none-too-rakish Randolph.

Let the games begin.

~

THE WHOLE of his frame bristled with nervous agitation as Dirk paced before the fireplace in the drawing room, awaiting the arrival of his mother and Rebecca. But as far as he was concerned, his tremors of excitement and anticipation stemmed from the new mission and had nothing to do with the spy with sad eyes. And while she had refused his earlier invitation, his disappointment with her absence derived from his inability to discuss their next move—not her rejection.

Footfalls in the hall interrupted his thoughts.

"I told Hughes to have the carriage brought around. Your *intended* is right behind me." His mother smiled as she pulled on her gloves.

Dirk rolled his eyes and heaved a sigh. "Mama, it is only pretense for the sake of her safety."

"Perhaps, but let us not abandon the idea." She averted her stare. "Rebecca is a charming girl, and her connections are impeccable."

"Yes, but—"

"Come along." She flicked an entreaty. "We do not wish to be late."

As the dutiful son, he followed her into the foyer and

helped her with her wrap. Although it was spring, the night air was chilly.

"I shall be in the carriage," the viscountess said as she crossed the threshold.

"Fine. We will be there momentarily."

Dirk checked his appearance in the wall mirror and smoothed a stray lock of hair. He straightened his cravat and adjusted the lace cuffs of his shirtsleeves. After consulting his timepiece, he re-pocketed it. The rustle of skirts caught his ear, and he turned to find Rebecca standing midway down the staircase.

And he nearly fell to his knees.

A vision in burgundy silk, she dipped her chin. "Good evening, my lord."

"Your dressmaker has my eternal gratitude." Heart pounding in his chest, he swallowed hard. "May I say you are stunning, my dear."

"You are rather ravishing, yourself." The corners of her mouth lifted.

She smiled.

And an invisible thunderbolt struck him in the gut, sending a wave of molten heat straight to his—

"Shall we?" Rebecca asked as she glided like an angel to his side.

"Indeed." He assisted her with a matching pelisse, then offered his arm in escort and made a mental note to keep his coat fastened or risk embarrassing himself and giving his mother an apoplectic fit.

"I must confess I am a trifle nervous about tonight," she said, blessedly oblivious to his aroused state, as he handed her into the equipage. "Do you mind if I avail myself of your breeches?"

Dirk tripped and fell into the squabs, face first. "I beg your pardon?" he inquired once he assumed his seat.

"I meant as protection." Rebecca hid the bottom half of her expression with an elegant fan.

"Are you all right, my son?" Was the woman who brought him into the world actually smirking at him?

Cursing his uncharacteristic clumsiness in silence, he dusted off his coat sleeves. "I am fine."

Thank God, the Lockwood townhouse was just around the corner.

When the carriage halted, Dirk paid careful attention as he descended. In the entrance hall, he escorted his mother and Rebecca into the drawing room.

"Why is there no receiving line?" Rebecca whispered with a squeeze of his arm.

"This is family." She seemed a trifle confused, and he winked. "No formalities."

While his mother made the introductions, Dirk concentrated on masking his irritation with his fellow Nautionnier Knights, who lingered a little too long over the spy's hand for his liking.

"Come, Rebecca. Let us sit with the women and discuss the latest embroidery techniques." The viscountess indicated an empty spot on a sofa at the center of the large chamber. "While the men enjoy vastly superior conversation detailing the merits of Spanish brandy over French."

The bawdy remarks ensued the moment the fairer sex moved beyond earshot.

"She is a succulent morsel." Lance wiggled his brows. "No wonder you wish to court her."

"Oh, I say." Blake clucked his tongue. "She is a tempting dish."

"Have you sampled her wares, brother mine?" With a

wolfish grin, Dalton flipped his lucky charm. "Tails, how appropriate. The interpreter does have a lovely—"

"One more disparaging comment in regard to Lady Rebecca, and I will permanently box your ears," Dirk stated in a low voice as he clenched his fists. "And stop tossing that infernal coin, else I shall shove it down your throat."

Damian whistled in monotone. "Someone is a tad sensitive this evening."

"Indeed." Rocking on his heels, Blake's eyes widened. "We are only expressing our sincere admiration for your temporary partner."

"We meant no insult," Lance said with the countenance of a saint.

"Gentleman, do not spoil my wife's dinner party, else I shall be forced to hang the lot of you from the *Hera's* highest yardarm. Come, Dirk." Trevor slapped him on the back and led him to the hearth at the far wall. "They are only spouting such nonsense for your benefit."

"I beg your pardon?" With an elbow resting on the mantel, Dirk studied the gentle curve of Rebecca's neck from across the room. "What benefit could I possibly derive from attacks on her person?"

Trevor vented a groan. "You really have it bad, old boy."

"I have—what?" The bodice of her burgundy gown accented her ivory bosom. How he wanted to bury his nose in the valley of her breasts.

"Do you not realize that your behavior is encouraging their rakish antics?"

"What behavior?" Dirk imagined her dark locks splayed across his pillow. "I have done nothing ungentlemanly."

"Then I suggest you stop undressing Rebecca with your eyes before you truly offend Caroline and the other ladies in attendance."

Dirk looked at him, dumbfounded. "Bloody hell, I do not know what is happening to me." Shock shivered deep in his chest, and he met the earl's stare. "Is it possible...can two people...do you believe in—"

"Love at first sight?" Trevor completed the thought with unnerving accuracy.

Dirk almost swallowed his tongue.

"I did not, until I found my wife." With a chuckle, Trevor shook his head. "'Course, it could have had something to do with the fact that Caroline was naked at the time."

Dirk blanched. "That is more than I wish to know."

"Right." Trevor cleared his throat.

He teetered. "I need a brandy."

"Follow me." At a side table, Trevor lifted a decanter and filled a pair of balloons. "Tell me something. Are your palms unusually damp whenever Rebecca is in your presence?"

"Indubitably, as those of an untried lad." And how he resented it.

"Does your heartbeat quicken when she enters the room?" Trevor queried, with a smirk.

"Like a salvo." As it did since they met.

"When you look on her, does it feel as though you were just punched in the gut?" Trevor had posited another eerily relevant question.

"I would describe it as a thunderbolt." And Dirk had been powerless to deflect the disconcerting plague.

"Has the mere thought of her provoked any uncontrollable salutes from your mainmast?"

With Rebecca in close proximity, his Jolly Roger had taken on a life of its own. "*Yeessss*."

"You are done for."

"Bloody hell." Dirk consumed the contents of his glass in one gulp.

"Easy, friend." Trevor whisked the crystal from his grasp. "While brandy might lessen your discomfort, it could dull your faculties, and you will need all your strength for the battle that is to come. And do not even try to convince me that there is not more to her story."

Dirk snapped to attention. "What battle?"

"The game of hearts." Trevor cast him an expression of unutterable pity.

"How can that be? We have only just met." Dirk speared his fingers through his hair. "It makes no sense."

"That is your first mistake." Trevor appeared to have captured his wife's interest. "There is nothing sensible about love."

Caroline glanced at a *chaise* tucked in a dimly lit corner, then peered at her husband.

"Is that a summons?" Dirk inquired.

"You are a quick study." After emptying his own glass, the earl set it on the table. "Do you want my advice?"

"Aye."

"Do not attempt to comprehend the incomprehensible." He straightened his lapels and then slapped Dirk on the back. "Thank whatever benevolent fate placed Rebecca in your jungle, and enjoy the hunt."

Dirk grinned as Trevor and Caroline settled in the far corner. He stifled a hearty guffaw when his fellow knight of the Brethren doused a nearby candle, whispered something in his bride's ear, and she giggled. The dinner bell sounded, and Dirk was positive the host and hostess, their heads together in quiet conversation, would be the last to enter the dining room.

"My lord, shall we go in?"

He gazed at Rebecca and sighed inwardly as his body reacted to her presence. But in light of his discussion with Trevor, he looked on his lady as would a predator assess a much desired prey. With a new attitude, he adjusted his cravat. Perhaps it was time to prowl.

"Dirk, are you not hungry?" she asked with cherubic innocence.

"Oh, yes."

But not for food.

THE DINING ROOM of the elegant Mayfair mansion of Lord and Lady Lockwood echoed with good-natured banter and unrestrained laughter. Bedecked in blue damask and a cream runner, the table boasted fine silver and elegant Sèvres chinaware, which shimmered in the glow of the ornate chandelier.

As the host and hostess argued over the place cards, Rebecca laughed. It seemed someone had moved the lovely countess from the chair at the far end of the table to a seat at her husband's immediate right.

"Blake does not mind sitting there." Trevor ushered his bride to her new position. "I want you next to me."

Caroline folded her arms. "But, it is not proper."

"Darling, this is family." Despite her protests, the earl settled his wife at his side. "And nothing about our family is proper."

"Bloody hell, are we ever going to eat?" The younger Douglas stomped a foot. "I am so hungry I could eat my gloves."

"Do not be so impertinent, Sabrina." Cara compressed her lips. "Mind your manners."

Rebecca studied the Douglas sisters, Cara and Sabrina. They were diametrical opposites, as were Dirk and his spirited, profusely charming brother, Dalton. Blake Elliott, Caroline's older sibling, appeared to share her fiery temperament, whereas Damian and Alexandra Seymour possessed an air of refined sophistication. And the Prescotts, Lance and his quiet cousin and ward, Elaine, seemed painfully shy and reserved. Other than the viscountess Wainsbrough, the elders in the group consisted of Sarah, the duchess of Rylan, and Admiral Mark and Lady Amanda Douglas.

After the decadent five-course meal, Trevor offered a toast in honor of his wife and their impending arrival. Rebecca studied each face and gathered mental notations regarding the various personalities, an inescapable habit of her occupation. The expectant mother was radiant, the father-to-be unabashedly proud. But what struck her most was the abiding intimacy and passionate puissance of their familial ties.

Once her brother Lucien had departed for Eton, which marked his transition into manhood, she had fabricated imaginary playmates to keep her company. The invisible companions shared her grief when Frederique, her beloved nanny, passed. They comforted her when her monthly courses first flowed, and they bolstered her confidence and determination as she faced danger and death as a member of the Corps. How marvelous it must have been to grow up amid such a large circle of friends. Never would she have been lonely. They were so candid, honest, and welcoming. Yet Rebecca belonged not in their esteemed presence.

Because she was a liar.

While they imparted personal reflections, she repaid their kindness with deception, and the ruse weighed heavily on her heart and mind. The men had been fed a bit of fiction, and the women, with the exception of the viscountess, welcomed her in complete ignorance. She was a spy, not a debutante or an interpreter for Wellington. For the first time in her tenure as an agent for the Crown, guilt gnawed at her conscience.

"You are woolgathering, my lady."

She gazed at Dirk and mustered a smile. "Your family is impressive and quite unique."

"Indeed, they are." He leaned close and said, "But you will not hold that against them?"

"Of course not." Rebecca claimed the last morsel of a strawberry tart. "I adore them."

"And what of me?" her partner inquired with a devilish grin.

So he was already fishing for compliments? "I have not decided what to think about you."

"Did you get my declaration?"

"You know I did." The simple pattern on the napkin provided a suitable diversion from his penetrating stare. "But I am a tad confused. Why the formality?"

"Because polite decorum demands it."

She traced the curves embroidered on the linen. "And you always do what polite decorum demands?"

"Indubitably." He shifted in his chair. "I am nothing if not honorable."

Across the table, Dalton repeatedly flipped a coin. Just then, he looked at Rebecca and winked.

"Your brother reminds me of Colin."

"He has no shame," Dirk stated in a disapproving tone.

"Perhaps, but he is charming and possesses the gift of spontaneity, which some women find appealing."

"I can be spontaneous."

Good heavens, the man was too easy. "Really?"

"Well, I can when my busy schedule accommodates such unplanned moments."

"I see." Laughter danced on the tip of her tongue, and she searched for an alternate topic for discussion. "Tell me about your relatives. Are you truly connected by blood?"

"Not exactly, but it is a long story."

"Out with it, Dirk." Sabrina snorted. "After all, Rebecca is one of us now."

Suddenly, she found herself in the spotlight.

"Sabrina, do not insert yourself into other people's conversations." Admiral Douglas lowered his chin. "Mind your manners."

The chastised party averted her gaze. "Yes, Papa."

"Oh, please. Do not feel as though you must forgo your usual rituals on my account." Rebecca glanced left, then right. "I should, very much, like to hear the tale."

"Go ahead, Dirk." Blake raised his glass in mock salute. "Enlighten the lady."

"Our five families share a history that dates to the fourteenth century. Our generation came together when Thomas, Elaine's older brother, drowned." His expression softened. "After his funeral, we gathered at midnight and swore an oath of friendship. That vow has stood the test of time, and we remain dedicated to our cause."

"How remarkable." She clasped her hands in her lap. "And what is the oath?"

The room grew eerily silent.

Dirk inclined his head. "That is a private matter."

"We could tell you." Dalton chuckled and tossed his coin. "But then we would have to kill you."

"I understand." Membership in the Corps required

similar loyalty, and Rebecca had taken a pledge of secrecy at the start of her service.

"If you were to marry Dirk, we would make the same vow to you." Tongue in cheek, Alex giggled. "You would be one of us."

"Behave, little sister." Damian arched a brow. "I apologize, Rebecca."

"Why are you apologizing?" Sabrina frowned. "She understands duty and honor."

"Brie, stop inserting your opinions into their conversation," Cara said as she wagged a finger.

"But, it is true." The younger Douglas humphed. "I heard Papa say she is an interpreter for Wellington, himself."

"*Sabrina Francis!*" The admiral steepled his hands atop the table. "Were you eavesdropping outside my study door again?"

"I might have been in the hall at an opportune moment." Sabrina picked at the hem of her sleeve. "Your voice carries, you know."

"I ought to heat your posterior." Admiral Douglas narrowed his stare. "Have you any idea of the gravity of the situation?"

"Oh, yes." Sabrina leaned forward. "If given half the chance, the traitor would no doubt murder Rebecca."

The admiral rubbed his forehead. "Bloody hell."

"Mark, is this true?" Lady Amanda inquired.

"Aye," her husband responded.

Surprised by the unfortunate events, and the chorus of feminine gasps, Rebecca attempted to soothe some raw nerves. "I am sorry—"

"Trevor, did you know about this?" Caroline folded her arms and glared at the earl.

The host cleared his throat and swallowed a healthy gulp of port.

Rebecca peered at Dirk. "Perhaps this is not such a good idea. I do not wish to cause trouble."

"Bother that." Alex covered her plate with her napkin. "You are no trouble. The problem lies with the men. They think women cannot keep a secret."

"Not true, sister." Damian rolled his eyes. "This is dangerous business, and there are lives at stake."

"But you could benefit from our help." Caroline thrust her chin in the air. "While the battlefields of France and Spain belong to men, women rule the *ton*'s ballrooms."

"Darling, I will not risk one hair on your lovely head, not to mention our child." It appeared Trevor could be as stubborn as his wife.

"I will not risk any of you." Rebecca pushed from the table and stood. "I refuse to place you in peril," she said to the ladies. "The traitor is after me. As a servant of the Crown, I must do my duty, but you are under no such obligation."

"Blast it all." Sabrina jumped to her feet. "We are with you, come what may."

Alex rose from her chair. "I second that."

"Third," Lady Amanda stated with a glance at the admiral, as though daring him to countermand her declaration.

The remaining women mirrored her stance.

The men looked on in palpable horror.

"It is settled." The duchess of Rylan lifted a glass in toast. "To a successful endeavor."

And just like that, *L'araignee* gained eight new, albeit unwitting and tad dainty, female partners in espionage.

CHAPTER FOUR

*L*ike a cannon shot, the ever-popular Netherton Ball signaled the start of the Season. In the lamplight, the long queue of carriages cast shadows on the graveled drive. The hum of the string quartet hung in the air as Rebecca ascended the entry stairs beneath the portico of the Palladian style mansion, and a shiver of excitement traipsed her spine as she smoothed the skirts of her emerald silk gown. In an instant, she reminded herself that she was working and tugged at her gloves.

"Nervous?"

"No." Rebecca tilted her chin and gazed at Dirk. Although it was customary for him to escort his mother at public functions until he took a wife, the viscountess had insisted there was no better way to introduce Rebecca to the family than to have her assume the prominent position. "Are you?"

With a smug smirk, he said, "Not in the least."

Despite his assertion, she suspected the contrary. "Then we are as one."

"Indeed." Dirk grasped her wrist and settled her palm

in the crook of his arm. "And I think now is as good a time as any to commence the charade."

"Ah, yes." The anticipation simmering under her petticoats had nothing to do with her assignment and everything to do with the man at her side. Why was she so attracted to her new partner?

"Rebecca?"

Do not look at his lips.

"Yes?"

"If you continue to frown, no one will believe you are in love."

With a flinch, she swallowed hard. "In love?"

"Aye." With a guileless expression, Dirk was devastatingly handsome in his black formalwear. "Else how will I convince the *ton* that you have accepted me?"

She adopted what she hoped was an adequate smile. "Is this good?"

"Too good." He returned the gesture, and her heart skipped a beat.

In the grand foyer, the viscountess, with Dalton at her left, paused. "Are you ready, my dears?"

"I suppose it is now or never." Rebecca clutched Dirk's arm. "Shall we?"

He nodded once and ushered her into the limelight. "All the world is a stage," Dirk said, borrowing the words of Shakespeare, as he handed a card to the butler.

"And we are merely players." She stared into the sea of silk, lace, and gems.

After reading the inscribed names, the manservant stood at attention, and his chest expanded to unimaginable heights. "His lordship, the Viscount Wainsbrough, and Lady Rebecca."

A hush fell over the magnificent ballroom.

Heads turned, hands covered mouths, and eyes grew wide as Dirk and Rebecca entered the fray. Pointed stares pierced her make-believe armor like a thousand bee stings, every whisper rang in her ears, and she stifled the urge to run. What powers had the strangers possessed? Why was she suddenly afraid?

"Are you all right, Becca?"

"Becca?" The informal sobriquet snared her interest and calmed her fears. "I am fine, thank you."

"The family has gathered at the back wall." He steered her through the crush.

Familiar faces came into view, and the countess of Lockwood neared. "What a stunning dress."

"On that note, I shall join the men." Dirk bowed, winked, and struck up a conversation with Lance, who stood on the fringe of the male set.

"How lovely you are, Rebecca." Alex gave her a gentle nudge. "I hope you have at least one more ball gown in your armoire."

"Why is that?" Rebecca inquired in earnest.

"Because we have secured vouchers for Almack's," declared Sabrina with a none-too-girlish back slap.

"Careful, Brie." Cara shook her head. "You might have hurt her."

"No harm done," Rebecca said on a gasp.

"See?" The younger Douglas grinned. "I told you she is tough, just like me."

"Well, I do not know about that." Rebecca clasped her hands to her chest. "So, I am going to Almack's? Goodness, I was seventeen when last I ventured into the Great Room."

"Wait a minute." Sabrina cast her a narrow-eyed stare. "I thought you had never been to a hall or had a season."

"That is correct." Rebecca dipped her chin. "You see, I was seventeen when my nanny passed. She had brought me to London for my come out, and I was permitted to dance my first waltz. But my uncle insisted I return to the country after Frederique died. It seemed he did not wish to be bothered with me."

"How tragic," Elaine murmured, her voice laced with sympathy.

"Well, you have us now." Alex wrapped an arm about Rebecca's shoulders. "We shall ensure you have a stupendous season, will we not, ladies?"

"Please, do not go to too much trouble." Rebecca's hair stood on end as Damian's little sister sported a mischievous grin. "I do not wish to be a burden."

As a child, she'd had few friends and had longed for a sister. But the death of her parents ended that dream and so many more. Never could she have imagined how it might be to form a friendship with a woman—let alone five spirited females.

If only she could truly confide in them.

"I have an idea." Cara peered at Rebecca and arched a brow. "What say we initiate her into our group, in our true fashion?"

Rebecca blinked. "I beg your pardon?"

"An excellent notion." Alex rubbed her gloved hands together. "Do you fence?"

As an agent of the Crown, she had been trained in combat with edged weaponry but, somehow, Rebecca was positive they were referring to the polite gentleman's sport. "No, I do not."

"Just what do they teach you in interpreter school?" Sabrina asked with a grimace of disgust. "Or do you go to school for such occupation?"

Recalling her defensive tactics drills, Rebecca replied, "I am not certain it qualifies."

"You know, we could ask Blake to tutor her," Alex said to Caroline. "Of all the men, he is most proficient."

"And most patient." Caroline nodded her agreement. "I shall check with Mama, but I am sure we could use the ball-room at Elliott House."

"Then it is settled." Cara turned to Rebecca. "Come to tea at Elliott House, tomorrow, one o'clock sharp."

"Tea?"

"Tea." The elder Douglas winked. "And bring suitable attire, if you follow my meaning."

"Excuse me, ladies. But I have come to collect my wife." With a smile Rebecca would describe as devilish, Trevor offered his arm to the charming countess. "Darling, they are playing our tune."

The handsome couple, obviously besotted with each other, made their way to the dance floor. How she envied their unveiled love and devotion and was seduced by the thought of having a man of her own to cherish. Could she relinquish her career for marriage? Trade her spy tools for a chatelaine's estate keys? Although the answers to her queries remained a mystery, Rebecca allowed herself to consider the possibilities.

She leaned toward Sabrina. "What is the significance of this dance?"

"There is no relevance other than to provide Trevor an opportunity to paw his wife in full view of the *ton*." Sabrina rolled her eyes and wrinkled her nose. "And Caroline lets him."

"Pardon me, but I believe this waltz is mine."

As Dirk pressed a palm to the small of her back, Rebecca shivered. "Indeed, it is."

She tried not to ponder the warmth of his embrace as he led her to the dance floor, tried not to anticipate the rippling of his taut muscles beneath her fingertips. But the first whirl in the light of the crystal chandeliers left her head spinning and her senses reeling. Dirk was holding her too close for polite society, but she could not muster a suitable protest. During a turn, they collided with another couple, and her hips met Dirk's.

Good heavens, he had a loaded pistol in his crotch.

Rebecca gazed at her partner through her lashes. He appeared unaffected, seemed almost bored.

"What are you thinking?" she asked.

"I...was...just pondering how much I am enjoying this dance."

Ah, he was not so unaffected, after all.

The warmth of a blush seared her cheeks when he hugged her even closer. "You are scandalous, my lord."

How could he impact her thus?

She was an accomplished spy, and he was a harmless seaman.

"What?" Dirk smiled with cherubic innocence. "We are supposed to be drawing attention to you, are we not?"

"That we are, but I do not believe Sir Ross would approve of your methods." Why was she complaining?

"And what about you?" He waggled his brows. "Do you approve, my dear Becca?"

Oh, how she approved. And she wanted him to—

"Let go of me, you bloody ridiculous fool," Sabrina bit off as she waltzed past while struggling in the arms of a stranger.

"Who is that man attempting to dance with Sabrina?" Rebecca asked, as the younger Douglas wrestled with a very handsome, albeit smug, male.

"Lord Everett Markham." Dirk chuckled. "He is an old friend of Trevor's and the new bane of Sabrina's existence."

"Why is that?" She giggled as the two circled the floor in a manner that could be described as anything but graceful.

"He seems to have a particular fondness for rankling Brie."

"I wonder if that is all he enjoys?" She laughed aloud as the waltz ended, and Sabrina unceremoniously stomped on Lord Markham's foot. When her unconventional friend sped past, Rebecca noted the well masked, but still visible, pain in her expression. "You should check on Brie."

"She and Markham are always fencing, so it is harmless fun."

But Everett appeared transfixed as he stood, motionless, and his gaze trailed Sabrina's flight. Theirs was not harmless fun. "Dirk, go—now."

"As you wish."

While Dirk set course in Sabrina's direction, Rebecca strolled to the terrace doors. A cool breeze wafted inside and invited her into the garden.

A mix of topiaries surrounded a large fountain, and Rebecca opted to explore a pebbled path. In the blue light of the moon, dark shadows sheltered clandestine trysts, and chirping crickets obscured the whispered declarations of lovers. Gooseflesh covered her arms, and she hugged herself as she ventured beyond a hedge.

The subtle scent of roses brought her up short, stopped her in her tracks, held her spellbound, and transported her back to the past, to a previous night, and another garden. With a hand at her throat, and her heart pounding in her chest, she closed her eyes and envisioned a face covered in blood.

Colin.

On a sob, her parents joined the morbid illusion.

"No," she whispered.

"How can you answer what I have yet to ask?"

Rebecca whirled around and discovered Dalton. "What on earth are you doing here?"

"Following you."

Before she could take him to task, Dirk's brother snaked an arm around her waist, pulled her near, and kissed her.

In a flash, she delivered a short punch sufficiently close to an important appendage, which induced him to free her.

"Easy, love." Dalton took a step in retreat. "You should not shut down the business until you have sampled the wares."

"I beg your pardon?"

"Come now. Do not even try to convince me that you are genuinely interested in His Dullship of Wainsbrough." He swaggered in her direction.

"Dalton, you are young and charming." In the silvery moonlight, she noted the hint of a smile and prepared to lower the boom. "Neither are qualities I hold in high esteem."

"Ouch." He halted mid-stride, and his smile curved to a frown. "Do you have to be so cruel?"

"I believe, with you, I do." She chuckled. "But I am equally certain you will have no trouble finding a balm to soothe your injured pride."

He quirked a corner of his mouth. "A kiss would do nicely."

"You, sir, are without shame."

"And usually lucky." Dalton pulled a coin from his pocket and tossed it into the air.

Quick as a wink, she snatched it from his grasp. "I make my own luck, and I suggest you try the same."

With that, Rebecca returned the token and charted a course for the main house. As she neared the hedge, the telltale snap of a twig gave her pause.

"Who goes there?"

"How exceedingly cruel of you, my dear." Blake emerged from behind a large shrub. "You ruined my surprise."

"And that would be?"

"This." He swooped.

The duke was fast but not fast enough.

Rebecca braced an arm against his chest and pressed a thumb into the fleshy spot at the base of his throat. The bold nobleman sputtered and choked.

"You are as bad as Dalton," she said once he released her.

"I beg your pardon?" The obviously offended aristocrat straightened his cravat. "Comparing me to that pup is an unforgivable insult."

"Perhaps, but I am certain you will get over it." With a giggle, she veered left from the path and wound up beneath a pergola in another part of the garden. Peering through the twisting vines overhead, she identified the various star clusters operatives used for navigation at night.

A hand covered her mouth, and an unknown person dragged her behind a thorny bush. Goodness, her would-be Romeo was serious this time. Could it be Damian? Or Lance?

Or, dare she think it, Dirk?

The heel of her shoe caught on an exposed root, tripping her and her prospective amour.

"Bitch."

L'araignee came alert in a flash.

With an elbow, she landed a jab to the ribs of her

attacker, and then stomped on a booted foot. Again, her assailant uttered a terse invective and immediately freed her.

The coat of scarlet cloth, with three rows of lace rounding the small blue cuffs, and gold lace rounding the coat and pockets, was adorned with gilt buttons set at exact distances. Even without benefit of sufficient light, she knew the buttons were ornamented with a sword and truncheon and encircled with a wreath of laurel. Completing the full dress uniform of an Army general was an impressive ensemble of white pantaloons and gaiters.

The man occupying the uniform was equally striking. Thick hair mixed with equal parts of black and grey fell unruly over a broad forehead. Eyes of pale blue, vaguely familiar, surveyed her with palpable dislike, and his patrician features were mottled with anger.

Then the mysterious stranger's stalwart demeanor broke.

"Where is my son?" He pleaded with upturned palms. "What have you done with him?"

"Your pardon, sir. I do not understand." Rebecca trembled and inched back, but she remained focused on her duty. "To whom do you refer?"

"Where is Colin?"

~

AFTER OFFERING Brie some comfort concerning her mysterious set-to with Markham, and summoning Cara, Dirk returned to the ballroom to discover Rebecca missing. Along the sidewall, three sets of double doors led to the terrace.

Had the operative ventured outside?

He weaved through the throng and crossed the threshold. As his feet hit the flagged surface, Dirk was almost plowed over by his brother.

"Dalton, have you seen Rebecca?"

"Aye." The scamp flicked his familiar lucky charm into the air. "The lady in question was ahead of me. Is she not in the ballroom?"

"No—"

"Ahem." Blake appeared as if from nowhere. "When last I saw her, she was walking toward the hothouse."

Dirk opened and then closed his mouth.

He glanced at Dalton, then Blake.

"What in bloody hell have you two been up to?"

"Who?" Dalton looked at Blake. "Us?"

"Er, I needed some peace and quiet," the duke said with a tug of his cravat.

Dirk folded his arms. "Tell me you did not accost Lady Rebecca."

"Now, I resent that, Dirk. Really, I do." Blake gazed at the sky. "I simply thought she might enjoy a tour of the Netherton's garden."

"You are well acquainted with a particular rose bush." Dalton elbowed Blake. "Just how did you get that nasty thorn out of your—"

"Enough." Dirk shifted his weight and considered the scene before him. "When last I saw Lance, he was dancing with Elaine. If the two of you are with me, that leaves..."

He whistled a Brethren signal, and a nearby evergreen rustled. Slowly, Damian emerged from the shadows.

"You called?" Blake's partner in nefarious enterprises asked.

"Gentlemen, you ought to be ashamed of yourselves."

Dirk dropped his hands to his hips. "If ever there were a damsel in distress, she is certainly such."

"Spare us the lecture." Damian chucked his shoulder, and then said to Dalton and Blake, "Did I miss anything?"

"No." Blake brushed his coat. "She is not very accommodating."

"I concur," Dalton added.

Dirk stared at the stars and prayed for patience. "Why do you not seek out a bottle of brandy and commiserate over your defeat?"

Leaving his fellow knights of the order to lick their wounds, he located the path leading to the orangery. As he closed in on the tiny structure, voices caught his ear. Through the glass, he spotted the spy in heated conversation with a man whose identity Dirk could not discern from his current position. His first inclination was to go to her assistance, but he reminded himself that Rebecca was no helpless woman. She was a member of the Corps on a mission and, if the traitor had contacted her, he was duty bound not to interfere. Dirk tiptoed to a decorative hedge and crouched down.

"Please, there must be some mistake," Rebecca said. "I have no knowledge of the person you seek."

"Lies! Colin mentioned your name in his last letter to me."

The stranger was none other than Lord Eddington.

Dirk bowed his head and closed his eyes. After Dirk's father had been killed in battle, Colin's sire had mentored the Randolph brothers. It was obvious Lord Eddington was privy to Rebecca's true occupation. So why had he not been informed of his son's death?

Had Sir Ross suspected Lord Eddington?

He lifted his chin and peered into the orangery.

"I beg you." Eddington grabbed her forearms and shook hard. "He is my youngest son. What has happened? I have not had a dispatch from him in a fortnight."

My lord, your son and my friend is dead.

"Unhand me, sir." She struggled to no avail. "You have no cause."

"I will show you cause."

When it appeared as though Colin's father was preparing to strike her, Dirk called out. "Rebecca. Darling, are you there?"

"I am in the hothouse," she replied.

Eddington released her before Dirk entered the orangery.

"My lord, I was unaware of your presence." He strode in with a hand extended in friendship. "I see you have met my lady."

"You guard this woman?" The general seemed confused as he ignored the gesture and stumbled backward.

"Aye." Dirk drew the lovely agent to his side. "She is mine."

"Do you know—have you any idea—I should return to the ballroom." Lord Eddington glared at Rebecca, then bowed. "I bid you a pleasant evening, Dirk."

Once they were alone, he ushered her to a daybed. She eased to the cushions but stopped him from doing the same.

"Pray, a moment." Rebecca retrieved an embroidery hoop, with a swatch of silks and a wicked needle, from the corner in which he was about to plant his posterior. "This could hurt something valuable."

"Oh, I say." He set the hoop and fabric on a small table and then joined her. "Are you all right?"

"Yes." She hugged herself. "So that was Colin's father?"

"Indeed." He rested his elbows on his knees. "Despite

what happened tonight, you should know he is the best of men."

"Of that I have no doubt. And he is worried."

"I gather Sir Ross has not told him of his son's demise?"

Rebecca inclined her head. "Why would he?"

"Because they are family."

"Members of the Corps have no kin insofar as the government is concerned." Her brow was a mass of furrows. "We are expendable. Thus Sir Ross has no duty to apprise the General of the situation or Colin's death."

"And what of honor?"

"Silly man." She pierced him with a lethal stare. "There is no honor in espionage."

A chill danced a merry jig down his spine.

"Do you honestly believe that? Can you be so callous?" When she averted her gaze, he cupped her chin and looked her in the eyes. "If you have no honor, have you no heart?"

"I loved Colin as I love my own brother Lucien," she said, her voice etched with sorrow. "Do not mistake my oversight for apathy."

In the dim light, Dirk had not seen her pain, had not noted her hurt. But he could not miss the single tear that rolled down her cheek.

"A thousand apologies, Becca."

At that instant, she clutched the lapels of his coat and buried her face in his chest.

"I am so tired, so very tired." His neck cloth muffled her words. "Why must I always be strong?"

"Lean on me." Dirk enveloped her in a secure embrace. "No harm shall befall you on my watch."

As she wept softly, he pressed a kiss to the top of her hair. She inched precariously close, and he tried to conjure pure, unimpassioned thoughts. Only the worst scoundrel would seduce a woman in such a delicate, vulnerable state. But when Rebecca settled herself in his lap, Dirk mentally sang the words to "God Save the King."

"There, there, Becca." He gave her a friendly pat on the back. "Perhaps we should meet with Sir Ross in the morning. He must tell Lord Eddington of Colin's death."

He stared beyond the glass walls of the hothouse and prayed no one discovered their impromptu tryst.

"Come now, love." Wedging a hand between them, he attempted to pry the spy from his body. "We should return to the ballroom before someone finds us."

With that, Rebecca lifted her head. "Are you so ashamed of me?"

"Of course not, I am merely thinking of your reputation." Dirk compressed his lips. "And would I have volunteered for this mission if I were?"

"That speaks to your sense of duty, but how do you feel about me?"

Could the woman possibly be more direct?

And how could he answer a question for which he had no answer? "Now is not the time—"

"There is no time like the present." Framing his face with her hands, Rebecca claimed his mouth in a searing kiss.

The unexpected assault caught him off guard, because never had a woman of his acquaintance been so bold. Dirk tried to protest, but she exploited her advantage by darting her tongue at his in rhythm with a repetitive sway of her hips. The suggestive motion left little to the imagination, and he was certain the world had tilted. Fire and desire pooled in his loins, passion rode hard in its wake. Just as he thought he might surrender, she readjusted her position. The mounting tension abated. Grasping at the last vestiges of his control, he almost cried when she slipped her fingers inside his breeches and caressed him where he wanted it most.

The salacious combination proved a potent elixir, and Dirk Randolph, no-nonsense Viscount Wainsbrough, was undone.

CHAPTER FIVE

"*I* never should have left your side."

"But I am more approachable when you are not there." Rebecca covered Dirk's hand with her own. "I believe garden tours provide an excellent opportunity for the traitor to make his move."

"I agree," said Sir Ross, as he steepled his fingers.

"Out of the question," Dirk replied.

So the stodgy lord feared for her safety?

His reaction went far to soothe her injured pride after their tryst in the Netherton's orangery the previous night. While Rebecca had been certain the no-nonsense noble would welcome her into his bed upon their return to Randolph House, the viscount had merely kissed her forehead and locked himself in his study. Most French generals invited her to their quarters after a single dance.

Why should Dirk be any different?

And this morning, he had remained stubbornly silent at breakfast and equally unresponsive on the carriage ride to Sir Ross Logan's office at the Ministry of Defense. How nice it was to see some signs of life in the handsome sea captain.

"*Rebecca!*"

She snapped to attention. "Yes, Sir Ross?"

Her commander arched a brow. "Glad you could join us."

"My apologies." She lowered her chin. "You were saying?"

"There appears to be some divergent opinion in regard to your tactics during this mission." The head of the Corps tapped a finger to the blotter. "Lord Wainsbrough believes you are in grave danger and thus require a constant companion. I, on the contrary, have faith in your ability to protect yourself and—"

"It is not a question of faith." Dirk leaped from his chair and loomed before the desk. "Why was Lord Eddington not informed of his son's death? Do you suspect him?"

"The decision not to apprise Eddington of Colin's demise was mine," Sir Ross explained. "Our turncoat may run if he discovers he has either directly or indirectly caused the death of a British agent."

Dirk folded his arms. "You do not think the villain already knows?"

"Colin was killed in France, and it is conceivable our Benedict Arnold is unaware of what has occurred on the Continent." With elbows propped atop the desk, Sir Ross tidied a stack of correspondence. "Regardless of the traitor's involvement, treason is a capital crime according to English law. I will not voluntarily provide the blackguard a warning."

"But you place us in a most precarious position." Dirk glanced at Rebecca. "How will she know from whom to defend herself? And how can I protect her? I cannot possibly watch everyone."

"We are monitoring the movements of the men that we

have determined warrant closer inspection, and you are not alone in the field, Lord Wainsbrough." Sir Ross raised a hand to halt Dirk's impending protest. "And I will not besmirch the name of an innocent man. You have no need of their identities."

"I disagree." Dirk pounded a fist to a palm. "I will not have her end up as did Colin!"

Shocked by the usually stolid nobleman's outburst, Rebecca immediately moved to his side. "Do not fret for my safety. You promised no harm would come to me, and I believe you."

"I do not care, as I still do not like it."

Sir Ross glanced at her, then Dirk. "Rebecca, give us the room."

She peered at her boss. "But—"

"That is not a request."

"As you wish."

Bloody hell.

Slowly, she strolled to the door. Just when things were getting interesting, she was relegated to the position of hall monitor.

Rebecca would much prefer to remain with her partner in espionage.

DIRK WOULD MUCH PREFER to remain with his partner in espionage.

As Rebecca exited the office, he could not stifle a frown.

"Have a seat, Wainsbrough."

"I prefer to stand."

"Suit yourself." Although Sir Ross smiled, he had not

appeared amused. "Tell me, how is the mock courtship progressing?"

"I am not sure." Dirk eased himself into one of the two chairs that sat before the large mahogany desk. "As I have never courted a woman before, I have no experience on which to assess the situation."

"Heed my warning." The Corps commander narrowed his stare. "Do not involve yourself, in truth, with my agent. Rebecca is a servant of the Crown. As such, your needs must perforce yield to those of His Majesty."

Dirk would have voiced an objection had the memory of the previous night's kiss not flashed in his brain. Annoying warmth in his cheeks had him exhaling in disgust. "I am tasked with her protection and am only trying to fulfill my duties."

"Have you bedded her?"

"I beg your pardon?"

"It is a fair question, Wainsbrough." Sir Ross opened a drawer and drew a cigar from a box. "Care for one?"

"No, thank you." The last thing Dirk wanted was another diversion to fog his brain.

Sir Ross slipped the cigar between his teeth. "Rebecca is a handsome woman and seems quite taken with you."

"Really?" Dirk bit back a retort that he doubted he could deliver in convincing fashion. "On what do you base your assertion?"

Why was he asking?

Because he wanted to know.

"This is not good." Sir Ross shook his head and pinned him with an icy gaze. "Rebecca is a professional, and she knows what she is doing. But I cannot have you distracting her. As God is my witness, I shall court her myself before I allow this mission to be compromised."

"I would never put Rebecca at risk."

"You already have," Sir Ross replied with unveiled anger. "Never has her attention wandered during a briefing, yet she drifted off like a woolgathering debutante, just now, in my office. You have captured her interest, as even a blind man could see, and could get her killed. She has to remain focused on the prize—to catch a traitor, not a husband. Do you understand?"

Bloody everlasting hell.

Never had Dirk considered that his attention, however innocuous, might put Rebecca in further peril. Then again, he had pointedly not pondered his attention to the delectable spy, because he had yet to reconcile her effect on him.

"Completely." Tension settled as a lead ball in his belly. "But why are you not telling her this?"

"And mark you as forbidden fruit? Not a chance." Logan chewed on the end of the unlit cigar. "Do I have your cooperation?"

"You may depend upon it." A cold chill pervaded his chest, and Dirk stood. "I will do nothing beyond that necessary to achieve our objective. I shall take great care not to advance a tendre with Rebecca."

～

"LUNGE, REBECCA. ATTACK!"

"Lean in."

"Thrust."

The women shouted encouragement as Rebecca staved off Dirk's aggressive offensive. He was backing her into a corner, but she was uncertain how to defend herself. Were it a dagger in her grasp, she could have run him through.

"Take the bit o' fluff in hand." Lance chuckled. "Show her you are the man."

Rebecca had thought Blake would be the only male joining their party. But when she mentioned to Dirk that she had been invited to tea at Elliott House, nothing would dissuade him from coming along. The other men, save Trevor, arrived soon after with the requisite equipment in tow.

"Watch out. Parry, *parry!*" Elaine winced and covered her eyes. "Oh, no. I cannot bear to watch. Someone tell me what happens."

Goodness, was her form that bad?

With a supremely arrogant smile, one to which she would take exception under better circumstances, Dirk parried her beautifully executed riposte with force sufficient to knock the weapon from her grip. He pointed his button-tipped foil at her throat and closed the distance between them.

"I shall accept your surrender."

Must he have been so cocky?

Well, Rebecca might be a beginner at the sport, but she was no babe in the woods.

With hands raised in implied submission, she bent her head and gazed at him through her lashes. She curved her lips as the thrill of the kill settled in her gut. When her prey neared, she moved, lightning fast.

On a sidestep, she landed a sharp jab to his ribs with her elbow. Grasping his outstretched arm, Rebecca planted her feet, centered her weight, leaned in, and hauled his six-foot-four-inch frame over her shoulder. Dirk vented an animal-like grunt as his posterior connected rudely with the polished marble floor. When he tried to put himself to rights, she quickly retrieved her weapon and pressed her booted foot to his chest.

"Just who is surrendering to whom?" Rebecca leveled the tip of her blade with his chin and smiled in triumph. "You are mine, my lord."

"Well done, Rebecca." Damian applauded her efforts and beamed, as would a proud sibling. "You are a fast learner."

"That was magnificent," exclaimed Caroline.

"Hoisted with his own petard," Sabrina said with a wink. "You are simply stupendous."

Cara and Lance halted their match.

"Could you teach me how to do that?" the elder Douglas asked.

"That will not be necessary." Lance pressed a hand to his left breast and looked on Cara. "I shall always be your champion."

Rebecca cursed the heat of a blush as she basked in their praise. Her heart swelled with emotion and, for the first time, she considered herself a member of the group. For a scarce second, she truly belonged.

"May I get off the floor, now?"

Rebecca surveyed the spoils of victory. "But you have not yet surrendered."

Propped on his elbows, Dirk cocked his head and cast her a lopsided grin. "I concede, my lady."

"And what do you concede?"

"What do you want?"

You.

Her thoughts raced in all directions, but she could not be so bold in mixed company. "Have I your word that you will honor my request?"

"You have my word as a gentleman, I will honor your request."

"Then I shall reserve my demand for a later date." And a more opportune moment. He could not have known it, but the stuffy noble had just landed himself in her lap.

A commotion in the hallway had her glancing toward the main doors. Suddenly, Lord Lockwood burst into the ballroom.

"Caroline!"

"Uh-oh." The countess skittered behind her brother.

"Coward," Blake said as she grasped his shoulders.

"The earl appears to be angry," Rebecca said to Dirk, who stood at her side.

"Perhaps he is upset because his wife is increasing with their firstborn." Dirk chuckled. "Which seems reasonable to me."

While the newlyweds argued, she studied her partner's profile. As Trevor fretted for his bride's health, Rebecca was certain Dirk worried about her safety. She would wager her dowry that, just like the soon-to-be father, the serious viscount would protect and defend his family.

And he would do the same for an agent of the Crown.

But could he ever see her as something more than a spy?

"What in bloody hell do you think you are doing?" Trevor inquired with a hint of panic.

"We were fencing." Caroline averted her gaze and bit her lip. "I left a missive with the butler."

"Yes, I know. Roberts stated you had gone to tea at Elliott House." Trevor planted hands on hips. "I happen to know that *tea at Elliott House* has nothing to do with the consumption of hot liquids and scones. For the love of Christ, Caroline, you are with child."

"Should we be hearing this?" Rebecca whispered to Dirk. "It seems a tad personal."

"What does it matter?" he replied. "We are family."

"I refuse to be confined for nine months while you come and go as you please!" Caroline stomped a foot.

"There is nothing to worry about," the earl explained, with a pained expression, to the group. "Dr. Handley said she might be a *little* moody."

Rebecca stifled a snort of laughter as five powerful men shuffled their feet and stared at the ceiling. None appeared inclined to help the expectant father.

"Darling, I am only trying to care for you and the babe." Trevor placed his hands on his wife's shoulders. "Perhaps I should spend more evenings at home."

"Ho-hum." Caroline yawned. "What does it matter to me?"

"Are you tired, sweet?" Trevor pressed a kiss to her temple. "What say we go home and take a nap?"

"A nap?" The lovely young countess seemed to soften in an instant, and her cheeks flushed a charming pink as she accepted her husband's proffered escort. "Well, if you insist. I do need my rest."

Rebecca stared in fascination as the lovebirds all but ran for the exit. "Why do I get the feeling their idea of an afternoon doze has nothing to do with sleep?"

With a shake of his head, Dirk chuckled. "At the pace those two have set, I would not be surprised if Caroline gives birth to twins."

Grinning, her heart light, Rebecca imagined how it would be to have someone watching over her with such doting affection and tender love. Never had she envisioned herself a wife and mother. Never had she considered having a family. But at that very second, Rebecca would give anything to occupy Caroline's slippers.

Only, in her dream, Dirk was her ideal mate.

But how could one catch a husband while attempting to trap a traitor?

INAUSPICIOUS SPECTERS of doom and gloom, their malevolent, twisted faces covered in blood, followed her, nipping at her heels, clawing at her flesh. No matter how fast or far she ran the sinister emissaries of the underworld, haunting and taunting, gave chase. And she was cold, so very cold.

Rebecca bolted upright in bed.

She glanced at the windows, then toward the door. After a few tense minutes, she gathered her wits and realized she had suffered another nightmare. Desolation and despair settled deep in her chest, as somewhere in the cavernous mansion a clock signaled the hour. It was two in the morning, and she was unharmed and safely ensconced in her chamber at Randolph House.

Earlier, with a curiously dour Dirk, she had passed the evening at yet another garish fete epitomizing the gross opulence that was the Season. Never had Rebecca danced so many unproductive waltzes. With nary a traitor in sight, she was restless, frustrated, and in need of something to soothe her frayed nerves. Tossing the covers aside, she dangled her legs over the edge of the mattress and eased her feet into her slippers. In the dark, she located her robe, draped it across her shoulders, and belted it tight at her waist.

Brandy was her elixir of choice as Rebecca stepped into

the hallway without the slightest sound. With the practice and expertise born of on-the-job training, she tiptoed down the hall and through the magnificent gallery. The painted images of Dirk's ancestors seemed to trail her movement, and she dipped her chin in tacit salute.

Quickly, she descended the grand staircase and veered in the direction of a full suit of armor occupying a corner in the foyer. Plush carpet cushioned her footfalls, and soon she stood at the entrance to Dirk's study. With a quick check of the hallway, she palmed the knob. As she eased open the door, a wave of gold light gave her pause.

Inside, a fire burned in the hearth, and the room was warm and inviting. In an overstuffed chair, Dirk sat with his nose in a book. The creak of a hinge announced her presence.

The viscount lifted his head. "Becca? What are you doing up at this hour?"

Seconds ticked past as she pondered her predicament.

Why in bloody hell had she ventured beyond the sanctuary of her chamber?

"I could not sleep." Clutching the folds of her robe, an immodest garment that left little to the imagination, she hugged herself. "I thought perhaps a brandy might help."

"Ah." Dirk closed the book and deposited it on a side table. "Brandy, we have."

"If it is not too much trouble." Like a giddy schoolgirl, she remained rooted to the floor and cursed the embarrassment searing her cheeks. "And I do not wish to intrude."

"None at all." Dirk stood and crossed the study. He lifted a crystal decanter from a silver tray and poured two glasses of the amber intoxicant. "And you are never an intrusion."

As she shivered in her night rail, though she was not

cold, Rebecca wondered how he could be so calm under the circumstances.

Could he not see her?

Was he not affected by her state of undress?

Dirk neared and presented the beverage. "Here you are."

His hand shook.

In that instant, everything changed.

A surge of confidence bolstered her resolve, determination formed an invisible shield, and feminine wiles functioned as her weapon. Hers was a script engraved in her memory, as the cocksure *L'araignee* emerged from within and charged the field with familiar derring-do.

"My lord, I believe you are in my debt." The veteran spy accepted the offering and sipped the liquid courage—not that she needed it.

The stoic noble blinked. "I beg your pardon?"

"Do you not recall our fencing match?" With a roll of her shoulders, she strolled to the hearth. "You promised to honor my request, did you not?"

"I did."

Anticipation licked at her senses, and fire danced a slow, sultry waltz in her veins. On occasions too numerous to count she played the provocative game of cat and mouse as an agent. But this was no game. And while the underworld of espionage had always determined her quarry, tonight, the choice was hers. After all, was not seduction a prelude to love and marriage?

"Are you prepared to pay the ferryman?"

"Aye." He cleared his throat. "What would you ask of me?"

L'araignee faced her prey and smiled. "I should like, very much, to take my brandy in your lap."

Poor Dirk choked violently.

She stepped forward. "You promised."

He retreated. "Becca, that is not—"

"You gave your word." She backed him in a circle about the chair in question. "Have you no honor?"

With a mighty frown, Dirk halted. "Sir Ross does not want you distracted."

"What?" She drew up short. "Is that what he discussed with you in private?"

"Aye." He nodded once. "Sir Ross believes we should avoid situations that might induce an attachment."

Daggers to the heart with frightful precision.

"And what about you?" Unaccustomed to rejection, because she always snared her man, the secret agent faltered, and disappointment weighed heavy. "Is that what you truly wish?"

He downed the brandy in a single gulp and pursed his lips. "I refuse to compromise your safety."

"Does that mean you will not compromise me?"

"I beg your pardon?"

With care, so as not to spook her prospective mount, L'araignee inched close. "Dirk, I want you."

≈

I WANT YOU.

The short but lethal refrain echoed in his brain. Set apart, they were three simple words, but taken together, as a whole, their meaning was anything but simple.

Without a word, Dirk took Rebecca's glass from her grasp, deposited both crystal balloons on his desk, and then reached for her. She wrapped her arms around his waist, and he hugged her tight.

"There is so much at stake." He stared at the ceiling as he held the beautiful operative in a protective embrace. Her confession, achingly sweet and freely bestowed, threatened to breach the limits of his self-restraint.

"I know," she responded with a squeeze. "But I cannot help myself. No man has ever affected me thus. Can you not comprehend my predicament? Is it not the same with you? Do you not want me?"

The woman would be the death of him.

How he wanted to lie, but for Dirk, with her, nothing would do but the unvarnished truth. "Aye, I want you."

She shuffled her feet and lifted her head. "Then what are we waiting for?"

Before he could reply, Rebecca framed his cheeks and kissed him.

Dirk had not known he had been praying for her to come through his door, until that moment. It was wrong, he knew it, and he cared not. Despite his attempts at self-reproach and admonishment concerning the incident in the Netherton's orangery, and a well-composed mental pledge not to repeat the mistake, the enchanting spy evaded his defenses and scored a direct hit in his loins.

To hell with honor and duty.

In less than a second, he swept her into his arms, sank into the chair, and positioned her in his lap, just as she had demanded. To her credit, the sly member of the Corps never allowed a hairsbreadth of distance between their lips, even as she shifted her knees to either side of his hips, and he drank, as a parched man dying of thirst, from the luscious enclave of her mouth.

Pulse points blazed to life, and torrid lust roared through his veins. A raging erection tested the durability of his breeches and his sanity. Dirk trailed the pearls of her spine with his fingertips, and then rested his palms on the twin swells of her derriere. A subtle tensing of her thighs signaled the start of a torturous dance.

With something between a sob and a sigh, he said, "Becca."

Unlike the shy debutantes of English society, with their restrained mannerisms and refined deportment, Rebecca moved as swift and dangerous as a jungle cat, and nothing escaped her caresses. In contrast with the stifled passion of a highborn maiden, she was ripe and juicy as a succulent pomegranate. And although she dressed in the silk and lace of a proper noblewoman, she was no less aggressive than a rake. Hers was an enticing combination.

With his fingers, Dirk walked a naughty path beneath her robe. His first contact with the tantalizing curls at the juncture of her thighs earned him an erotic, feminine moan. As she suckled his tongue, she thrust her hips, and his world rocked. How he yearned to peel the flimsy nightgown from her body, spread her atop his desk, and fill her. The urge to lose himself inside her honey walls, to taste the delights she freely offered, tempted him beyond any delectable confection he had ever before sampled.

Had he wanted her?

Desperately.

Painfully.

Unequivocally—yes.

Through his wool breeches, Rebecca teased his tumescence, and he shuddered. Again and again, she spurred his arousal, summoned the beast. Breaking their kiss, she grasped his wrist and flicked her little pink tongue to the flesh at the inside of his thumb, then brazenly tickled the length of his finger. The implication was unmistakable.

Dirk almost spilt his seed.

Through a haze of desire, a warning rang in his ears.

And then it hit him.

Reality struck him in the face as a bucket of cold water.

Somewhere in the back of his mind an indisputable truth deflated his passion and something else.

"Stop," he said with a flinch.

"What is it?" Rebecca asked. "What is wrong?"

"We should not be doing this." He withdrew his hand, moist with the proof of her desire, from between her legs. "If Sir Ross—"

"Sir Ross can go to the devil." The operative inclined her head. "And he is not the reason you are rejecting me."

"I am not rejecting you, Becca." Of course, he was, and the reason left his senses reeling and his shame reaching impressive heights. "I am merely suggesting we forestall exploring whatever we have begun until the villain is caught and our mission complete."

The agent searched his eyes, and he feared she might discern the cause of his behavior.

"You make it sound so methodical, as if emotions can be placed on a schedule." She slid from his lap and narrowed her stare. "What will happen to us when this is over?"

"It is late, and we must prepare for another ball." Dirk stood and sidestepped the spy and her perplexing query. "You should return to your chambers—now."

Save the ticking of the mantel clock, the room grew silent as a tomb.

"I see." The pain in her expression cut to his core as Rebecca clutched the folds of her robe. "I bid you a pleasant rest, my lord."

"And I bid you the same, my lady." He bowed and averted his gaze.

When a definitive click sounded her exit, Dirk checked

to make sure she had indeed quit the study. He poured himself a brandy, drained the glass, and chased it with another healthy gulp directly from the decanter. Through the window he stared at the stars. A chill of dread shivered down his spine, and gooseflesh covered him from head to foot. Shock tore through his gut, and every fiber of his existence screamed a denial. But he could not refute the evidence.

The spy with sad eyes possessed the experienced touch of a courtesan.

CHAPTER SIX

"*B*loody hell, Dalton, it is not that funny."

Dirk scowled at his younger sibling who was, at the moment, convulsed with laughter.

"Ah, but I disagree," Dalton said between guffaws and then collapsed in another fit of hilarity atop the four-poster. "My, but you are lovely."

Refusing to take the bait, Dirk stood, uttered a mental prayer for forbearance, and frowned at his oh-so-dapper reflection in the long mirror.

"What with your knee breeches, you are quite the dandy, old man." His younger sibling pressed a hand to his belly as he howled. "I say, all you are missing is a tail feather."

"I am not an old man," he replied between gritted teeth.

As he studied his profile, Dirk suffered in silence. The truth was he agreed with the scamp—he looked like a peacock. How he loathed the ridiculous ensemble. There was only one person on earth for whom he would don the humiliating attire. In short, Rebecca was attending a ball at Almack's.

No doubt the patronesses had installed such requirement in order to test the devotion of ardent admirers, because no chap ventured inside the hallowed halls without first suiting up. Though many a rake avoided the legendary establishment, Dirk welcomed the distraction from his perplexing predicament, which centered on the early morning events in the study.

Neither a brisk ride in Hyde Park nor an afternoon round of fencing had eased his mind in regard to the lady spy and her knowledge of the sensual arts. If it were any other woman, his interest would have surely faded, yet the operative remained rooted in his thoughts, an undeniable fact that spoke volumes. Which begged the question: Should her past entanglements matter? Should he concern himself with men he had not known?

Noting a crooked cravat, Dirk neared the mirror and tugged at the yard long swath of linen. A knock at the door had him glancing over his shoulder.

"Come."

"What is going on in here?" his mother inquired as she entered the chamber.

"Mama, your youngest child seems to find my garb cause for unrestrained jollity," Dirk said dryly.

With hands on hips and chin rapidly reaching dangerous heights, a sure sign the woman who gave him life was not pleased, she stated, "My dear, you are devastatingly handsome. Rebecca will surely swoon, as will at least a dozen other young ladies, tonight." Then her icy gaze shifted to Dalton. "And why are you not dressed? You will not be permitted into the Great Room without knee breeches."

With an expression of utter horror, Dalton rose from the bed. "Mama, I am not going to Almack's. Rebecca is Dirk's responsibility. And I ship out tomorrow night on another supply run. I need my rest."

Whether based on suspicion or past behavior, Dirk doubted his brother's veracity.

"Be that as it may, Lady Rebecca requires your assistance. And I am well aware of your impending departure. But, as you stated, you do not depart until tomorrow. Thus you are available to help us, tonight."

With that, the viscountess turned and walked toward the door. As she opened the oak panel, she said, "My darling son, life is a series of unforeseeable sacrifices, and I take pride in your service to the Crown. Now, get into your knee breeches before you make us late."

As their mother quit the room, Dalton snorted in obvious disgust. "Well, that is just swell dandy fine."

It was Dirk's turn to laugh, but since he considered it bad form and, judging from Dalton's countenance, a matter of self-preservation, he merely chuckled. "Do not rip at me, little brother. You brought her in here with your riotous laughter."

"This development is exceedingly cruel." Dalton flipped his lucky coin into the air then slapped it to his palm. "Tails. How appropriate, as I shall enjoy none prior to weighing anchor, thanks to Mama's edict."

"I do not follow."

"I had arranged an assignation to get my wick trimmed by a prime piece." As a child deprived of a favorite toy, Dalton stomped past. "Now I must pass the evening with a bunch of witless chits and their marriage-minded mamas, while eating stale cakes and drinking ratafia."

As his sibling stormed from the chamber, Dirk sighed and again adjusted the folds of his neck cloth.

In the quiet of his quarters, an erotic image flashed before his eyes, and a feminine cry echoed in his ears. Skin soft as a velvety peach, a sultry memory, teased his fingertips. The sweet taste of brandy, sipped from lush lips, danced on his tongue. The beast below his belly button roared.

"Stop this nonsense," he chastised his reflection.

Fisting both hands at his sides to cease their trembling, Dirk muttered a curse. Never had his body or his life seemed so beyond his control; and the source of his affliction appeared to share his malady, awareness of which only intensified his torment. Yet despite all efforts to the contrary, he could not stop wondering about the lady's history.

With layer upon layer of intellect and emotion, Rebecca was an enigma. Like a many-sided prism, the seasoned agent portrayed an endless combination of colorful personalities. She could be a charming escort, a restrained noblewoman, a vivacious vixen, or a lethal government operative depending on the situation. But which personality was truly hers? And if she offered him a glimpse of her genuine character, would he know it?

Dirk studied his image in the mirror.

Had not most people two faces?

He certainly had a public and a private persona and, at times, the two were quite different. Thus far, he was positive the daring temptress that had kissed, groped, and attempted to seduce him in various locales was none other than *L'araignee*—not Lady Rebecca. Indeed, it was the war-hardened spy who had taken him in hand, literally and figuratively, and led him in a salacious waltz through the London ballrooms. Dirk had not known why he suspected as much, he just had an inkling.

Yet he was the man and she the woman. In the sensual

arena, feminine susceptibilities had always deferred responsibility for dictating terms of surrender to the stronger sex. Perhaps that was the reason he felt rudderless on a ship without an anchor. Custom, and male pride, if truth were told, demanded he reverse their positions, but how to go about it?

The solution, when it came to him, was surprisingly simple.

"Of course." He smiled at himself.

Mapping his strategy as though it was a mission for the Crown, he adopted a professional approach marked by order and precision. Like a conqueror preparing to seize a much-desired prize, he dressed for battle. After adjusting the lace-edged kerchief in his pocket, Dirk smoothed the lapels of his coat. Summoning the rakish expertise honed in the arms of some of England's most provocative paramours, he mentally bolstered his licentious weaponry and then went in search of his prey.

It was time the hunter became the hunted.

Measuring one hundred feet long by forty feet wide, the Great Room at Almack's was filled to capacity. The nondescript décor was a bit more frayed about the edges, and many faces had aged, which contrasted with the gilt and glitter of the cream of London society. Upon closer inspection, Rebecca decided little had changed since she last ventured inside the hallowed halls. To her surprise, the patronesses were very welcoming, and Lady Sefton offered a pointed, but polite, admonishment regarding Rebecca's lengthy absence.

As it was early in the Season, the marriage mart boasted

a brisk business. Despite attempts to blend in, Rebecca could not ignore the narrow-eyed stares cast in her direction. Although no one dared cut her, it was evident that more than one mama mourned the apparent loss of Viscount Wainsbrough, eligible bachelor.

"A penny for your thoughts."

Rebecca fingered the sapphire and diamond choker the viscountess had lent her for the ball and gazed at Dirk. "I am worried."

In an instant, his casual expression sobered. "Have you identified suspicious activity?"

She had, but not the kind to which he referred.

The curious thoughts filtering through her brain centered not on the elusive traitor but on her partner in espionage. For some reason she had yet to ferret out, the normally reserved lord had mutated into something best described as...wolfish.

"Heavens, no." She shivered as his countenance shifted to one more akin to a rapacious barbarian. "I am afraid I might forget myself and damage your mother's jewels."

Dirk blinked. "You cannot be serious."

"But I am." With her hand tucked in the crook of his arm, she gave him a squeeze. The muscle beneath her palm tensed, and her nerves charged with renewed anticipation.

After her attempt at seduction in the study, and his subsequent rejection, Rebecca had thought Dirk disinterested. What man, sane or otherwise, would decline a feminine dish of carnal delights delivered on a proverbial silver platter?

One either indifferent or dead.

Only this morning, she had accepted defeat and retired the field. In spite of her initial character assessment, it seemed she had been wrong about the no-nonsense noble.

His polite mannerisms and boyish charm signaled nothing beyond high breeding. That afternoon, she had shed more than a few tears and sought solace in a tin of Belgian chocolates. It appeared her surrender had been a tad premature, because the stoic viscount was stoic no more.

But Rebecca never could have foreseen Dirk's sudden change in tack.

A subtle caress of her derrière through her gown, a sneak attack hidden from the crowd by the portly figure of Lady Kleinfeld, heralded a new contest.

"My lord," she said in a low voice, hoping her stare conveyed ample rebuke at such shocking behavior.

Dirk cast her a devilish grin and quietly replied, "*En garde.*"

So the dashing sea captain wanted to play? When he abandoned her to the company of the long-winded Lady Kleinfeld, and entered a conversation with a nearby aristocrat that she guessed was the mate to the frumpy matron, Rebecca decided to answer the challenge.

It took considerable effort to maneuver into position, and prevent detection, but she returned fire with a bold but brief fondling of Dirk's bottom using her own body as a shield. Expecting, demanding, a puissant response, she was disappointed to garner nothing more than an over-the-shoulder glance and an arched brow.

When, moments later, Dirk claimed her hand and deposited it in the curve of his elbow, he deftly, yet discreetly, trailed a finger along the curve of her bodice. Rebecca gasped and shuddered, and then she met his gaze.

And her knees buckled.

As she checked her balance, the perplexing viscount chuckled and lent his support. "Are you all right, Becca?"

"I am quite fine, thank you." Swallowing her trepidation, surrendering to temptation, she again looked him in the eyes.

The intensity, the fire, the raw passion she noted had not been a product of wishful thinking or imagination. Desire burned bright as the sun, warming her from top to toe and pooling at the juncture of her thighs. There was a curious power, an unmistakable force that held her in thrall, capturing her senses. Locked on his stare, she inhaled a sharp breath as an invisible, but nonetheless potent, connection snared her mind and body.

In a miracle of flesh that defied reason, and Rebecca had never thought possible, the confounding man managed to touch her without touching her. And, oh, what she felt.

But Dirk merely inclined his head and smiled.

The strains of the first waltz had couples rushing to the dance floor, and Rebecca was positive his daring game was at an end. But the innocuous party ritual proved an affecting experience. In a brilliant flanking assault, Dirk slipped an arm about her waist, and his hips engaged in a naughty dance of their own. And through it all, her partner never missed a step, never faltered. Each reverse was superbly performed, every whirl effortlessly executed.

A tantalizing hunger burgeoned in her belly, and fire simmered beneath her skin.

She was acting like a debutante, and it was silly.

His was the most recent pursuit of those too numerous to count, and he followed in a long succession of would-be romancers. She was a veteran agent of the Crown, not an untried flibbertigibbet. Yet her pulse raced, and her cheeks burned as tinder set aflame.

"Are you enjoying yourself, Becca?"

"Oh, yes." She was grinning and giddy but seemed

powerless to restrain herself. "So much that I forget my duty."

"But you have not." His lips curved even more. "You are doing precisely what Sir Ross commanded."

Confusion tempered her happiness. "I am?"

"Indeed." Dirk clutched her tighter, bent his head, and whispered, "You are supposed to portray the much-adored woman that—"

"Lady Rebecca, so good to see you in our fair city. It has been a long time."

Rebecca jerked back and peered at the interloper. A silver-haired giant with harsh features and icy blue eyes smiled at her. Embarrassed, she realized the waltz had ended, but neither she nor Dirk had noticed.

"I beg your pardon, sir." She swallowed hard. "Have we been introduced?"

"In a manner, yes." The distinguished gentleman bowed. "Lord Varringdale, at your service. Might I have the honor of the quadrille?"

"My apologies. Your reputation precedes you, sir." Though his address seemed genuine, his chilly countenance aroused her suspicions. "Although I do not recall the face, the name is legendary."

"Wainsbrough." Lord Varringdale dipped his chin. "Surprised to see you doing the pretty."

"I could say the same for you, Varringdale." Dirk extended a hand, which was accepted in the customary fashion, and then he said to Rebecca, "I shall await you by the Roman bust."

As she settled into the dance, assuming the correct position among three other couples, Rebecca studied her temporary partner. "I am afraid you have me at a disadvantage, my lord," she said as they joined hands.

"Oh?" A brow arched, he stared down his nose. "How so?"

She traded places with another lady and nodded a greeting to her new escort. Strolling in a slow circle, each pair shuffled again. After completing a full rotation, she returned to Varringdale's side.

"I do not recall our introduction," she stated, as her thoughts raced.

The curious lord clutched her fingers, and they entered the line. "We met in Paris."

In an instant, Rebecca stiffened.

Glimpses from her past missions flashed before her, an array of images coursed her mind, but she could not place him. Yet something seemed oddly familiar. Had he worked for the Corps? Had he been disguised? As the dance concluded, she realized Dirk was at the opposite end of the ballroom.

"Allow me to escort you back to Viscount Wainsbrough," Varringdale said with a sickeningly sweet smile, which deepened when she acquiesced without protest. "I can see by your expression that you do not remember me. It is rumored about the Ministry of Defense that I am the most secular member."

"Of course." The pieces of the puzzle fell into place, her frazzled nerves calmed, and she stopped in her tracks. "Colin spoke highly of you, my lord. He lauded your thesis on the finer aspects of cover and concealment."

"Ah, young Eddington." Sorrow ever so briefly colored his features, only to be masked by effusive charm. "His is a terrible loss. Has it been difficult for you, my dear?"

"Quite." She inhaled a shivery breath as the vision of Colin's corpse, lying amid the rose bushes, revisited her memory. "We were very close, and I know he thought fondly of you, my lord."

"Flattery is unnecessary." Varringdale covered her hand with his. "I doubt you two had much time for intelligent conversation, given the nature of your liaison."

Rebecca almost swallowed her tongue.

He knew not her true occupation.

The man had assumed she was nothing more than a mistress—a whore. The revelation provided solid ground on which to plant her feet, and in the blink of an eye, *L'araignee* reevaluated her game plan.

Clinging to her faculties, the cunning operative revisited her script and her part to play. "Colin and I shared a variety of interests, but none fascinated me more than his exploits for the Corps."

"Eddington must have trusted you, to have imparted such a secret." Surreptitiously, Lord Varringdale scanned the crowd. "Perhaps he divulged his discovery? The one that cost him his life?"

False concern tainted his words; the spy wanted to trounce his toes. "Nay, my lord. I have not a clue."

As if he had not believed her, Varringdale narrowed his stare. "I see."

"It is a pity, really." Like a seasoned agent baiting a hook, she inclined her head and averted her gaze. Ah, the devil plays the best tunes. "I have lost a most generous benefactor."

Varringdale tensed beneath her palm, and his countenance shifted noticeably. "Indeed? Have you chosen your next guardian?" He leaned near. "I should be too happy to accommodate you."

Not a chance.

"My lord, please." Drawing on the reality of her situation, Rebecca glanced left, then right, and frowned. "If my youthful dalliance were known about town, my brother would bear the ruin."

"Of course." He patted her hand. "You have my word as a gentleman, your confidence shall never pass my lips. But I would have a favor in return, a boon for my discretion."

His word as a gentleman?

The man made her skin crawl, and she struggled to suppress a shudder, though the situation was nothing new. "And that would be?"

"Should you change your mind, you will grant me the opportunity to plead my case."

Well-honed instincts rushed to the fore, and warnings tolled like the bells in a Wren steeple.

Varringdale was testing her veracity.

Through the elegant formalwear, Rebecca caressed his arm. She would play the arrogant lord as a violin and pluck his strings. "Currently, I am a guest of the Viscount and Viscountess Wainsbrough. Beyond that, I have no plans."

"Excellent." He all but licked his lips. "But we must save that topic for another discussion. Even now, your host approaches."

Ah, candy from a babe.

She peered over her shoulder and nodded an acknowledgement to Dirk. Displaying signs of concern and, dare she think it, jealousy, he portrayed the perfect suitor.

Under her breath, she said, "Lord Varringdale, I shall weigh your offer with due diligence."

It was late when the Wainsbrough town carriage bobbed along the quiet London streets. Because his mother had departed the ball with the Duchess of Rylan, Dirk enjoyed Rebecca's company, unfettered. Nestled in the squabs opposite him, with her eyes closed, the spy had not uttered a single word in regard to her conversation with Lord Varringdale. When he could tolerate her silence no further, he shifted to sit beside her.

"I wondered how long it would take you to make your move."

"Are you not sleeping?" he asked as he draped an arm about her shoulders.

"No, I am merely positing tonight's developments."

Although he desperately wanted to discuss one development in particular, Dirk would not press her. "Was it a fruitful evening?"

"Exceedingly so."

Frustrating seconds ticked past.

"Then Sir Ross should be pleased at our next debriefing." He clamped his mouth shut, reining in the urge to conduct his own interrogation of the pensive operative.

The steady clip-clop of hooves filled his ears, and he bit his tongue and prayed for patience.

"Varringdale generously offered to stand as my next benefactor."

"He did what!"

"Shh." Rebecca giggled and slipped into his lap.

And Dirk recalled his carefully charted course. It was just the anchor he needed to ground himself. "So, did you accept him?" he inquired as he took the helm and set a palm to her clothed thigh. She said she wanted him.

"Of course n-not." She stuttered as he flexed his muscles, and her eyes flared. "But I discerned that Colin did not fully confide in his one-time mentor. Lord Varringdale believes I was Colin's mistress, in truth."

"Really?" He skimmed his hand over her skirts, letting it rest on her knee, before blazing a naughty path to her shapely calf. He was rewarded with a telltale shiver. "Did Colin often speak of Varringdale?"

"No." She shook her head, and then let her gaze fall to his wandering fingers as he prowled beneath her gown. "I know Varringdale trained him but nothing more. However, he asked if Colin had shared the discovery that resulted in his death."

"Bloody hell." Dirk toyed with a garter, inched higher and traced flirty circles on her bare skin, and she gasped. "How did you respond?"

The agent opened her mouth—just as he brushed the little curls at the apex of her thighs.

In that moment, the veil lifted.

Gone was *L'araignee*, the agent provocateur of the Counterintelligence Corps. Slowly, Becca, his soft and sweet lady, emerged. With something between a sob and a sigh, she met his stare as he touched her most intimate flesh, moist with the proof of her arousal. When he parted her, shock and a hint of fear filled her expression. If it had been anyone else—a virgin—Dirk would never have been so bold, would have retreated. But Rebecca possessed knowledge to the contrary.

So there was no reason to temper his sensuous assault.

In a single fluid stroke, he navigated her supple sheath. She was amazingly tight, scorching hot, and he fought the urge to drive his length into her pliant folds.

Panic evident in her demeanor, she flinched, drew back, and crossed her arms over her chest. "W-what are you d-doing?"

"As if you do not know." Dirk chuckled and seized her mouth.

Soul-stirring passion ignited the instant their lips met. Slivers of exquisite sensation shivered over his skin, pleasure poured through his veins. He angled his head, intensified the kiss, suckled her luscious tongue, and his wanton vixen hummed low in her throat. Fire burned in his loins, insatiable lust charged every nerve. He was gentle, he was restrained, but, heaven help him, he was hungry.

Never had he wanted any woman as much as he wanted her.

Before he lost himself in the voluptuous tide, and with her that was a definite danger, Dirk ruthlessly grabbed the reins and held himself in check. Summoning the finesse of a lifetime, he focused on Becca and let her responses dictate their erotic journey. After a few breathless minutes, she fisted her hands in his hair, bit his lower lip, and shifted her hips to meet his questing fingers.

As he made to withdraw from her sumptuous flesh, she cried, "No."

"Patience, my dear." He could not help but smile. "I will set you free soon enough."

At her quizzical glance, he eased down her bodice, then tugged the ribbon of her chemise. Baring her breasts, he brought her own warm honey to a furled nipple. Slowly, deliberately, he pinned her gaze and licked the essence of her desire from the taut bud.

On a moan, Becca rested her head on his shoulder. With a lilting singsong of pants and sobs, she lauded his efforts.

And Dirk savored every sound. Ached to hold her naked in his arms. Yearned to lose himself inside her. Longed to bask in the pinnacle of surrender, as the ultimate fulfillment claimed her.

How many years had he denied himself such indulgence?

He was proper.

He was dependable.

He was the saintly Dirk Randolph.

And he was a bloody fool.

"Becca." He whispered against her lips, "I want you."

Returning to the oasis between her legs, he played a sultry rhythm. In a decadent slip and slide, he let her fly.

As she soared, she gifted her cry of completion into his mouth and gazed into his eyes with helpless adoration and something he could not quite understand. Had he not been on the receiving end of her unique talents, he would have thought her an innocent. But it was a powerful and humbling experience, nonetheless.

"You are so beautiful." With tears welling in her brown depths, Becca cupped his cheek and said, "Thank you."

She buried her face in his neck, and it was then that Dirk noticed he was trembling. Sinking in the cushions, he stared at the roof of the carriage and exhaled. Despite his intent to seduce the lady, he waited for regret, shame, or some other admonishing emotion to take hold of his senses. Instead, sated languor pervaded his limbs, suffusing his frame with perplexing satisfaction.

Perplexing because his cannon was loaded for battle.

With a fist, he pounded three times on the interior side of the equipage—signaling his coachman to start for Randolph House. If he had any lingering doubts concerning his chosen art of war, his temptress had just vanquished them. Convinced he was on the right path, Dirk celebrated his first victory.

His plan worked perfectly.

CHAPTER SEVEN

A harsh smack sounded as leather connected with flesh, heralding an intense but friendly fight. At the center of the main ring in Gentleman Jackson's Boxing Salon, Dirk flexed his pugilist prowess while pondering his passionate pursuit of a professional agent provocateur.

Last night's tryst in the carriage had been a singular success. Never in his wildest imagination could he have anticipated the blissful rapture of Becca's awakening. The raw vulnerability evident in her expression, the happy tears she shed, and the sweet cries of surprise mixed with unmasked joy conveyed a tale of which he had not foreseen. While it was evident the lady spy possessed experience in the voluptuous arts, it was equally obvious he had introduced her to something new.

Damian struck a glancing blow to his midsection, and Dirk responded with a one-two combination.

"Ouch!" Blake winced from the sideline. "That had to hurt."

Although it had not seemed possible, and not in a million years would he have thought it likely, Dirk realized the seductive operative, during all her missions for the Corps, might never have tasted the fruits of her labor and enjoyed the unmatched force of completion. Perhaps her previous forays into the sensual realm had occurred only as a result of necessity, born of duty. In light of her reaction to his strategy, it was a sensible conclusion. The prospect left him melancholy and giddy at once.

Melancholy because hers was a virgin release.

Giddy because hers was a virgin release.

And it was he who had fed Becca her first heavenly delight.

Spellbound, captivated by the decadent memory, Dirk dropped his fists. Damian clipped his chin, and Dirk answered the attack with a solid punch—which landed a little too south for his lifelong comrade's comfort.

"Watch it, brother." Bobbing and weaving, Damian arched a brow. "I must still get myself an heir."

"My apologies." Dirk bent his head, assumed the correct stance, jabbed with his left hand, then his right, and followed with a left hook.

"By the by, how goes it with the luscious Lady Rebecca," Lance inquired. "She is a prime piece."

"Do tell," Damian said between strikes. "And spare us the lecture on propriety and honor."

"Oh, I say." Waggling his brows, Blake elbowed Lance. "Nice duty, if one can get it."

Stumped by their queries, Dirk paused to consider his reply. His adversary seized the advantage and caught him with a vicious uppercut that had Dirk backing into the ropes.

"I greatly esteem her." He stalked to the center of the ring, butted fists with Damian, and squared off in another round.

"Balderdash." Dalton clucked his tongue. "You did more than waltz on the dance floor at Almack's."

Ignoring the inappropriate accusation, which, knowing his scamp of a sibling, was founded on envy rather than truth, Dirk mentally charted his courtship of the female agent, wrestling with pesky details while physically pounding his opponent in the ring. With every thrust, jab, and punch, he crossed an item from his imaginary task list. Whenever a particularly thorny issue snared his concentration, thus muddling his romantic machinations, Dirk simultaneously vented his frustrations on Damian.

After a punishing combination dropped the duke, bottom first, to the canvas, an obviously stunned Damian shook his head and jumped to his feet. "You are in rare form, my friend."

"Perhaps that intense energy stems from a bit of nocturnal jousting," Dalton said with a wink. "What say you, brother? Have you docked your ship in Lady Rebecca's harbor?"

"Now see here—" Stars twinkled, blurring his vision, as Dirk sustained a bruising blow to the cheek. With a gloved hand, he rubbed his now aching jaw and glared at Damian. "That was a cheap shot."

"I beg your pardon?" With high dudgeon, the duke rested fists on hips and frowned. "You have no cause for complaint, after almost clipping my wick."

"Bloody hell, I said I was sorry." Again, Dirk lowered his chin and prepared to strike. "If you cannot take the pain, perhaps you should consider needlepoint?"

"Oh, that was fine form. And might I suggest you bed Lady Rebecca?" Damian lunged. "Perhaps then you would cease behaving like a horse's arse?"

"I will show you a horse's arse." Exchanging blow after

brutal blow, desperate to defend Becca's honor and good name, Dirk marveled at the anger pulsing through every vein, surging in every muscle. Amid shouts for calm and cool tempers, he charged one of his oldest and dearest friends.

Ignoring pleas for civility, he trained his thoughts on the vulnerable member of the Corps and set his sights on his opponent. All his doubts surrounding her sexual history knotted his insides, gnarled his emotions, and flooded his senses. A rush of power soared through his right arm, homed in on his knuckles, and, in Damian, Dirk found a convenient outlet.

The duke fell to the canvas in a lifeless heap.

"Christ, Dirk." Blake jumped into the ring. "Are you trying to kill him?"

"He was only fooling, damn fool." Lance knelt and cradled Damian's head.

"What was I thinking?" Ashamed at his utter loss of control, Dirk dropped to his knees. "Is he injured?"

"It is obvious you were not thinking. He is out cold," Dalton said in an uncharacteristically admonishing tone.

Stunned by his reaction to what had been nothing more than harmless banter, Dirk mentally flayed himself. How was it possible for a single person to upend his life so completely? His obsession with Rebecca had reached dangerous depths. He wanted the spy with sad eyes, yet he could not consummate their relationship until he knew the extent to which she had been compromised and the necessary vows were spoken.

"Should I fetch a doctor?" Dirk inquired in earnest but garnered only speculative stares. "Believe me when I say I did not intend to hurt him."

At that instant, Damian groaned, furrowed his brow, and his eyelids fluttered. "Wainsbrough, are you there?"

"Aye." Dirk leaned near. "What is it, brother?"

In a flash, the usually levelheaded duke punched Dirk in the nose.

"ARE you ever going to tell me what happened to your face?" Rebecca smiled and elbowed Dirk in the ribs. "Or is it a matter of national security?"

He adopted the expression he used whenever he wanted to convey ire without uttering a word. As a rule, the look could make the most stalwart sailor cringe and cower.

Becca merely giggled.

"It is nothing," he replied with open irritation. "Just a scratch from my weekly pugilistic exercise."

"What did you do, beat your adversary with your nose?"

This time, she laughed.

As he surveyed the throng currently squeezed into the ballroom at Richmond House, Dirk tried not to consider his offended appendage, which was swollen to almost twice its normal size, and managed to scare off a young dandy circling the agent's skirts.

"Lady Rebecca, may I have the pleasure of this dance?" Lord Albemarle asked, and then nodded a greeting, which Dirk returned in kind.

"Of course," Rebecca replied with a dip of her chin.

"I shall wait here," Dirk said. As Albemarle ushered the operative into the rotating sea of couples, he stood next to a pedestal bearing a vase filled with an array of exotic blooms.

A quick scan of the crowd revealed Varringdale, who

appeared to be studying the spy's moves with unmasked interest. Near the terrace doors, Dirk discovered Sir Ross Logan. The head of the Corps seemed lost in discussion with a prominent member of Parliament, if not for the occasional furtive glance in Becca's direction. But when he spotted Clarkson, the lowly secretary, mingling with the Hogart twins, he almost knocked the flowers from the pedestal.

What was an unranked clerk doing at one of the *ton's* galas?

"Are we not a fine pair?" Damian asked from behind.

Dirk peered over his shoulder and noted the nasty bruise encircling his friend's left eye. "I still cannot believe I did that."

"I could say the same in regard to your nose." Damian grinned. "It is not broken, I hope?"

"No." Dirk again gave his attention to the dance floor. Clarkson had disappeared, and, mid-turn, Rebecca cast him a charming smile. "But I had it coming."

"Nonsense." The duke moved to his side. "Wielding the woman's reputation as a weapon, I resorted to schoolboy teasing and deserved to have my head lopped off. In my defense, your little brother can be quite provoking."

"Some things never change," he said with a huff. "Ever since we were in shortcoats, Dalton has found sport in my attachments."

"Is that the way the wind blows?"

"Aye."

"You know, until this very second, I doubted your sincerity where the lovely interpreter was concerned." Damian leaned close. "Thought you were merely dedicated to the mission."

Denial traipsed the tip of his tongue.

But Dirk saw no reason to deny the truth.

"Doubt me no longer."

The dance ended, and Albemarle returned Rebecca to Dirk's care.

"That was a fruitful waltz." His partner in espionage opened a fan with a flick of her wrist. "Goodness, it is warm in here."

"Did you learn something?" he queried as she tucked a stray tendril behind her ear.

"Indeed. The portly lord is a treasure trove of gossip on London's elite—" Becca's mouth fell agape. "*Lucien!*"

"Hello, beautiful." As the lady spy stepped into her brother's arms, Lucien Wentworth, sixth Earl of Calvert, glared at Dirk. "Wainsbrough."

"Lord Calvert." Although they shared a civil handshake, Dirk got the distinct impression he had just been put on notice. "I did not know the *Intrepid* was in port."

"We sailed into Deptford this afternoon. I understand my sister is currently residing in your home." Calvert narrowed his stare. "Why is that?"

"Lucien." Rebecca elbowed her elder sibling. "The viscountess invited me to stay with her and partake of the Season. It was a generous offer, and I did not wish to refuse."

"Rumor has it you are courting my sister."

"Oh?" Dirk had not so much as flinched. "I rarely heed rumor."

"If you besmirch her character I shall call you out," the young navy man warned.

"Rest assured, my intentions are honorable." And then it hit him. Dirk realized just what he intended, knew well the inevitable conclusion of his declaration.

Perhaps Lucien understood too, because his expression softened. "Take care of her."

"You may depend upon it."

"Is my first lieutenant bothering you, Wainsbrough?" a booming voice, laced with humor, inquired.

To the undiscerning onlooker, Rebecca gauged the masculine interplay with unimpaired aplomb, but inside her heart skipped a beat at Dirk's declaration.

"Bless my soul, it is a ghost from the past." Dirk chucked the naval officer on the shoulder. "How long has it been? Five years?"

"Captain, allow me to present my sister, Lady Rebecca." His tone bespoke admiration, and Lucien beamed, as would a proud parent.

Rebecca studied the impressive blue uniform festooned with braided epaulets that declared his rank. Standing over six feet, with guinea-gold hair and impossibly blue eyes, the man rivaled her brother's military resplendence. And from the chorus of feminine whispers, it was evident many noblewomen shared her assessment.

"Captain Jason Collingwood, commander of the *Intrepid*, at your service." He bowed with a flourish that drew several breathy sighs from the young ladies nearby. "Please, call me Jason."

"And you must call me Rebecca," she said as he pressed a chaste kiss to her gloved knuckles. But as he made to stand upright, the captain paused. A ripple of awareness passed from his fingers to hers.

"Might I beg a favor?" Jason compressed his lips.

Intrigued, she nodded. "Of course. What would you have of me?"

"An introduction." He motioned discreetly. "To the lady in red."

After a wink at Dirk, she gazed at the individual in question and smiled. "Pray, a moment."

Strange, she would never have imagined her well-honed spy instincts could be put to such use. As she waited for an appropriate opportunity to insert herself into the conversation, Rebecca pondered Jason's potent reaction to a certain party. Had Dirk suffered a similar response when they first met aboard his ship? If memory served, he had stuttered.

And then the bloody French had attacked the *Gawain*.

War was so inconvenient.

With a whispered summons, Rebecca secured the female in demand.

"Lady Alexandra, may I present Captain Jason Collingwood of the Royal Navy." Rebecca stepped back. "Lucien serves him aboard the *Intrepid*."

As Jason kissed Alex's hand, the highborn daughter of a duke giggled and said, "You are lovely."

To wit the obviously surprised seaman replied, "Not half so lovely as you. Shall we dance?"

"That was smoothly done." Dirk slipped an arm about Rebecca's waist.

"Will Damian mind?" She bit her lip.

"No. Collingwood is not a stranger in our circles. Still, we should probably guard them." Dirk led Rebecca into the mix of whirling partners.

"Surely he would not think of accosting her here." She rethought her matchmaking machinations.

"Jason is not the one who worries me."

Just then, the duo in question circled near, as Alex inquired, "Tell me, Captain, is your vessel very large?"

"Ah, I see." Rebecca laughed and settled into the dance.

As always, waltzing with him proved a powerful experience.

"Your efforts appear successful." Dirk chuckled. "Alex and Collingwood seem lost in a world of their own."

"I can hardly take credit for that." But she noted the couple's proximity, which tested the limits of propriety. "Mutual attraction played a small part."

He arched a brow. "Mutual attraction?"

"Indeed." Their hips met on a turn; she brushed a telltale bulge and gasped. She glanced down, and then caught his stare. "Do you not feel something?"

"Aye." In the light of the crystal chandeliers, Dirk blushed. "I feel it."

Rebecca could have shouted for joy.

Despite the proper façade and polite manners, the no-nonsense viscount wanted her. The undeniable proof rode hard against her belly. And she was determined his passion would not go unrequited. Dirk had to know she desired him.

Tonight.

∽

"Join me in the study for a brandy?" her prey inquired as Rebecca gave her cloak and gloves to the butler.

"What a marvelous idea." Canting her head, she smiled at Dirk. "We can continue our conversation."

They would share a delicious intoxicant, all right.

But not the sort poured into a glass.

"An excellent notion." The handsome nobleman ushered her down the hall. "I was wondering if you had ever met Wellington?"

"Indeed, I have." A hint of cigar smoke teased her nose

as she entered the masculine domain. "He is a formidable military strategist, and his prowess is unmatched on the battlefield."

"I hear he also has a way with the ladies." After closing the door, Dirk walked to a side table, lifted a crystal decanter, and filled two balloons. "Of course, that could be mere conjecture."

"There is more to it, I believe," Rebecca said as she spread her fingers and warmed her palms by the fire.

"Oh?" The curious lord joined her near the hearth and offered her a glass. "Do you know someone with firsthand experience?"

Barely stifling laughter, she was certain Dirk was asking whether or not Wellington had dallied with her. On a side-glance, she clucked her tongue. "I am not one to gossip."

"And never would I encourage you to engage in such behavior." He appeared befuddled as he narrowed his stare. "But—have you reliable confirmation of Wellington's abilities?"

The poor man was an easy mark.

"Really, Lord Wainsbrough." Somehow, she managed not to grin. "Such naughty conduct from a heretofore impeccable gentleman."

"I beg your pardon." Dirk tugged at his cravat, and then swilled the contents of his glass in a single impressive gulp.

Following his lead, Rebecca downed her brandy, accepted his empty balloon, and set it with hers on the mantel. It was high time to make her move. Summoning all her experience with the opposite sex, the siren spy, the one who never failed to catch her man, emerged. Social conventions and polite precepts fractured, scattering on the floor as autumn leaves.

L'araignee took a bold step in his direction.

He retreated.

Again, she inched forward.

Dirk backed into a chair.

The operative moved, swift and sure, grasped his neck cloth, and quickly untied the folds of linen.

"Becca, what are you about?" His brow furrowed as she drew the yard length of starched fabric and flung it aside.

"Is it not obvious? I am making you more comfortable."

"Oh?" The usually stuffy lord appeared on the verge of protest.

"Certainly, you did not believe we were going to extend our debate of edged weapons versus firearms." Clutching the lapels of his elegant formal coat, she slipped the wool from his shoulders, freeing the garment and dropping it to the rug.

"I must c-confess I d-did," he stuttered as she unbuttoned his waistcoat and stripped it from him in much the same fashion. "It was an intellectually stimulating discussion."

"Perhaps I have another method of stimulation in mind." She unhooked the shirt fastener at his throat. "One that will prove a pleasurable interlude for us both."

"But—" Myriad emotions invested his expression. A hint of shock mixed with hesitance, and Dirk opened and then closed his mouth. A single brow arched, he grinned. "Really?"

On her tiptoes, *L'araignee* gently kissed his bruised nose. "Indubitably."

Desire flashed in his amber eyes.

Before her quarry could object, she pushed him into an overstuffed chair. After kicking off her slippers, the secret agent hiked up her skirts, straddled his thighs, and eased to his lap. Brushing aside the ruffles of fine lawn, she set her lips to his. Dirk groaned into her mouth as she twined her fingers in his hair and held him to her. She could have cried like a baby when he prodded her with his tongue and suckled hers.

For a few heated, desperately groping minutes, she merely sat there and let the normally restrained nobleman ravish her. With both hands grasping her bottom, he anchored her close and rocked his hips in an illicit rhythm, teasing her with a very promising erection. Passion nipped at her senses, blazing a trail straight to her loins, and delicious fire sang in her veins. When he broke their kiss, bent his head, and buried his face in her bosom, she stared at the moulded ceiling and moaned in appreciation.

Prior to this night, in terms of the male species, *L'araignee* had always trusted her spy instincts. As a member of the Corps, she had been trained to distance herself from the physical demands of espionage. That included various trysts born of duty to the Crown. For her, licentious behavior was simply a tool of the trade, a useful tactic to evade a target's defenses and gain secrets pertinent to national security.

But not tonight.

For good or ill, the seasoned operative was determined to put her talents to work in an all-together different contest. And when she finished, the high and mighty lord would consent to visit her bed. How badly she wanted to release the rapacious barbarian lurking amid the polite decorum, wanted to revel in the raw power masked by the proper façade, wanted to taste the uncontrolled lust of the man beneath the elegant attire. It was all there, burning as an unquenchable flame, just beyond reach. Patience stretched thin; she would seize her prize.

And *L'araignee* knew just how to go about it.

As Dirk hovered dangerously close to a nipple, she drew herself up and slid from his lap.

"Becca, did I hurt you?" he asked in a raspy voice.

"No, but remain where you are." From a daybed she retrieved a pillow, which she dropped on the floor at his feet. Pressing his thighs further apart, she knelt between his legs. Now was her opportunity. This was her gift from fate, and she was going to claim it.

"What are you doing?" With a countenance of curiosity and confusion, he leaned forward. "Is something wrong?"

"Relax, my lord." Palms to his chest, *L'araignee* urged him to recline. Grasping his wrists, she settled them on the arms of the chair. "Promise, no matter what happens, you will not move."

"But—"

"Give me your word, as a gentleman."

"Now, see here—"

"Swear on your viscount's coronet."

"All right." With a frown, Dirk dipped his chin. "I vow, I will honor your request."

In a flash, she nipped at the skin stretched taut across his ribs and speared his navel with her tongue. At his sharp intake of breath, *L'araignee* chuckled and moved lower to catch the waistband of his trousers with her teeth. Drawing imaginary circles along the inner sides of his thighs, she traced a naughty path to his crotch and caressed the mound of hardened flesh burgeoning beneath the fabric. Conscious of his intense scrutiny, she peered at him, and he favored her with a boyish grin and a shrug of his shoulders.

"Are you ready for me?" she inquired as she unfastened the hooks and freed his fully aroused length.

Dirk blinked, as would an owl. "Ready for what?"

L'araignee knew exactly what she was going to do as she

stared at him through half-open eyes. She had partaken of the act, had committed the deed countless times on men she would never have touched outside her occupation, her life as a spy. In return for the pleasure she gave numerous strangers, she gained priceless bits of information for Wellington and his generals. But never had she derived any enjoyment, in kind.

Tonight would be different.

Because the recipient of her talents was one of her choosing, for no other reason than she wanted him. And how she wanted him.

Slowly, deliberately, she smiled, bent her head, and flicked her tongue to the plum-shaped tip.

"*Good God,*" he exclaimed with something between a sob and a sigh. "Rebecca, you cannot mean to—"

"Remember your promise."

With a furrowed brow, he appeared to contemplate his predicament. She narrowed her stare as she worked him with her hand, pumping at an enticing pace. When Dirk closed his eyes and sank into the chair, *L'araignee* commenced the decadent, delicate dance.

Moving over him, she took him into her mouth, loving him with all she had and for all she was worth. She knew well the rhythm, the tantalizing slip and slide that would make him howl in delight, and he manifested a succulent treat of unmatched masculinity, a fact that spurred her on, emboldened her anew. The thrill, the sheer power of holding something so potent, yet so fragile, in her tenuous grasp was overwhelming, a point she had never pondered.

With fistfuls of her hair, he thrust his hips in opposition to her movements. The momentum grew, the cadence quickened as Dirk ravaged her lips and, somewhere in the back of her mind, *L'araignee* realized she had lost control of the situation. With fire and desire simmering beneath her skin, wild and wanton passion and anticipation burned in her belly, and she licked and suckled his miracle of flesh as she would a flavored ice from Gunter's.

As a sultry summons, his low, steady groan heralded his climax. Quickly, she snaked her arms under his thighs and took him deeper still. In a staccato of bursts, his impressive display of virility left her senses reeling as she drank from him.

Suddenly, without warning, nerves charged, and a series of sweet spasms between her legs sent wicked shivers down her spine, not unlike those that had wracked her body in the carriage the previous night. And as before, wave upon wave of heretofore-unimagined bliss rushed over her skin from head to foot, and she floated in a make believe sea of sensuous euphoria. At long last, *L'araignee* found pleasure in the pleasure she gave.

Weighted with sated languor, she pressed on Dirk a final kiss, then sat on her heels, wrapped her arms about herself, and closed her eyes against welling tears. Never in her life had she experienced anything quite so lovely as her seduction of Viscount Wainsbrough.

Could the upright noble resist making love to her now?

WAS THERE anything quite so lovely—or erotic—as the sight of Becca seducing him? At that precise moment, Dirk peered at Rebecca and smiled.

Sparing a minute in silent rebuke at his complete loss of self-control, his thoughts swiftly turned to marriage.

He was Dirk Randolph, Viscount Wainsbrough and oh-so-responsible eldest son of the equally conservative Brent

Randolph. Like his sire, he led an orderly life and was a creature of habit, traits for which he would never apologize.

But it seemed Becca had found a chink in his armor.

She had discovered something primitive, unrefined, and untamed in his person, and he rather enjoyed it. Problem was, whatever she had unearthed, the beast would no longer be caged; and he had thoroughly compromised her. And while he may not be her first lover, he would damn well be her last. But honor demanded he speak the vows before consummating their relationship, and he was nothing if not honorable, so she would have to wed him.

The spy with sad eyes.

Therein lay the only impediment to his happiness.

Dirk had not wanted a government agent for a wife, yet Rebecca would be his wife.

CHAPTER EIGHT

*T*he previous night should have been a momentous occasion. Rebecca had taunted and tempted her conquest yet, in the end, she had slept alone. If not for intimate knowledge to the contrary, she might suspect Dirk was a eunuch.

"I trust you enjoyed an undisturbed rest?"

Dirk's rich baritone startled her, and she tripped on the uneven pavement. "I b-beg your p-pardon?"

"Careful." He gripped her elbow and smiled. "I simply asked if you found your accommodations agreeable."

Could the man possibly be more formal?

He spoke to her as though nothing licentious had occurred between them. As if she had not held his rather impressive erection between her lips. Rebecca gazed at the curious viscount and considered her next move.

"Ah, I slept like a babe."

Surely, it was easier to lie than to explain the truth?

She had bared her soul to him the previous night, and he acted as if they had done nothing more than share polite conversation over a spot of tea. Her spy instincts and common sense counseled that what happened was perfectly natural for two people attracted to each other, but her cheeks burned with uncharacteristic timidity.

An essence of self-doubt nipped at her skirts as they neared the park, their mounts in tow. Dirk wrapped his hands around her waist, sneaking a quick kiss as he lifted her to the saddle, which more than lifted her spirits.

The horse whinnied in protest and shot forth as if possessed by some malevolent entity.

An attenuated cry of surprise escaped Rebecca as her tenuous grip tangled the reins.

"Hold on!" Dirk shouted from behind.

The world passed in a blur, and claw-like tree limbs threatened to upend her at every turn. *L'araignee* was an expert rider, but she was accustomed to mounting astride in breeches. Sidesaddle, dressed in a proper habit, she bobbed perilously atop the frazzled horse. If only she could slip her booted foot in the stirrup, she might be able to secure her position and slow the usually docile mare. As it was, the saddlebow provided her only anchor, and it was not enough to abate the brutal excursion.

"I am almost there!" Her knight protector hollered.

The thunderous clap of hooves sounded an impending rescue, and Rebecca bit her lip as she jostled violently. Serpentine fear danced a sinister jig at the tip of her tongue, pervading every tightly wound nerve when she spied a low-cut hedge, fast approaching. Under any other circumstance, she might have managed to clear the hurdle, but not after such a punishing jaunt.

"Dirk—hurry," she cried.

Every muscle screamed in protest as she fought to maintain her precarious perch. Blood was a bitter pill in her mouth, and she prayed that would be the only blood spilled as an oak claimed her riding cap. Mere seconds from disaster, she cursed the hedge that would, no doubt, end the domestic fantasy she had enjoyed of late. The mare tensed beneath her, preparing to jump, and Rebecca closed her eyes.

"Hold fast," Dirk cautioned.

The unyielding vise that snatched her from the saddle had not diminished the shriek of terror that had taken up residence in her throat. The peal of horror burst forth as a cannon blast, as they soared over the hedge atop her no-nonsense knight's bay. They landed hard, but alive and unharmed, on the opposite verge. Fear was soon replaced by shame when Rebecca realized she was shivering uncontrollably in Dirk's comforting embrace. Tears of embarrassment mixed with some as yet unidentifiable emotion, and she buried her face in his chest.

"You are safe, darling." Dirk kissed her hair, then pulled back and cupped her chin, bringing her gaze to his. "Are you all right?"

"I am." She mustered a smile. "No small thanks to you."

Just as she thought it safe to let down her guard, she noted a crimson stain marring his white linen shirt. It was blood from the wound on her lip. A prescient awareness of impending doom sliced the calm, settling as an emotional knife through her heart.

What was it that had concerned Sir Ross regarding her relationship with Dirk? The handsome captain might distract her. No one considered the impact on her should some unforeseen disaster befall the charming viscount. How selfish she had been in her amorous pursuits not to ponder the unwarranted attention that might result from her interest. She could never live with herself if the traitor targeted her new partner to get to her.

"Becca, where are you?"

She blinked. "What?"

"I called you three times, but you simply remained still in my lap." With a pointed stare and a brow full of furrows, Dirk cocked his head. "Where did you go?"

"Do not be silly." She offered a less than enthusiastic chuckle. "I am right here, my lord."

"No, you are not. And you are hurt." He gripped her arms and gave her a cursory survey.

"It is nothing. I bit my lip." Bilious terror pooled in her throat. With Lucien aboard the *Intrepid*, safely under the protection of Captain Collingwood, how had she failed to consider her lone remaining vulnerability? The no-nonsense Viscount Wainsbrough was her Achilles' heel because she cared for him. And how she cared for him. "It was quite an unusual ride."

Framing her face with his hands, Dirk caressed her lower lip. Suddenly, without warning, he bent his head and traced her lips with his tongue. Playfully he suckled, engaging her in a frisky duel. Sinking into his strong frame, Rebecca set about showing her hero how much she appreciated him—the best way she knew how. In full view of polite and proper society, she pressed on her partner very impolite, very improper kisses.

To hell and the Reaper with the *ton*.

～

"I BEG YOUR PARDON, MY LORD."

Dirk looked up from the estate ledgers he'd been reviewing. "What is it, Hughes?"

"Timmons requests a moment of your time. I believe it

has something to do with the incident in the park this morning."

"Send him in." He closed the log and set it aside. "Oh, and Hughes, have Lady Rebecca join us, at once."

"Yes, my lord."

As the door to his study closed, Dirk stood, stretched long, and walked to the window.

Below, the sidewalk of Park Lane was a beehive of activity. Fashionable Londoners scurried in all directions, running errands and meeting with friends, or simply strolled to see and be seen. Ignorant of the danger lurking in their midst, indifferent to the horrors of a war fought in another land, they carried on with their daily routines because they knew not otherwise.

In short, life happened.

Oh, to be so lucky.

Tormented by the truth, he marshaled his emotions with ruthless command. Heaven help him if he faltered. Despite the unsettling events of the day, he could not, would not ponder a future without Rebecca. Yet only that morning he could have lost her, forever, had he failed to save her.

The spy with sad eyes.

In his mind he recalled the moment they met aboard the *Gawain*, when she pulled back the hood of her black cloak, and the deck shifted beneath his feet. In that instant, everything changed. She called to him, to his sense of honor and duty, to his need to protect and defend, but that was not all. To his inexplicable amazement, the beautiful agent touched him in ways he could never have imagined, summoning soul-stirring passion and molten desire unlike any he'd ever known.

And yet her mystical magic could end in a singular fragment of time.

Because *L'araignee*, the sought-after secret agent, put Rebecca, his ladylove, in the perilous sights of an as-yet unknown villain.

"You sent for me?" Rebecca asked.

Oh-so lovely in her powder-blue morning dress, just seeing her set his heart racing.

"I did indeed." Dirk smiled. "Please, have a seat."

From his desk, he retrieved the latest edition of *The Times* and handed it to her. "I thought this might interest you."

Myriad emotions danced in her countenance as she scanned the headline, and then gave her attention to the accompanying article, and he wondered how she'd managed to become one of England's most notorious spies when he read her with such ease. Could it be that she felt comfortable enough to reveal her true self when in his company?

"The infantry not only defended Fuentes de Oñoro, but also forced Massena's troops to re-cross the Agueda River." Her eyes flared with unabashed enthusiasm. "Oh, Dirk, it says Wellington has taken the garrison of Almeida."

"You must be pleased," he declared with pride.

"Of course, I am." She folded the paper and met his gaze. "As any English citizen would be."

Modest to a fault, a quality he found most charming in his future wife.

"I meant because of your dispatch. The intelligence you secured gave Wellington an edge," Dirk pointed out. "You ensured the success of our troops."

"My lord, you grossly overstate my contribution." Shaking her head, Rebecca sighed. "My information merely apprised them of impending attack. I did not fight their battles, because victory is never owed to one person. Our brave fighting men succeeded because of their determination, spirit, and hard work. War is never as simple as black and white. You, of all people, should know that."

"Well said, my lady." Not that he expected any less. "Then, I suppose, you would not be amenable to a little celebration of your efforts."

"A celebration?" She blinked and all but leapt from the chair.

Standing before him, with face aglow, she crossed and uncrossed her arms, and then clasped hands in front of her in a desperate attempt at feminine deportment, which might have worked, if not for her visible tremors of excitement.

"What have you planned? What should I wear? Perhaps I need a new gown." She bit her lip. "Oh, I hope you have not gone through too much trouble."

"It is a surprise." Dirk laughed as he playfully tapped her nose. "And you need only present yourself, love."

"Then I shall endeavor to gift you a companion worthy of your efforts, my lord," she purred.

"How considerate of you to make it appealing, Becca, but entirely unnecessary, I assure you."

"As you wish." She turned to leave but paused and then reversed course. "Dirk, may I ask you a personal question?"

"I am at your service."

"What is your government affiliation?"

"I beg your pardon?" Bloody hell, he had not wanted to lie to his bride-to-be.

"As we both know you are not a member of the Corps, in which branch do you serve the Crown?"

A common response shot to the fore. "Well, I completed a commission in the Navy."

"Then, if you are decommissioned, why did Sir Ross

send you to convey me to London? Why did he not dispatch a military transport?"

Why was he not surprised that the usual rejoinder had not sufficed? "Perhaps because I was already tasked with a supply run."

"All right." Becca looked her skepticism. "If that is your story."

Were she a gentleman, he would take insult and demand satisfaction.

"And Colin and I were old friends," Dirk added for good measure.

"As you said the night we met." She retreated a step. "Then I bid—"

"No, do not rush off." He caught her elbow. "I would ask a favor, in kind."

"I stand ready." Sparks flared in her velvety brown eyes.

"Tell me, have you any aspirations once your mission is complete? That is to say, have you any plans for the future, when the war is over?"

For a moment, she pondered his query in silence.

After several seconds, she said, "While nothing is set in stone, I believe it fair to say I have aspirations."

"And they are?" Dirk held his breath in anticipation of her answer, because her reply could render his courtship the shortest in history.

"I should like, very much, to marry and have a family," Rebecca declared, with a ghost of a smile. "I want to know how it feels to wake up in the morning and have nothing more important to decide than what color dress I will wear. I want to bathe in perfumed waters every day, without fear that my scent will betray my presence on surveillance. I want to fashion my hair in the latest style, and attend events of the Season for no reason other than to waltz the night away in the arms of my beloved."

"Really?" He could have danced a jig, because her achingly tender testimony was music to his ears. "One would think the excitement and intrigue of espionage would know no competition."

The very instant he uttered the statement Dirk regretted his choice of words. In a flash, the spider spun its web, veiling the elegant noblewoman in the gossamer armor of a spy.

"Actually, Lord Wainsbrough, service to the Corps is not what you might think." *L'araignee's* smile faded, as had her effuse effervescence. "Agents live on borrowed time, always looking over their shoulder, wondering who is watching whom," she explained. "Most of their assignments are spent crouching in dark alleyways, or in some equally enticing locale no normal person would willingly inhabit. The work is hard and dirty, neither glamorous nor exciting, and they do things most sane people could never conjure in their most disturbing dreams, all in the name of King and Country."

Dirk cursed himself repeatedly, as the operative deteriorated from delight to despair.

Wringing her fingers, she frowned. "You must think me selfish for wanting to abandon my profession."

"On the contrary." He took her hands in his and pulled her into a hug. "I marvel at what you have accomplished these last five years. You have earned my utmost respect."

"I am not certain that I deserve your respect." She snuggled close, burying her face in his chest, and he pressed a kiss to her hair.

"Becca, believe me when I say you are the bravest woman I know."

A knock at the door brought them apart.

Rebecca blinked and cleared her throat.

Dirk cursed softly and tugged at his cravat. "Come."

"Your pardon, my lord." Timmons, the groom, entered the study. "I thought you would want to know what caused poor Alice to bolt like she did. One of the undergrooms found her grazing in the park and brought her back." In an outstretched hand, he held a prickly, gnarled bur. "Found this beneath the seat, tucked just under the edge of the cantle."

"No wonder Alice ran." Dirk studied the nasty looking seedcase, letting it roll in this palm. He glanced at his groomsman. "Any idea how it got there?"

"None, my lord." Timmons shrugged. "May I ask, which of the undergrooms saddled the horses this morning?"

Brows arched in surprise, Dirk cocked his head. "They were saddled when we entered the mews. Since I spoke with you yesterday about taking Lady Rebecca riding, I assumed you left word to have them ready for our morning exercise."

"No, my lord." Timmons scratched his ear. "I thought you would send for your mounts, as usual, so I was surprised to see you walking them out yourself."

Dirk considered the possibilities as he held the bur in his fingers. "Timmons, post a guard at the mews. Not a single mount is to go out that you have not personally saddled and inspected."

≈

"SO YOU BELIEVE this was an attempt on Rebecca's life?" Blake narrowed his stare, as he appeared to consider the latest *cause célèbre* of their mission.

The Nautionnier Knights, including Dalton and Lance, who'd recently returned from their quick supply runs, huddled in a private room at White's.

Dirk nodded once. "Aye, I do."

Dalton shook his head. "Has anyone else made contact with her besides Eddington and Varringdale?"

"No." Dirk frowned and raked a hand through his hair. "It is hell trying to protect her from a villain we have not, as yet, identified."

"What does Sir Ross think of the situation?" Damian asked.

"That is the most frustrating part." Dirk drew hard on his cigar and exhaled a cloud of smoke. "You would think we were simply exchanging pleasantries. The man hardly raised a brow when I told him Rebecca could have been thrown from her mount and killed."

"But you said she was unharmed," Damian declared, earning a reproving glare from Dirk.

"That is not the issue."

"No." Lance held a hand up to forestall Dirk's impending protest. "The fact that she is an interpreter in service to the Crown is the issue."

"Brother, everyone in this room has taken risks for the good of our country." Damian stared at Dirk over the rim of his glass of brandy. "Lady Rebecca is no different, and she has served since before you met."

"I for one admire her bravery and devotion to duty," Trevor added.

"Would you feel the same if it were Caroline at risk?" Dirk asked, his tone laced with sarcasm.

"I would never let Caroline become an interpreter in the first place." Trevor sat back in his chair. "And, as Damian pointed out, Rebecca was an aid to Wellington when you met her. Besides, Caroline is my wife."

"And Rebecca is going to be mine."

The words were spoken before he realized it. Truth and determination rang, clear as the finest crystal, in his voice.

The room fell eerily silent.

Dirk caught Blake and Damian exchanging their 'I told you so,' expressions.

Nonplussed, Dalton was not so subtle. "You cannot be serious."

"Once this business if finished, if she will have me, I intend to marry her," Dirk responded in a manner he hoped left no doubt of his sincerity.

"And our lady soldier is in agreement?" Dalton leaned forward, resting elbows on knees. "You are certain she wants the same?"

"I believe she is equally disposed to such proposal." He looked each brother in the eye, challenging anyone to gainsay him.

The lifelong friends exchanged wary glances.

"Well then, I believe a toast is in order." Damian held his glass high. "To your lovely bride-to-be. May we finish this dreadful affair and capture the traitor so you might just get yourself leg-shackled."

"I will drink to that." Though Dirk attempted to portray unshakeable conviction in his plans to wed the beautiful operative, he struggled with unanswered questions.

Rebecca was a spy and had seen and done things of which he could only wonder. For good or ill, her work was part of her past and her present. But once they married, espionage would cease to be an integral component of their lives.

There was no room for the Corps in their future.

As the Brethren departed, some boasting more illicit endeavors, Dirk waved farewell to Blake and Damian. His young scamp of a sibling offered a ribald comment, tossed his familiar lucky coin, waggled his brows, and followed suit. But there was one member of their party whose counsel he required.

"Trevor, a minute."

"What is it, brother?" asked the newest Nautionnier Knight.

As Dirk had sailed with Trevor on his first mission with the Brethren of the Coast, and watched in awe as Caroline's husband rescued a member of his crew during a vicious storm at sea, he felt a genuine kinship for the veteran seaman. And although he surmised he could have sought Admiral Douglas's opinion on the topic foremost on his mind, Dirk would rather share his misery with someone who had just survived a similar circumstance.

"I need a little direction," he explained. "Some advice, if you will."

"What can I do for you?" Pondering his empty glass, Trevor motioned for a refill. "As if I cannot guess."

Bloody hell, his partner in crime was not going to make things easy. Dirk shifted in his chair and thought of Rebecca, soft and feminine in his embrace, and a wave of sensuous warmth permeated his polite attire.

"Oh, no, I know that look."

"What?" Dirk snapped to attention. "To what are you referring?"

"That stupidly content expression you are sporting." Trevor chuckled. "If it makes you feel any better, I have spent every day of my life on the other side of that face since I met Caroline."

"Now see here—"

"And you deny it. A sure sign that another man has fallen victim to perfume and petticoats."

"I resent that, Trevor, really I do."

"Oh, give over. It stings like a hornet when you first get hit. But, take my word, it does not last long, provided you manage to keep your head out of your arse."

Dirk blanched. "Gads, do you think the rest suspect?"

"What? That you are indubitably smitten with the charming Lady Rebecca?" He snorted. "Not unless they have ever suffered love themselves. Though they probably have some inkling."

"Suffered love? You make it sound like a battle wound."

"Oh, I say, the initial pangs of love are, by far, the most brutal, and it is a lethal cut to the heart, but, before you know it, you hurt so good."

"Are you purposely trying to confuse me?" Dirk scratched his temple.

Trevor burst into laughter. "Brother mine, I could tell you the unvarnished truth, but then you would probably sail for the Horn, and you would miss something truly special that defies all logic."

"I do not follow."

"My wife once told me that love is a gift, not an obligation, and I must confess her statement confounded me, at the time. But since that day I have come to discover her meaning."

"Pray, continue."

"Dirk, if love has found you, then you need only accept it, and the sooner the better for your sanity."

"You make it sound so appealing."

"Any less, and I would do you grave disservice. So, what did you want to ask me?"

"Well, I was wondering how one goes about courting a woman?" Dirk stretched his legs and studied the polished toes of his boots. "My experience leans decidedly toward the seduction of the fairer species. You know how it is in the Navy. Barmaids and doxies tumble into your lap with little, if any, effort. Of course, that usually involves sharing a bed for only a night or two. I must admit, I haven't the foggiest notion how to go about enticing a lady into my bed for the rest of her life. Not that I expect Rebecca to spend the rest of her life in my bed. Well, not that I intend us to have separate bedchambers—"

"Enough." Trevor held up a hand, ceasing Dirk's nervous rant. "You know, it is painful to watch another man go down."

"And I am going down?"

"Like a sinking ship."

"Bloody everlasting hell."

"Come now, it is not that bad." Trevor snickered. "Take my word for it, there is a fine line between seduction and courtship. The goal is still the same, if only a more permanent arrangement. The difference is you have to do the pretty for the sake of the *ton*. It all happens out in the open."

"What?" Dirk choked on his brandy.

"The courtship, you ass."

"My mistake."

"Take her flowers, and buy her chocolates. Compliment her appearance, but be careful, that can be a deadly trap. Tell her she is lovely, her hair looks nice, her dress is pretty, and she has great shoes. But leave it at that." Trevor wagged a finger in warning, "Try to get fancy, and you will end up in a world of trouble."

Puzzled, Dirk shook his head. "I do not understand."

"For instance, you profess sincere appreciation for her new style. Instead of taking it as a compliment, she will want to know why you did not like her the way she was. Then she will be angry with you, and that could go on for a fortnight."

Dirk pressed his hand to his belly and stared at the ceiling. "How the deuce am I to tell the difference?"

"Just do as I said, and keep it simple." Trevor slapped his thigh. "Oh, and buy her scads of useless trinkets. Women have a particular fondness for knickknacks that serve no purpose other than to gather dust."

"Really? Then why encourage them?"

"Gratitude, brother." Trevor grinned. "I would buy my wife a whole house full of dust collectors for one of her 'thank yous.'"

"That really is more information than I want to know about a woman who is, for all intents and purposes, a sister to me."

"Sorry."

"So, flowers, chocolates, useless knickknacks, parochial compliments, and I will win the woman."

"Count on it."

"Trevor, you are a bloody genius."

CHAPTER NINE

The roses arrived at noon.

Ensconced in her sitting room, and failing miserably in her attempt to master needlework, Rebecca cursed another imperfect stitch and spared a quick peek at the large bouquet perched atop the side table. The exquisite red blooms had become a potent, painful reminder of Colin's death, and their haunting scent often invoked her darkest demons. Yet the artful arrangement, which also featured purple snapdragons, had achieved a decidedly different effect. Perhaps the sender had some-thing to do with the nervous excitement simmering beneath her skin.

The accompanying card, stark in its simplicity, bore no name or seal, but she recognized the telltale conservative script in an instant. Then there was the beribboned tin, marked by identical importuning correspondence, of deca-dent chocolates that arrived only half an hour later. And the message, three elementary words when considered on their own, but taken together as a whole, a powerful request, a sultry summons impossible to deny.

Think of me.

Silly man. Had Dirk not realized she had done little else since that remarkable night in his study? Against her better judgment, Rebecca set aside her mangled mess, snatched the tin from the table, inched the strip of emerald satin from the box, lifted the lid, plucked a tempting morsel from its nest of cotton, and tossed the confection into her mouth. The richest, creamiest milk chocolate mingled with the subtle tartness of strawberry, and she moaned her appreciation. Standing, she walked to the center of the room, closed her eyes, and hugged herself.

Fanciful dreams materialized from thin air, whimsical images straight from the stuff of fairy stories, and a chorus of chubby cherubs sprang to life, letting fly a shower of mystical arrows and serenading her with a naughty ditty of love. And how she loved. On a giggle, she stretched out her arms and whirled, again and again, gaining speed with each successive turn, like a giddy schoolgirl wearing a brand new dress.

Until a strong male arm encircled her waist and lifted her feet from the floor.

Anchored firmly in Dirk's embrace, she touched her nose to his. "My lord, what are you about?"

Amber eyes twinkling with amusement, he grinned. "I take it my modest offerings to your beauty please you?"

With calm deliberation, Rebecca locked her arms behind his head and let her lips express her gratitude. But she was the grateful recipient of their shared kiss. She was thankful for his hands, one shifting lower until he cupped her bottom and pressed her to his hips, while the other inched up and came to rest at the nape of her neck, fingers twining in her hair. Oh, the erotic heat of him, the sumptuous taste of him, sweeter than any store-bought treat, sent her spiraling to the dizzy heights of passion.

"I should ply you with flowers and chocolates more often, love." Dirk pressed his forehead to hers. "Or is there something else you prefer?"

"You." Her heart skipped as he eased his grip, letting her slide down the front of him. "Only you."

"That goes without saying." He reached into his pocket and retrieved a small parcel. "Then I suppose you are not interested in this?"

"Another gift? You spoil me." She accepted it without hesitation and opened it at once. Inside, on a bed of snow white satin, was a porcelain rosebud. "Oh, Dirk. It is lovely. But, what is the occasion?"

"The answer is simple, really." He rocked on his heels. "I had thought to keep fresh flowers on your night table, but I may not always be here to do so. Now you have a bloom that, like my affection, will never wither or fade."

"My lord, I am confused." Actually, his bold declaration both stunned and thrilled her. "Unless you perceive the traitor to be hiding in my chambers, there is no need to maintain the pretense of our courtship behind closed doors. And Sir Ross—"

"Can go to the devil." Dirk trailed a finger along the curve of her cheek. "What say you, my darling Becca, if I am in earnest?"

Devoid of fluff, bereft of superfluous sentiment but nonetheless powerful, her plainspoken suitor made her an offer she dared not refuse.

She exhaled a shaky breath. "Viscount Wainsbrough, am I to understand that you wish to pay court, in truth?"

"Indeed." He seemed so calm and equally certain. "Have you any objections?"

And just like that, he set the world at her toes.

"I must confess it is my fondest wish." How she wanted to shout inexpressible elation, yet one thing held exultation at bay. "But I am still an agent of the Crown, and I must complete my mission before I can entertain any proposal."

No doubt that would temper his plans.

"Is that your only impediment?" He narrowed his stare.

"I can think of none other." She held her breath against rejection.

"Then you will have me?"

Rebecca launched herself into his arms.

IT WAS THE FASHIONABLE HOUR, and, as had most London society, Dirk and *L'araignee* participated in the pompous spectacle that was the promenade. Clutching his arm, she dipped her chin to the various matrons of the *ton* and was always surprised to discover another claimed acquaintance, when she had spent the better part of the past five years on the Continent. Occasionally, her partner in more ways than one cast her a charming grin or a wicked wink, reminding her of their shared secret.

Yes, the no-nonsense, oh-so noble Viscount Wainsbrough had declared his intent to wed Lady Rebecca. And while she was still reeling from his modest proposal, he accepted her consent with unimpaired aplomb. So, as the gossipmongers whispered of the latest courtship to snare their attention, as Sir Ross lingered somewhere in the shadows, and as an unidentified villain lurked in places darker still, the spy traipsed an imaginary tightrope between reality and illusion.

On the surface, they could have passed for a carefree

couple, planning their future with reckless abandon. In truth, they enjoyed no such luxury until the traitor was in custody. Beneath the elegant formalwear and carefully composed demeanor, they played a lethal game of cat and mouse, with *L'araignee* as bait and Rebecca's most fervent hopes and dreams on the line.

"I met with Logan this morning," Dirk said in a low voice. "I thought it prudent to inform him of the minor alteration to our mission."

"You did what?" *L'araignee* paused mid-stride.

"Calm yourself, darling, else you will provide fodder for the scandal sheets." He covered her hand, anchoring her firmly in the crook of his elbow. "And it had to be done."

"Forgive me, my lord." Now she came to a dead stop. "Am I to understand that you met with my commander, on my behalf, to inform him of a commitment sworn by me, without my knowledge or assent?"

"I did."

"For the love of all creation, why?" She scanned the area and pulled him aside, ensuring a modicum of privacy.

A brow arched, he replied with more than a hint of arrogance, "Suffice it to say that you are to be my wife."

"That may be, but I did not surrender my cloak of office." She checked her tone, so as not to risk accidental discovery. "How dare you usurp my position."

"My dear Rebecca, I would have you know that I am only too aware of your current occupation." Dirk shifted his weight. "What you conveniently overlook is that, given your promise, all prior obligations must perforce yield to mine, as I am your future husband.

"Well, my dear Viscount Wainsbrough, I would have you know that if you ever interfere in my work again, you will yield more than a promise."

L'araignee turned on a heel, prepared to make a brilliant exit, and ran straight into Lord Eddington.

"Lady Rebecca." Colin's father glared at her, anger laced with pain, and grasped her forearms. "What news have you of my son?"

As the operative studied the patrician features marred by distress, she lamented the burden born of duty. Espionage demanded discretion that exacted a high price often paid in blood or at the unintended expense of those most innocent, the survivors. Since the veteran military man remained a suspect, she could not divulge the facts. Her gut-wrenching duplicity only contributed to the caustic stain on her conscience.

"Lord Eddington, believe me when I say that nothing I could tell you would ease your mind or bring you comfort."

"May I be of assistance?" Dirk inquired, as he assumed a protective stance at her side.

Immediately, the general released her. "Wainsbrough, have you no honor? Have you no shame?"

"I beg your pardon?" her partner asked with unveiled incredulity.

"You consort with this heartless harlot," Lord Eddington spat.

"Careful, old friend," Dirk said quietly. Too quietly. "You insult my bride-to-be."

"You are to be married?" The elder man paled.

"Indeed." Dirk inclined his head. "Wish us merry, Eddington."

"I will do no such thing." To *L'araignee* he said, "This is not over, Lady Rebecca. I know what you are, and your time will come."

∿

"My lord, just what are you about?" Blindfolded, Rebecca stretched taut her arms, flicked her fingers, and all but bounced with unconcealed excitement. "Hurry, Dirk. I want to see."

"Just a minute." Standing behind his ladylove, he grinned and waited for the servants to quit the dining room.

After their impromptu and unpleasant row in the park, and the subsequent odious scene with Lord Eddington, Becca had retreated to her secret agent persona, wrapping herself in a cloak of reticent melancholia every bit as imposing as the hooded black garb of the Corps.

In short, the spy with sad eyes had resurfaced with a vengeance, and Dirk's heart ached for her.

So, with his mother at the Douglas residence for the evening, and his scamp of a brother chasing some unfortunate skirt, he was determined to put his courtship back on smooth waters with the promised celebration of the operative's efforts.

"Are you ready?" he whispered to the crest of her ear.

"*Yes.*" She trembled visibly. "I am uncontrollably excited."

"All right, love." A quick tug freed the simple knot, and the sash slipped away, revealing the fantasy he had created just for her.

Bathed in the soft light of tapered candles, the usually utilitarian, but still somewhat elegant, dining room boasted a jungle of roses in every conceivable color. The finest linens of white damask trimmed in old gold blanketed the grand table, which bore only two place settings, one at the head and the other to its left.

"Oh, Dirk, never have I seen anything so beautiful."

With the grace and ease of a gently bred noblewoman, his Becca visited each and every bouquet, pausing to caress a delicate petal or press her nose to a particular bloom. Having completed a turn about the room, she stood before him, happy tears filling her brown eyes. Slowly, she smiled, and in that simple affectation unveiled a face aglow with shimmering ebullience that rivaled the sun.

And Dirk could have cried.

Without a word or warning, she threw herself at him, her arms encircling his waist, and hugged him so tight he could scarcely draw breath. On a sigh she relaxed, unutterably soft and feminine, and he bent his head and kissed her hair.

While unfinished business loomed beyond the walls of his London residence, and they would resume their mission soon enough, tonight Rebecca was not a member of the Corps. Tonight she was not in search of a traitor. Tonight she was nothing more than his future wife, to be adored, cherished, and indulged. He could give her that—would give her that—if only for tonight.

"May I say you look lovely this evening?"

"Do you like my dress?" Rebecca stepped back and circled once. "I noted your preference aboard ship and here, in your home, so I wore it just for you."

Trevor's words of wisdom rang clear, as Dirk just stopped himself from explaining that burgundy was his father's favorite color, and, as such, his mother had decorated everything with it. "Darling Becca, you are a vision. Now, shall we dine?"

Dirk held her chair as she settled herself, and then claimed his place at the head. As he draped his napkin across his lap, she asked, "And what do you think of my hair?"

For several seconds, he studied her. Had she done

something different, or was it the same? Again, invaluable advice echoed in his brain. Keep it simple. "A masterpiece."

"But, it is not my usual style." She toyed with a long curl that hugged her neck. "Do you really like it?"

Bloody hell, was hers a trick question? "My dear, your hair is a work of art in any style."

"Why, Captain Randolph, are you not the charmer?"

Over a sumptuous feast they traded opinions on the close quarter use of flintlock pistols, the advantages of swords versus daggers, and hand-to-hand combat. While Dirk would have preferred less provocative topics, Rebecca took to the discussion as though imparting a new gardening technique, and he marveled at the depth of her knowledge.

For dessert, ah, dessert was a memorable experience. As the staff had been dismissed, Dirk retrieved the covered dish from the sideboard, intending to serve two bowls of the decadent peach jam pudding, but his lady had other plans. Planting her shapely bottom firmly in his lap, with a few wicked wiggles of her hips, Becca handed him a spoon. Bite by succulent bite, he fed her, claiming an occasional sugary kiss in payment for services gladly rendered. Finally, they adjourned to his study, where Dirk had one more surprise.

"Another present?" She accepted the brown parcel with both hands. "Goodness, it is quite heavy. But you really should not have, as you are spoiling me horribly."

"Is that not the purpose of courtship?" Although Trevor had not specified the sort of dust collectors to which women were partial, Dirk thought his latest selection fit the requirements to perfection.

"I would not know." With great care, she pulled the ribbon from the box and lifted the lid. "And I have had no prior experience with which to compare."

Silence settled uncomfortably in the room, and he

wondered if he'd erred in his choice. Perched on the edge of his desk, he waited for some sign, a hint of any kind, of her reaction. At last, she met his gaze and burst into laughter. Just when he thought she might manage a word in response to his gift, she collapsed in convulsive hilarity.

When he could no longer tolerate the suspense, Dirk asked, "Have I done something wrong, my dear?"

"Heavens, no," she said between giggles, and then held up the knickknack in question. "My sweet Captain, you bought me a paperweight." With that, she hugged the large prismatic crystal to her chest, reclined in the chair, and once again surrendered to unrestrained mirth.

Blister it, he was bound to fail, sooner or later, but he'd hoped for later—after they wed. With arms crossed in front of him, he frowned. "If it does not meet with your approval, I can return it to the vendor."

At his remark, all jollity ceased.

"You will do no such thing." She set the trinket on the table and stood.

In one swift move, she stepped between his outstretched legs, grasped his wrists and brought them to either side of her hips. Framing his face in her hands, she kissed each cheek. "Thank you." Then she paid homage to his forehead. "Thank you." The tip of his nose was the next fortunate recipient of her attention. "Thank you." Finally, she said against his lips, "Thank you," and came at him with sufficient force that he had to prop them up, just to keep from falling back on the desk.

Ah, it was good to be a man.

His fiery bride-to-be nipped at his flesh and suckled his tongue in appreciation. Hell, for her brand of acknowledgment, he'd buy her two housefuls of paperweights. For several desperate, heated, unspeakably tender minutes, Dirk just sat there and reaped the luscious fruits of his labor. Until his bold Becca reached between them, her fingers walking a naughty path straight to his—

"Darling, it is late." To his infinite thanks, as if on cue, the mantel clock signaled the midnight hour. "We should retire."

The smile with which she favored him warmed him to his toes. "My lord, I could not agree more."

"Shall I walk you to your room?" He adjusted a lace cuff.

With a delightful incline of her head, she clutched his elbow. "Are you always so noble?"

There was nothing noble about the hammer in his crotch. "Well, I try to be when circumstances permit."

"Why am I not surprised?"

Together they entered the hall, strolled into the foyer, and then turned right to climb the stairs. While Rebecca chatted about their upcoming engagements, Dirk tried in vain to cool his blood. Painfully aroused, he was positive he could bounce guineas off his Jolly Roger, because, at that very moment, his Roger was dangerously jolly. Every stick of heretofore-innocuous furniture presented enticing possibilities and alluring scenarios he mentally filed for future reference.

"Dirk, are you listening to me?"

"I beg your pardon?" He snapped to attention.

"What has you otherwise occupied?"

Should he apprise her of his bawdy plans for the cushioned, two-seater bench in the gallery, which might just spontaneously reanimate his ancestors for sheer inventiveness, alone?

"I was merely wondering what you intended to do with your gift?" He handed her the box. "Careful. Do not drop it."

"Never, my lord." She opened the door to her chambers. Just as she crossed the threshold, she turned and sighed. "I hope you know how much I enjoyed tonight. It was truly the most wonderful time of my life."

And with that she was once again in his arms, searing her initials on his heart with a soul-stirring kiss.

Warning bells pealed in his ears, and he retreated before she ended up on her back. "Oh, love, I am in complete agreement. And we have only just begun." With a most proper bow, and most improper thoughts, he said, "Until next we meet, lady mine."

Her brown eyes sparked. "You will not have long to wait."

Self-restraint in tatters at her innocent declaration, Dirk all but ran for the safe haven of his quarters. Crossing the room in mere strides, he untied his cravat and dropped the linen to a nearby chair, and then paused to splash cold water on his face at the washstand. After shrugging out of his jacket, he flung it aside. Closing his eyes, he inhaled and exhaled, inhaled and exhaled, and rolled his shoulders. When that had not born serviceable results, he vented a long-drawn groan and marched to his bed. Sitting at the edge, he yanked off his boots, flinging them one after the other to the floor, and then toppled to the mattress. Sleep would be hard won, because visions of a chestnut-haired beauty danced in his head.

How he wanted to reverse course and spend the night in Rebecca's arms, to nurture what he hoped would be a deep and abiding love, but he'd promised himself that he would wait until they had spoken the vows. While he wanted her, ached to claim her, he wanted something more than seduction. Dirk did not know why it mattered to him, why he cared, he just did.

Filling the bed at his bachelor lodgings had never been a problem, but the activity in which he had previously engaged involved experienced women, superficial attachments, and basic human needs. Although he was keenly aware that his intended bride was not an innocent, which she confirmed in a most elemental fashion that spectacular night in his study, that should not mean they could not make a virgin start together, as husband and wife.

A soft click caught his ear, interrupting his internal dialogue, followed soon after by padded footfalls. Dirk sat up—and froze.

Standing in the center of his room, a silk-encased goddess, with long flowing locks draped effortlessly about her shoulders, seemed to float in the air. Only a single mother-of-pearl button at the throat fastened the diaphanous robe, more an afterthought than a functional garment. He blinked repeatedly, hoping that his mind, no, not his mind, but another more insistent aspect of his anatomy was playing an exceedingly cruel joke.

"Rebecca?"

CHAPTER TEN

"*M*y lord." Swimming in nervous anticipation, the heights of which she had not experienced since her first mission, Rebecca licked her lips and took two tentative steps, yet she was making a giant leap toward the future she dreamed to share with her own personal knight in shining armor. "I hope I did not keep you waiting too long."

"My God, woman, just what are you about?" Dirk averted his stare, and she halted. Was he angry? "I do not recall granting you free access to my chambers."

"I misunderstand." What were the roses, dinner, and paperweight if not a prelude to seduction? Confused and hurt by his hostile response, she clutched the folds of her robe in an attempt to cover herself. "Do you not want me?"

"It is not a question of what I want." He raked a hand through his hair. "It is a matter of honor. I do not wish to be another one of your conquests."

She flinched, as though physically struck by the weight of his statement.

"*How dare you.*" The floor beneath her feet shifted, as

his words cut a lethal wound deeper than the sharpest dagger.

"Rebecca, get out of here." His tone bespoke ire and something she could not identify, and still Dirk would not look at her. Was she so repulsive? "We can discuss this in the morning."

"No." Wild horses could not drag her from his presence. "You've made an accusation, and I would have you explain yourself, now." To avoid further miscommunication, she added, "Tonight."

"I made no accusation." He paced like a caged lion and then stopped. "I merely stated a fact of which we are both aware."

Mentally, she replayed their brief courtship, the none-too-subtle stares, the provocative caresses, and the passionate kisses. Was hers an unsuccessful seduction? What had she missed? She inched closer. "And that would be?"

Dirk faced forward, steadfastly refusing to meet her gaze. "That you are no innocent."

Bullet to the heart with deadly precision. Over-whelming shame traipsed her spine, and seething anger sprinted in its wake. "Draw breath to define what you refer to as innocent."

On a groan, he dropped his head back and stared at the ceiling. "You have known other men."

What had he expected of the lone female spy in the Counterintelligence Corps? "There are many men of my acquaintance—"

Once again, he paced. "That is not what I mean, and you know it."

Dumbfounded, Rebecca spread her hands. "Actually,

Lord Wainsbrough, I am at a loss to comprehend your allegations."

"Oh, come now. Must we play this game?" With fists at his sides, his amber eyes impaled her on the spot. "If you prefer I be blunt, then so be it. What have you done in the line of duty? How many men have you pleasured, or can you say with any real accuracy? Have you any children? If not, then what do you use, a patent shield or a womb veil? Is your conscience so unencumbered, madam, as to pretend a virtue you no longer possess?"

She gasped at his brutal charge but recovered, setting her jaw squarely against his attack. As realization dawned, the relevance of his interrogation sank in, and *L'araignee* stood tall and uninhibited by her lack of dress. "Are you quite finished?"

"My apologies," Dirk said in a low voice. "I have no right to ask such questions."

"But you have, and I will answer them," she said with calm determination.

"No." He turned his back on her. "I do not wish to know."

"Ah, but you do, my noble Captain," she purred. "And answers you shall have. So, where to begin? Perhaps, as I started out, so you may understand my gradual degeneration from lady to spy."

"You do not have to do this."

"Yes, I do."

"I do not wish to know the gory details."

"Do you want to hear this or not?"

"Tell me."

With a long drawn sigh, *L'araignee* wrung her fingers, because hers was not an easy task. She had hoped to avoid comingling her past with her future, but Dirk left her no

162   BARBARA DEVLIN

choice, so she prayed the benign inception of her career might temper the later, more lurid details. "As the only female in a branch of the government with approximately eighty sworn personnel, I learned the invisible but none-theless valid rules of espionage one mistake at a time, because my male counterparts had no interest in my excuses or me. But, as I proved myself in the field, I gained a measure of respect from those who knew of my existence."

Dirk looked at her. "Were you trained prior to your first assignment?"

"Yes, I received the standard protocol." *L'araignee* nodded and arched a brow. "But, as you are a Navy man and can, no doubt, relate to my situation, the common texts of counterintelligence provide only the most general knowledge a spy uses in trade. The practical lessons learned in the back alleyways or during the seduction of a particular French general constitute survival training, at its best."

Lips compressed, he frowned. "Were you afraid?"

"Every minute of every day, but fear is one aspect of which no agent speaks yet every agent understands." A chill settled in her chest, as sordid images flashed before her.

Countless bodies bearing various wounds.

Hand-to-hand combat; fighting to survive.

Nameless male enemies licking their lips in anticipation.

The young girl lying abed, still clutching a stuffed toy, as though fast asleep—if not for the multiple stab wounds in her chest.

"It is the reason I vomited repeatedly in the twelve hours following my first kill. It is the reason I strap a dagger to my thigh. It is the reason I had once thought I would never marry or have children. It is the reason I hesitate to plan beyond today."

His gaze traveled the length of her body, and at last he moved in her direction. "You are not wearing one now."

"No. I did not think I needed protection from you." Neither cowering nor retreating, *L'araignee* held her ground. "Another grave mistake, I am afraid."

"I beg your pardon." Dirk stilled. "I would never hurt you."

"My lord, you already have."

For several minutes, they simply stared, eyes locked. His features hardened, and she summoned all her strength. He exhaled audibly, and she lifted her chin a fraction higher.

His brow a mass of furrows, Dirk shifted his weight. "Becca, I am sorry. I am so sorry and so very ashamed. In haste, I spoke out of turn. You see, I want us to begin our life together as husband and wife, if only to distinguish our marital bed from your prior liaisons for the Corps."

"My *prior* liaisons?" On the heels of an apology he added further insult? "You must think me truly despicable."

"It is not your fault, really." Again he paced. "I am certain your tenure as a spy has required great sacrifice, as I am equally positive that you surrendered your body under the gravest of circumstances."

"How easily you judge me." Her knight had not known it, but he had just fallen from his horse, and she would die before she told him. "And how quickly we return to the question foremost on your mind."

Dirk faced her. "I rescind my queries."

"Ah, but that I will not allow. Let me see, how many men have I pleasured?" *L'araignee* tapped her fingers, as if calculating the sum. "I cannot say, as I stopped counting in a selfish undertaking to save my sanity. But I can tell you of the first, though I do not recall his name." Fresh in her mind in all its depravity, it seemed like yesterday, and she shook her head. "On a terrace, overlooking a manicured garden, I knelt at his feet. It took mere minutes, but the effects lasted days." She folded her arms across her chest and quivered. "I could not eat or sleep, and I scrubbed my flesh raw in an effort to rid myself of the ensuing revulsion and self-loathing."

Dirk cast her a piercing glance, and what she saw there cut to marrow. She had not wanted his pity. "But, you were only doing your duty."

"Yet you have instigated this rather insightful exploration of my past, but I digress." Desperate to break the intimate connection, and in need of refuge, she peered out the window. A crescent moon, partially shrouded in clouds, beckoned the spectral demons that haunted her without mercy. In a morbid waltz they gathered, forming a visual tapestry of horrors. "Some months later, my assigned target resisted my attempts at seduction, as his tastes inclined to more violent pursuits."

"What happened?" he inquired softly. Too softly. As if he cared.

"He broke my jaw." Venting a half-sob, she brought a hand to her throat. How unfair it was that the memory, so vivid after all that time, could travel with lightning speed, reach through to the present, and hurt her again. "You see he gained pleasure in the pain that he gave. I cannot convey the relief that washed over me, despite excruciating agony, when Colin burst in and helped me fight my attacker. However, my relief was short-lived when, a few days later, I learned of our loss at the Battle of Maria de Huerve and our subsequent defeat at Belchite."

"But that was not your fault." Her errant knight sounded so sincere.

"I might have prevented it, or at least given our fighting

men a chance, but we will never know, because we killed my quarry before gleaning any tactical intelligence." *L'araignee* carried that stain, one of many, on her conscience.

"Becca, you take too much on yourself."

"Perhaps, but my job is to ferret information, and in that I had failed. Yet I learned a valuable lesson. I discovered how insignificant I am in the grand scheme," she stated flatly. "From that day forward, I began to distance myself, to detach myself from the actions of *L'araignee*, but I could not escape the filth."

"I do not follow," he whispered.

"I felt dirty." A torturous vise locked tight about her chest, as she prepared to impart her most embarrassing secret. "And as I despaired that I might never be clean again, a group of crusty sailors rowed me from shore to sea, whereupon I met you, and you taught me otherwise."

"How so?"

"You made me believe in that which I had thought existed only in fairy tales. You gave me hope as I had never known, and how I hoped." The walls closed in, imprisoning her in an invisible hell. With a heavy sigh, she rested her head in her hands. "At least, I did. Yet nothing seems clear. How could I have been so wrong?"

"You were not wrong."

"Oh, but I was, my lord. I am a fool, and I deserve to suffer." Rejection was a bitter pill. *L'araignee* turned and made for the door. She had to get away; she had to return to the familiar, the underworld of espionage, where hope was an exercise in futility, and the steely spy ignored said emotion. "Now, if you will excuse me, I must wake the servants and have my things packed."

"Why? Where are you going?"

"Home, I suppose." With a gallantly mustered air of

nonchalance, she shrugged. "I will not stay where I am not wanted, nor will I spend another night under your roof."

"Rebecca, wait."

"Make up your mind, Viscount Wainsbrough," she said over her shoulder, as her imaginary spy's cloak, her conjured armor, fractured. "Not long ago you ordered me out of your room, a command I now obey." And then *L'araignee* ran straight for the door. Her hand on the knob, cool metal against her moist palm, she twisted and pulled.

"It is your turn to listen." Dirk reached from behind her and slammed the oak panel shut.

"I am not interested."

For a few uncomfortable minutes, an awkward contest of wills ensued, as *L'araignee* fought to flee Dirk's company, and he steadfastly refused to let her go. They pushed and pulled, grunting and panting, as they waged a tug of war. When she could stand no more, she elbowed him in the ribs.

"Oomph." He doubled over, and as he attempted to recover, she planted a heel to his bare toes.

Lightning quick, she opened the door, but he kicked it shut before she could escape. So she tried another shot to his midsection, but he deflected it.

"Rebecca, stop." He caught her wrist.

"Unhand me." Then she recalled her successful maneuver during their swordplay, but he anchored himself stubbornly to the rug, so she resorted to kicking his shin.

"You know, it would have been much easier to take you to bed." Dirk wound an arm about her waist, lifting her, leaving her feet dangling.

"No, thank you. And put me down this instant." With his chest pressed to her back, her targets were limited. As he carried her to his four-poster, which was fast approaching, she bent her knees and tangled her legs in his, sending them tumbling to the floor, her facedown and him sprawled atop her.

"Are you all right?" he asked, the coarse stubble of his jaw grazing the crest of her ear.

"I would be fine if you would kindly remove yourself from my person." Wound tight as a clock spring, she bucked as an unbroken horse, ever aware that each thrust exacted payment in the precious coin of self-control.

"Not until you calm yourself." Dirk eased to the side, lifting much of his weight but keeping her firmly in check.

"What do you mean? I am calm." She squirmed to no avail, and black desolation welled in her heart, spreading slowly, weakening her already tenuous defenses. "If I lose my temper we will both be in trouble."

He chuckled, deep and throaty, which only compounded her misery. "Very well, but first I would have you promise to hear me out."

"No."

"Then we shall stay here all night, love." Nestling close, he draped an arm possessively across her hips, and the contact left her trembling. "My, what a delectable pillow you make."

Helpless, at last *L'araignee* shattered.

With a wresting sob, and despair so compressed the most brilliant sunlight could not penetrate it, Rebecca yielded. Black ice surged in her veins, enveloping her in cold, dense sorrow as thick as London fog. In seconds, the dam burst, and she let forth years of anguish.

"Becca, please, do not cry." Dirk swore under his breath and massaged her shoulders. "I am not worth the salt in your tears."

As he whispered words of regret and begged forgiveness,

she could not elude the unutterable melancholy that imprisoned her. Face pressed to the carpet, Rebecca conjured magical vignettes of the life to which she had dared aspire, and in the next second mourned her short-lived fanciful hopes and dreams, as they whirled in a dark vortex of desolation, before scattering like so much dust in the wind.

"No more." Unbearable tension clawed at her nerves, and she shuddered. "I can take no more."

In a single swift move, Dirk rolled her over, cradling her head in one hand and cupping her chin with the other. "Hush," he said against her lips, and then added, "Hold me."

And Rebecca obeyed, just as his mouth covered hers.

Surrounding warmth suffused her limbs, relaxed her muscles, and melted the oppressive chill beneath her flesh. Unfailing strength beckoned, anchoring her, drawing her from the murky shadows of endless dejection. And then she was floating in blissful oblivion, her mind vacant of a single gloomy thought.

When a palm settled on her breast, long fingers caressing, sending her senses reeling, she opened her eyes and met her rescuer's amber gaze. What she saw there, undeniable passion, sent her spiraling ever higher.

Dirk wanted her.

The knowledge worked on Rebecca in ways she could never have imagined, and just when she entered the fray, suckling his tongue, intensifying their kiss, he lifted his head.

"Are you sure you are all right?" He gave her a cursory glance. "Did I injure you?"

She frowned. "Not as you might think."

"Darling Becca." He sighed so heavily that she felt it to her core. "What am I to do with you?"

She traced the curve of his cheek. "You know what I want."

"My dear, I understand that your profession has encouraged a certain boldness of spirit." The planes of his face hardened, and his jaw locked. "Perhaps that is why I would have our marital life distinguished by observing all strictures."

"Dirk, would you explain yourself in greater detail, because, from my vantage, it sounds as if you do not want me. And before we enact another scene, I would have you clarify your position."

"Somewhere, we are not connecting," he stated with a grimace.

"Oh, I know we are not connecting."

"Ever the vixen," Dirk said with a lopsided grin. "What I am trying to explain is that your sexual history is of no consequence. Only, I am not sure how to declare it without offending you. So, if you think about it, would I court you if your lack of innocence were a factor? To put it simply, I envision our wedding as a rebirth, of sorts, for us both."

At last, realization struck, and Rebecca could only laugh at the absurdity. "You mean, you believe I am no longer—"

"—A virgin."

"And you would marry me despite that?"

"Despite that," Dirk responded without hesitation, and her knight had just regained his horse.

"Why?"

"Because I care for you." And his armor shone bright as the finest silver.

With his grudging confession, her heart positively sang, vanquishing the pain and disappointment at what she had thought was rejection. "Silly Captain. You think me incompetent not a whore." Rebecca huffed in relief. "Colin and I expended considerable effort to protect what we could of my virtue."

"I do not follow."

"My lord, my education in sensual arts extends only as far as what I did to you in the study. As an agent of the Corps, when locale necessitated further measures to safe-guard my body, I drugged my targets with laudanum, and they enjoyed only a good night's sleep, in some instances without achieving completion."

"Wait a minute." With an expression of utter shock, Dirk sat up, and she followed him. "Am I to understand that—"

"Yes." She placed her hand on his arm. "I retain that which is mine to give."

"But, you are so bold, so passionate." Brows almost reaching his hairline, Dirk blinked. "How is it possible?"

"Practice? Ingenuity? Pure luck?" She shrugged. "I would not venture a guess. But there is no such thing as a missish spy, and I approached each assignment always cognizant that I might be required to sacrifice maidenhood for the good of the Crown."

"I cannot even imagine what you have endured." He met her gaze, eyes searching, and then asked, "And none of your targets ever suspected the truth?"

"Some did, but men are so predictable and quite easy to placate. You see, in the face of doubt, I needed only to proclaim my curious conquest a most proficient lover, and there ended the questions. And when Sir Ross suggested I rid myself of my maidenhead, which he considered a dangerous distraction, Colin approached an old friend—a roommate from his days at Eton, to do the deed, but the gentleman declined."

"I do not believe it." He shook his head. "Would it surprise you to know that I am that man?"

"And once again you refuse me."

"Dearest Rebecca." Dirk cupped her cheek. "You are the bravest woman I know."

"Praise, indeed." She kissed his palm. "Now will you take me to bed?"

"Absolutely not." He scrambled to his feet and then helped her stand.

"But—why deny me?"

With indefatigable sangfroid, which she found indefatigably irritating, he said, "Because, in light of recent revelations, I could not, in good conscience, violate your honor."

"To hell and the Reaper with honor. I want you, and I will have you tonight."

"Why so persistent, love?"

"I cannot believe you have to ask. Do you not realize that we live on borrowed time? At any moment, the villain could strike, and all that we are, everything that we have could end," she pleaded. "I would have you—now."

Dirk exhaled audibly. "And I would wait until the vows are spoken, and we are husband and wife."

"No." She shook her head. "That is unacceptable."

"Becca, there is more to your insistence." He set her at arm's length and then planted hands on hips. "What are you not telling me?"

She hesitated, and then frowned. "I am afraid."

"Of what?" Concern rang clear in his voice.

"Of dying. Of losing you. Of never knowing what might have been." Stepping close, she brushed the backs of her fingers along his ribcage, skimmed his taut chest, and finally locked her arms behind his neck. "In the past, my work has left me nauseous and dirty. But with you, it is different;

perhaps because I do not consider it work. Thus far, the Corps has determined my seductions. Just this once—if only this once, I want to spend the night in the arms of a man of my choice. I choose you."

"Becca, you humble me." Dirk set his forehead to hers, as he hugged her so tight she could barely draw breath. "If I take you, there is no going back. The rules governing our respective positions in society are very explicit. You will have to marry me. Do you understand; I will be your only option?"

"Then we are in agreement, because you are the only man I have any interest in touching—or having touch me."

"So, you accept me?"

"Yes."

"You will marry me?"

"*Yes.*"

Without word or warning, Dirk grasped her wrist and made for the door. Shocked that he would make such a bargain and then renege, Rebecca wanted to scream, but she held her tongue. Tears welled, and her throat constricted. She had said her part, had made her argument, and she felt no shame. But when her knight slid the bolt with a definitive click, nervous excitement shivered over her skin.

CHAPTER ELEVEN

*L*eaning against the oak panel, Dirk pulled her into a warm, reassuring embrace, and she softened, melting slowly, sinking into him. He lowered his head, favoring her with a long, lingering, inexpressibly tender kiss, and Rebecca wanted to cry. Desire sparked, a quiescent flame simmering beneath her flesh as it spread, tickling her senses, charging every nerve. The urge to touch him, to work her magic, pooled in her belly, then found convenient outlet in her hand, which she inched between them.

Making quick work of the hooks at his waist, she discovered Dirk fully aroused, scalding hot, and she caressed him in broad, sweeping strokes, at hurried and then lazy intervals. He groaned, an elementally male celebration of her efforts that emboldened her. Rebecca released him, broke their kiss, bent, and took him into her mouth.

For several minutes, she loved and teased him with her tongue. Then she dropped to her knees and set her palms to the twin swells of his bottom, kneading and prodding an urgent rhythm. When he speared his fingers in her hair, holding her in place, and thrust, harder and faster, emitting guttural grunts in time with their fevered pace, almost attacking her mouth, Rebecca hummed in triumph. Focusing on his face, studying his expression, she marveled at the erotic power she wielded. Indeed, the oh-so noble Viscount was hers.

"Enough, else this will be over before it starts." In a flash, Dirk stepped back and swept her into his arms. "Darling, promise me something."

"Your wish is my command," she said, as she scored her nails to the nape of his neck.

"Just for tonight, try not to do anything too encouraging." He grinned.

"But—why?"

"Because your first time should be a memorable experience, and you know I cannot resist you." Dirk nipped playfully at her nose. "Later, you may come at me to your heart's content, and I will sincerely enjoy honing your skills, love."

"All right. But, will it hurt?" she inquired, as he set her on her feet and unfastened the single mother-of-pearl button of her robe, letting the filmy garment slide to the floor. Standing before Dirk as God fashioned her, Rebecca inhaled a deep breath and glanced at the monstrous four-poster bed to her right.

"Only once." Dirk bent, grasped the ends of his breeches and tugged them swiftly to his ankles, before kicking the garment to the rug. Equally naked and thoroughly erect, her knight favored her with a half-smile. "But if I do my job properly, your pain will be minor and soon forgotten."

"Then, by all means, do your job properly, my lord." For some reason Rebecca could not fathom, she was suddenly overtaken by uncharacteristic timidity. Perhaps it was because she had been both instigator and navigator of her previous experiences with the male form. She had always determined when to act, what to do, and how far she would go.

Not so, tonight, she mused.

"Are you frightened?" Dirk trailed a finger along her cheek.

Pondering his question, she exhaled. "A little."

He inclined his head. "Do you trust me?"

"Implicitly," Rebecca responded without hesitation.

With outstretched arms, Dirk said, "Then come here."

In an instant, she stepped into his embrace. Naked, skin to skin, he pressed his hips to hers, letting her feel the hot and hard proof of his desire. Then his lips covered hers, and her fear was forgotten. For a long time, Dirk simply kissed her, but there was nothing simple about his kiss. With a lengthy, lingering communion of flesh, her gallant knight sailed her into erotic seas with an expertise she had not expected of her noble captain. By the time he backed her to the bed and eased her to the mattress, she was breathless.

Resting between her legs, he licked and suckled her breasts before inching lower, blazing a naughty trail to her belly. "Lift your knees," he said as he skimmed his nose through the crisp hair at the apex of her thighs.

Staring at the canopy, she gasped. "Why?"

"Do as I say, love."

Despite thoughts to the contrary, Rebecca complied. "What are you going to do?"

"The same thing you did to me in my study."

"You cannot be—*oh*."

Determined to prevail as an active participant, she fought the compulsion to lose herself in the sensations spearing through her, but hers was a futile gesture. With his tongue as a decadent weapon, Dirk waged a succulent assault on the intimate center of her existence, and reality slipped its anchor. Wave upon wave of pleasure lapped at her nerves, as his head bobbed and weaved in sweet torture. Almost instinctively, she braced for the usual revulsion and self-loathing that accompanied her licentious forays for the Corps, but the discomfiting emotions remained conspicuously absent. Instead, she soared to some heretofore-foreign yet mystical realm, where she felt no shame or regret.

Delicious fire simmered in her limbs, before burning a sumptuous path to the very point where Dirk pressed on her caress after glorious caress. Fisting her hands in the bed linens, Rebecca moaned, as everything inside her seemed to twist and turn in unison, surrendering to the blissful oblivion that beckoned. Suddenly, she could not breathe, and deep within her, something shattered as passion claimed her, and she screamed his name.

Seconds later, in the dark recesses of her mind still capable of coherent thought, she was vaguely aware that her wicked captain had shifted, nudging her thighs further apart as he settled his weight over her. Through a lusty haze of sated torpor she noted the barest stab of pain, which was quickly replaced with an unfamiliar fullness not altogether uncomfortable. When she surfaced, returning to the mortal plane, she discovered Dirk nibbling her lower lip.

"Hello, my lord." Rebecca smiled.

"Hello, yourself." He rubbed his nose to hers. "How do you fare?"

"Better than I expected." She smiled and brought her hands to rest on his shoulders. "So, is this where it hurts? Should I prepare myself?"

"You tell me," Dirk said, as he grazed her jawline with

his teeth, before flexing his spine, withdrawing from her body, and then fluidly thrusting his hips, driving his flesh deep within hers once again. "Feel anything?"

Oh, what she felt. Ecstasy. Elation. Exhilaration. Mustering what strength she had left, Rebecca could manage nothing more than a half-strangled cry in response.

"Praise, indeed, my lady." With a supremely arrogant grin and a chuckle, Dirk began the illicit rhythm.

Again and again, he repeated the erotic dance in an achingly monotonous cadence. Just when she thought she could take no more, he shifted, reared up on his arms, angling each successive penetration ever so slightly, and she feared she might swoon. But her captain kept her grounded, as his gazed locked on hers, and she cradled his face in her hands.

Holding nothing back, Rebecca bared herself in more ways than one, all but begging him to love her.

The noblewoman and the spy.

And his eyes remained focused on hers, as their world collapsed into a sensuous cocoon of ardent whispers and tender caresses infused with unspoken but nonetheless potent devotion. Again and again, Dirk took her to the brink of ecstasy, only to turn tide and leave her wanting more, until she could bear it no longer.

"Do not stop." She twined her fingers in his hair. "Please, do not stop."

Resting on his elbows, he pumped hard and fast, and then froze. With a lusty groan, he whispered her name, and Rebecca was lost.

≈

HOURS LATER, as the last of the candles guttered, Dirk stared at his future wife, who slept, curled to his side, a wisp of hair across her forehead. In the dark, he frowned. The revelations of the night had left him reeling.

Physically, he was content.

Mentally, he was spent.

Rebecca's unexpected innocence, coupled with the wild streak she brought out in him, had again turned his ordered world on end. The barbarian she had unwittingly unleashed took her without considering the consequences, and of that there were many.

Circumstances required they wed in haste.

They may have already conceived a child, and Dirk would brook no question of his heir's birthright. While the lady had consented to marry him, she had not specified a suitable date for the ceremony. And she remained an operative in the employ of the Counterintelligence Corps. Add to that the fact that a traitor lurked in their midst, presenting a threat to Dirk's bride-to-be, and nothing seemed certain, yet he craved certainty.

Recalling their discussion, it was clear Rebecca had not intended to remain an agent in the King's service, but what could he do in the meantime? And what if she changed her mind? He had not wanted a spy for a wife, but he was keenly aware that he might have no choice in the matter, if the two were indelibly enmeshed.

If so, God help them.

~

"MY DEAR, you have the smile of a well-pleasured lady."

Shocked by Lord Everett Markham's forwardness, Rebecca fought to maintain her composure as she circled the elegant dance floor of Howard Hall in the arms of the devilish rogue. Concerned for her safety, in regard to the as yet unknown villain, she tried but failed to summon sufficient spy instincts to disguise the emotions assailing her senses, so she sought diversion in an unsportsmanlike attack.

"Lord Markham, you are positively shameless." And he was an easy target, as Rebecca seized on his weakness. "No wonder Sabrina refused to dance with you."

His arrogant smile morphed to a brooding frown as Everett caught sight of the subject in question, currently fumbling through a waltz with the equally graceful Sir Kleinfeld.

"Have you declared your regard?" she inquired, tongue in cheek.

"I beg your pardon." Unadulterated horror invested his handsome features. "I know of no such regard."

"And you deny it. Could there be more convincing evidence of your interest in Miss Douglas?"

"My dear Lady Rebecca, I would have you know that I am currently plotting the pursuit of a particular ace of spades. Of course, to say more would be ungentlemanly, and I am, if nothing else, a gentleman."

"Indeed."

"Indubitably."

"If you say so."

"I do say."

"All right, my lord." Despite efforts to the contrary, Rebecca giggled. "If that is your story, you had best stay with it."

"It is, and I believe you have inaccurately assessed the situation."

"Oh? How so?"

"You see, Miss Douglas is infatuated with me. She simply cannot resist my estimable charm, therefore she wisely does not put herself in situations where she would be tempted."

Rebecca emitted a rather unladylike snort. "You cannot be serious."

"Oh, but I am. She adores me," he insisted.

"Of that I have no doubt."

"Truly? Then we are in agreement?" Was it her imagination, or had Lord Markham seemed hopeful?

"It appears we are, because Sabrina cannot stop looking at you." Rebecca counted to four and then added, "Just as you search for her with each successive turn we make on the floor."

"Bloody hell."

Now she laughed aloud. "No worries, my lord. I can assure you that your secret is safe."

"Lady Rebecca, I tell you, that Sabrina Douglas is the most fascinating woman I have ever known." He paused and then rolled his eyes. "She is also the most frustrating, foul-mouthed, bungling creature of my unfortunate acquaintance."

"And still you fancy her."

For a moment, Everett simply gaped at her. At last, he furrowed his brow. "I admit nothing."

Rebecca wanted to tell him that, despite his best efforts, his demeanor betrayed the truth in vivid detail. In the underworld of espionage, ferreting information was her specialty. It was her well-formed opinion that the very attempts to conceal the deepest and darkest confidences of the human condition often led to their discovery. In short, the more people tried to hide, the more they revealed, and the rakehell nobleman was no different.

Just then the music stopped, and the dance ended.

"Come, my dear." Extending his arm, Everett pointedly avoided her stare. "I shall return you to the unabashedly besotted Viscount Wainsbrough."

The mere mention of Dirk's name brought telltale warmth to her cheeks, and delicious memories of their night, of his hands, of his mouth, wreaked havoc on her nerves, searing a path straight to her belly, and she tripped.

"It would appear you and Miss Douglas share the same affliction and, dare I presume, for similar cause?" Lord Markham arched a brow and smirked. "Worry not, Lady Rebecca, for I shall keep your secret, too."

"Then we are mutually beholden." She smiled as he realized, however late, that he had just confirmed her suspicions.

As Everett handed Rebecca to Dirk's care, he quickly turned and claimed Sabrina from Sir Kleinfeld. "My dance, Miss Douglas."

"No." Sabrina stood stock-still with hands fisted, and Rebecca pondered a warning but remained silent.

"But I insist." With an arm at Sabrina's waist, Lord Markham steered her toward the dance floor.

"We both know I will only trounce your toes."

"Perhaps I am in the mood to have my toes trounced."

Rebecca winced, because their exchange was truly painful to watch, and she would wager the suave nobleman would soon regret his words.

"Well, Lord Markham, allow me to oblige you." Sabrina stomped hard on Everett's foot and relented as he made it clear he would not be refused.

"Do you think we are that obvious?" Rebecca asked her knight protector.

"Of course not." Dirk shifted his weight and frowned. "We are far too sophisticated for such romantic nonsense."

"Romantic nonsense?" She giggled and inched close. "My lord, are you so immune? If memory serves, you were quite overcome, last night."

A charming red flush spread from his neck to his cheeks, as her not-so-unaffected viscount narrowed his stare and smiled. "That may be, but I believe you are the one who screamed."

"I seem to recall that you made quite a bit of noise, yourself, my lord." With a gentle sashay of her hips, she nudged his very impressive erection. "And mine was merely a humble expression of joy. Let me assure you, I can scream much louder."

"Really?" he whispered. "We should put that to a test. Tonight."

"Oh? An intriguing offer, Captain. But not very...hmm, what is the word I am looking for?" She tapped a finger to her chin and counted to five before meeting his heated gaze. "Romantic."

"Dearest Becca, you are, as always, a challenge." Dirk compressed his lips. "We shall see what I can muster at this late hour to tempt you."

"Only if you are up to it, my lord."

"I believe I have already demonstrated my ability to rise to the occasion, Lady Rebecca."

"I hate to interrupt this touching scene, but we have a mission to complete." Sir Ross scowled at Rebecca. "Do you intend to dawdle all evening, or are we going to work?"

"Sir Ross, what are you doing here?" she asked with a quick search of their immediate area.

"Ensuring that you remain focused on the task at hand."

he replied icily. "My position affords me regular invitations to such droll affairs, but I usually decline."

"If that is the case, how are we to explain your sudden presence without suspicion?" Mind racing, Rebecca clutched Dirk's arm. "There must be a reason for your impromptu affiliation."

"Perhaps I can be of service?" The quietest member of the Brethren stepped forward and cast a shy smile.

"Where did you come from?" Sir Ross snapped in a most ungentlemanly fashion, which gave Rebecca pause.

"Why, I was standing right behind you," the young woman responded with the poise and ease of a gently reared noble. "And you should check your tone, sir."

"My apologies, if I have caused offense." The venerable head of the Corps blushed. "I do not believe I have had the pleasure of your acquaintance."

"Lance will kill me if she is harmed, but I can think of no better justification for your connection to my family." Dirk glanced at Rebecca, then Sir Ross, and back to Rebecca. "Lady Elaine, may I introduce Sir Ross Logan."

Elaine maintained a regal stance, until Sir Ross bowed with a flourish of which Rebecca had not thought him capable. "It is an honor, Lady Elaine."

"Indeed, it is, Sir Ross." Elaine extended a hand. "Now, if it is not too great an imposition, perhaps a waltz will satisfy the gossipmongers and put your fears to rest?"

Sir Ross opened his mouth and then closed it. With a nod, he escorted Elaine to the dance floor, just as Trevor appeared with a visibly faltering Caroline.

"Trevor, stop doting on me." Caroline fanned herself. "It is just a bit warm in here."

"I am doting on two." With a worried expression, Trevor

placed a protective arm around his wife's shoulders. "Please, sit, if only for a moment."

When Caroline swayed, both Rebecca and Dirk reached to steady her.

"Enough. We are going home." Trevor flagged down a passing servant. "Have the Lockwood carriage brought around." To Dirk, he said, "Will you help me get her out of here?"

"Of course." Dirk stepped forward.

"That is not necessary," Caroline insisted. "I can walk." As if to prove her point, she took a rather shaky step and teetered again.

"Hold hard." Dirk assumed a position of support at Caroline's side, opposite her husband. "Lean on me." To Rebecca he said, "Will you be all right?"

"Certainly." Studying the care and concern her intended displayed for his friend left Rebecca deliciously giddy.

Often conveying an air of casual indifference, especially aboard ship, Dirk seemed terminally in control. While there was something to be said for self-discipline, she rather preferred the rapacious barbarian that claimed her most intimate gift. Prior to last night, never would she have guessed that her no-nonsense lord possessed a wild streak that could rival the most licentious operative of the Corps. Almost instantly, a masculine chorus of lusty grunts and groans filled her ears, erotic images flashed in her brain, and her heart pounded. The hair rose on the back of her neck, and she shuddered.

L'araignee came alert and scanned the room.

Near the back wall, Mr. Clarkson, the oily secretary from Sir Ross' office, smiled and raised his glass. Strange, he acted as if he knew her, but she had always worn her cloak when visiting the headquarters of the Corps. To the best of her knowledge, he had never seen her face. Had Sir Ross enlisted his aid to protect her?

Mentally, the spy shook her head. Clarkson was not a trained operative, a person of estimable rank, or a titled member of the peerage to garner invitation to one of the *ton's* most exclusive celebrations. Yet, there he was, mingling with the crowd. Had not Dirk claimed that he had seen Clarkson at the ball at Richmond House, earlier in the Season? At the time, she had thought it rather farfetched and had dismissed Dirk's assertion, as had Sir Ross. So how could she explain his presence at another social function?

A mix of partygoers obscured her view, and she lost sight of the secretary. When the crowd parted, *L'araignee* was nonplussed to discover him gone. The gentle movement of drapery snared her attention, and she made her way to a pair of French doors, which hung slightly ajar to allow the cool night air into the somewhat stuffy ballroom. With a quick glance over her shoulder, she sidestepped to the small terrace.

Silvery moonlight cast an eerie mosaic of shadows from the rail and overhanging tree branches on the tiled floor. A mix of crickets and all manner of night creatures weaved an audial tapestry that reached a fevered pitch as *L'araignee* closed her eyes to acclimate her vision. It was a trick of the trade that never failed. Gooseflesh covered her from head to toe.

She was not alone.

Fear surfaced in an instant, and she dipped her chin in insouciant salute. Fighting every natural instinct to flee, she held her ground and waited. When the cold, steel end of a gun barrel pressed into her back, she forced herself to remain calm.

"Lady Rebecca, you should not have returned to London."

The voice of her assailant was unnaturally deep, masking the subtle nuances, as if he knew how to disguise his true identity. Rolling her shoulders to keep distracting tension at bay, *L'araignee* inhaled and asked, "What do you want?"

"You know what I seek. For your sake, I hope you have not already surrendered it to Sir Ross."

"There must be some mistake," she replied with child-like innocence. How would a noblewoman respond to such a situation?

"There is no mistake."

"I beg your pardon?" And then she seized on an appropriate reaction. "Is this a robbery? You may take my jewels. I will not resist you."

"Do not play coy with me, because I know of your connection to Colin Eddington, and I am immune to your charms. I can kill you right now and sleep as a babe tonight."

"There must be some mistake." Very slowly, *L'araignee* lowered her head and began a tortoise-like turn to the left.

The barrel jammed hard into her shoulder blade.

"Face forward, or you are dead."

She swallowed hard. "You would not shoot me here, not with so many witnesses nearby."

Myriad maneuvers beckoned, but she was unsure of her success, so she made no move. And she pondered how long Dirk would be gone. When he found her missing, would he search for her and imperil himself? And where was Sir Ross?

"Your confidence will be your downfall."

"Your carelessness will be yours," *L'araignee* snapped and then bit her tongue against further outburst, lest her temper betray her.

"At last, a glimpse of the much touted spirit." The villain gave vent to a sinister laugh. "So the whore fancies herself a worthy adversary? How enticing, and what I would like to do to you. A pity that your protector was stupid and reckless, leaving you to bear his burden."

In silence, *L'araignee* breathed a sigh of relief, because her attacker had no knowledge of her true occupation. He believed her nothing more than a wealthy man's mistress, albeit in possession of some unknown item of value, which was an important clue, so she played into the ruse.

"How dare you speak ill of Colin. He was brilliant."

"Not so brilliant as to escape death."

Despite all her training, she was still human, and her emotions got the best of her.

"I swear I will find you."

"That day will be your last."

"You can run but you cannot hide." *L'araignee* had to keep him talking. Surely Sir Ross was watching and waiting to make the arrest.

"You are the one who should hide, not that it will do you any good. Ignorance will not save you, Lady Rebecca, and my associates are not the patient sort. We will get what we want from you—with or without your cooperation."

"I have no intention of hiding, and you cannot take that which I do not have."

"No, but we can bleed you. We can hurt you until you beg for mercy. And even after we have obtained what we want, we can hurt you for our pleasure."

"But I do not know what you seek." She needed to do

something, had to make some attempt to discern the identity of the traitor.

"Then you had better find out and soon. You will hear from me again, and you should be more forthcoming if you value your life. Colin can no longer protect you."

The weapon shifted, the pressure eased, and *L'araignee* seized the opportunity. In a flash, she turned, only to be stopped by an agonizing blow to the back of her head.

Then there was no pain.

CHAPTER TWELVE

"Open your eyes, love." Dirk stared at Rebecca's limp form. "You are safe and home."

His future wife mumbled incoherently before sitting upright in a rush, with fists flailing and legs kicking wildly.

"Hold her, Lord Wainsbrough." Dr. Handley pinched her nose, and when she opened her mouth to gasp for air, he forced a healthy dose of laudanum down her throat.

Bucking, as would an unbroken horse, her head jerked violently from side to side, as the thick, syrupy medicine seeped from the corner of her lips, and she moaned in protest.

Damian and Dalton each caught an ankle, while Dirk pressed his palms to her forearms, leaned over her, and eased her to the mattress.

Why had he left her alone?

That singular question had repeated itself a thousand times in his mind, a castigating refrain, ever since Sir Ross appeared from nowhere, tapped Dirk on the elbow, and informed him that Rebecca was injured. Fear for her life ripped through him, overwhelming guilt rode in its wake, and a world of regret anchored on his shoulders.

It had taken mere minutes to convey Caroline to the Lockwood carriage, but Lady Jersey had waylaid him in the foyer, with an endless stream of queries regarding his relationship with Lady Rebecca. Ever the gentleman, he had endured the impromptu interrogation with unimpaired aplomb. When he returned to the ballroom, he discovered the spy curiously absent. In an instant, he learned that years of ingrained civility and polite decorum could exact a heavy toll.

And Rebecca had paid the price.

Somehow, Dirk knew he would never erase the image of her motionless body, sprawled on the tiled floor of the terrace at Howard Hall, after an unknown assailant had attacked her. A chill had traipsed his spine as he lifted her head, cradled her in his hand, and the slick ooze of blood seeped between his fingers. An unfamiliar rage shredded all semblances of control and rational thought, and Dirk wanted to kill. Wanted to tear the unidentified blackguard's throat out with his teeth. Indeed, desire for revenge was a powerful inducement, almost as intoxicating, as seductive as lovemaking.

"Dirk," she murmured, barely intelligible.

In a flash, fury yielded to concern. "I am here, darling."

With something between a sob and a sigh, she called him again and relaxed.

"The lady needs rest, Lord Wainsbrough." The doctor bent and monitored her breathing and heartbeat and then stood tall. "I shall check her condition in the morning."

Studying her face, so graceful in repose, Dirk asked, "Will she be all right?"

"It is nothing more than a goose egg and a nasty scrape

on the noggin, which always bleeds to excess," the elder physician assured. "I daresay her fitful reaction is a delayed response to the assault. You'll see, she will be better when she wakes."

From the shadows, Sir Ross stepped forward and frowned. "Send for me when she is lucid, as she must be interviewed." He sketched a curt bow. "Dr. Handley, shall we take our leave?"

"Thank you, Sir Ross." Retrieving his black bag, Dr. Handley rubbed his furrowed brow. "Lord Wainsbrough. Sir Dalton. Your Grace. I bid you good night."

At the threshold, the physician paused, gazed at Rebecca, and shook his head. "A female interpreter? Whoever would have suspected such an outlandish notion? One would think Wellington could find enough men to speak the enemy's language without involving a woman in this infernal war. The next thing you know, our ladies will want to wear breeches."

"If you need anything, know you shall have it." Damian tugged his cravat loose and unbuttoned his waistcoat. "I will convey the news of her condition to the others." With a nod, he followed Dr. Handley and Sir Ross and closed the door behind him.

Quiet, neither peaceful nor comforting, settled on Rebecca's chamber. As Dirk remained a sentry at her bedside, countless emotions prevailed on his heretofore-unshakeable self-control, and he pressed a clenched fist to his mouth lest he embarrass himself.

"How are you, brother mine?"

"I am no mood for levity, Dalton."

"Oh, of that I have no doubt.

"What do you want?"

"Only to offer support."

Dirk met his sibling's stare and was nonplussed to see no hint of the usual inappropriate humor. "I am sorry. I have no quarrel with you."

"No worries, old man." With a lopsided grin, Dalton chucked his shoulder. "It is altogether discomposing to see you so undone. If memory serves, you weren't half so over-wrought after my most grievous infraction, when I got loaded to the gunwalls and hid under the bed in your bachelor lodgings while you weighed anchor in Lady Spencer's harbor. Even then, you found sport in the absurdity of the situation. Tell me, how does it feel?"

"How does what feel?"

"To be in love." It was a statement, not a question.

For a scarce second, Dirk toyed with denial, but he had to consider the facts. The reality was he could neither command nor, at the very least, manage his emotions. It was as if some invisible force dictated his every move, and each successive charge placed him in greater peril of running amok. He was not ready to put a name to his affliction, but he was too smart to ignore the possibility. "Do you really want to know?"

"Yes."

"As if I am rudderless in stormy seas." Dirk grimaced and raked his fingers through his hair. "As though my innards have been devoured by a wake of buzzards. Like someone ran a ramrod up my—"

"I get your meaning, and how appealing it sounds, though it differs somewhat from the stuff of poets." Dalton wrinkled his nose.

"Believe me, brother, I would not wish this on the worst reprobate of my acquaintance."

"So what do you intend to do about it?" Dalton pulled his lucky coin from his pocket and repeatedly tossed it in the air. It was a habit that Dirk found annoying, but, in light of the circumstances, it barely registered.

"I haven't the faintest clue."

"Oh, I say." Dalton's eyes grew wide. "You are done for."

"How can you be so certain?"

"Because never have I known you not to have a plan." Dalton snorted. "Even when we were in shortcoats, while I often squandered my monthly allowance in a week, you always saved your money, spending no more than the income from the high-interest loans you made to our classmates."

Plagued by uncharacteristic indecision, Dirk pushed away from the bed and paced, stopping only to glance at Rebecca before reversing course. Pondering one maneuver after another, he could seize no viable solution to his quandary. "This is all my fault."

Dalton arched a brow. "You blame yourself for what's happened?"

"I most certainly do." Dirk paused and retraced the evening's events. "I am tasked with her protection, and I left her alone to trade mindless chitchat with Lady Jersey."

Rebecca shifted and whispered his name. Dirk froze until she calmed, yet he was anything but calm. Wound tight as a clock spring, he wanted to roar. Every attempt to marshal his temper only compounded his anger and something else. Some powerful emotion he had yet to fully distinguish held him captive as it took up residence deep in his chest, rendering him weak, shaken, and bewildered.

"Who found her?" Dalton inquired in a low voice.

"Lord Varringdale."

"How did he come upon her?"

"Claims he was in the garden with a friend and unwittingly witnessed the altercation."

"Unwittingly?"

"He saw two silhouettes and thought it was nothing more than a rendezvous, until one struck the other."

"Did he get a look at the traitor?"

"No." Dirk shook his head. "It was too dark, and the villain's face was obscured in the shadows. Varringdale alerted Sir Ross, and they found Rebecca." He fixed his gaze on the ceiling and shuddered. Why, oh, why had he always followed the straight and narrow path? "She could have been killed as a direct result of my exacting obeisance of social strictures."

"Wait a minute, brother. You cannot assume responsibility for someone else's crime, and Rebecca is a servant of the Crown. She knows the risks involved and has accepted the mission. In any case, she is never going to lure the traitor with you by her side, but there may be a way to provide protection without your physical presence." Dalton rounded the bed and, with shoulders squared, faced Dirk. "Are you certain you want to marry her?"

"I will have no other," he responded without hesitation.

"Then we must capture the turncoat if you are to have any future together," Dalton pointed out. "You cannot spend the rest of your life constantly looking over your shoulder."

"I do not care about that."

"And what of children? You have always wanted a family." Dalton inclined his head and frowned. "Are you willing to risk your heirs?"

"It does not signify." Dirk clenched and unclenched his fists. "I can protect what's mine."

His younger sibling cast a glance at Rebecca. "What if it signifies to her?"

"Why are you doing this?" Dirk settled his hands on his hips. "Why are you saying these things?"

"Someone has to be the devil's advocate, because you have the devil in your wake." Dalton compressed his lips. "Best to consider all the possibilities."

"Believe me, I have thought of everything," Dirk replied with a heavy sigh.

"All right, then here is my proposal." Dalton lifted his chin. "Marry her."

"I intend to."

"No, brother, I mean marry her—now. Put the full weight of the Brethren behind her. Our extended familial allegiance is well known, and the double-dealer will think twice about bashing her skull when next they meet."

As much as Dirk hated to admit it, the scamp's logic was sound. "Do you really believe it would make a difference to a criminal?"

"Think about it, brother. When Trevor stole Caroline from my ship, Blake and Damian cut to the chase, stemmed the tide, and caught him in the middle of the open ocean." Dalton grinned, his cocky, oh-so-confident grin. "If you were the traitor, would you want us on your tail?"

STANDING on the doorstep of Calvert House, Dirk handed his card to the butler and was immediately granted an audience. In the dining room, at the head of a long table, sat Lucien Wentworth, Earl of Calvert and Rebecca's elder brother, dressed in trousers and a black satin robe, his hair still wet from a bath. With a quizzical expression, he waved a welcome.

"Have a seat, Wainsbrough. Have you eaten?"

"I have." Dirk looked on with amusement. Oh, to be so unencumbered, yet such ease would not be long-lived once he shared the truth of Rebecca's occupation. "It is a bit late in the morning for breakfast."

"Ah, well, what can one say?" Lucien smiled with self-satisfied smugness. "I was otherwise engaged last night, if you get my meaning, and returned to find my house filled with Runners."

Dirk gasped. "Bow Street Runners?"

"Indeed." The young lieutenant dabbed the corners of his mouth with his napkin. "It appears we have had a break-in, though I have yet to discern what, if anything, was stolen."

"Really?" An ominous chill settled in the pit of his stomach, and Dirk shuddered. "Then how do you know you had a break-in?"

"The chamber was a bloody mess." Lucien took a liberal gulp of coffee. "Even the mattress was turned. Daresay, it will take the servants several days to put everything right."

Tapping a finger to his chin, and pondering the curious development, Dirk sat back in his chair. Perhaps the incident was nothing more than an unrelated coincidence. "Why would someone go through your bedchamber?"

"Oh, not mine." Lucien set his napkin on the table and scoffed. "It was Rebecca's quarters. I suppose the bounder had a sick preoccupation with women's fashions." He steepled his hands. "So, tell me, to what do I owe the honor of your company? I presume this has something to do with my sister."

"It does, and I may be able to make some sense of your break-in." Dirk took a deep breath and met the young man's piercing stare. "Have you ever wondered what Rebecca did to busy herself after you joined the Navy?"

In stupefied silence, Lucien listened as Dirk told him of his sister's chosen profession, her tenure in the Counterintelligence Corps, the events surrounding Colin's death, and the extent of the threat to her life. Lucien blanched and winced when Dirk detailed their current mission, how the courtship began as a ruse, and part of the plot to catch a traitor, which presented suitable cover for her temporary residence in his home and offered her a modicum of safety. Most difficult to explicate was his now earnest courtship, the previous night's assault, and Dirk's intent to wed Rebecca as soon as his petition for a special license was granted.

"My God." Lucien leaned forward, with both elbows on the table, and cradled his head. "She has never gotten over the death of our parents. But never would I have imagined this." He looked up; his eyes glistened with tears and determination. "Tell me what I can do to help protect her."

"I need your support."

"Wainsbrough, I am at your service." Lucien offered an outstretched hand, which Dirk accepted with a firm grip. "But I thought you said Rebecca already accepted your proposal. Is my sister being willful?"

"She has agreed to marry me." Dirk nodded. "But we have discussed a ceremony at the end of the Season, contingent upon capturing the traitor. I am not certain she will be amenable to hasty nuptials, and I am equally unsure of her regard. Perhaps you could provide assistance with the matter."

For several seconds, Lucien studied Dirk. At long last, he shifted and sighed. "Do you care for my sister?"

It was inevitable that her brother would ask the one question guaranteed to perplex Dirk, and he knew he could not evade the query were he to secure the much-required allegiance. Numerous responses formed in his brain, none of which calmed his nerves or his racing heart. In a flash, his world spun out of control, an annoying affliction that occurred with greater frequency of late. Composing an answer would offer no measure of comfort, so he opted for heavily varnished honesty.

"While I am compelled to wed Rebecca for reasons other than emotion, I will not deny that I hold her in high esteem."

An uneasy quiet fell upon the room, as Dirk again became the subject of Lucien's scrutiny. Swallowing the urge to press his suit, Dirk summoned patience that ought to qualify him for sainthood. Mentally, he ticked off various options, one by one, should his scheme fail.

"I will speak to my sister, but I must do so this afternoon." Lucien stood. "I sail with the *Intrepid* on tomorrow's tide, and we will not return to port for another two weeks, at least."

After securing a gentleman's agreement, Dirk left the earl to finish his breakfast, though it appeared Lucien had lost his appetite.

Regaining his curricle, Dirk flicked the reins and headed for his next destination. Like a man preparing for battle, he was gathering his defenses, and there was one more party to enlist in his campaign. One more person to convince his plan was for the best—before facing Rebecca.

As he merged into the lane, he tried not to consider the nagging doubts plaguing his subconscious. He was acting impetuously, rashly even, and such behavior was uncharacteristic for him.

Constancy and preparation were key elements of his persona; they were ingrained in his psyche. Never had he acted without a well thought plan and a reasonable, attainable goal. Given the unpredictable nature of his present mission, Dirk could determine no definitive conclusion. Yet he remained entrenched in the belief that his course was correct.

While he desired control, he desired Rebecca more. The beautiful agent was his, already promised, if only he could keep her alive until they discharged their task. No fear for his own mortality bolstered his motives, because he had faced death numerous times as a knight of the Brethren. Rebecca's demise he could not comprehend, at all. It was his duty to protect her—by any means necessary.

But would she see it that way?

And if she could, would she be willing to embark on a life that would require her to sever all ties with the dark world of espionage? It was a conversation that had yet to be spoken, but he was fervent in his position. Though he was marrying a spy, he would not allow his viscountess to remain in service to the Crown. Which begged the question: What would he do if the two were inseparable?

SITTING in the morning room at Randolph House, Rebecca arched a brow in question and eyed Dirk with unfettered skepticism that visibly increased in epic proportions when he sidestepped to permit Lucien and Sir Ross entry. Setting aside her needlework, she clasped her hands in her lap in a calculated display of feminine deportment that had not fooled him for a minute. Dirk was grateful when she focused on Sir Ross. For his plan to work he needed to remain in her good grace, so he was content to blend into the background, and let his co-conspirators do their worst.

"Why is my brother here?" Her voice was clipped and accusatory.

Sir Ross stood before her, hands on his hips. "After what happened last night, I have determined that he is also at risk."

"Precisely what does my getting hit on the head have to do with Lucien?" she snapped.

"Sir Ross is referring to the break-in at Calvert House," Lucien inserted into the conversation. "Specifically, your room was targeted and completely dismantled."

That brought her swiftly to her feet. "Are you all right?" Grasping her brother by his forearms she looked him over, top to toe. "Did they harm you?"

"Did they harm me?" Lucien took hold of her shoulders, shaking her roughly. "You dare ask if they harmed me? You nearly got your skull cracked, and you are worried about me?"

"Lucien, please, you do not understand." Rebecca half-sobbed.

"Make me understand." He shook her again, lifting her till her feet barely touched the floor. "You've been traipsing the Continent as an operative for His Majesty these last five years, doing God knows what, risking your life time and again, and you have the audacity to ask if I am all right?"

"I had to do it." Tears welled in her eyes. "For Mama and Papa."

As her brother gave her another jolt, Dirk placed his hand on the young man's shoulder. "Easy, Lucien."

Just as fast, Sir Ross halted Dirk's interference. Together, they retreated and let brother and sister work through their differences. And, as such, allowed their strategy to run its intended course.

"Did it ever once occur to you to tell me of your occupation?" Lucien pushed her away as if he'd been scalded. "Christ, Becca, when I think of all those times you saw me cast off, standing there on the docks. Always reminding me to be careful and to come home safe." His eyes narrowed, and he pinned her with his stare. "You little hypocrite."

"But I was only thinking of you." She spread her hands wide in supplication. "I did not want you to worry."

"You did not want me to worry?" He folded his arms in front of him, adopting a stubborn stance. "What the devil do you presume I do while at sea? Do you believe I simply sail away and forget about you? Sister, you are never far from my thoughts. As it is, I am shipping out tomorrow. How will I ever be able to concentrate on my duties?"

The contretemps played before Dirk as a well-orchestrated affair, but could Lucien deliver the final blow? With each successive point made, her brother wore her down, as evidenced by her quivering chin and ever-slumping shoulders. Confidence in the outcome grew by leaps and bounds, when Dirk noted the first tear fall.

Lowering his head, Lucien gave her his back and sighed audibly. "After everything we have been through, the loss we have endured. How could you, Becca?" he asked in a melancholy tone. "How could you do something so dangerous without confiding in me? How could you risk your life, without even saying goodbye? Have you no care for me? You are all I have left in the world."

"Forgive me, please." With a tentative step, Rebecca hugged her brother from behind and pressed her cheek to his shoulder. "I swear, I will do anything to make it up to you."

Beyond her view, Lucien met Dirk's gaze, winked, and smiled a sly smile that gave Dirk gooseflesh. "Anything?"

"Anything, I promise."

"Perfect!" Lucien whirled around. "I have a solution that will serve us well." He cupped her chin in his palm. "I understand Lord Wainsbrough has offered for you?" When she nodded her agreement, he continued. "I approve of the match and give you my blessing. As a small request, to soothe my delicate nerves, I urge you to wed with all possible haste, sister."

Before Rebecca could reply, Lucien made a show of addressing Dirk directly. "Lord Wainsbrough, while I know it is an imposition to ask, and I would not do so were the situation not of the gravest importance, would you consider marrying Becca immediately? I would feel much better knowing she has your protection."

"*Lucien*." Rebecca appeared aghast at his suggestion. "I will not marry Lord Wainsbrough merely to procure a bodyguard."

"Oh, I say." With both brows raised, and fighting a wicked grin, Dirk summoned a wide-eyed impersonation of cherubic innocence that never failed to fell his mother. Their scheme was working better than he had hoped. "I had not thought of that, but your idea has merit."

Completely ignoring Rebecca's ever-growing protests, Lucien then turned to Sir Ross. "Do you think it would impede her mission in any way?"

"You cannot be serious." Rebecca elbowed Lucien in the ribs.

Sir Ross averted his stare and pretended to give the matter due consideration. "No, I do not think it would frustrate our villain in the least. After last night, I would venture to guess he is growing more impatient and desperate by the hour. In fact, this might just provide the impetus needed to motivate the blackguard."

"Sir Ross, please," Rebecca pleaded. "Surely you cannot agree with this insanity."

"Actually, your brother makes a valid point, Rebecca."

Tapping a finger to his lower lip, Sir Ross paced with the grace of a jungle cat. "There have been two attempts on your life, your home has been burgled, and we have every reason to believe these crimes are connected. Perhaps when his efforts to dispose of you proved unsuccessful, the traitor chose to invade your dwelling, which put your brother at risk. In any case, as Viscountess Wainsbrough you would have a formidable defense.

"Our villain lives in the shadows, using anonymity as a shield. Killing the wife of a peer would instigate a search for a murderer such as London has rarely seen. It would be lunacy. Whoever we're dealing with would be aware of that fact. Thus your nuptials would work to your safety and our advantage."

Wringing her fingers, she gazed at the floor. "All right. I—"

"Wonderful." Lucien beamed at his sister. "You can be married as soon as Lord Wainsbrough secures a special license." As Rebecca opened her mouth to speak, he added, "Oh, Becca, my spirits are much improved. Now I can sail content in the knowledge that you are secure."

"Lucien, wait—"

"You accepted him."

"I did."

"You said anything."

"Yes, I did."

CHAPTER THIRTEEN

*I*t was late in the afternoon when Hughes informed Dirk that *he* had been summoned to *his* study. His initial response was intense irritation. No one, not even his mother, dared commandeer his domain, which left only one person currently residing beneath his roof with gumption sufficient to execute such brazen stratagem; and that possibility gave him pause to reflect.

Under normal circumstances, he might have been angry at having his authority so audaciously usurped; yet he could muster no ire. When he found Rebecca, wringing her hands, muttering incoherently, and pacing before the window, he could only smile. The spy with sad eyes was overset, and he decided he liked her overset.

With nary a sound, he closed the door and leaned against it. "You sent for me, love?"

With a start, she whirled around. "My lord, I would have a word."

"My lady, I would have more."

In a mere handful of strides he closed the distance between them. Rebecca took two steps back—to no avail.

He hauled her into his arms and ravaged her luscious lips. Struggling and squirming in his grasp, she pulled her mouth from his, so he gave his attention to the sensitive crest of her ear, tracing the delicate arc with his tongue and nibbling playfully on the fleshy lobe.

"Dirk, you must stop," she said breathlessly. "I cannot think."

"Then do not think," he murmured against her temple. "Just kiss me."

She acted as he bade, and memories of last night besieged his senses. Fearing for her safety, and unwilling to leave her side, Dirk had climbed into her bed in the wee hours of the morning, with no licentious intentions. But his agent provocateur had intentions of her own.

At some point Rebecca reached for him, and he reached for her. It mattered not who made the first move, only that theirs was a shared goal; mutual reassurance found in mutual pleasure. And she came at him with a hunger he had never before experienced. Acquiescing to her whispered request to let her have her way, he relinquished the helm and marveled as she steered him into heretofore-unrivaled erotic seas. He recalled her nimble fingers, her naughty tongue, and her sultry cries of ecstasy. Even now, just thinking of her wanton but unschooled maneuvers summoned a stout salute from his Jolly Roger. Indeed, Dirk was sincerely looking forward to his wedding night.

When next he came up for air, he pressed his forehead to hers and sighed. "I have ordered my staff to move your belongings to the viscountess's suite."

"What?" She frowned as if to chastise him, but he wasn't fooled for a second. "But we are not married. And where will your mother stay?"

"Believe me, she was more than happy to vacate her

rooms." He pressed his hips to hers and thrust ever so slightly. "Besides, I want you near, where I can protect you."

With an arched brow, she cast him a flirty smile. "Are you certain it is protection you wish to offer me?"

"Perhaps close cover is more apropos." He rocked again. "Very close."

"My lord, you are distracting me, and there is something of importance I wish to discuss."

"All right." Reluctantly he freed her from his grasp. "If you insist on working, tell me what is wrong."

"About last night. Did you see Sir Ross when you returned to the ballroom?"

"No. Why?"

"Because he was supposed to be guarding me, yet he was curiously absent when I was attacked." Now she frowned in earnest. "I expected him to burst on the scene and arrest the villain, but he never appeared."

"Perhaps he was diverted by Elaine."

"But the sole purpose of his presence at the ball was to monitor our mission, and he is a past master at espionage." She tapped a finger to her chin. "And there is something else I haven't told you. I spotted Clarkson at the event."

"Logan's secretary?"

"The very one." She rubbed her arms. "And the way he looked at me...as though he were aware of my occupation."

"If memory serves, he attended the ball at Richmond House, too. What would a man of his standing be doing at another one of the *ton*'s premiere galas?" Dirk mulled the possibilities, searching for a plausible explanation. "Would Sir Ross enlist Clarkson's aid?"

"I wondered the same thing, and it makes no sense. Clarkson is not a trained operative, and we could just as easily secure another spy, so why was he there?"

"I cannot fathom. Did you mention it to Sir Ross during the debriefing?"

"No."

"Why not?"

"I am not sure," she said with a shrug.

"Do you suspect him?"

"Oh, I do not know what to think." She paced. "My previous missions involved a designated target and a clearly defined goal. Colin and I strategized, formed a plan of attack, and executed it, without fail. Our assignment is utterly foreign. It is frustrating to battle an enemy I cannot see, and it is even worse to sit idly and wait for the traitor to make his move. The situation is beyond my control, and I do not like it. If only we could recruit additional agents without alerting Sir Ross."

"I suppose such conjecture is justified." Dirk raked his fingers through his hair. "But why would he charge me with your protection if he intended to harm you?"

"To deflect attention from himself and thereby provide the means to strike."

At her unsettling revelation, a shiver of dread traipsed his spine. "Logan is in a position to obtain the most intelligence and inflict the greatest damage."

"For all we know, he could be Denis. Perhaps that is why none of our agents has ever been rescued alive."

Dirk swallowed hard and purposely ignored the grievous implications of her conclusion. "I say, you do suspect him."

"Yes, and I feel terrible about it."

"So what do you require, lady mine?"

"Assistance." With chin held high, Rebecca met his questioning gaze. "Could we trust your friends were we to divulge all the facts, including my true occupation, surrounding our mission?"

"Aye, that is just what I would suggest."

"Are you absolutely certain of their reliability?"

Bloody hell, he had secrets of his own to share, and he was infinitely unsure of her reaction. "More than you know."

"Then I shall leave their briefing to you." Rebecca paused and then faced him. "And there is something else."

For some reason he could not explain, Dirk shuddered. Perhaps it was her dour expression that chilled him to the marrow and set his nerves on edge. "And that would be —what?"

"We need to discuss our arrangement."

"Our *arrangement*?" he asked. "Perhaps you are referring to our impending nuptials."

In an abrupt change of tack, she gave him her back. "In regard to our wedding, there is one condition upon which we must agree, or I will not marry you."

"But you have already accepted my proposal, and you promised your brother." Anger surfaced, slow and steady, but he clenched his fists and managed to speak calmly. "Are you reneging?"

"No." She shook her head. "I will marry you—with a stipulation."

"And that would be—what?" he prompted, steeling for her response.

"Should either of us desire it, a divorce may be obtained once the traitor is caught, and the mission is complete."

"What!" Dirk shouted in unveiled anger. "Have you no honor? I made you an earnest offer—one you accepted. Do not think you can change your mind now."

"I am not changing my mind," she insisted. "I merely seek to make the situation more convenient for you."

"For me or for you?" Dirk replied, his voice dripping sarcasm. "We are not even married and already you seek freedom. Are you so encumbered?"

"Please, you misunderstand. Do not think me ignorant of your motives." Rebecca reached for him and grasped his hand in hers. "You have an uncommonly strong sense of duty, and you have been tasked with my protection. As I feel I have come to know you quite well, I believe you would do whatever necessary, even if it meant sacrificing your own happiness, to fulfill your obligation. I care for you too much to secure my future on the ruin of yours."

Shaken to his core, Dirk could only stand there and process the significance of her declaration. At first glance, Rebecca had spoken to him as a man desirous of ridding himself of an importuning mistress. But there was more to her request, as evidenced by her last statement. "You care for me?"

Her eyes flared as she kissed his palm. "How could you doubt it?"

Because she had not been very forthcoming in her attachment.

"Yet you think me indifferent?"

"Given the passion we have shared, I will be forever in your debt," she said quietly. "But I am not so naïve to equate lust with love."

"And if I am not indifferent?" He bit his tongue against further spontaneous confessions and shifted his weight. Everything that had seemed so clear when he entered his study was suddenly muddled. Was he nothing more than her lover to be cast aside when she had no need of him?

Rebecca blinked but remained stubbornly silent, and Dirk had never felt more uncertain in his life. He hoped for a sign or, at the very least, some validation of his bold but unplanned admission. In that moment, words failed him, because his course was no longer firmly set in place.

Driven to distraction, and thoughts focused solely on escape, he stomped to his desk, yanked open the top drawer, and retrieved a tiny parcel. After tossing the box haphazardly atop the blotter, he marched to the door but halted, truly regretting what he was about to say.

"Once our business is concluded, if it is your wish, you may have your divorce."

UPON ENTERING the dining room the following morning, Rebecca was disappointed to find it as empty as the right side of her bed remained the previous night. Had she known her generous offer to grant Dirk a divorce would result in much unexpected and equally unappreciated forced abstinence, she would have reconsidered her course or abandoned it altogether. The wee hours seemed to last an eternity, as she tossed and turned in a valiant but vain effort to sleep. Thus her nerves were on end as she pressed a hand to her upset belly. Despite her lack of appetite, she made quick work of dry toast and sent for a mount.

Hyde Park was aglow in the golden light of the rising sun. The landscape was resplendent, as the dew-covered grass glittered, and a chorus of birdcalls formed a delicate serenade, but Rebecca concentrated on her search for Dirk. With a nudge of her mare, she set off for the sandy track and was disappointed to discover it virtually deserted.

Blast, blast, blast!

Sometime during the night, she pondered her successful tenure with Colin. So in tune to each other's thoughts and moves, they were as honey on a hot scone. In every sense save one they were a dynamic duo. Now she understood her late colleague's advice regarding romantic attachments and work. Despite her training, she had crossed an imaginary line and made a mess of her current partnership.

She could not sleep.

Could not eat.

Could not think.

In short, she had not a chance in hell of capturing her prey. Instead of watching for any sign of the traitor, her attention was commanded by Dirk Randolph, not that it mattered.

The villain was a sly one.

Based on years of experience and knowledge, she surmised the turncoat was purposefully waiting, watching, and studying, which heightened her anticipation and kept her on tiptoes. Constantly guessing at the enemy's next move, she was completely off balance. It was a brilliant tactic; one she had used many times.

In the past, when missions became inordinately stressful, she and Colin played poker, wagering late night surveillance shifts and all manner of unsavory work. At that very moment, her game of choice had nothing to do with cards and everything to do with one very stubborn viscount and a four-poster bed...or the plush chair in his library. Thanks to her bright idea, her anxiety had increased tenfold. Heaven help her if he petitioned for a divorce when their task was complete.

Rebecca mentally kicked herself.

If Dirk had come to her with such a proposal, she would have drawn her pistol and shot him in a rather sensitive spot, before putting a bullet between his eyes. Well, she might not have done anything quite so dramatic, but she would've been furious all the same.

Pounding hoofbeats brought her alert in an instant.

Rebecca turned in the saddle—and froze. Every muscle tensed, and she stiffened her spine, sitting fully erect and mustering a half-smile. Instinct told her to run; yet she could not afford to give offense, in light of her task. Still, she wondered why the approaching rider affected her thus.

"Lord Varringdale, how lovely to see you this morning."

He reined in, bringing his mount scandalously close to hers, and she would have called him out if not for the fact that he thought her a highly paid whore.

"Lady Rebecca, or should I say Lady Wainsbrough-to-be. Felicitations, my dear, on your good fortune." With an elegant flourish, he tipped his hat, yet his expression was anything but elegant. "Many a fair face has sought the prize you now claim. No doubt your *persuasive abilities* far surpassed previous contenders."

"Thank you, my lord," *L'araignee* replied with an air of whimsy, despite his insult, and she gritted her teeth against a rapier retort. "I am very happy."

"Care to join me for a ride?" he inquired in a tone that suggested the activity he proposed would not involve horses. "I have been told I am quite skilled."

"Oh, of that I have no doubt, my lord, but I must decline your rather intriguing offer, because Viscount Wainsbrough is expecting me, and I am already late."

"Another time, perhaps." Lord Varringdale nodded. "I am, most definitely, at your service." Kicking his heels, he headed for Rotten Row.

Desirous of a bath after the nasty exchange, Rebecca gave the park one more cursory search before she drew rein and set her mount for the mews. As she navigated the London streets, she examined her predicament.

For all intents and purposes, her current mission was an unutterable disaster. At odds with her partner, her efforts to identify the traitor, thus far, had been unsuccessful. But how could she right her predicament? As she could not actively hunt the villain, she could only focus on that which she could hunt. In other words, it was time to swallow her pride, apologize to Dirk, admit her mistake, and make amends.

After stabling her horse, she strolled past the carriage house and into the alleyway leading to the main walk. She was to marry on Saturday, which gave her two nights to correct the situation. Her aching heart eased, and she hummed a happy tune as she tugged at her calfskin gloves, while carefully considering her next move.

A dark figure leapt from the shadows.

Rebecca shrieked and then quickly recovered. Hiking her skirts, she reached for the dagger she kept tied to her thigh and came up fast, bold, and unafraid, catching her would-be-attacker by surprise.

"If you want me, you will have to take me by force," *L'araignee* declared with unwavering resolve.

The masked blackguard seemed hesitant. When she half-lunged, he flinched and splayed both hands, revealing no weapon. At that point, she charged her assailant, and he turned and ran.

Slowed by the weight of her riding habit, *L'araignee* flew in a frenzied froth of petticoat fluff.

"Halt!" she shouted as they neared Park Lane. "Someone stop that man!"

The rogue sprinted to the walk and tripped over an unfortunate passerby. He glanced over his shoulder; realized she closed the distance between them, and shot across Park Lane. With nary concern for her safety, *L'araignee* gave pursuit.

Bestial cries erupted like the hounds of hell. Thunder roared, and the ground shook beneath her feet, as a heavy town carriage drawn by a team of six steered directly at her.

"Watch out!" The coachman waved a warning and shouted a slew of expletives.

Rebecca stood stock-still and clutched her throat. And then the world disappeared in the shadow of a large form that flashed before her, snatching her from death's cold hand at the last possible second. With feet planted on *terra firma*, she eased from the suffocating vise that held her, took a minute to compose herself, and shook out her skirts. Only then had she spared a glance at a familiar expression of fury.

"Good morning, my lord." She swallowed hard. "I was looking for you."

His fingers a manacle at her elbow, Dirk dragged her up the entrance stairs and into the house.

"I scoured the park, but you were not to be found." He walked so fast she nearly ran to keep up with him. "Beautiful weather to share a ride, do you not think?" She half-giggled. "No? Well, if you wish to be alone, I am sure I can find something to occupy my time."

He strode to the entrance of his study, with her in tow, and swung the oak panel wide. With a whip of his wrist, he yanked her inside and slammed the door behind her.

Then she was in his arms, a punishing kiss bruising her lips. She dropped the dagger to the floor, pressed her body to his, licked the inside of his cheek, and moaned. Urgency, hunger, and desire welled, and her heart beat a rapid salvo. Sumptuous heat suffused each taut muscle—until she was unceremoniously released. Again the earth teetered beneath her feet, and Rebecca fought to remain upright.

For several seconds, Dirk paced the floor. He faced her, his mouth opened then closed. He gave her his back and raked a hand through his hair. Then he turned on her, and she scarcely had a moment to brace herself for the fiery demon.

"*What in bloody hell were you doing!*" he roared. "Would you rather be trampled to death than marry me?"

With a step in retreat, Rebecca gulped. "As I said, I was looking for you."

His eyes narrowed, and he stalked her. "And you thought to find me beneath the wheels of a carriage?"

"No." She shook her head and bit her lip. "I was chasing a masked man. He assaulted me as I returned from the mews."

The weapon resting innocuously on the carpet ensnared his attention. In an instant, his irascible disposition surrendered to care and concern. And when he took her in his arms again, his embrace was one of comfort.

"My brave Becca, you could have been killed."

"But I was not injured." For several seconds, she hugged him close, and he hugged her with equal fervor as she nuzzled him. "I should send word of the attack to Sir Ross."

"Do you think it wise, given your conjectures?"

"If I am correct, and Logan is the traitor, then he would already know what has happened, and failure to apprise him of the situation could arouse suspicion before we plan our next move."

"Smart lady." He sighed heavily and kissed her temple. "I will be glad when this dreadful affair is finished, and the spy trade is nothing more than an interesting chapter in your past. Daresay I have half a mind to tell Sir Ross that you are quitting the Corps, and he must capture the villain without you."

"You do, and you will be lucky to have half a brain when I am through with you." Rebecca brought her hands to his chest and shoved hard but could not break his hold. "My profession was no secret when you proposed, so I do not understand your objection now. You have no right—"

"I have every right as your husband." He kept her firmly anchored in his grasp. "Do you honestly believe that I will allow my viscountess to court danger as a spy? Do you expect to continue service to the Crown as you bear my children? I will not live in constant fear for the safety of my wife and my heirs. Do I make myself clear?"

Simmering with frustration and anger, Rebecca glared at her future husband. "As you have been so good as to apprise me of your stance, my lord, allow me to make my position with equal clarity," she spat. "I have sworn an oath to protect my country—an oath I do not take in jest. As previously discussed, I shall consider resigning the Corps once I have completed my final mission—as long as I can do so without threat to your person. You have my word, as a lady, and I intend to keep it. Be that as it may, know that I will do whatever is necessary to catch the traitor, even if it means putting myself and our future in harm's way."

Dirk stood stock still, as though processing her declaration. Sensing a possible breach in his defense, she stomped his booted foot and gained her release.

"That was a cheap shot," he groused with a frown.

"I doubt it left a mark." Beyond his reach, she paused before the door, a hand on the knob, and half turned to face him. "In any case, those are my terms. You will live with that, or you will not live with me."

"When is the happy occasion?" Admiral Douglas rounded his desk and leaned against the edge. The Brethren of the Coast sat in a half-circle of high-back leather chairs.

"Saturday next." Dirk gazed at the mirror shine of his Hessians and tried not to think of his heated discussion with his bride-to-be. "An announcement will appear in tomorrow's *Times*."

"That is awfully soon, brother mine. Are you sure about this?"

Casting his sibling a look that would have withered many a man, Dirk could only frown at Dalton's lopsided grin.

"I am marrying her."

"And the lady is so inclined?" Blake canted his head. "She shares your enthusiasm?"

"Of course." Dirk braced for a lightning strike. "She wants what I want."

"What about her occupation? Will you allow her continued service to the Crown?" Trevor asked. "Were she my wife, I'd halt such endeavors, posthaste."

"Cannot believe she is a spy for the Corps." Lance rested his chin in his hand. "Even harder to stomach the fact that you deceived us."

"He was under orders," Damian, the voice of reason, explained.

"I do not see how she could expect to work once we are wed." Somehow, though he had not the foggiest notion how to obtain her resignation, he would persuade her to leave the Corps. "I plan to start a family as soon as possible."

"Doing so all by yourself?" The admiral smiled. "Or were you going to enlist Rebecca's aid?"

"I beg your pardon?" Dirk scoffed.

"Do not take offense." Admiral Douglas chuckled. "I merely suggest you consider speaking with your intended prior to the wedding. She may have other ideas for her future as your wife that do not include the immediate introduction of children. Contrary to popular male opinion, women have a mind of their own." He rolled his eyes. "Especially our women."

"You can say that again," Trevor added. "Something altogether unsettling happens when you put a ring on their finger."

"Aye." Admiral Douglas compressed his lips. "And time does not improve their condition."

"Oh, I say." Trevor downed a healthy gulp of brandy. "You just answered a question I had not yet summoned sufficient courage to pose, and I take issue with your response."

"Gentlemen, neither of you inspire confidence."

DIRK'S own words revisited him in a mocking refrain when he entered the foyer of his home. After polite apologies for his rude behavior, he enjoyed dinner with his bride-to-be and anticipated a memorable night, but the lady had other plans. Soon, the truth of Admiral Douglas's warning rang clear. Sitting in his study, enjoying the current conversation even less than their previous one, the singular observation undermined every argument he made with the beautiful but maddening spy.

"The solution is simple." Rebecca rested hands on hips. "We shall refrain from further sexual activity until such time as the traitor is apprehended."

"Bloody hell, you cannot be serious."

"Indeed I am." She stood firm, her countenance one of insuperable determination. "I blame myself for such carelessness. I have been trained to prevent conception in the line of duty, and in my haste to share your bed I overlooked that one important detail. Thank you for bringing it to my attention."

Dirk could kick himself in the arse.

"Rebecca, this is not about children, and you know it. The point of contention is your position as a spy and the fact that once our mission is finished, you will retire."

The expression on her face declared he had just grossly overstepped his bounds.

"I will retire? And who decided my future for me? You? Lucien?" With shoulders squared, she gave vent to an unladylike groan. "I will not be dictated to by you or my brother. You have no right."

"I have every right." In a valiant attempt at intimidation, he stood toe-to-toe with his unutterably stubborn woman, his nose mere inches from hers. "As your husband, your welfare is my responsibility. I will not have you skulking in dark corners, ferreting out villains. I will not allow you to continue your mock seductions. Do you truly believe that I shall sit idly, mothering our children, while you chase information to further the King's war effort?"

"No. I thought we would share the upbringing of our young. I understand you will be called upon to transport members of the Corps." Her brow a mass of furrows, she tapped a finger to her chin in an impatient rhythm, and what little confidence he had went up in smoke. "Tell me, my lord, in what capacity do you serve His Majesty? You were commissioned to the Royal Navy, you still accept orders from the Crown, and yet you wear no uniform. You work in concert with the Corps, but you are not an agent."

The world teetered on edge, and Dirk feared he might swoon.

"Perhaps you should have a seat." He shuffled his feet and prayed for calm. "There is something I need to discuss with you."

"All right." In high dudgeon, she claimed his desk chair and folded her arms before her, as if she were the Queen of England. "I am listening."

"I am not what you think I am," Dirk began. Spilling his secrets, one at a time, he revealed the existence of the notorious band of Nautionnier Knights known as the Brethren of the Coast. How their ancestors descended from the Templar mariners, the warriors of the Crusades.

After King Philip the Fair of France conspired with Pope Clement V to ban the Templars, the mariners escaped persecution, torture, and certain death by fleeing to England. Granted asylum by Edward II, the Order of the Brethren of the Coast was formed to serve the King and his successors.

In silence, Rebecca gazed at the solid gold badge of the ancient order. Fashioned in the shape of an eight-point wind-star, the compass of ancient seafarers, a large, blue diamond twinkled at the center, with the Latin phrase *Nulli Secundus* inscribed beneath.

"Second to None?" Her brows rose in question.

"Our motto," Dirk explained. "Our way of life."

"To be the best?" She placed the noble insignia on his desk.

"Aye." He nodded once. "To give all in service to the Crown." Wave upon wave of emotion crossed her lovely face. "Becca, what are you thinking?"

"Hypocrite." Without warning, she jumped to her feet, knocking the chair to the floor. "You are a knight of the Crown, and I am a spy. Where is the difference? We both take great risks in the war effort. How dare you insist I retire the Corps."

"Darling, it is not the same." He leaned forward and rested his palms on the blotter. "It is my responsibility to protect and defend our family." Gauging her demeanor, her incessantly tapping foot, and her compressed lips, Dirk realized he had erred again. He was in trouble—big trouble.

"Is that so?" Her searing tone could melt butter. "And as your wife, just what do you expect of me?"

In the interest of self-preservation, Dirk retreated and strategized his next move. The spy with sad eyes was not likely to fall prey to heavy-handed tactics, so he considered his target and chose his words carefully.

"My dearest Rebecca, I ask you to be my partner, the mother of our children, and the guardian of our home in my absence. As your husband, I commit myself to you, encompassing all sorrows and joys, all hardships and triumphs. It is a promise made in love, kept in faith, and lived in hope."

At that point, the angry secret agent yielded as the gently bred lady emerged, rounded the desk, and flew into his arms. "I am sorry we quarreled."

With a heavy sigh he held her close. "I have been waiting my whole life for you to step aboard my ship."

"Dirk, I know you are worried, but I swear I will be careful." She lifted her chin and met his gaze. "As a knight of the realm, you must understand my obligation to the Crown."

Dirk frowned. "I do not want to, but I do."

"Then there will be no more arguments, and we will cease our physical relationship until we have captured the traitor."

"What about our wedding night?"

Rebecca shrugged. "You are no stranger to sacrifice."

CHAPTER FOURTEEN

*T*he sun shone brilliantly on a crisp, clear morning, heralding Rebecca's wedding day. As she strolled down the grand staircase of the stately home, it dawned on her that when next she entered the residence, she would be its mistress.

In the past, when she had dreamed of the momentous occasion, she imagined taking vows with no doubts or hesitation. Of course, her fanciful visions had never included a traitor and the Counterintelligence Corps. Nagging trepidation lingered, and she sighed. Would Dirk ever acknowledge that he was marrying *L'araignee*, as well as Lady Rebecca?

"Ready to face the enemy?" Dalton cast her lopsided grin.

"I beg your pardon?" She blinked and almost tripped.

"Not too late to run." He snickered. "After all, my brother has the personality of a tabletop—a very dull tabletop, at that."

"You, sir, are incorrigible."

"And correct." The younger Randolph clucked his

tongue. "Or do you take issue with my assessment, dear sister-to-be?"

"Indeed, I do." Against her better judgment, she accepted his escort. "As I find your brother rather...stimulating."

"Stimulating?" Chuckling, he handed her over the threshold. "Are we discussing the same person?"

"It might surprise you to discover that Dirk is infinitely fascinating." With a giggle, Rebecca stepped into the carriage, eased to the bench, and checked the folds of her Alençon lace gown. In a flash, salacious images danced in her head. Lusty male grunts and groans filled her ears, strong hands skimmed her thighs, and then there was that naughty tongue—

"I do not believe it."

"What?" She snapped to attention.

"His high and mighty of Wainsbrough has weighed anchor in your harbor." Dalton shook his head. "And he has not yet spoken the vows."

"Now see here."

"Oh, do not bother denying it. If there is one thing I know, it is the look of a well-pleasured woman. The charming flush in your cheeks betrays you, my dear."

"If you breathe one word, so help me, I will not be responsible for my actions."

"Just what do you intend to do?" With hearty guffaws, Dalton grasped the edge of his seat and leaned forward. "Spank me?"

"You, sir, are without shame." Rebecca crossed her arms and humphed. "I am marrying your brother."

"And that matters?"

"It does to me."

"Why?" He adjusted his cravat.

"Because I love him," she blurted before she realized what she had said. Silence fell heavy between them, as the carriage gently rocked. In that very moment, it dawned on her that she'd spoken the unvarnished truth. "You have my word as a lady, I love Dirk."

"I am happy to hear it." All trace of levity vanished from his expression. "Because I do not want to see the old man hurt."

"You have my solemn promise, I would give my life for him."

"I believe you would." Dalton pounded twice on the ceiling of the carriage and shouted, "To the church."

A few minutes later, they arrived in Hanover Square, where a small crowd gathered on the steps of St. George's, and she waved to cheering children until she ventured beyond the Corinthian columns. Waiting just inside, Lucien stood tall in full military dress.

"I was not sure you would make it." She ran into his welcoming embrace.

"Captain Collingwood kept his promise, but my leave is only for today." To Dalton, Lucien said, "You had better hurry. Your brother will wear through the carpet if he paces much longer."

"On my way." The younger Randolph clicked his heels and saluted. "Good luck."

Rebecca considered Lucien's presence a harbinger of glad tidings, so she took her place at his side with no regrets, save one. "I wish mother and father were here."

"I would wager they do too, as do I. Shall we?" Lucien led her to the double-door entrance of the nave. Just then, the pipe organ signaled the start of the show. "They are playing your tune, sister."

The crowd rose to their feet as she walked the aisle.

Before her, Dirk smiled, and she responded in kind, because, for the first time in years, she had hope. Hope for a future she had never planned, but a life filled with possibilities that she desperately wanted.

With their hands clasped, her captain pledged, "From this day forward, my heart will be your shelter, and my arms will be your home."

With a surprisingly thorough kiss, Dirk sealed their union and left Rebecca's senses reeling. When her new husband hugged her, she whispered, "My lord, I want you."

To wit he nuzzled her and responded, "My lady wife, at this moment, I could make love to you as fifty men."

"Then perhaps we should forgo our agreement, just for tonight."

"I like the way you think."

BECAUSE THEIR WEDDING was the first of the Season, the *crème de la crème* of the *ton* turned out in force for the reception. One by one, luxurious carriages, each bearing a coat of arms unique to its occupant, stopped at the entryway. Ere long, the ballroom at Randolph House filled to capacity.

A sea of impressive gems shimmered in the sunlight filtering through the long windows. Elegantly dressed ladies wore gowns representing every color of the rainbow, while dapper dandies and ravishing rakes circled their feminine prey in a rousing game of cat and mouse.

The Brethren dined, danced, cut the cake, and downed bottle after bottle of champagne. They toasted and roasted the handsome couple, all in good fun, of course. Soon, the various guests disappeared, leaving only the odd extended family Rebecca inherited with marriage to Dirk.

"Bring on the brandy, cheap bastard." Blake slapped her husband on the back. "It is time for the real celebration."

"The real celebration?" A flurry of activity commenced, as the Nautionnier Knights shuffled furniture in various directions. "Gentlemen, just what are you about?"

"Patience is a virtue." Lance resituated a chair.

"And what happened to Dirk and Trevor?" Caroline rubbed the small of her back and sat on the sofa.

"They were in the foyer," Sabrina explained. "No doubt they will join us shortly."

"Join us for—what?" Rebecca could glean no hint as to what lay in store for her.

"Your initiation." Blake winked. "You do not faint at the sight of blood, do you?"

"Has anyone seen the dagger," Dalton chimed.

"What?" Rebecca swallowed hard. "Am I to be skewered?"

"Darling, he is joking." Dirk slipped an arm around her waist and kissed her temple.

"Indeed." Trevor offered Caroline a glass of milk and said to Rebecca, "You are getting off easy. They made me walk the plank."

"Given that you kidnapped my sister, you are no one to complain." Blake glared at Trevor and snorted. "Be grateful you maintain the ability to father children."

"Now I resent that, Blake, really I do."

"Gentlemen, I believe it is all blood under the bridge. And tonight is about our new sister, not long-resolved injuries." Damian held a worn, leather-bound book, bearing Latin script. "Gather round, everyone."

"Let us be done with it." Lance swaggered near. "Because the happy couple has a marriage to consummate."

"Hear, hear." Dalton tossed his lucky coin. "Tails. How appropriate, as it is high time my brother caught some—"

"That is quite enough." Dirk chucked his younger sibling's shoulder.

"Are they always like this?" Rebecca asked Caroline.

"Worse," the countess replied. "Especially when we are all present and accounted for."

"Are we ready?" Blake tugged at the lace trim of his sleeves and adjusted his cravat.

Damian cleared his throat. "My brother knights and estimable sisters, we gather to welcome another member to our family, as we would not repeat the error we made with our most recent entrant."

Lance cast Trevor a side-glance and nudged him, and the Earl of Lockwood grinned. The unspoken regard and playful banter Rebecca found unutterably endearing, as it reminded her of Lucien, and she wished her own brother were in attendance. But Lucien had already returned to the *Intrepid*.

"Gentlemen, settle down." Damian rolled his eyes. "Where was I? Ah, yes. Love, honor, and devotion were the beginning of our Order. Bonds of kinship and friendship all-important. We uphold these principles embrace for embrace, desire for desire, for one, for all. For King and Country we stand, for love and comradeship we live."

"How lovely." As happy tears beckoned, Rebecca smiled. "I do not know what to say."

"That is the ancient oath first pledged to our ancestors." Damian closed the volume and clutched it to his chest. "It is the same we declared on a moonlit night as children, and a vow we now pledge to you." He knelt before her, took her hand in his, and kissed her wedding band. "On my honor, I am at your service, my lady."

One by one, the Knights of the Brethren dropped to a knee and repeated the momentous gesture, and Rebecca was touched beyond words, especially when Dirk pressed his lips to her flesh, then pulled her into a loving embrace. For the second time that day, he sealed their pact with an inexpressibly sweet kiss.

Hoots and hollers brought them up for air, and she laughed, until Dirk whispered, "Save that for later, love."

"If I may, allow me to thank you—all of you, for the warm welcome," Rebecca said with a sniff. "Please know that I shall do my utmost best to fulfill my responsibilities as a member of your set."

"Brave lady, you have already exceeded expectations." Blake passed a tray laden with filled brandy balloons. "Your service to the Crown is astonishingly extraordinary."

"Oh, I say." Cara tucked a stray tendril behind her ear. "Had you been born to the Brethren, you could not be more worthy of such distinction."

"Blast it all." Sabrina clucked her tongue. "You are bloody well splendid."

"I do so admire your strength." Elaine, the quietest member of the odd extended family, hugged the shadows. "I could never be so bold."

"Praise, indeed." Unaccustomed to such effuse appreciation, Rebecca's cheeks burned with embarrassment.

"Come, brothers and sisters, and let us toast." Blake held his glass high. "To the Brethren of the Coast."

"*Nulli Secundus*," they proclaimed in concert.

The ballroom echoed their cheers, and again her new relations surrendered to harmless but spirited repartee.

"So, what did the ladies do last night?" Dalton asked. "As we considered it our solemn duty to drag His Dullship of Wainsbrough to the Muddy Rudder."

"We enjoyed our own initiation." Alex shot Rebecca a telling glance and smirked.

"Oh, really?" Trevor frowned. "And what did this initiation consist of?"

"The same thing we did the night before you married Caroline," Sabrina interjected.

"Which would be?" Trevor persisted.

"None of your business." His wife elbowed him in the ribs.

"My friends, while I should be content to spend the evening in your company, I believe it is time for us to take our leave." Dirk drew Rebecca to his side. "My bride and I have urgent business."

"I would wager you do, brother mine." Dalton waggled his brows and tossed his coin. "Tails, again. Luck favors you."

A few minutes later, Dirk and Rebecca ran the Brethren gauntlet to a waiting coach. Tucked, safe and sound, in the elegant equipage, she folded her arms.

"My lord, I do not wish to appear ungrateful, but I would consider it the height of neglect were I not to point out the obvious." He hauled her to his lap, but she remained steadfast. "We have not completed our mission. We cannot depart—"

Dirk silenced her with a kiss.

"How charming." Standing on the dock at Deptford, Rebecca gazed at an evergreen adornment, listing in the breeze, amid the rigging of the *Gawain*. "But you know we cannot sail."

"That is a wedding garland, love." Hugging her from

behind, Dirk nuzzled her temple. "It is a centuries old Navy custom to announce the marriage of a crewmember. And I do not intend to sail. I thought, perhaps, we could spend tonight aboard ship, as it is where we first met."

"Oh, Dirk, what a lovely, sentimental gesture."

"Well, I cannot take credit, as it was Trevor's suggestion. He and Caroline consummated their vows in his cabin, on the *Hera*. It struck me as a good omen, and I must admit my motive is not so gallant, as I have long desired you naked in my bunk."

"Scandalous." She swatted in play at him. "But, if memory serves, you were unfailingly noble when you rescued me."

"My dear wife, I may be noble, but I am not dead."

Rebecca laughed, turned in his embrace, and set her lips to his. A few desperate seconds later, Blake and Damian drew rein, which drew the newlyweds up short, and she pressed her face to Dirk's chest.

"Your sheets are not getting any warmer, brother." Blake dismounted.

"Worry not, lovebirds." Damian followed suit and sketched a mock salute. "We have your back."

"Gentlemen, I would have your promise to remain here, at the gangplank." Dirk frowned. "Until dawn."

"Oh, come now." Blake snorted. "Do we look like a couple of curious virgins?"

"Indeed." Damian wrinkled his nose. "We have no interest in your connubial interlude, insofar as it remains uninterrupted."

A spectator to the awkward exchange, Rebecca could only giggle.

"Your word, brothers." Dirk tapped his foot.

To Damian, Blake said, "You know, I do not believe he trusts us."

"You may be right," Damian replied.

"Now." Dirk set Rebecca at arm's length.

"Oh, I say." Damian nudged his partner in crime. "You have our word."

"Indubitably." Blake bowed. "We are fixed in your wake. Go to it, man. Rock the boat."

"Aye, aye, Captain." With nary a warning, Dirk swept Rebecca off her feet and all but ran to the main deck. In mere seconds, he carried her into the captain's cabin. The quarters remained much as she recalled but not quite so conservative.

Bathed in the saffron hue of candlelight, the once utilitarian bunk now boasted a velvet counterpane of deep burgundy, matching satin sheets, and plush down pillows. Crystal vases filled with red roses perched in every nook and cranny. But what struck her as odd was the cushioned, two-seater bench sitting before the bunk, which looked vaguely familiar.

"My lord, is that the same one—"

"From the gallery?" Dirk traced her jawline with his nose, nipped her chin, and then set her down. "It is."

"What, pray tell, is it doing here?" She tried but failed to suppress a shiver of delight.

"Ah, I have special plans for that—and you." With grace and ease she envied, he untied his cravat and tossed the yard-length of linen to the floor. "'Step into my web,' said the spider to the fly."

"Oh?" Pulse points blazed to life, but she stood mesmerized, unable to move. "Who is the spider, and who is the fly?"

"Does it matter, as long as we are together?" He doffed his coat, and his waistcoat soon followed.

"I do not suppose it does. But what if I do not wish to be pursued?" Goosebumps covered her from top to toe. "What if I choose to pursue?"

"You may chase me anytime, my lady wife. But I warn you, I am an easy mark where you are concerned." Clothed only in his trousers, he smiled a wicked smile and extended his arms. "Now, come here."

Trembling with excitement, Rebecca obeyed without hesitation. As they had already shared a bed, the telltale sting of a blush puzzled her. And the finesse of a seasoned spy abandoned her. She licked her suddenly dry lips and inhaled a shaky breath.

Dirk met her stare and arched a brow. "Are you afraid?"

"Of you?" She shook her head. "Never. But I am afraid for us."

"Rebecca." He pulled her close, enveloping her in the comforting warmth of his body. "I will let no harm befall you."

"But what about you? I could not bear it if the villain caught you in his sights." There was something she wanted to say to her new husband, but she could not compose a suitable declaration. "And you must be worried, otherwise Blake and Damian would not be on watch."

"That is merely a precaution." He hugged her tighter, and she thought she might swoon. "I will brook no inter-ruptions tonight."

"Dissemblance is not in your nature, and I know you are troubled." Finally, she summoned courage, swallowed hard, and looked Dirk straight in the eye. "I love you so much, that I would give my life for you."

"Darling Rebecca, I love you, too. And, if must needs, I would sacrifice myself for you."

"Please do not feel that you must respond, in kind. While I will admit I would be disappointed to discover you do not share my affection, I will not be angry. I would rather you be honest."

"You doubt me?"

"Well." She bit her lip. "Everyone knows it is not fashionable to love one's wife, and our courtship was anything but usual."

"Hell and be damned with fashion, and what care I for courtship. I do love you, else I never would have married you."

For a minute, they simply stood there, resting forehead to forehead. Slowly, he smiled. She responded, in kind. At long last, Dirk set his mouth to hers in an inexpressibly sweet affirmation of an intangible, yet nonetheless powerful, commitment.

And Rebecca surrendered.

Desire simmered beneath her skin, and undeniable hunger burned in her belly. She broke their kiss, wrenched from his embrace, and gave him her back. "Dirk, if you do not fill me soon I will scream."

"That will give Blake and Damian something to talk about." He tugged at the laces of her gown and groaned. "What the devil are you wearing? It will take a sennight to get you out of this infernal contraption."

"The modiste said it was all the rage." She swayed left and then right, as he battled her gown.

"For what, an insane asylum?"

"Poor darling." She could not help but laugh.

"Bloody hell, this is an exercise in futility. Grasp the back of the chair, love." She complied as he bade, and Dirk ripped apart the laces of her wedding gown.

"My dress."

"Relax. I tore the seam, so we can have it repaired." He inched the bodice to her waist and then shredded her undergarment.

"That chemise was brand new."

"I will buy you another one—hundreds of them." A pool of lace encircled her feet, as he stripped her bare. With his hand he skimmed her breasts and then blazed a naughty trail to a far more delicious target. At the first touch of her most sensitive flesh, she dropped her head back and sighed —until he came to an abrupt halt.

"What is this?"

In an instant, she realized he had discovered the thread attached to the oval sponge she used to prevent conception. Although she dreamed of growing a family with Dirk, she refused to expose an innocent babe to the dark world of espionage.

"Please, do not be angry. We have an agreement." Rebecca held her breath. Braced for a prime male temper tantrum, she was genuinely surprised when Dirk chuckled. "My lord, I am relieved you find humor in the situation."

"You mistake me." He cast her a boyish grin. "If I find humor in our predicament, it is because we are on the same page."

"We are?"

"Indeed." He shifted his weight. "You see—I procured some sheep skins."

"You did not."

"I did."

"Oh, Dirk." In concert, they burst into laughter. "I do love you."

And then Rebecca pounced. She wound her arms about

his neck and scored her fingernails to his nape, earning a lusty grunt as reward.   In a flash, her no-nonsense nobleman devolved into a marauding barbarian, as he tossed her to the bunk.   Inching to the center of the mattress, she extended her arms and flicked her hands in bold entreaty.   In response, Dirk practically tore his trousers from his limbs.   Naked and aroused, he flung himself atop her, and she reveled in his apparent loss of control.

Somewhere, in the tiny recesses of her mind still capable of coherent thought, she reminded herself to take her time, as it was her wedding night.   But a spy enjoyed no guaranteed tomorrows.   So she let go the reins and ravished her man, in kind.

The room filled with a sensuous, audial tapestry of her feminine sighs and his husky groans.   When they joined their bodies, passion glimmered and then crystallized, annihilating all persistent doubt.

Rebecca had done the right thing.

Their marriage would be a success.

CHAPTER FIFTEEN

"*Our marriage is an unutterable failure!*" Rebecca lashed out with a hand and moaned in frustration. Drowning in a haze of anger, she paced the office of Sir Ross. "You should have seen him. The stubborn fool hovered the entire night. The devil, himself, would not dare approach me."

Compressing his lips, Sir Ross leaned forward in his chair. "Well—"

"The man is impossible. It was our first ball as husband and wife, and he treated me as if I were the villain. Daresay I could not catch a cold with him lurking about." She came to a halt before his desk, foot tapping an impatient beat, and arms folded in front of her. "You must help me."

"All right." Sir Ross pointed a finger in emphasis. "Perhaps I can—"

"I cannot work under these conditions." She resumed pacing. "I thought the man was reasonable. There is not a reasonable bone in his body."

A knock at the door silenced her tirade. Quickly,

Rebecca pulled the hood of her black wool cloak over her head.

"Hold hard." Sir Ross arched a brow. "Come."

"Viscount Wainsbrough to see you, sir," said Mr. Clarkson.

Rebecca humphed.

"Well this should prove entertaining." Sir Ross rolled his eyes. "Send him in, at once, and make yourself scarce."

Clarkson nodded.

Seconds later, Dirk stormed through the door, slammed it forcefully behind him, and halted when his gaze met Rebecca's. "I should have known I would find you here."

Riding a wave of righteous indignation, she shook her fist. "I have every right to be here."

"In that I will not argue, but I take issue with your hasty retreat from our home." Stretching to full height, he stared down his nose at her. "I will not have you running like a scared rabbit when it suits you. In future, when we disagree, you will face me."

"How dare you call me a coward." With hands on hips, she thrust her chin. "You are an old woman."

"Better an old woman than a dead woman."

"That is not fair." To Sir Ross she said, "Would you tell him he is ruining our mission?"

In turn, Dirk glared at the head of the Counterintelligence Corps. "Would you tell her to stop taking unnecessary risks?"

"Enough." Sir Ross stood and rounded his desk. "May I remind you that you insisted on marrying in the middle of this assignment? And I supported the idea because it seemed in Rebecca's best interest, given that she remains our only hope to lure the traitor. The Season is nearing its end, and there is no time to change our strategy."

"Is there news from the front?" Dirk asked with a frown.

"Soult has advanced on Wellington's position, but I believe we have reached a turning point in the war, so I will not jeopardize our effort for the sake of a lover's quarrel. Whatever your differences, resolve them—now."

With that, Sir Ross quit the room.

Alone with her husband, Rebecca sought refuge along the rear wall and pretended to examine a framed antique pistol. How she hated fighting with Dirk.

"I have had my fill of staring at your back." With his hands on her shoulders, Dirk whirled her about to face him. "I am your partner in all enterprises. Talk to me."

"My orders are to catch a traitor."

"And mine are to protect you."

"I have a duty to the Crown."

"Your duty is to me." He pressed his fist to his chest. "I am your husband and, as such, claim your allegiance. All prior claims must perforce yield to mine."

"That is not fair." Her heart sank. How could she tell him what he had not wanted to hear? That while she wanted nothing more than to free herself from the hell of espionage, it might not free her. "You knew I was a spy when you married me, and we agreed that I would complete this mission before deciding whether or not I would retire."

"That is not the conversation I recollect."

"What do you mean?"

"Do you remember what you said in my study, because I recall every word. 'I should like, very much, to marry and have a family. I want to know how it feels to wake up in the morning and have nothing more important to decide than what color dress I will wear. I want to bathe in perfumed waters every day, without fear that my scent will betray my presence on surveillance. I want to fashion my hair in the latest style, and attend events of the Season for no reason other than to waltz the night away in the arms of my beloved.' Were you lying to me? Did you say those things because you thought it was what I wanted to hear?"

"I would never lie to you."

"Then I would have your promise to end your career as an agent of His Majesty."

"I cannot. I simply cannot." Should she share her fears? Would he understand her reluctance to sever ties with the Corps? "You cannot force me to quit."

"If must needs, I can do just that."

"Why?"

"How often do you wake, in the middle of the night, screaming in terror?"

"Do not say it." She bowed her head and closed her eyes. "Please. If you prefer, I can sleep in my chambers."

"Like bloody hell you will. I want you in my bed." His voice softened. "Darling, all those things you want for your-self—I want them for you, too. It pains me to see you suffer, Becca. I ache for you."

"Dirk, I do not deserve you. I am sorry we quarreled." She started when he pulled her into his arms, and she met his gaze. "Perhaps you should not have married me. If you seek a divorce, I will not contest it."

"My dear disillusioned wife, there will be no dissolution of our marriage." He cast her a lopsided grin. "Even if I have to post in *The Times*, for all to see, the number and ways, which are rather impressive, if I say so myself, I have taken you."

"You would not dare."

"Do not tempt me." He brushed her nose with his.

"Including the two-seater bench?"

"Especially the two-seater bench."

Standing in the Danford ballroom that night, Rebecca navigated the cavernous hall, stopping to share a bit of conversation here, and partake of a choice piece of gossip there. To all eyes, she appeared to be nothing more than a young socialite, newly married, happy, and harmless. Oh, how looks could be deceiving.

Wedded bliss had mutated into conjugal hell.

One minute she and Dirk made passionate love in the library, and the next they were barely speaking. Her stomach was a mass of jumbled nerves, and for once, she appreciated the prying eyes of the *ton*, because they drew her mind from her troubled marriage.

"Excuse me, your ladyship." A footman paused before her, holding a silver tray. "You have a message."

Rebecca retrieved the envelope and navigated to the back wall. Sheltering behind a large bust, she removed the card.

Meet me in the gazebo at midnight, and come alone. If you do not obey, your husband will not live to see the morn.

A dark sense of foreboding traipsed her spine. She rolled back her shoulders and eased the ominous note down the bodice of her gown and under her chemise. Glancing from side to side, she joined the Brethren.

Dirk was nowhere to be found.

She scanned the dance floor, hoping to spot him as he passed, but there was no sign of her husband.

In an instant, she panicked.

Had the villain taken Dirk? Was he held prisoner, only to be released after she cooperated? And what was it the traitor sought? She had nothing to give them because her hasty departure from France afforded her no opportunity to pack.

"Blake, have you seen Dirk?"

"Well, last I—"

"What is wrong, my lady wife?"

Rebecca nearly jumped out of her skin. Facing what she considered her decidedly better half, she fought the urge to crawl into his arms. "Where have you been? I looked everywhere for you."

"Since you find my presence suffocating, I thought to safeguard you from afar." Dirk frowned and cupped her chin with his hand. "What is the matter? You are as white as a sheet."

How could she tell him what she felt without undermining her position and instigating another argument? No doubt his answer to all her concerns would follow the same tired diatribe—quit the Corps. As if it were that simple. At that moment, her needs were basic. She needed the warmth and security of his body surrounding her. She needed his strength and support. She needed him.

"Dance with me, please?"

"As you wish." Cold and distant, he offered his escort but no solace as he steered her to the crowded expanse. But when he turned and pulled her close, fire ignited beneath her flesh, which settled into a slow, ever-constant flame, soothing her frazzled nerves and calming her fears. As they waltzed, she pressed her breasts to his chest and her hips to his. In mere seconds, she relaxed.

"What are you doing?"

The tension returned with a vengeance.

"I thought it rather obvious." She sighed. "We are sharing a dance."

"That is not what I mean, and you know it." He arched a brow. "You are practically throwing yourself at me. What game are you playing?"

"My lord—" Rebecca choked on a sob, and tears welled in her eyes.

She wanted to divulge the news of her midnight rendezvous, wanted to warn him of impending danger. But if she alerted Dirk, she could jeopardize him further. When he cursed under his breath and led her from the dance floor, she had not protested. At the back wall, they slipped between a pair of velvet drapes to a small private balcony overlooking the gardens, where darkness enshrouded them.

"All right." Dirk stood tall, hands on hips. "What are you about?"

"This is difficult for me." Burrowing her face in his coat, she wrapped her arms around his waist and hugged him tight.

"Rebecca." In an instant, he enveloped her in a warm embrace. "You are trembling. What has upset you?"

"I hate when we are at odds. I have always worked alone, except for Colin. But he was a member of the Corps and could take care of himself, or so I thought. In the end, he was killed, and I was powerless to stop it." She nuzzled closer. "I will not lose you."

"You are worried about me?" Surprise rang clear in his voice. "I assure you, madam wife, I can take care of myself and you."

Rebecca reached up, wound her fingers in his hair, and brought his lips to hers. She sashayed her mouth over his, thrust her tongue, flagrantly inciting him. She held him to her, clung to him in raw desperation.

Finally, after several reckless, wild, incredibly intense minutes, whereupon anyone could have walked in on them,

Rebecca broke their kiss and buried her face in the crook of his neck.

"Dirk."

"What?"

Should she tell him he had been threatened? Should she tell him he was in peril?

"Hold me."

~

EVER SINCE THEIR tryst on the balcony, Dirk had been concerned for his wife. The urgency with which Rebecca had come at him gnawed at his instincts, and he had not liked it. Despite attempts to convince himself otherwise, he would swear he had tasted a lamentable farewell in her kiss. Almost as if she believed it would be their last, and that troubled him.

Because Rebecca was afraid of nothing.

But she was definitely frightened of something. He wondered what had brought about the change. As he completed another turn on the dance floor with Alex, he craned his neck to keep his wife in sight.

At the terrace doors, she paused to survey the ballroom before crossing the threshold. Seconds later, Sir Ross followed in her wake.

Dirk came to an abrupt halt, and Alex to crashed into his side. Grasping her forearms, he kept her from falling.

"Sorry, Alex. I need to check on Rebecca. Can we continue our dance another time?"

The younger Seymour smiled and patted his cheek. "Of course we can."

Where the Brethren gathered, Alex joined the ladies,

while Dirk caught Blake's stare. In a flash, the Nautionnier Knights came alert.

"What is it," Damian inquired.

"There are games afoot."

MOONLIGHT FILTERED THROUGH THE TREES, and dark shadows danced an eerie kaleidoscope on the walkway, as pebbles crunched beneath her slippered feet. A gentle breeze teased the curls of her hair and ruffled her skirts.

Rebecca moved slowly, listening for any hint of the traitor. Mid-stride, she halted. Standing perfectly still, she detected the telltale thud of footfalls on the grass, over the muted strains of music from the ballroom.

Someone stalked her.

I know you are there.

Gooseflesh covered her arms, and nervous anticipation settled in her chest. Rebecca closed her eyes and breathed deeply. Focusing on her pounding heartbeat, she found comfort in the repetitive rhythm and rolled her shoulders, easing the tension investing her frame.

Clearing her mind, she erased Dirk from her thoughts and recalled her training. After a few minutes, she unclenched her fists and twittered her fingers. Cool night air penetrated her gloves, bestowing an icy kiss to her damp palms. Fear loomed as a taunting apparition of impending doom, and, as she always had, she saluted the imaginary but nonetheless potent wraith and set it aside.

The spy within emerged.

L'araignee smiled, opened her eyes, and methodically scanned the area before her. Assessing every possible advantage, she plotted her course, knew the tack she would take. Like a reveler in search of a brief respite from the noisy gala, she strolled toward the gazebo, setting a relaxed pace, thereby luring her prey. The pursuer had resumed their pursuit.

Stepping onto the flagged surface of the summerhouse, she extended her arms, feeling for obstacles she could not see in the dark.

The villain was there.

She could sense his presence as a storm cloud on the horizon. With grim resolution, she waited for the traitor to make his move.

"Viscountess." An unforgiving vise encircled her waist, and the cold blade of a knife pressed to her throat.

With the instinct of an assassin, *L'araignee* raised her hands but suppressed the urge to resist. For the blackguard to be of any use, she had to capture him alive.

"Please, do not hurt me. I will not fight you." Had she sounded appropriately traumatized? "Take my jewelry. I will not tell a soul, I promise."

"Is that what you think?" Her anonymous attacker chuckled in a rich baritone that seemed vaguely familiar. "Once again, you make the same mistake."

"What else could you want?" She gasped with feigned ignorance.

The traitor trailed his fingers from her waist to her breast. "You are a very attractive woman."

"No, please. Not that," *L'araignee* implored. "I am newly wed."

"What difference does it make to a whore such as yourself?"

Though she was certain her assailant had been altering his tone to disguise his true voice, it was obvious he let his emotions get the best of him. For a second,

L'araignee was certain the mask had slipped. She seized the opportunity, replaying his words in her mind. "I am at a loss—"

"Do you have it?" He tightened his grip, crushing her tender flesh.

"You are hurting me," she cried in pain.

"Stop stalling. When last we met, I told you to expect another visit. Did you find what I seek?"

"No." With the blade he cut her skin, and it burned as a firebrand on her throat.

"I am losing patience."

"You may as well kill me," she said with resignation. "I know not what you require. I was Colin's mistress, and he told me nothing."

"You lie."

"He did not confide in me, I swear." *L'araignee* tilted her head back, as far as possible. If the turncoat would relent just an inch, she might be able to take him into custody, but he pressed the weapon close. "Can you give me a hint or a clue, as I know not what to look for?"

The blackguard sighed, and she knew, without doubt, they shared an acquaintance. She needed to keep him talking.

"Should I search for clothing? Jewelry?" No response. "A painting or document?" He tensed, a subtle flinch, when she mentioned the last item, and she committed that vital tip to memory.

Finally, after what seemed an interminable silence, he spoke. "It may be several papers—or a small journal. It will be written in French. If you want to live, do not attempt to read it."

L'araignee closed her eyes as he dug the knife into her flesh.

"How am I to contact you?" A trickle of blood trailed her chest.

"I will find you."

"What if I am unable to locate the item?"

"Then your husband will die."

DIRK HAD SEARCHED HIGH and low, and there was no sign of Rebecca or Sir Ross. Standing on the gravel path, he was just about to return to the main house when voices caught his attention. It was a heated conversation, not the soft murmur of lovers.

He focused, trained his ear, and let the quarrel guide him. A small walkway veered from the main path, and he missed it on first inspection. He glanced left and then right, before navigating the sandy course. The dispute grew louder the further he ventured. At last, amid the tall hedges, a gazebo emerged. Inside, he could barely make out a silhouette, which he thought odd, because he distinctly heard two voices—that of a man and a woman.

Something was wrong.

He crept closer, hunkering down when the argument commenced, and his blood chilled.

An anonymous aggressor held Rebecca captive. Thinking only of her safety, Dirk stepped forward and cursed when a twig snapped beneath his foot.

"Who goes there?"

"It is Viscount Wainsbrough," he called out. "I am looking for my wife. Have you seen her?"

"She is here, and I believe she is ill. Perhaps you should help her?"

Dirk retrieved a pistol from the waist of his trousers. Palming it, he walked inside the garden structure.

A shadowy figure all but launched Rebecca at him.

He caught her and turned, shielding her with his body. The mysterious man fled, and they gave chase.

"This way." Rebecca hiked her skirts. "He took to his heels in this direction."

In a clearing, the path widened to reveal a maze.

"You must be joking." Dirk halted, but a rustling in the bushes spurred him into action. "Over there," he whispered.

In the expansive labyrinth at the heart of the garden, they ran in one direction, only to meet a dead end. Reversing their course, they plowed over Damian.

"Bloody hell, watch where you are going." Damian righted his coat.

"Where is Blake?" Dirk asked.

"Right here." Blake brought up the rear. "And I have our man."

Rebecca gasped when Sir Ross stepped into the moonlight.

AT RANDOLPH HOUSE, the Brethren gathered to interrogate Sir Ross. Myriad questions swirled in her brain, as Rebecca struggled to comprehend recent events. Although she had suspected her boss might be the villain, she had not truly believed the worst until Blake took the head of the Counter-intelligence Corps into custody.

"You are in error." Sir Ross scowled. "I am no turncoat."

"Then what were you doing out there?" Dirk folded his arms.

"The same thing you were doing—protecting my asset." Sir Ross leveled his gaze on Rebecca. "And I would like to know what led you to the gazebo, in the first place."

Suddenly the center of attention, she stared at her hands, tightly clasped and white-knuckled. It was the moment she dreaded. "I received a summons."

She retrieved the note from the bodice of her gown, which her husband promptly snatched from her grasp. As he read the message, he furrowed his brow, and then met her gaze. "Why did you not tell me of this?"

Searching for a plausible excuse for her behavior, one that would leave her pride and marriage intact, Rebecca failed to compose a suitable response. Never could she admit the truth; that love for her husband clouded her judgment. At last, she settled for a small measure of verity.

"I did not want you to alarm the traitor." She struck a conciliatory tone. "I know you mean well, but we must make contact if we are to capture him."

"You do not trust me?"

"My lord, it is not a question of trust." She inclined her head. "Had you known of the threat, you might have clued the villain to our plan, and where would that leave us? As I am experienced in this arena, you must defer to my assessment."

"Indeed." Dirk shifted his weight. "I suppose that explains the scene on the balcony."

Embarrassment burned in her cheeks as the memory of their encounter flooded her consciousness. How she had clung to him as a frightened little girl. "I am sorry that I did not confide in you. That was rather unprofessional."

The long-case clock in the hall sounded the hour. It was three in the morning.

"Unprofessional?" Dirk smirked. "We all need comfort at some time or another. Even *L'araignee*."

And there it was, the heart of their quandary. Could he not understand that, while she may desire to resign the Corps, the Corps may not allow her to resign? Would he ever acknowledge that his wife and the spy were one in the same? Her husband had not known it, but he hurt just then, and she would die before she confessed it. So she sought refuge in diversion.

"Sir Ross could not have accosted me in the gazebo."

"How can you be certain?" Blake lowered his chin. "I saw him follow you."

"Because the blackguard was waiting for me." She revisited the events in her mind. "And I believe I heard Sir Ross in my wake."

"How did you know her destination?" Damian inquired, with a side-glance.

"I received a missive, as well," Sir Ross explained. "To the rose garden." He searched his coat pocket but came up empty. "It was right here. Must have lost it as I ran the hedges."

"How convenient," Dirk remarked in an icy tone that left no doubt of his suspicions.

Sir Ross shot to his feet. "Now see here, Wainsbrough—"

"Stop it, both of you." Rebecca intervened before the two men came to blows. "You are behaving like children."

"We all have our shortcomings." Dirk glared at her, and she shivered. "Are we finished?"

"Until tomorrow." Sir Ross nodded and stood. "I believe so."

"May I have a word in private with Sir Ross?" Biting her lip, she crossed and uncrossed her arms.

"As you wish." With an expression hard as granite, Dirk raked a hand through his hair. "I am done for tonight."

As the Brethren exited the study, Rebecca considered her next move. Thus far, her efforts to catch the turncoat had failed. Worse, her career represented a very real barrier between her and Dirk. She had to decide what meant more, her marriage or her mission, children or the Crown?

Could she sacrifice the prospects Dirk offered for a lonely existence in the filthy trenches of espionage?

Could she surrender her soul for service, love for duty?

The answer, when it struck her, seemed so simple. For good or ill, it was time to stand for the future she desperately desired.

"Sir Ross, I want out."

CHAPTER SIXTEEN

*a*s she had since her wedding, Rebecca woke the
following morning and reached for her husband.
Finding herself quite alone, she frowned. Dirk had not
roused her, as had become his custom and to which she
looked forward with each successive sunrise. Much to her
chagrin, it appeared he had chosen a ride of a different sort.
Tossing the covers aside, she leapt from the bed, traversed
the tiny corridor adjoining their chambers, crossed her
room, and tugged hard on the bell pull.

By the time her lady's maid appeared, Rebecca had
coiffed her hair. After donning her riding habit, she headed
for the dining room. Disappointed to find it empty, she
breakfasted on toast and coffee, before sending for a mount.
Unaccompanied and undisturbed, save the clip clop of the
mare's hooves on the cobblestone, she mulled last night's
events.

Given their heated discussion in Dirk's study, and
fearing rejection, she had not the courage to join him in his
bed. Instead, she shivered beneath the covers in her suite,

refusing to don a nightgown because it impaired her ability to move.

At some point during the wee hours, her husband entered her room, swore under his breath, flung aside the sheets and blanket, and lifted her from the mattress. Call her a coward, but she feigned sleep. In no time, he carried her to his quarters, conveyed her to his four-poster, and eased beside her. And although they had not made love, he had held her close.

For once, no one chased her in her dreams.

As she approached Hyde Park, she surveyed the area and noted the sandy track was virtually deserted, save a lone rider. From atop his impressive stallion, Dirk studied the sky. She slowed the mare to a trot just as her husband spied her. Though she longed to see his brilliant smile, which never failed to set her heart pounding, she knew he was still angry. The rigid posture, clenched jaw, and hardened features betrayed him, and to her disappointment, he frowned.

"Good morning." She drew rein.

He dipped his chin but made no effort to welcome her.

While she had not expected him to make things easy for her, she had not anticipated utter indifference.

"Dirk, do not turn away from me."

"I beg your pardon." He snapped to attention, and his heated gaze scorched her to the saddle. "I believe you are the expert in that arena."

"I have apologized, what more would you have me do?"

"I would have your promise never to keep secrets from me again," he said without hesitation.

"Know that you have it."

With a snort of skepticism, he narrowed his stare. "Why do I not believe you?"

"Dirk, please." A gentle heel to the flanks of the mare brought Rebecca closer to his stallion. When she placed her palm to her husband's thigh, his muscles flexed beneath her touch. "I swear, I will never again keep anything from you."

After a long, painful silence, which had her biting her tongue, he took her hand in his and brought it to his lips. "Why does it feel as though for every step forward, we take two steps back?" he asked with a heavy sigh.

"I get your meaning." Rebecca winced. "And I fear it is entirely my fault. Forgive me."

"There is nothing to forgive, Becca." He met her gaze. "The state of marriage is new to us both, and I do not claim to be a master in this realm. I just wish we could embark on our new life absent the added stress of our mission."

"Then we are on the same page, because last night, after you left the room, I informed Sir Ross of my intent to resign the Corps." She inhaled a shaky breath. "I only want to be your wife."

With a downturned mouth, Dirk inclined his head. "Are you sure about that?"

"Yes."

"My dear, perhaps we should not be too hasty in our decision. Once the traitor is captured, we can determine how best to proceed."

"Have you changed your mind?" Rebecca pressed a fist to her chest and swallowed hard. "Do you want a divorce?"

He rolled his eyes. "How many times must I tell you there will be no divorce?"

"Then you must know that I am equally determined." She lifted her chin. "I have no interest in any endeavor that takes me from you. I promise, I will quit the Corps once our business is finished."

"Can you be so sure?" he inquired softly. "Oh love, it is

wrong of me to demand that you give up part of your life that has meant so much to you."

"My lord, do you not see, spying was important because it was all I had. It was my contribution to the war effort and means to avenge my parent's death." Rebecca wanted to cry. "However naïve that may sound."

"You are not naïve." He cast her a boyishly sweet smile. "You are the bravest woman I know, and you have my utmost admiration, as well as my heart."

"Praise, indeed." Her pulse pounded in her ears, and when he leaned forward, she met him halfway, accepting the kiss he so readily bestowed. "I missed you this morning," she said against his lips.

"And I you." He nipped her flesh.

"Then why did you not wake me?"

He whisked a stray tendril from her face, and then caressed her cheek. "Because we cannot resolve all our problems in bed."

"And is this problem resolved?" In expectation of his answer, she tingled from top to toe.

"I hope so."

"Then where does that leave us?"

"Waiting for the turncoat to make his move."

A SENNIGHT PASSED before Rebecca received the much-anticipated summons from the traitor. In that time, she and Dirk resumed their lives as though everything were normal, as though they had no more concerns than the usual newlywed mishaps. How she enjoyed the whimsical role of viscountess, composing menus and selecting silverware, while engaging her husband in after dinner discussions of such enthralling topics as tactical surveillance and close combat maneuvers. Just as she had adopted the comfortable routine of societal ingénue, the underworld of counterintelligence beckoned. All too soon, she and Dirk, along with the rest of the Brethren, gathered in Sir Ross Logan's office at the Ministry of Defense.

"When did it arrive?" Sir Ross examined the curious missive.

"This morning." Rebecca clasped her hands in her lap and fought the fast rising tension investing her shoulders. "Hughes found it on the floor, in the foyer."

"Must have been slipped under the door." Dirk propped his elbow on the armrest of a wingback chair. "Which troubles me, given that we made the social rounds with the expressed intent of providing the blackguard ample opportunity to make contact in public."

"Our villain grows desperate." Lance frowned.

Damian nodded once. "Then we have no time to lose."

"What is the plan?" Admiral Douglas inquired.

"I have taken the liberty of collecting various communiqués seized by our agents on the Continent." Sir Ross indicated a stack of dispatches bundled on his desk. "*L'araignee* helped decipher most of them, and they are authentic, which should lend credence to our ruse."

"How will you deliver them?" Blake asked.

"Dirk and I are to attend this evening's performance at Vauxhall," Rebecca replied. "At midnight, I am to proceed to the end of Hermit's Walk, where our turncoat will be waiting, and I shall convey the documents I have discovered as a result of my supposed search of Colin's belongings."

"Were there any effects?" Damian tapped a finger to his chin. "Any hint of this mysterious item?"

"None." She shook her head. "As my retreat from

France was rather hasty, there was no time to gather personal possessions. And the traitor clearly stated that he sought papers or, perhaps, a journal."

"So it is entirely plausible that the document in question was, in fact, buried with Colin." Dalton repeatedly tossed his lucky coin. "Oh, the irony."

"And what do we know of this Denis character?" Admiral Douglas rested a shoulder on the sidewall and furrowed his brow. "You have not been very forthcoming on the enemy."

"Denis is an animal." Sir Ross perched on the edge of his desk. "Beyond that, we know nothing, as none of our agents has survived contact with him."

"Have you any description of his appearance?" Trevor asked. "Are you certain he is French?"

"No." Sir Ross shrugged. "So I suppose we cannot, in good conscience, rule out the possibility that he is English."

"I can speak to his brutality." Rebecca shivered, and Dirk took her hand in his. "A couple of years ago, Colin and I recovered the remains of one of our operatives after Denis had done his work. The poor man was unrecognizable."

"You are referring to Egglesfield." Sir Ross compressed his lips and gazed at the floor. "I remember him. His body was nothing more than a twisted lump of bloody flesh and broken bones. Even his eyes were dislodged from his head."

The room grew silent as a tomb.

In that moment, for the first time since she had joined the Corps, Rebecca wished she had never become a spy. Given what she deemed trivial contributions to the war effort exacted at an unfairly high price, she would give anything to go back to the past and undo that hastily made decision. Then again, if she were not a secret agent, she might never have met Dirk. She studied the no-nonsense sea captain who had changed her life for the better. Finding himself the subject of her scrutiny, he offered a half-smile and winked.

"Gentlemen, pray tell, how are we to safeguard my wife?"

THE AIR WAS thick and humid, as *L'araignee* tiptoed Hermit's Walk, and a gentle breeze kissed her hair and rustled the hedges on either side of her. Moonlight above cast her shadow on the graveled surface, reminding her that she was not alone, as Sir Ross and the Brethren trailed her movements from a close but discreet distance. Wrapped in the evening's playbill, and tucked in the crook of her arm, was the cache of documents Sir Ross had prepared for her, in accordance with the turncoat's demands. As the Pastorale from Handel's *Messiah* filled her ears, she scanned the area and cursed under her breath. The music effectively shielded any telltale sounds of a stalker.

Yet she would swear she could hear her heart beat.

The traitor had chosen an excellent night and location for a rendezvous, given the thousands of revelers in attendance of the *al fresco* entertainment at Vauxhall Gardens. It was a brilliant strategy, as a sea of innocents afforded ample opportunities for cover and concealment. And therein lay his mistake, as the crowd could also impede any attempted escape.

I know you are there.

As always, the taunting specter of fear danced a merry jig, and she dipped her chin in insouciant salute, setting aside her trepidation in order to perform her duty. Against all logic, rhyme, and reason, and drawing on years of experience, she put one foot in front of the other, ever encroaching on the kill zone of espionage, where she would capture the villain.

Indeed, once she had the traitor in her sights, she would not yield. Her mission would end right there on that very night, because *L'araignee* was determined to resign the Corps. No more would she pleasure French generals in exchange for bits of information. Dirk was the only man she had any interest in touching—or having touch her. Never again would she lurk in back alleys, with the rats and refuse of humanity for companions, in search of her prey, or gaze on the lifeless remains of war combatants, friend or foe. If she met her fate in her sleep while abed, after a long, uneventful, and peaceful existence, she would be happy.

At last nearing the end of the dark and deserted walk, she noted its namesake transparency in the hermitage and prepared for the impending assault. Nerves tingled and muscles clenched, as she surmised the turncoat would approach from the rear in an attempt to intimidate her, and *L'araignee* primed for battle.

When the first thunderous roar of the fireworks display reverberated, she flinched in earnest. In that instant, an unknown attacker covered her mouth with his hand and encircled her waist with his arm. Swallowing the urge to resist, she relaxed her body as he dragged her behind the hedge.

"Have you found what I seek?" His breath was hot against her neck. Focusing on his voice, she scrutinized his dialect and immediately realized that something was amiss. He released her with a warning: "Stay where you are, or I shall be forced to shoot you."

"I brought what met your requirements from when last

we spoke." She held up the packet of papers. "There was nothing else."

"Excellent." The blackguard snatched the documents from her grasp, and *L'araignee* was surprised and furious to discover that he wore the familiar black cloak of the Corps.

How could one of their members betray Colin? Given their oath of office, their history of distinguished service to the Crown, and the inherent sacrifice demanded of their trade, she vowed he would face justice for his treachery. The urge to strike settled as a bitter pill in her throat, and she swallowed hard, lest she foul the plan and lose her quarry.

Somewhere in the vicinity, Sir Ross and the Brethren stood alert and waited for the ideal moment to pounce. She need only do as told, distract the scoundrel, and keep him talking.

Papers fluttered as the traitor reviewed the decoys.

"These are worthless," he snapped. "Where is the item we seek? What have you done with it?"

"I do not know what you mean." The unforgiving end of a pistol gouged her back, and she fought the fast rising panic. "I have given you what I found, I swear."

"Liar." The assailant grabbed her throat and pressed the barrel to her temple. "I should kill you."

"The shot would frighten the crowd." The only thing standing between *L'araignee* and death was the simple flex of a finger on the trigger. "Do you want to sound the alarm?"

"Shut up." He laughed. "You think that the only means at my disposal?"

As if to prove his point, he tightened his hand at her neck, and she choked. Frantically, she scratched at his wrist and kicked his shins, and his fingernails dug into her flesh. Desperate for air, her lungs seized and violent paroxysms rocked her from top to toe. She reached for his head and wrenched his hair, but he relented not. Aching for precious oxygen, her chest burned, and the rush of a waterfall echoed in her ears. Twisting and turning to no avail, she tried but failed to scream, and her knees weakened.

"You there, hold hard!" Admiral Douglas shouted above another volley of fireworks.

Dare she hope?

"Stay back, or I shall kill her." The villain jerked and let go her neck, but he kept her firmly anchored in his grip. "I mean what I say."

Holding to consciousness by mere tenterhooks, L'araignee sucked in a deep breath, and then another. In a matter of seconds, her vision cleared. Gathering her wits, she reassessed her position and adapted her strategy.

"Please, do not hurt me," she cried in an attempt to confuse the situation. If she could draw the turncoat's attention, she might afford Admiral Douglas the opportunity to act, but she had to be careful.

The traitor still held a gun to her head.

"I am a married woman." Again she inhaled. "My husband will pay a handsome reward for my safe return."

"Shut up," he barked. "Else I will silence you for good."

"Calm yourself, man. I am unarmed." Admiral Douglas splayed both palms for inspection. "Let the lady go. I am sure this has been an unfortunate misunderstanding."

Retreating further into the gardens, her assailant hauled her with him, and L'araignee dug in her heels to slow his escape. Ignoring her instincts and desire to fight, she slackened her muscles, burdening the turncoat with her full weight.

"Come now," Admiral Douglas kept pace, measure for measure. "One bit o' fluff is not unlike the other."

"Do you take me for a fool? Do you think me an idiot? No doubt Sir Ross hugs the shadows, and, at this very moment, I am surrounded."

The blackguard knew of their plan.

Had he discerned the extent of her involvement? Had he discovered her identity? Had he known that she was *L'araignee*? If so, everyone she cared about could be at risk. Dirk and Lucien would be in grave peril.

"Who is Sir Ross?" Admiral Douglas neared. "Let us settle this dispute as gentlemen. The woman is of no use."

"Oh, I beg to differ. She is my ticket to freedom." The traitor licked her cheek. "Where I go, so too goes she."

Riding a wave of nerves and nausea, her stomach heaved.

"What is wrong, dove?" He groped her breast, squeezing cruelly until she cried in pain. "Do you not fancy my touch? Perhaps I should keep you for my enjoyment."

The vocal mask slipped, and she recognized the voice in an instant. Searching her mind, she tried to envision his face. Slowly, she peered left and glimpsed his profile from the nose down, as a mask and hood shrouded the rest. The angular lines of his jaw and the firm set of his chin teased her memory.

"Surely you do not believe you can evade notice, with a hostage in tow." Admiral Douglas squared his shoulders. "Release her, and all is forgotten."

"Like bloody hell, I will—"

Suddenly, the villain dropped the pistol and fell limp.

In a flash, *L'araignee* bent, hiked her skirts, retrieved the tiny dagger from the sheath strapped to her thigh, and prepared to lunge. Whirling about, she halted in her tracks.

There, standing before her, was Dirk.

Wearing a coat of impeccable Bath superfine, a pristine

white cravat tied in a precise mathematical, fawn-colored breeches, and glossy Hessians, he cut the perfect picture of a refined English nobleman, if not for the weapon clutched in one hand and the unconscious double-dealer in the other. "Are you hurt, my lady wife?"

Incapable of coherent speech, Rebecca shook her head.

As if from nowhere, Sir Ross appeared with the remaining Brethren, took custody of the traitor, and conveyed him to the ground.

"I struck him with force sufficient to render him harmless." Though Dirk addressed Sir Ross, his impenetrable stare never left hers. "He is not grievously injured."

When Dirk spread his arms wide in welcome, she ran into his embrace.

"Have you any idea how hard it was to let you depart our supper box without so much as a kiss goodbye?" he asked softly.

"Have you any idea how hard it was to depart our supper box without so much as a kiss goodbye?" she responded in kind.

At his prompt, she lifted her chin in invitation, which he readily accepted. As he set his lips to hers, she closed her eyes and savored the taste of her gallant knight. The adrenaline surging in her veins found a convenient outlet in the passion of that elementary but potent affirmation of their union.

"While I hate to break up this heartfelt reunion, we have work to do." Sir Ross cleared his throat. "Our charge must be remanded for interrogation."

"Who is our snake in the grass?" Lance knelt beside Sir Ross.

"Oh, I say, pull back the hood." Blake squatted. "Let us have a look at the enemy."

"The bastard ought to be keelhauled." Dalton flipped his lucky coin. "Heads. Perhaps the guillotine is more appropriate."

"That can be arranged," Damian added.

"At long last, my dear." Dirk smiled. "Our mission is over."

"So it seems." Giddy with excitement, she bounced.

"Tomorrow, we journey to Lyvedon," Dirk said with a sigh. "And not a day too soon."

"Oh, my god." Admiral Douglas blinked.

Rebecca stared in horror at her attacker. "It cannot be."

"But it is." Dirk furrowed his brow and pressed a fist to his mouth.

"Bloody hell." Sir Ross sat back on his heels, the mask in his grasp. "It is Clarkson."

CHAPTER SEVENTEEN

*L*ooming over his personal secretary, Sir Ross shook his head in astonishment. "How could I not have known?"

"You cannot blame yourself." Rebecca massaged her sore neck. "We were all deceived."

"I am the head of the bloody Corps." His jaw muscles flexed as he gritted his teeth. "Yet I allowed a turncoat to run my office." He stood, righted his coat, and motioned to Trevor and Dalton. "Get him out of here. I want him in interview as soon as I return to the Ministry."

"Of course." Trevor grasped Clarkson under his arms and to Dalton said, "Take his feet."

"I do not like this." Sir Ross grimaced and glanced at Rebecca. "The man was my secretary. He had the intelligence of a gnat, which is why I hired him. Not for minute do I believe him capable of masterminding a coup of this magnitude."

"Do you suspect someone else is involved?" Dirk asked.

"I know there is." Rebecca crossed her arms.

"How can you be sure?" Dirk raked a hand through his hair.

"His speech was off," she explained. "The man who approached me at the Netherton's had a much deeper voice, and he disguised it better." She tapped a finger to her chin and shook her head. "No. I am certain it was not Clarkson. In fact, I would stake my life on it."

Sir Ross narrowed his gaze. "You are that sure?"

"I am positive." She nodded once.

"Then perhaps you should join me in interrogation." Sir Ross offered her his escort.

"Agreed." Rebecca took a single step in his direction.

"Wait just a moment." Dirk caught her by the elbow and swung her to face him. "You cannot let Clarkson know you are a member of the Corps. It is too dangerous. What if he alerts his accomplice?"

"It is a risk I will have to take as—"

"You mean it is a risk we must take," Dirk asserted. "As you are my wife, our collective fate is inextricably intertwined. Your actions affect us both. As such, we need to discuss our next move."

"I beg your pardon, Viscount Wainsbrough." Sir Ross sketched a curt bow, and then addressed Rebecca. "I will have my carriage brought to the front gate. Should you choose to participate in Clarkson's interview, and continue the investigation, I will give you ten minutes."

Caught in between two powerful men, each with their own agenda, Rebecca could only stand there and ponder her predicament. At her left, Sir Ross represented the ugly past, rife with deception and death. To her right, Dirk stood as a physical manifestation of the promise and possibility of the future she desperately desired—but that future relied

on her ability to break free from the bowels of counterintelligence.

"My lord, I am well aware of our connection, but I have a
mission to complete, and what I do as an agent of the Crown
is my affair." She wrenched from his grasp. "I will not walk
away simply because you command it."

"Wrong on both counts. Your work is concluded, and
the traitor is in custody." Stretching to full height, he arched
a brow. "You vowed to leave the Corps—a vow to which I
hold you. As my viscountess, you must obey me."

"Dirk, please, be reasonable. In obeisance of your terms,
I have tendered my resignation, contingent upon the turncoat's capture." Rebecca splayed both arms in supplication.
"Can you not see that our assignment remains incomplete?
As I once told you, victory in war requires more than one
person acting in concert with another, as does conspiracy.
There must be more persons involved in this treasonous
plan. There must be a top-level schemer, a predator every
bit as dangerous, if not more so, than Clarkson, and he must
be caught, else we will never be safe."

"Let Sir Ross and his men round up the others. I want
you with me." He pressed a fist to his chest and compressed
his lips. "Come to Lyvedon, our ancestral home, where we
can start our new life apart from this nasty business and
leave the past behind."

The desperate plea in his voice broke her heart, but
Rebecca resisted the urge to surrender her cause. She had
to be strong, even if it killed her, and it might.

"Would that the answer were that uncomplicated." With
a heavy sigh, she shuffled her feet. "We have to uncover
those with whom Clarkson was in league. And I would
wager our villain knows of my involvement, though he may
not be aware of the extent to which I am connected with the

Corps. In all honesty, you have to admit we cannot move forward until we truly finish the task at hand, as we would forever be looking over our shoulders, and that is no way to live."

"Neither is this." Dirk inclined his head. "Will you always make excuses? Will you always invent reasons to delay your resignation? Do you ever truly intend to leave the Corps?"

"Of course, I do." Conscious of the minutes ticking down, Rebecca retreated. "For now, Sir Ross is waiting, so I must go. I know you are angry, but this is neither the time nor the place for that discussion. We can talk it over when I come home. Will you wait up for me?"

"No."

"Then we will discuss it tomorrow."

"That will not be possible." He flicked a speck of dust from his coat sleeve. "I journey to Lyvedon."

She stiffened. "You would go without me?"

With casual indifference that has not fooled her for a second, Dirk folded his arms in front of him. "If must needs."

"Then I, too, will do what must needs." Rebecca turned on her heels and departed his company without so much as a backward glance.

THE FOLLOWING EVENING, as the sun sank below the yardarm, Dirk stared at his sleeping wife. After spending the night at the Ministry of Defense, presumably questioning Clarkson, she had arrived home in the late morning hours, exhausted and starved. Leashing his temper, they barely exchanged two words. Instead, he placed her welfare before his pride, ordered a light repast, of which she made quick work, and tucked her in his bed.

Despondent over their situation, he could not decide whether to throttle her or kiss her silly, as he had indulged her occupation to the point of madness. Worse, he suspected that, if he said nothing and remained complaisant, she would birth his heir in some back alley-way, while spying on a French general. So he needed to do something, had to make a stand.

Careful not to make a sound, he crossed the room. With one last agonizing look at her motionless form, he grasped the knob and opened the door. In mere minutes he gained his curricle and sped through Mayfair, fueled by a wave of anger and frustration.

Despite his intent to depart London, he made it as far as White's, where he found Trevor and Everett.

"May I join you?"

Trevor glanced at Everett and then arched a brow. "Be my guest."

Settling himself in a comfortable chair, Dirk leaned forward, but just as fast, changed his tack and reclined. After a few seconds, he crossed his legs. Then he uncrossed his legs. A second later, he folded his arms in front of him, before reversing course and resting an elbow on the armrest.

"Something troubling you, friend?" With a half-smile, Trevor signaled for an additional round of drinks.

"No, no." Dirk tugged at his coat sleeve, cleared his throat, and shifted his weight. "Everything is fine." An uncomfortable silence twisted the knot in his stomach even tighter. "Why do you ask?"

"You seem a tad out of sorts." Trevor handed Dirk a glass of brandy.

"Discord in connubial paradise, Wainsbrough?" Everett

inquired with a chuckle, which faded quickly when Dirk shot the second son a lethal stare.

"Oh, I say. You are in bad shape." Everett slapped his thigh. "Such a sad sight." To Trevor, he said, "Reminds me of the night you showed up at my doorstep, when you discovered Caroline attended—"

"I fail to see how I figure into the equation." Trevor scowled. "And if memory serves, you promised to be the soul of discretion."

"Now do not get snippy with me." Everett rolled his eyes. "Was it my fault that you jumped to unsupported conclusions weaved from whole cloth and landed yourself in the proverbial doghouse?"

"No." Trevor grimaced. "But you can blame no one but yourself when I break your nose."

Misery truly loved company, Dirk realized, as he found comfort in the revelation that Trevor also struggled with a willful wife, and he sighed. "Gentlemen, is there a purpose to this conversation?"

"May I offer a bit of unsolicited advice?" Everett peered at Trevor and then Dirk. "Mind you, I speak as the veteran of a heated campaign. Have your staff stow your most treasured valuables."

"Lord Markham, while some may indulge in uncontrollable outbursts, I can assure you that I am immune to such behavior." Dirk fortified himself with a healthy gulp of liquid courage. "Trust me, it is not in my nature."

"Glass is of particular concern," Everett stated flatly and then gazed at the ceiling. "Someone reduced my entire collection of erotic Oriental figurines to rubble after a wicked row with his bride."

A telling flush crept across Trevor's cheeks. "I apologized for that."

In that instant, Dirk wished he were somewhere—anywhere, else. "I have never surrendered to unrestrained fits of rage."

"I would extend the warning to include fragile items," Trevor added. "You do not want anything near that can be broken."

Exasperated, Dirk revisited the argument with Rebecca. She had valid reasons for remaining in London, just as he had valid reasons for quitting the field. Although he understood her perspective and admired her devotion to duty, she had to accept that his chief concern was her welfare. He had to defend his family. If anything happened to her, he would never forgive himself.

"Have you told her you love her?" Trevor queried in a low voice.

"Are you out of your mind?" Everett hissed. "You do not ask a man if he is in love, especially with his wife. Do you want to get us both killed?"

Trevor arched a brow. "And just what do you know of love?"

"Bloody hell." Everett winced. "I still shudder when I recollect your reaction to the same question posed quite innocently by me."

"Oh, well we know just how experienced you are with that delicate brand of warfare polite society more commonly refers to as marriage."

"Did I or did I not get you to the altar, Jolly Roger intact?"

Reason and logic were cornerstones of Dirk's existence, yet there was nothing reasonable or logical about Rebecca's occupation. And she resisted his authority. Could his predicament get any more humiliating? He huffed a breath and drained his glass. "Once again, gentlemen, I ask you, what is your point?"

"Apologies, brother." In an instant, Trevor sobered. "If I may be so bold as to suggest that you consider a few relevant facts."

At the end of his tether, he acquiesced. "I am listening."

With a finger, Trevor gestured in emphasis. "First, I admit that Caroline is my life."

Dirk dipped his chin. "As Rebecca is mine."

"Second, my chief concern is her safety."

"And Rebecca's is mine."

"All right." Trevor glanced at Everett, as if choosing his words carefully, because his friend was not privy to their mission, and then met Dirk's gaze. "Given your current situation, and the observation that you are, at present, here. Who guards your wife?"

As the Wainsbrough town carriage rocked gently to and fro, Rebecca yawned and rubbed her weary eyes. It had been a long day, and nothing had gone right, as Dirk held true to his word and departed for the country before she woke.

How could he abandon her?

Whether or not he agreed with her stance, he could have stayed and talked to her. They should have discussed the situation, as they were partners. Was he not the same man who had followed her to the Ministry and decreed, in front of Sir Ross no less, that when their opinions conflicted they should conduct a calm and rational examination? Apparently, such edict only applied to her.

Well, for good or ill, she kept her word.

Before leaving the Ministry of Defense, she tendered her resignation from the Counterintelligence Corps. Her career in espionage was terminated, and, much to her surprise, it was a chapter of her life she found remarkably easy to close. Sir Ross accepted her decision with a distinct air of fatalism, assuring her there would always be a place for *L'araignee* should she decide to return, but that was no longer an option.

Tomorrow presented a new beginning, in more ways than one.

Of course, it was all for naught if she could not mend fences with her husband. The carriage halted and she roused from her reverie. With infinite gratitude, she accepted assistance from the footman.

Hughes opened the door as she reached the entrance. "Good evening, your ladyship."

"Hughes." She dipped her chin and tugged off her gloves. "Would you have a tray sent to my sitting room?"

"I shall see to it at once, your ladyship."

As though weighted with iron shackles, her legs shook as she ascended the grand staircase. Gaining the peaceful solitude of her bedchamber, she dismissed her maid and undressed herself. If she could not be with Dirk, she preferred to be alone. Staring at the dour image in the mirror of her vanity, she pulled pins from her long brown hair, and the locks cascaded over her shoulders. Her heart was heavy in her chest, and her mood as black as the night sky.

Resting her head in her hands, she sighed. "Tell me it is not too late."

With a mournful groan, she pushed away from the vanity and strode to the armoire. Donning an ebony silk robe that practically swallowed her, because it was a man's garment, not to mention Dirk's favorite, she cinched the belt at her waist. She took a step and froze. A hint of sandal-wood teased her nose, aroused her senses, and an image of Dirk materialized in a flash. How she missed her stubborn husband.

For the umpteenth time, tears welled, and she sniffed. Well, at least now she understood her wayward emotions of late. But how would he react to her news? Would he be happy? Would he be sad?

She hoped for the former but feared the latter.

Never had he tempered his fierce dislike of her occupa-tion. When discussing what he desired in a wife, Dirk had been open and honest, and above all consistent, from the beginning. And she had told him she wanted the same.

Had she lied?

After entering the sitting room, she closed the door behind her and leaned against the oak panels. For a moment, she rubbed her temples and stared at the carpet beneath her feet. With a sigh, she crossed the room and stood at the table bearing her dinner. Lifting the silver cover, she inspected the fare and wrinkled her nose.

Although she was not hungry, it was important that she ate something. So she sat herself down and polished off the roasted chicken, green peas, and carrots. With a pleasantly full belly, she walked to the window and stared at the starry sky. If Dirk were outside, he would have glimpsed the same view. The thought was comforting.

"Ho-hum." She yawned.

Once again in her room, Rebecca peered at her bed and frowned. Then she stared at the portal that connected her suite with Dirk's. So he was not in residence. Had that meant she could not sleep in his bed? She navigated the tiny corridor before she realized she had moved. At the end of the hall, a sliver of golden light emanating from beneath the door gave her pause.

Why was the fireplace lit in his chamber?

Quick as a wink, she turned the knob and tiptoed into his room.

Bare-chested, beautiful, and no doubt still angry, Dirk sat in bed, with the sheets pulled to his waist, as he read a book. Aching to touch him, her fingertips tingled, and her heart raced.

"You are home," was all she could say as her knees weakened, and she feared she might swoon. Perhaps she should simply fling herself atop him and take refuge in his warm embrace.

He glanced up. "As you see." He stared at her and arched a brow. "Is that my robe?"

She gulped and clutched the silk folds to her chest. "It is." Her voice wavered, and she cursed herself.

He closed the book and set it on the bedside table. "Have you misplaced your night apparel?"

She lifted her chin. "I have not."

Clasping his hands in his lap, he opened his mouth and then closed it. "You look tired."

"I am." Projecting a placid demeanor, which was nothing more than pure deception, she walked to the fireplace, gazed into the flames, and rubbed her forearms. "It has been a trying day."

"How are things progressing with the case?" he inquired with an acid tongue that had not escaped her notice. "Has Clarkson divulged the names of his partners in crime?"

"He was found dead in his cell this morning." But despite the double-dealing clerk's demise, Rebecca feared she might never be free of her past as a spy. "So he will not be telling anyone anything, ever again."

"Suicide?"

She shrugged her shoulders. "Who knows?"

"How did he die?"

"We suspect poison, but it will be at least a week before the autopsy report is complete." Nerves got the best of her, and a wave of nausea had her leaning against the mantel for support. "He foamed at the mouth, and the surgeon believes it was arsenic."

"What will you do now?" Dirk asked.

It was now or never. "Nothing."

"I beg your pardon?"

"I will do nothing, because I surrendered my commission." Inhaling deeply, Rebecca closed her eyes and prayed for strength. "I resigned the Corps and am no longer an agent for the Crown."

Telltale footfalls on the carpeted floor declared her husband had vacated his bed and come to stand directly behind her. "Why?"

"Because I will not risk an innocent."

"What?"

"You heard me."

Dirk grasped her shoulders and brought her to face him. Naked as the day he was born, he traced her chin with a finger, and then brought her gaze to his. "Becca, what are you telling me?"

"I am pregnant." She hoped he was pleased, because she needed his kindness at that moment.

In an instant, his expression softened. "Are you sure?"

"Dr. Handley confirmed it this afternoon, though I was not surprised. I immediately returned to the Ministry and met with Sir Ross, to help him tie up as many loose ends as possible before leaving—for good." Swamped with a heady mixture of uncertainty, anxiety, and longing, Rebecca fought in vain to keep the tears at bay. "I did not know what went wrong, because I used the sponge to prevent conception, but then I recalled that we used nothing the first few times we made love."

"If I remember correctly, you were in a rush to meet your fate, darling." Was it wishful thinking, or was he teasing her? "In fact, you quite swept me off my feet."

Relief washed over her and eased her worried mind, but the adrenaline was too much to bear. With the weight of the world still entrenched on her shoulders, Rebecca broke.

"No, Becca. Do not cry." Dirk pulled her close and kissed her.

It was an olive branch, an achingly tender caress meant to soothe, and after a few minutes she relaxed in his arms. The tears flowed, as would the ocean through a breached hull, and she sobbed with unrestrained abandon and without pride.

"Why did you come back?"

"Can you not guess? I could not stay away from you, and it was wrong to leave as I did." He chuckled and gave her a squeeze. "You have turned me into a doting husband. Heaven help me when I return to sea."

"Are you pleased?" She wiped her nose on her sleeve and hiccuped. "I mean about the baby? Is this what you want?"

"Oh, love." He cupped her cheek and smiled. "You carry our child. How could I not be pleased?"

"I was coming to Lyvedon. I planned to depart at dawn." She whimpered. "I am so sorry I chose Sir Ross over you. It will never happen again."

"My dear, I owe you the apology." He bent, lifted her from her foot, and carried her to the bed. Perched on the edge of the mattress, he cradled her in his lap. "Never should I have forced you to choose sides."

"Dirk, I do not deserve you." She nuzzled his chest.

"Again, you are mistaken, as I do not deserve you." When he tipped her chin, she followed his lead and accepted the kiss he so tenderly bestowed. Their tongues met, and he tasted her slowly, intimately. The stress of the day yielded to undeniable passion, and she moaned.

"I want you." With exploring fingers, she searched for his most delicate protuberance.

"Not so fast, my lady wife." He caught her wrist and frowned.

"It has been too long—"

"I would not injure the babe."

"But Dr. Handley said—"

"You need to rest." With a gentleness of which she had not thought him capable, Dirk tucked her beneath the covers. "Sleep, angel, while I make preparations. We shall journey to Lyvedon soon enough."

CHAPTER EIGHTEEN

*T*he next morning, Rebecca woke to breakfast in bed, and to her abiding delight, Dirk fed her every morsel, alternating bites of food with sweet kisses. Later, he bathed her, toweled her dry, and brushed her hair for the better portion of an hour. Happier than she would have ever thought possible, she reveled without complaint in the attention her overprotective husband shamelessly lavished on her.

Since it was early in her pregnancy, he had not forbid her to partake of their morning ride, which she had dearly missed. He had, however, held her to a conservative trot— no galloping permitted. And when they returned to their home, and he adjourned to his study to review estate accounts, he kept her at his side, encouraging her to read or work on her needlepoint. In short, wherever he went, she went, too.

While the staff prepared their trunks and mustered supplies for the journey to Lyvedon Hall, the Wainsbrough ancestral pile, she was forced to recline on the *chaise* and keep her feet elevated. Conscious of the whispers and ever prying gaze of the *ton*, she tried to shoo Dirk off to one of his clubs, but he would not let her out of his sight.

Since the Season was well nigh at an end, he decided they would remain in residence in the evening, with dinner served in his bedchamber. And despite her assurances that she had, indeed, remembered how to put a fork to her mouth, she dutifully huddled in his lap and consumed everything he offered her. When he insisted she retire early, she objected vehemently—until he proceeded to keep her awake for a few hours, with his particular brand of sumptuous divertissement.

Lost amid an enthralling potpourri of love and devotion, it never occurred to Rebecca that there was an ulterior motive to her husband's excessive fussing. Her recently retired spy instincts never tweaked, because it seemed a natural reaction to impending fatherhood. After all, Trevor doted on Caroline, as Dirk doted on his wife. She presumed his attentive behavior bespoke concern for the baby.

"Viscount Wainsbrough, sir." Sir Ross Logan's new secretary announced Dirk's arrival and then excused himself.

"Why am I not surprised?" The head of the Counterintelligence Corps stared up from the report he had been reading and extended a hand in welcome. "Have a seat, Wainsbrough."

"Sir Ross, thank you for seeing me on such short notice." Settling into one of the high-back chairs that faced the large desk, Dirk wondered how best to proceed. "Perhaps you can guess my reason for calling."

"Is it fair to assume you are not here to bemoan the

weather?" Sir Ross cupped his chin in his palm and frowned. "Out with it."

For several seconds, Dirk simply studied the patterned rug on the floor. Though he dreaded the answer, he had to pose the question foremost on his mind. "How serious is the threat to my wife?"

"Well, it depends on the depth of corruption in our forces, which I have yet to fully determine." Sir Ross leaned back and sighed. "With no idea of the number or rank, I do not know who I can trust. And then there is the mysterious item our villain believes Rebecca possesses. Something for which he is willing to kill to obtain."

Other than the necklace, which was little more than a harmless keepsake, Colin had given Rebecca; she carried nothing aboard the *Gawain*. She had no papers or journal. His heart sank in his chest, and Dirk cast a narrowed glance. "Do you believe Clarkson committed suicide?"

"No." Sir Ross shook his head. "I think he was poisoned."

"Just as I feared." A shiver of dread traipsed his spine, as he realized the gravity of the situation. "Someone within the Ministry?"

"Yes," Sir Ross stated without hesitation. "At the very least, our chief turncoat has access to the Ministry and the offices of the Corps. Our profile suggests he is well known, he blends into our personnel, and his presence does not arouse suspicion. As to his motive, we are clueless."

"Bloody hell." Dirk grimaced. "That could be anyone."

"Precisely. And because of that, he could not risk having Clarkson in custody. All members of the Corps are schooled in the tactics of interrogation we employ." Sir Ross lifted his chin and caught Dirk in a lethal stare. "I would have broken Clarkson."

"Rebecca has asked me to take her to Lyvedon Hall." Dirk stood and paced the floor, and then he halted. "What do you suggest?"

"The open landscape and isolation of the country would leave you vulnerable to attack." Sir Ross pressed a clenched fist to his mouth and paused. "Is there any chance you would be willing to talk Rebecca into returning—if only to help us uncover the conspiracy? I need someone I can trust."

Dirk walked to the edge of the desk, placed his hands on the blotter, and stared down his nose at Sir Ross. "My wife is pregnant."

With an expression of utter shock, Sir Ross blinked. "Commiserations."

"I would rather you congratulate me."

"Felicitations, of course." Sir Ross steepled his hands. "I understand your concern, Wainsbrough. This definitely changes our situation. However, I still believe your wife is our best shot at luring the villain into the open. Would you consider delaying your trip to the country for a week?"

"What have you in mind?"

"I can guarantee her safety."

"You cannot guarantee the safety of your own people."

"Point taken."

"Just tell me what you want."

"It is simple, really. Stay close to your wife."

"Done," Dirk replied in a hairsbreadth of a second.

"Take her to the last few engagements of the Season." Sir Ross stood and righted his coat. "Patronize the theatre and the opera. Circulate. See and be seen. But keep me abreast of your schedule."

"I warn you, Sir Ross." He pointed in emphasis. "I will not put Rebecca or our child at risk. If you think I will stand idly by while you dangle her as bait for a murderer, you are mistaken. The bastard will have to get through me to get to my wife."

"It will not be necessary for her to contact the blackguard, as I will shadow your footsteps, watching to see who is watching you. I give you my word; no harm shall befall Rebecca on my watch. I will surrender my life, if necessary."

The urge to protect and defend his wife and child ran as a river of molten steel in his veins, and Dirk had never felt so mighty, so invincible—so helpless, at once. As if he had just struck a bargain with the devil, a chill of foreboding unease settled in his chest, and his heart raced. For good or ill, he was about to place the center of his universe in the sights of an unknown, deadly adversary.

"Tell me your plan."

AFTER COMPARING NOTES, strategizing, and checking each and every detail, Dirk gained his carriage and set off for his next destination, praying he had done the right thing. With any luck, his hastily scripted dispatches had found their mark, and the men would be waiting. His entire future relied on their participation and success. To his chagrin, there was not much he could do, but watch and wait for the traitor to strike.

In the world beyond the window, the signature maple trees of Hyde Park stood tall as sentries, and the stately homes fronting Park Lane, his own included, cast an elegant divide of brick and mortar. By all accounts, everything seemed as it should be, and nothing appeared out of place or abnormal. How he wished that were true.

When the equipage turned onto Upper Brooke Street,

grim acceptance settled as a lead ball in the pit of his belly. Stopping at the residence that bore the placard inscribed with the number 24, Dirk recalled the first occasion on which he enlisted the aid of the Knights of the Brethren of the Coast to protect Rebecca. At the time, she was nothing more than an intriguing woman he hoped to know better. Now, she was his world.

In mere seconds, he skipped up the entrance stairs, doffed his hat and gloves, gave them to the butler, and then turned right and strode down the hall to the familiar bastion of the Brethren. To his relief, the knights were in full attendance, and he was the last to arrive.

The casual greetings, lightheartedly bestowed, barely registered in the conflicted miasma of his brain. Lost in a haze of anger mixed with fear, he had not quite grasped the Admiral's call to order.

"Dirk, are you all right?"

"Yes." He snapped to attention and discovered himself the subject of intense scrutiny. "I am fine."

"As I was saying, the directive from Sir Ross provided ample detail." The admiral fixed him with a sympathetic stare. "Son, yours is a precarious position, and I do not envy you."

"It is regrettable business, brother." Damian compressed his lips. "Given recent events—the revelation of the impending expansion of our family."

"Congratulations, old boy," Blake offered. "You can rely on us. We will do our part to keep your wife and child from the line of fire."

"Hear, hear." Lance smiled.

"In light of your cooperation to capture the traitor, the Lord High Admiral has seen fit to suspend all pending assignments for the Order." Admiral Douglas rested an elbow on the blotter of his desk. "Henceforth, we are to commit our resources to safeguarding your viscountess."

"I am grateful, Admiral." Though he remained calm on the surface, inside Dirk was a jumbled mass of nerves, wound tight as a clock spring. And again he wondered whether or not he should confide in Rebecca.

As she was with child, he had insisted Dr. Handley verify her good health the previous morning. When he escorted the doctor to the door, Dirk inquired as to the effects of added stress and understood full well the hazards. He was gambling with their lives, not to mention that of their firstborn, and their entire future was at stake.

"Will you brief Rebecca?" Trevor asked. "Were I in your boots, I would not want my wife to know—not in her present condition."

"No." Dirk shook his head. "I cannot tell her the truth."

Trevor sighed. "It is for the best."

"So you intend to make the rounds of the final events of the Season? Perhaps we should enlist the aid of our sisters." Lance scratched his chin. "After all, social drudgery is their *forte*. And they will be hot as a hornet's nest if we do not ask for their help, and they get wind of our plot."

"You cannot be serious." Dalton snorted. "They would only get in the way."

In that instant, Admiral Douglas' head shot up, and he narrowed his stare. With a finger pressed to his lips, he forestalled the conversation and softly crept to the entrance of his domain. Quick as a wink, he grasped the knob and yanked open the door.

The youngest Douglas offspring toppled over, landing flat on her face.

"*Sabrina Francis!*" Admiral Douglas shouted. "What the

devil do you think you are doing?"

"Ought to tan her hide."

"She needs a good beating."

"Lock her in her room for a fortnight."

"Get her a husband."

"I was merely inspecting the rugs." Faced with such threats to her freedom and posterior, Sabrina managed to appear contrite, and she shuffled her feet. "It might be time to have them cleaned, Papa."

Admiral Douglas folded his arms and stood stock-still.

Clutching fistfuls of her skirts, Sabrina rocked on her heels.

Although no one said a word, Dirk was ready to explode.

"All right—I was listening." She stomped her foot. "But before you toss me out, at least do me the courtesy of hearing what I have to say."

"Against my better judgment, you may proceed." Admiral Douglas made an elegant sweep of his hand, permitting her entry.

Marching right in, as if she owned the hallowed men's retreat, Sabrina perched on the edge of her father's desk.

"As I see it, the trick to this plan is getting Lady Wainsbrough out in public, without arousing her suspicions. I should think a few invitations from myself, Alex, and Elaine would accomplish your objective in brilliant fashion."

She paused for a moment and wrinkled her nose.

"As Sir Ross will be guarding her from afar, the danger would be minimal. Surely he will trap the scoundrel before he gets anywhere near Lady Wainsbrough. Then this whole nasty affair will be concluded, with Rebecca none the wiser."

Sabrina grinned from ear to ear, and it was obvious she was quite proud of herself.

At first, Dirk wanted to throttle her. But as he mulled her proposal, and assessed her logic, he could not surmise a single counterpoint. Propping an elbow on the armrest of his chair, Dirk rested his chin in his hand. "Brie is right."

"What?"

"Are you mad?"

"You are as crazy as she is."

"You cannot be serious."

"Hear me out, brothers." Though he loathed admitting it, the plan was just outlandish enough to succeed. "Rebecca will never accept that I have suddenly acquired a fondness for the opera, or any other such pursuit. I have never gone for that sort of thing, a fact she knows. Were I to approach her with myriad engagements, her well-founded instincts would be clamoring with incredulity. In short, she would know something was wrong."

"I agree." Admiral Douglas reclaimed his seat. Leaning forward, he clasped his hands atop his desk. "Well then, we will need to coordinate our efforts with the women."

"Save Caroline," Trevor insisted. "Sorry, Dirk. But I do not want her involved in this ugly endeavor."

"Oh, I concur," Dirk assured him.

"Well then." Lance stood and stretched. "It would appear I am in need of a box for the opera."

"And I should consult the theatre offerings." Damian adjusted his cravat and slapped Blake on the back. "Come, brother."

"Sabrina Francis, call your mother in here." Admiral Douglas gazed at the ceiling as if in expectation of divine intervention.

"Right away, Papa." Sabrina paused at the door. "And Cara, as well?"

"Indeed," the Admiral replied.

"Bloody hell." Dirk tugged loose his cravat. "I need a drink."

~

"ARE YOU A MORNING PERSON, TOO?" Rebecca asked Sabrina as they strolled, parasols in hand, through Hyde Park. The sun had barely crested on the horizon when the youngest Douglas appeared with an invitation to walk the sandy track.

"On occasion." Sabrina shrugged. "Both Mama and Cara are late risers, and I enjoy having time alone with Papa."

"I see." Lilting birdsong filled her ears, and Rebecca smiled. "Are you very close with your father?" She had always wondered what her relationship with her sire would have been like had he lived longer.

"Very." Sabrina laughed. "Mama always says I am my father's daughter."

Riding ahead, Dirk sat high atop his stallion. Rebecca marveled as he exercised his horse, knowing he would be an excellent patriarch, doting endlessly, and no doubt a stern disciplinarian.

And now that she had resigned the Corps, her child would not live in fear of losing its mother. As the matriarch of her growing family, she would celebrate every milestone, from the first word, to the first steps, to the first session at Eton; to the day he took a wife.

While there were no medical tests to confirm her instincts, she believed she was carrying a boy. The spy trade had taught her to trust her inner voice, and it proclaimed, loud and clear, that she increased with Dirk's heir. Absently, she pressed a palm to her belly.

"How does it feel?" Sabrina queried in a small voice tinged with awe.

Rebecca blinked. "I beg your pardon?"

"To have a life growing inside you? Does it tickle?" Sabrina chuckled, and then her expression sobered. "Does it hurt?"

Faced with such charming naïveté, Rebecca could only smile. It was too soon for her to evidence any physical change, but she felt different, yet it defied explanation.

"No, it does not hurt. Though I have heard it can tickle when the babe begins to move. Still, it is a tad early for that." At that moment, Dirk waved, and she blew him a kiss. "Daresay my condition has had greater impact on my husband, as he has been constantly underfoot."

"Oh?" Sabrina frowned, and Rebecca wondered if she had overstepped her bounds. "How so?"

"We have been to Drury Lane twice, the opera," she said, counting off the events on her fingers. "And he even escorted me to a musicale at the Hogart's, which I would rather he had eschewed."

"Bloody hell." Sabrina wrinkled her nose. "Not the twins."

"Oh, yes." Rebecca grimaced. "After all the talk, which I must confess I thought exaggerated, I have finally suffered the distinct privilege of enduring their unique brand of entertainment."

"You give them too much credit." With a hand to her mouth, Sabrina leaned in to whisper, "Miranda Hogart sings like a braying ass."

Rebecca burst into laughter.

Just then, a swarthy, oily looking man stepped from behind a large maple. He swept up his arm in a flash.

Startled, Rebecca shrieked.

Shouting the alarm, Sabrina positioned herself between Rebecca and the stranger. Fast as a whip, she raised her parasol and conked the man directly on the head. With his mouth agape in surprise, he stood frozen and then slumped unconscious on the ground.

As if from nowhere, Sir Ross, Damian, Blake, and Lance magically appeared, with Dirk bringing up the rear on his stallion. After quickly dismounting, he ran to Rebecca.

"He had something in his hand," Sabrina said breathlessly, as she held a fist to her heart, the parasol still clutched tightly in the other.

Squatting, Sir Ross bent over the motionless figure and retrieved a small spray of wildflowers. "Is this what gave you cause for concern, Miss Douglas?"

"Uh-Oh." Sabrina shuffled her feet.

"It is all right, darling." Dirk snaked an arm around Rebecca's waist and hugged her close, but she was no mood for his particular brand of comfort. "You have nothing to fear."

She glanced at Dirk, then Sabrina, then Sir Ross, and then Dirk again. "My lord, if you wish to maintain the use of your arm, release me this instant."

He had done so, dropping both hands to his sides.

Frightened and furious at once, Rebecca lifted her chin. "Would someone care to tell me just what is going on here?"

AFTER PROFUSE APOLOGIES to the unfortunate flower peddler, the group reconvened in Dirk's study. With a calm deportment, Rebecca inclined her head as Sir Ross explained the motivation for their efforts. Not for one minute was Dirk fooled by his wife's outward demeanor. She stood at the center of the room, a subtle warning that while she might understand their actions and sympathize with their cause, the man sitting behind the desk enjoyed no such affinity and would not escape her wrath.

"We searched Clarkson's residence," Sir Ross explained. "We discovered correspondence which indicates he was in direct contact with a French operative. I thought it necessary to keep you in a protective custody, of sorts, and your husband was kind enough to cooperate."

"I am sure he was," Rebecca said sweetly. Too sweetly. "Tell me, Sir Ross. In the time you have had me under surveillance, has anyone shown unusual interest in my movements?"

"No." Sir Ross shook his head. "There has been nothing to suggest you are being stalked. In light of Clarkson's death, our villain may have feared discovery and fled the country."

"Well then, I suppose there will be no opposition to my journeying to Lyvedon tomorrow." It was a statement, not a question.

"Of course not." Sir Ross cleared his throat. "If the individual we sought has escaped, then the danger to you is non-existent."

"How fortunate," his wife said in a high-pitched singsong that gave Dirk collywobbles.

"Rebecca, I am sorry for my part in the deception." Sabrina shifted her weight. "I was genuinely concerned for your safety and was only trying to help."

"Do not worry yourself one bit, my dear." Rebecca placed a kiss of sisterly affection on Brie's cheek and then exchanged a handshake with Sir Ross. "I am not angry with either of you."

Behind her, Dirk reclined in his chair, as the implication

of her words confirmed the fact that he alone bore the brunt of her ire.

"Now, if you will excuse us, I would like a word with my husband."

His study cleared with remarkable efficiency, as his fair-weather friends abandoned him to the firing squad. With a piteous glance and a pained expression, Sir Ross departed, at last. No sooner had the door shut than Rebecca faced him.

"How dare you conspire to use our unborn child as a carrot before the horse?" She pounded a fist to the blotter. "And you lied to me. How could you deceive me?"

"Becca, darling—"

"Do not '*Becca, darling*' me."

"I know you are upset—"

"*Upset?*" She set hands on hips. "You think me upset?"

"Easy, love." In a flash, Dirk stood, rounded his desk, and grasped her arms. "Think of the babe. You—"

"Do not touch me." In high dudgeon, she wrenched free and stomped to the window. "I am not upset. *I am bloody well furious!* How could you do it?"

"Neither you nor our child were ever in any danger."

"You do not know that." Her eyes flared. "And I thought you a kind and considerate husband."

"I did what I thought best." He reached for her, but she quickly skittered beyond his reach, taking refuge behind a chair. "I did not want you to worry."

"So you plotted with Sir Ross to continue the mission without my knowledge?" Rebecca emitted a cry of sarcasm. "Tell me, my lord, did you laugh at my ignorance behind my back? Did you find sport in your duplicity?"

"Of course not." When he shoved the chair aside, she turned and ran from the study. "Becca, come back here."

"Leave me alone," she cried over her shoulder as she flew up the stairs.

"We are going to discuss this, my lady wife." Dirk took the steps, two at a time.

"I am through talking to you." She gained her room, slammed the door, and slid the lock home with a defiant click.

"Well I am not through with you," he muttered under his breath. Standing before the entry to her chamber, Dirk grasped the knob and shook it hard. At the same time, he banged a fist on the oak panel. "Rebecca, open this door."

"Go away, you addled ass," she shouted in response.

And then it hit him. He was a no-nonsense man who preferred an orderly existence defined by logic and reason. Yet there was nothing logical or reasonable in his actions. With a chuckle, he released the knob, strode down the hall, crossed his chamber, and ever so quietly slipped through the little corridor adjoining their apartments. With nary a sound, he entered his wife's quarters and smiled.

With her back to him, and an ear pressed to the door, Rebecca stood. Stealthily he stalked her. In mere seconds, Dirk swooped and whisked her into his arms just as she screamed.

"Let go of me." Tears coursed her cheeks, and he cursed himself for making her cry. As he retraced his steps, carrying her to his bedchamber, she folded her arms in front of her. "Do not think you can seduce your way out of this."

"I do not intend to," he replied with genuinely good humor. "We are going to talk this through calmly and rationally, and then I am going to seduce you."

"No."

"Yes."

Dirk walked to the edge of his mattress and eased her down. Before she could scramble away, he covered her.

Rebecca squirmed and kicked, and with both hands she pushed at his chest. "Get off of me."

Framing her jaw with his fingers, he covered her lips with his and then seized her mouth. He licked and suckled her tongue, engaging her in succulent play—an appetizer to the main course. As her resistance faded, her legs stilled, and her body relaxed beneath him.

"I did what I had to—for you," he murmured against her flesh.

"For me?" Rebecca asked, and her breath hitched as he nibbled at her throat. "I would have thought your heir of paramount concern."

"I would do anything to protect you." Dirk lifted his head and gazed into her turbulent brown depths. "You are my life, Becca. Without you, I am nothing."

The truth rang clear in his voice, startling even him.

Resting his forehead to hers, he sighed. "I love you."

How striking was it that three simple words, honestly spoken, could wash away the ire in the blink of an eye?

Favoring him with a flirty, feminine smile, Rebecca wound her arms about his neck and scored her nails to his nape. "My lord, I love you, too."

With nerves charged, passion shimmered like the finest crystal, igniting the air about them. Fueled by a wicked erection, and the base desire to join with his wife, he inched her skirts to her waist and then unhooked his breeches.

"I thought you said the seduction would come later." Rebecca swallowed hard. "After our discussion."

Dirk nipped the tip of her nose. "I changed my mind."

CHAPTER NINETEEN

*I*n the weeks since they journeyed to Lyvedon Hall, Dirk counted himself a fortunate man as his wife blossomed amid the lush landscape of their country estate. The dark circles beneath her brown eyes paled, the underlying strain in her deportment faded, and at last, she relaxed. With the energy one would expect of a secret agent hunting information vital to national defense, Rebecca dove into household management, expressing an unrivaled zeal for menu planning. Much to his relief, she no longer found it necessary to strap a dagger to her thigh.

And although he had remained on guard, should some unexplained, infelicitous misfortune strike his bride, it seemed his concerns were for naught. With each passing day, the traitor occupied less and less of his thoughts. As such, Dirk and Rebecca settled into a comfortable routine.

Professing an avid appreciation for the backwater, she accompanied him on the weekly jaunts to visit their tenants, and he marveled at her natural ability to ferret out the minutest deficiency. When Rebecca declared that, while London was fine for a time, she would much prefer to spend her days on their principal estate, Dirk was not about to argue. Keeping his beautiful wife tucked in the woods might seem a bit draconian to some, but he thought it the perfect environment to nurture their marital relationship, because he so wanted to be a good husband.

Climbing the back stairs to the morning room, Dirk shrugged his shoulders in an effort to relieve a nagging twinge. For some reason he could not fathom, he had suffered an uneasy night. When he recalled the inventive measures his resourceful viscountess had undertaken to soothe his restlessness, he could not help but smile.

Sitting on the *chaise*, attempting to master needlework, the only skill she had yet to conquer, she cast a charming pout and peered at him as he entered the room. "My lord, pray tell. How do women find the patience for such tedium?"

Dirk laughed and sat beside her. "I had thought to spend the afternoon shooting." He gave her a playful nudge. "Unless you would rather remain here and indulge your fondness for embroidery, would you consent to join me?"

"Oh, my love. I can think of nothing I would prefer more." Eyes effervescent with unabashed joy, she twined her arms about his neck and kissed him on the mouth with a resounding smack. "Give me five minutes to change my clothes."

Without hesitation, she tossed aside her silks and leapt from the *chaise*.

"I shall await you in the foyer." It was his luck to marry a woman who preferred guns to a needle and thread.

∾

WITH A SQUEAL OF DELIGHT, Rebecca brushed out the skirts of her new red riding habit, which she had ordered a week before departing London. How she had fretted that it might not arrive in time for her to bring it to Lyvedon, but a stodgy character delivered it with nary a second to spare. And she had been waiting for the perfect opportunity to surprise her husband.

Checking her image in the long mirror, she appraised her appearance and giggled. "The man will not know what hit him."

In a froth of petticoats, she skipped down the stone staircase that led to the foyer, where Dirk waited. Midway, she paused. Wearing tan corded-breeches tucked into gleaming Hessians, an ivory lawn shirt sans cravat, and a dark green hacking jacket, her husband looked only slightly dangerous. When he turned and spied her, his jaw dropped, and her belly flip-flopped.

He said nothing. Merely extended a hand. She glided to a halt before him and dutifully twirled for his perusal.

"Is this a new outfit?" He pressed his lips to her palm.

"It is." She dipped her chin.

"Perhaps we should reconsider our afternoon entertainment?" He pulled her hips to his and thrust, every so slightly. "What say you?"

"My lord, you are shameless."

"And aroused."

"But our horses are saddled." She tugged on her gloves. "I do so look forward to our rides."

"Oh, I can promise you a ride."

"*Dirk.*" Thrilled with his enthusiastic response, she swatted playfully at his chest. "There is always tonight."

"All right." He cast her a lop-sided grin. "But I would

have your word that only I relieve you of this delicious confection."

"If you insist," she said with a laugh, as they stepped into the sunlight.

"Indeed, I do." He lifted her into the saddle and then reached beneath her skirt to caress her calf. "Damn. I knew I should have had Hughes pack the two-seater bench."

"But you are so inventive." Quick as a wink, she grasped him roughly by the neck and kissed him hard. "I am certain you can improvise."

"Rebecca, by all that is holy, I am going to make love to you like fifty men."

"Is that a promise?"

"You may depend upon it."

"Then let us away, as the sooner we venture, the sooner we return." She flicked the reins and set a furious pace.

With Poulson, the loader, following at a discreet distance, they steered their mounts for open country. Charging hell bent for leather through the meadow, Rebecca taunted her husband, urging him faster still. In a clearing, targets perched at various distances provided ample sport, as well as the opportunity to best her no-nonsense captain.

"Hell and the Reaper." Dirk studied her pattern and marked bullet placement in chalk. "Remind me never to quarrel with you when there are firearms within reach."

"Well, your smooth bore pistol projects a curve ball, so I aim with recoil, in mind," she stated, matter-of-factly.

"My dear, you are an excellent markswoman." He chucked her chin. "Should we have another go?"

"Yes, please." Basking in his praise, so freely accorded, she smiled and nodded eagerly. "I must confess it is your flintlock rifle that I am most anxious to try."

"I should warn you, it has quite a kick." Dirk retrieved the weapon in question. "Perhaps I should help you?"

"Show me." She assumed the proper stance.

"Grasp it by the stock, and tuck the butt into your shoulder, pulling it in tight." He made a few adjustments. "Rest your cheek to the flat of the butt, else you risk a nasty bruise to your lovely face."

"Like this?" She followed his directions to the letter.

"Perfect. Now, take aim." Standing at her back, he checked her form. "Rotate to full-cock, but be careful, as that releases the safety lock."

She performed as he bade. "What is next?"

"You are ready to fire. Do not be afraid."

"I am not afraid." Rebecca inhaled a deep breath and held it. Ever so slowly, she eased her finger to the trigger and then tugged hard. The force of the blast nearly set her on her bum.

"Beautiful shot, Becca."

After a few additional rounds, her hand went numb, her shoulder ached, and her belly rumbled with pain of a different sort. "Dirk, I fear all this excitement has worked on me as I had not intended. I am quite famished."

"Actually, I am not surprised, given that you eat for two." He narrowed his stare and grinned. "Come, as I would not have my viscountess withering. We are past due for our noon meal, and, it just so happens, I have provisions."

"We are to picnic?" She blinked.

"Precisely."

A nearby grove of trees offered a shady spot for lunch, and he spread a blanket on the ground, as she untied a sack from his saddle and grimaced. "This is heavy."

"Careful, darling." Dirk accepted the parcel and knelt. "There is chicken, cheese, bread, grapes, and white wine."

"Sounds delicious." After unpacking the simple fare, she sat, situated her skirts, and draped a napkin over her lap. "You are so thoughtful. Thank you, for today."

"Only ensuring the health and welfare of my wife and child." He winked. "Of course, should you choose to express your gratitude tonight, I will not complain."

"My lord, you may depend upon it."

Serenaded by the local birdlife, they fed each other small bites intermingled with tender kisses. Afterward, Dirk stretched out beside her, with his arms crossed beneath his head.

"I am so happy." Without thought, Rebecca crawled atop her husband and covered his mouth with hers. In an instant, he flipped her onto her back and slid a hand into her bodice. Fire erupted in her thighs, and searing heat burned in her veins—which yielded to bone chilling cold.

Abruptly, she ended their kiss and came alert in a scarce second. "Someone watches us."

"Relax." Dirk trailed his finger along her jaw. "It is only Poulson, and he is not that close."

"Are you certain?" The spell broken, she resituated her riding habit.

"It is all right, my dear. However, I do not wish to make a spectacle of my wife." He whisked a wayward tendril from her face, stood, and brought her to her feet. "So let us away, else you will lift your heels for me here."

With the sack repacked, the blanket rolled and retied to the saddle, Dirk settled her atop her mare. Heeling the sinewy flanks of his black hunter, he directed her through a copse of trees and toward the forest. As they neared the edge of the woods, he slowed his mount, and Rebecca followed suit. A bridle path opened before her, and they trotted through the dense foliage, until they entered a small clearing.

Reining to a halt, Dirk peered back. "We should wait for Poulson."

As the minutes passed, her husband grasped her wrist and suckled a fingertip. "Remember, I, alone, have the honor of peeling you out of that luscious ensemble."

To wit she bubbled with laughter. As she made to offer a naughty reply, Poulson appeared.

"Shall I reload your weapons, your lordship?"

"Not now. Her ladyship and I—"

The telltale cough of gunfire pierced the calm.

Every muscle in her body flinched, and gooseflesh covered her from top to toe, as she glanced from side to side. Fear clawed at her throat, but she maintained control —until Dirk slumped forward. Clutching his shoulder, he groaned, as blood oozed between his fingers.

"Rebecca, go back to the house," he said through gritted teeth. "Now."

"No." She shook her head furiously. "You are injured. I will not leave you."

Additional shots rang out in rapid succession.

Rebecca slid from the saddle, just as Dirk teetered precariously and then fell to the ground, his body hitting the earth with a heavy thud. Poulson leapt from his mount and knelt beside her husband.

"Must be poachers nearby." The loader pulled a handkerchief from his pocket and placed it over Dirk's wound. "What a horrible accident, your ladyship."

Another barrage sounded, and Dirk's horse bolted.

"That is no accident." She hunkered as bullets sliced the air. "Where is the pistol?"

"In Lord Wainsbrough's saddlebag, your ladyship."

Poulson brushed aside a lock of hair matted with blood from Dirk's forehead. "This does not look serious. It is a graze, your ladyship."

"Then why is he unconscious?"

"Perhaps his lordship hit his head in the fall."

An eerie sensation of *déjà vu* shivered up her spine.

In the blink of an eye, she transported to a different place and time. The hazy glow of moonlight, the delicate scent of rose petals, the stains on her peach gown, the once boyish expression rendered devoid of emotion, the stone cold flesh of death. Arriving too late, she could not save Colin.

But she would save Dirk.

A relentless salvo echoed in the woods.

Rebecca sprang into action. Regaining her mount, she held tight to the reins.

"Guard his lordship with your life," she commanded. "I will draw their fire."

"But, your ladyship." Mouth agape, Poulson stared at her. "You do not know what is out there. You could be shot."

"It is a risk I am willing to take." For a hairsbreadth of a second, she gazed at Dirk's face, committing every detail, every nuance to memory. "Forgive me, my love."

Rebecca kicked her heels and sent the roan flying down the bridle path. Although she had resided at Lyvedon for a few weeks, she had never ridden that particular tract of the estate. The narrow trail twisted and turned, requiring all her concentration as she hugged the verge. In her wake, thunderous hoofbeats spurred her faster.

Fear and panic ravaged her senses, but Rebecca remained focused as horse and rider soared as one along the course. The trees thinned as she neared a glade, so she dropped the reins, gave the mare her head, leaned forward and clutched the saddle, and the animal charged into the field.

Her heart pounded in her chest, and she thought she might explode at any moment. An image of Dirk, deathly pale with haunting red eyes, appeared before her. It was the same nightmarish visage that Colin had assumed.

"No," she muttered into her sleeve.

Ahead, the path split in two, leading back into the woods, in opposite directions. With a glance at the sky to check her bearing, she noted the sun's position and veered left, hoping the trail led to the main house, where she could raise the alarm. Then, against all rhyme and reason, she took a quick peek behind her.

Six cloaked riders rapidly gained ground.

"Oh, no."

Again, she let go the reins, stretched long, and clung to the roan's neck. They raced through the dense forest, and low-lying branches snagged her hair and habit. Purposefully, she rode in the center of the path, praying the narrow course kept her pursuers at bay. But her prayers went unanswered, as the perilous verdure cleared to reveal a wide expanse, and Rebecca cursed. She had ridden the mare for an hour before the band of villains gave chase, so she was not going to outrun them—not in the open.

To her right, the coppice closed in, offering safe haven. Though there was no visible path, she decided it would be wiser to brave the trees than attempt escape via the meadow.

Grasping the reins, she reared up and steered the mare toward the edge of the forest. Behind her, the ominous hoofbeats grew louder. In a tactical error she would live to regret, she glanced over her shoulder.

The men were on her tail, preparing to overtake her.

A quick check of the sun told her she was headed in the wrong direction, as the estate house was to the north. When she turned her attention to the terrain before her, she spied a grove that presented much needed concealment. The roan had not missed a beat, and she galloped like lightning into the heavy foliage.

It was too late when Rebecca noted the decumbent branch.

At full force, she rode straight into it, slamming it squarely with her chest. Her lungs seized, as she gasped for air, and pain ripped through her muscles. Horse and rider separated, and she landed prostrate, unable to move. The mare disappeared into the brake. Staring at the cerulean sky, she fought unconsciousness.

Six sinister figures loomed over her, their faces shrouded by their hooded cloaks, and she tried but failed to stifle a plaintive cry. The rush of a waterfall filled her ears, starbursts shimmered beneath her heavy eyelids, and all coherent thought collapsed as she plunged into blackness.

WITH A FIERCE ACHE in his head, and another below his belly button, Dirk groaned. Instinctively, he searched the sheets for the warm soft body of his wife, because she usually cuddled close. As he reached with his left arm, pain seared his shoulder, bringing him fully alert, and he opened his eyes.

Dim light cast barely imperceptible shadows about the chamber, as the curtains were drawn. Yet, through a haze of confusion, he inventoried his surroundings. There was the tallboy that once belonged to his father, the long mirror adorned with mother-of-pearl insets, his four-poster, and various appurtenances, all the familiar comforts of home. But those items held pride of place in his suite at Randolph House—in London.

When he sat upright, the room spun out of control, and he slumped in the pillows.

"Easy, Lord Wainsbrough." Dr. Handley perched on the edge of the mattress.

Dirk squinted and rubbed his forehead. "What am I doing here?"

"Recovering," the physician replied. "You were lucky, as the bullet passed clean through your shoulder."

"You gave us quite a scare." Admiral Douglas stood at the foot of the bed. "How do you feel, my boy?"

"Three sheets to the wind." He grimaced. "What happened?"

"Best I can tell, you hit your head in the fall." Dr. Handley held up his hand. "How many fingers do you see?"

"Three." Dirk massaged the back of his neck.

"Follow my movements, your lordship." Dr. Handley traced an imaginary path with a finger. "Excellent. There do not appear to be any lingering deficiencies."

"Will someone please tell me what the devil is going on?" He blinked in a valiant but failed effort to clear the fog.

"Admiral Douglas, I shall take my leave." Dr. Handley gathered his physician's bag. "If his lordship presents additional symptoms, send for me, at once. Otherwise, I will check his condition in the morning."

"Thank you doctor." Admiral Douglas weighed anchor in a bedside chair. "Now, if you can manage, I should like, very much, to know what you recall of your last day at Lyvedon Hall."

"My *last* day?" He cleared his throat. "And where is my wife?"

"Take your time, son."

Something in the admiral's demeanor troubled Dirk, but he was not sure why. On the advice of the man he had come to consider a second father, Dirk closed his eyes and foraged the miasma of his memory for pieces of the reality that defied him. Slowly, a collage took shape from the still forms of his life, until the images assailed him in staccato blasts.

The journey to Lyvedon Hall.

The gunfire no one anticipated.

The terror in Rebecca's expression.

"I indulged my wife in a round of shooting, as she favors the sport. Poulson, my loader, trailed us." Dirk pressed a fist to his mouth and relayed the remaining events, to the best of his recollection. "After I fell from my horse, I lost consciousness, and then I woke here."

"Blake and Damian questioned your man, and your account matches his."

Blood ran cold in his veins, and dread shrouded his heart. With a deep breath, Dirk opened his eyes and met the admiral's stare. "What happened?"

"From what we have gathered, Rebecca thought you gravely injured, and she was still taking fire from an unknown adversary. Your horse bolted, leaving her and Poulson defenseless. To spike their guns, she rode off, which allowed your loader to seek assistance." His brow a mass of furrows, Admiral Douglas sighed. "She saved your life, that wife of yours."

"My viscountess is the bravest woman of my acquaintance." Dirk compressed his lips. "I am fortunate, indeed. But I will have words with her, as she is increasing and should not take unnecessary risks."

Stretching beneath the covers, Dirk yawned. He shifted his weight and resituated a pillow. And then he snapped to attention.

"Admiral, what have you not told me?"

The veteran naval officer frowned. "The mare returned to Lyvedon Hall, later that night."

Dirk swallowed hard. "Only the mare?"

Admiral Douglas dipped his chin.

Had Dirk thought he was in pain?

Drowning in a tidal wave of nausea, he suffocated as agony tore at his chest. With his jaw clenched, he gritted his teeth, sat upright, and steeled himself to pose the question that imprisoned him in his own private hell.

"Where. Is. Rebecca?"

CHAPTER TWENTY

*L*ocked in a stone cell small enough to prevent her standing upright or reclining to full length, Rebecca shivered and drew herself into a corner. The villains had stripped her naked before imprisoning her in the tiny enclosure, but unconsciousness had spared her the humiliation. Now, she huddled amid the stench of damp earth mixed with urine and prayed for the strength to endure.

In the dark, she searched her memory and drew on her training as an agent for the Corps. In the lonely solitude of her confinement, she recalled the various tactics deployed to break captives of war, so her current situation was not entirely unfamiliar. The nudity, the base brutality of her cage, and the meager fare of water and stale bread portended evil. But it was what she could not surmise, the length and hardship of her incarceration, that most frightened her.

How long had she been there? And where was *there*? Judging from the number of meals, Rebecca guessed it had been two days since the attack at Lyvedon. Of course, thoughts of the grand estate conjured images of its owner, her husband. In the blackest hours of her ordeal, when she despaired her perilous predicament, she pictured Dirk, hale and hearty, with the wind in his hair as he barked orders to the crew aboard the *Gawain*. Instinctively, she placed her palm to her belly and smiled. With their babe tucked safe inside her, she was not alone.

Therein lay the heart of her courage, because she knew without doubt that Dirk, no matter the extent of his injuries, would come for her and his heir. Despite the traitor's intent, Rebecca need only survive, so she resolved to persevere.

Although she was not hungry, she ate every scrap and drank every drop. For exercise, she bent her knees and flexed her muscles. Closing her eyes, Rebecca prayed the nightmares plaguing her slumber would not return, because she desperately needed rest. But when she slept, she dreamt.

Running, bare-footed, naked, and so cold, she fled. Hoofbeats thundered, and she glanced back, but nothing gave pursuit. Before her, a dreary forest loomed as a specter of doom, with trees bereft of foliage standing as gnarled sentries. Absent grass, flowers, and ivy, the woods bore no sign of life. Amid dense fog, five shrouded figures emerged, their heads bowed. When four apparitions lifted their chin, she recognized the mournful wraiths and gasped in horror. Their faces the gray pallor of death, and eyes blood red, Dirk, Colin, and her parents stared at her. Then the last hooded phantom revealed a sinister skull, which laughed in a hideous squall.

With a hand to her throat, Rebecca jolted awake and immediately convulsed. Pain tore through her belly, and she seized violently. Curled in a fetal position, she bit the fleshy side of her hand and searched, unseeing, the confines of her stone prison. Inhaling deeply, she willed herself to relax, and her racing heartbeat slowed. Laughing at herself, she realized it had been nothing more than a bad dream.

Until another vicious paroxysm ravaged her gut.

Though she tried to scream, the agony strangled her cry. Gasping for air, she clenched her jaw and dragged herself, inch by excruciating inch, to the door of her cell.

"Help. Someone help me."

A wave of nausea left her heaving hard, and spasm after relentless spasm devastated her. When a rush of fluid oozed between her thighs, Rebecca screamed.

"Oh, God." A particularly piercing torrent seemed to tear her in two. "Help me, *please!*"

Banging her fist on the wooden door, she gritted her teeth against a vile bitterness. Warm wetness streamed her face as she wept, and she pressed a hand to her belly as she retched. Then she lay, wide-eyed, in the darkness.

The wooden door opened.

Unaccustomed to the luminous glow, torchlight scorched her eyes, and ensuing tears blurred her vision, as unknown jailers wrenched her from the cell.

"Who are you?" Rebecca moaned. "What do you want with me?"

The world spun on its end, until she noticed the change in her surroundings. Stretched on a long table, with her arms and legs tied to various corners, and a white sheet spread across her torso, she cried as a wresting cramp had her bucking as an unbroken horse. Trapped somewhere between unendurable consciousness and blissful oblivion, she studied the stranger who tended her.

"Try to relax," he said in a curt voice. "It will go easier for you."

"What is happening?"

"Do not concern yourself." He tossed a bloodstained rag to the floor.

"Am I dying?"

"No."

Rebecca licked her dry lips. "May I have some water?"

The man paused, as if to assess her condition, and then moved out of her field of sight. When he returned, he slipped his arm beneath her head and held a glass to her mouth.

"Not too much, else you will vomit," he warned.

With a nod of assent, she sipped the cool liquid, and it soothed her sore throat. After a few minutes, the pain ebbed, and she floated as if separating from her mortal shell. It was too late when Rebecca realized she had been drugged.

The stranger packed a black physician's bag and bowed, at what she had not known. And then he was gone. She tugged at her restraints but could not loosen them.

"Lady Wainsbrough, welcome to my lair."

A menacing figure, with his identity hidden by a leather executioner's mask, stepped from the shadows.

"Who are you?"

"In Mother England, I am known by a rather unremarkable name." He stood at tableside. "But in the hallowed halls of the Counterintelligence Corps, I am called Denis."

Despite her stupefied state, she trembled in fear of her captor. "What do you want from me?"

"Are we really going to play this game? It is becoming quite tedious." He reached beneath the table, and the rasp of an unhinged latch snared her attention. "Perhaps you require motivation."

All of a sudden, a panel she had not known existed

dropped from the table, and her head fell back, dangling precariously. "Please, I do not know what you seek."

"Wrong answer, my dear." The villain held a large bucket from which he poured a deluge over her face.

Water filled her nose and mouth, which dammed her throat, as she fought to free herself. Struggling to breathe, she jerked from side to side, but straps at her chest and forehead held her firmly in check. Just when she was certain she could take no more, and she would drown, her punisher ceased his torture.

"Now then. Is my lady in a mood to cooperate, or shall we continue our fun?" He hovered near. "Where is the item Colin stole from General Villatte's courier?"

Choking and sputtering, she heaved. "I swear, I do not—"

The torrential flood recommenced, and Rebecca plummeted into a vortex of terror.

"Sɪʀ Ross Logan to see you, my lord." Hughes bowed.

"Come in." Dalton extended a hand in welcome. "Thank you for answering my summons so quickly."

Shielded by an antique Oriental screen, Dirk scrutinized the head of the Corps, as a hastily scripted scene played in his study at Randolph House.

"I was grateful to receive it." Sir Ross greeted Admiral Douglas and Lance and then sat in a high back chair. "News of your brother's demise filled the front page of today's Times. I am more sorry than I can say. But the article made no mention of Rebecca. How fares my lady spy?"

"What do you know of Lord Wainsbrough's death?" Lance lowered his chin and arched a brow.

"Only what I read." Sir Ross adjusted his coat and glanced at Dalton, then Lance, and then Admiral Douglas. "That unknown poachers killed Viscount Wainsbrough in an unfortunate accident. Why do you ask?"

"Sir Ross has not left London," Lance said to Admiral Douglas. "In fact, his routine remains surprisingly predictable, as he supervises an agency that trades in espionage."

"Have I been under surveillance?" The head of the Corps snapped to attention. "Has this something to do with the search for the traitor?"

"We do not know," Admiral Douglas replied. "We thought you might enlighten us."

"Do you still suspect me?" Sir Ross stood. "Where is Rebecca? I would speak with her."

"As to your loyalties, we were unsure, given the elusive nature of our villain, and his uncanny ability to evade us at every turn," Dalton declared with an air of morbid finality. "And my sister-in-law is missing."

That was the pivotal moment for which Dirk had been waiting. He needed to gauge Logan's reaction to Rebecca's disappearance. So, despite the urge to throttle the man, Dirk held his tongue and shifted his weight.

For several minutes, Sir Ross simply gazed at the floor. Then the secret agent conducted himself, as Dirk had not expected. Acting completely out of character, the veteran spy dropped to the chair, slumped forward, rested elbows to knees, and buried his face in his hands.

"Never should I have allowed her to join the Corps, but she would not be dissuaded, so I trained her, myself. And although our ages did not support such a relationship, I considered her a daughter. When she successfully concluded her first mission, I was very proud." He sighed.

"But, to be honest, I was never so relieved as when she resigned her commission."

The spontaneous confession, freely offered, convinced Dirk that his fears regarding Sir Ross were unwarranted, so he carefully strategized his next move.

"Have you any recent developments in your investigation of the turncoat?" Admiral Douglas inquired softly.

"One of significance. I enlisted Lord Somerset's aid, as we served, together, in the Light Dragoons." Sir Ross sat upright, retrieved a missive from his coat pocket, and surrendered it to Admiral Douglas. "He found a connection, although it is remote, to Clarkson. I had thought to send two agents to reconnoiter."

"Cousins?" The admiral passed the correspondence to Lance. "Several times removed, but a relation nonetheless."

"Admiral, at the first sign of trouble, why did you not contact me?" Sir Ross asked, with a pained expression.

"We are contacting you now." Dirk emerged from his hiding place. "But I needed to know I could trust you."

"Hell and the Reaper." Sir Ross leapt from his chair, and his jaw dropped. "You are alive?"

In mere minutes, Dirk relayed the events surrounding the attack at Lyvedon, the true extent of his injuries, the ominous return of the riderless mare, and Rebecca's inexplicable absence.

"Are you certain she has been abducted?" Sir Ross narrowed his stare. "She could be lying about in the woods, incapacitated and in need of medical attention."

"Blake, Damian, and Trevor made a thorough search of the estate," Dalton explained. "There is no sign of her."

"And Poulson insists that more than one person fired upon them." Lance scratched his cheek. "Damn nasty affair."

"We planted the newspaper story to confuse the traitor and buy us the time to act." Admiral Douglas frowned. "But I believe the situation grievous, thus we haven't a second to spare."

"And there is something I have not shared." In silence, Dirk prayed his logic was sound, because he was about to show his cards. "Colin gave Rebecca an item, with the expressed intent that it be delivered to me."

"You said there was nothing." Lightning fast, Sir Ross charged Dirk and grasped fistfuls of his shirt. "What have you concealed? Do you realize you may have secured her death sentence?"

"We kept it from you because Rebecca and I had our suspicions where you were concerned. And it does not meet the traitor's requirements." Dirk winced in pain from his shoulder wound. "Hold hard."

From his desk he retrieved Colin's lone personal effect.

"A necklace?" Sir Ross exclaimed with incredulity. "That is what he gave Rebecca?"

"Now do you understand why we neglected to mention it?"

"Sorry, Wainsbrough. I get your meaning, but I would like to examine it." The head of the Corps fingered the chain and then turned the pendant in his palm. "A shako. Eddington loved the infantry."

"There is a mounting plate on the back, presumably to stabilize the medal." Dirk pointed to the small detail.

"Had Colin never discussed the necklace with you?" Admiral Douglas queried, as he held a candlestick, while Sir Ross produced a leather pouch from his coat pocket. "Could it be a clue or hint to something of importance?"

"No." Dirk compressed his lips. For the umpteenth

time, he wracked his brain, pondering the conceivable significance of the military adornment. "I am at a loss."

With a magnifying glass from his collection of tools, Sir Ross made a thorough inspection of the medallion. "This is interesting."

"What is it?" Dirk peered over Sir Ross's shoulder. "What have you found?"

"Why would a mounting plate require a spring and hinge?" Sir Ross splayed his palm. "Lord Wainsbrough, would you be so kind as to hand me the tweezers?"

"Of course." Suspense wreaked havoc on his nerves, as Dirk retrieved the requested utensil. "Do you honestly believe something is secreted in that miniscule nook?"

"A spy knows no boundaries when it comes to smuggling evidence. I once recovered military battle plans, including a map of the grounds and troop placement, from the hollowed tine of a woman's hair comb." The veteran agent grew deadly silent. "What have we here?"

"Out with it, man."

"Tell us what you see."

"What have you discovered?"

"Patience, gentlemen." Sir Ross stood upright and offered Dirk the magnifying glass. "Have a look for yourself."

"All right." Dirk explored the panel of gold welded to the pendant. "What am I missing?"

"It is the plate that I find rather curious," Sir Ross replied. "At first blush, it appears to be nothing more than what you suspected—a stabilizer for the shako, to keep it from bending."

"And the infinitesimal pin protruding from the corner?"

"That, Lord Wainsbrough, is the question." With his

thumb, Sir Ross held one side of the medal stationary, while he used the pointed end of the tweezers to depress the small, seemingly inconsequential prong at the top left of the plate.

The tiny panel popped open, revealing equally diminutive parchment.

"Sheer genius," Sir Ross whispered.

"What are they?" Dirk raked his fingers through his hair.

"Pray, a moment." Again, Sir Ross employed the magnifying glass, as he carefully collected three dotted squares and set them atop the blotter.

Rife with tension, Dirk shuffled his feet. Finally, frustration got the best of him. "What is it?"

"It cannot be." Sir Ross dissected each individual piece of intelligence and then repeated his perusal. "But it is."

Dirk vented a sigh. "Sir Ross, if you do not—"

"Check for yourself." Sir Ross handed Dirk the magnifying glass. "It is a marvel."

Pausing at each square, Dirk analyzed the script, a haphazard and incoherent gibberish, which meant nothing to him. "Is it fair to assume this is some sort of code?"

"Aye, it is. But not just any code. It is *Le Grand Chiffre*," Sir Ross declared.

"The Grand Cipher?" Dalton asked.

Sir Ross dipped his chin. "Belonging to the man himself —General Bonaparte. It is his personal code, worth an untold fortune, and something for which they would be willing to kill to keep from us."

"How do you know it is Napoleon's code?" Puzzled, Dirk scratched his temple. "It could be a decoy to mislead you."

"The primer in the top right corner of the first parchment is Zeus," Sir Ross explained. "Every general in the French military has a code name, as do we in the Corps.

They assume personas of the Greek gods. For instance, Soult uses Adonis, supposedly because he has a way with women. Bony is Zeus."

"Colin must have stumbled upon a communiqué intended for Bonaparte," Dirk surmised. "He was a master of decryption."

"No small wonder they want it back." Admiral Douglas shook his head. "This could change the war."

Lance frowned. "And they believe Rebecca is in possession of such?"

"So it seems." Sir Ross folded his arms in front of himself. "Which means the threat to her safety is worse than I thought."

"When you searched Clarkson's residence, you uncovered evidence that he was in league with the French," Dalton stated. "Do you suspect Denis is involved in this affair?"

"I think it a sure wager," replied Logan.

"And Denis uses primitive methods—torture," stated Dirk.

"Conjure your most heinous fear, and then double it." Sir Ross nodded once. "That is Denis."

"Gentlemen, we must away." Dirk shuddered as he considered the obvious. In the navy, he had faced death on occasions too numerous to count, including the infamous Battle of Trafalgar. Rebecca's death he could not fathom, at all. "The lives of my wife and child are at stake."

"What is our destination?"

"Our reconnaissance suggests he is at his estate in Hampshire, south of Portsmouth."

"I would caution you, Lord Wainsbrough." Sir Ross adjusted his cravat. "My lead is, at best, a long shot. You must prepare yourself. We could be riding into a dead end."

"I do not care." Dirk clenched his jaw. "I want to leave immediately."

In his haste to reveal the necklace, and the subsequent developments, Dirk realized he had not viewed the missive Sir Ross provided.

"And what of this mysterious relative?" Dirk accepted the note from his brother and scanned the contents. As he read and reread the correspondence, and digested its significance, cold dread settled in his marrow. He stared at Sir Ross. "Bloody hell, she knows him."

The head of the Corps nodded. "And if he is our traitor, he cannot risk discovery."

Dirk swallowed hard. "Should he reveal his identity, he cannot set her free."

"Which means—"

"He must kill her."

CHAPTER TWENTY-ONE

*C*old water splashed her face, and Rebecca came fully alert in an instant. When her vision cleared, she discovered she had again been relocated, and her new quarters were not much of an improvement on the last. With braziers mounted at equal distances on the stone walls, the room was quite large. Antiquated but sturdy racks of wood and iron occupied half the chamber and gave it a decidedly medieval, somewhat barbaric, aura. Pegs embedded in the rock sported a nasty collection of chains and manacles, all manner of confining devices.

Iron restraints suspended from the ceiling shackled her wrists, and her toes barely touched the floor. If she relaxed her feet, her wrists bore the entirety of her weight, and excruciating agony ravaged her arms and shoulders.

Just to her left sat a table bearing a dubious array of bladed and pointed instruments, lethal in their appearance. Though she summoned courage, Rebecca could not stop the tremors investing her body, as memories of the vicious water torture she had suffered at the hands of her captor flooded her consciousness. And once again she prayed for the strength to endure the impending hardship.

The leather-masked executioner approached.

"So glad to see you could join me, Lady Wainsbrough. Must confess you have presented quite a conundrum, as you are the first woman to grace my house of horrors, and you have proven an unexpected delight." Denis stepped into view, clutching an object she could not discern, at first, until he let go the leather thongs and repeatedly slapped the cat o' nine tails to his thigh. "Bigger men have fallen with less inducement, but you remain defiant. I had hoped to spare you the usual, brutal motivation I favor; else I will spoil your pretty face, but there may be no avoiding it. Now, whatever am I to do with you?"

"Please, I am innocent." The drugs having long since worn off, Rebecca girded herself with the staunch belief that her husband would come for her and the babe. She had only to survive. "Colin gave me nothing. Had I anything that met your requirements, you would have it."

"Why am I not convinced?" He chuckled malevolently. "Perhaps because you have told me naught. But I have a bit of enticement that just might suit our purpose."

From the pocket of his leather apron her tormentor produced a newspaper. He unfolded the section and smoothed the wrinkles before holding it for her to read. *The Times* headline snared her attention in an instant.

Viscount Wainsbrough Killed In Tragic Accident

"No," she said through gritted teeth.

"Your husband succumbed to his injuries." Denis tossed the paper to the ground and grabbed her chin, bringing her gaze to his. "You were not hoping for a rescue, were you?"

Speechless, Rebecca's imagination ran riot as she revisited the last day at Lyvedon Hall.

The red riding habit. The rapid gunfire. The blood oozing from Dirk's shoulder. The eerie calm of his expression after he fell from his horse. It was just like Colin.

"No."

"Wrong answer, my dear."

When the crude whip rent the air, she braced for the first strike—and screamed as the leather thongs sliced her flesh.

"What did Colin tell you of the code?"

Rebecca whimpered.

Again he flogged her, and again she wailed.

"Where did he hide it?"

She could only moan in response.

Denis flayed her repeatedly and then stopped.

"Help yourself, my dear." He grabbed a fistful of her hair, wrenched hard, and pressed his lips to the crest of her ear. "Give me what I seek, and you shall have a quick death. Toy with me, and I can promise you a long, arduous end. Would you not rather enjoy a hasty reunion with your husband and child?"

Husband *and child*?

Slowly, his words penetrated the dark recesses of her brain still capable of coherent thought. The cramps. The blood. Now it made sense. All her training, all her experience could not have prepared her for the loss of her babe. Immeasurable grief enveloped her, and incomprehensible pain feasted on her insides. Rebecca blinked and flinched but could not speak.

"At last, the lady stumbles. In our earlier conversations, you were not very forthcoming." Twirling the whip, Denis prowled in a wide circle about her. "I hope for your sake, you are prepared to be more cooperative."

Choking on anguish mixed with fear, Rebecca could not form a response. One by one, with each successive beating, she shed the hopes and dreams that had sustained her, as autumn leaves fall from trees, until nothing remained except desolation and despair. Heedless of the shackles biting her flesh, she collapsed, dangling as a rag doll from the ceiling. Blood trailed her arms as tears streamed her face, and how she sobbed.

She had lost everything.

Her parents, her husband Dirk, her unborn child, and her partner Colin were gone. Yes, she had Lucien, but he had the navy. In that moment, Rebecca broke.

With her stare fixed on the wall, she asked in a small voice, "What do you want to know?"

"That is much better." Still masked, Denis cupped her chin and tilted her head. "Tell me of the code."

"I know not of any code," she responded in an emotionless monotone.

"With whom did Colin work?"

"We worked alone."

"Who is the spy called *L'araignee*?"

Through the misery, the solution to her problem rang clear. Salvation resided in the answer to his question. She need only divulge that secret to ensure her death, whereupon she would reunite with her family. Rebecca licked her lips and swallowed hard. Though her mind screamed defiance, her heart shattered, and she bared her soul.

"I am *L'araignee*."

Aware that she had just sealed her fate, she succumbed to hysterical laughter.

"I am *L'araignee*."

Her body shook with unhinged mirth.

"I am *L'araignee*."

"Lady Wainsbrough fancies herself a spy? A novel concept—absurd but novel. The British Army would never hire a woman to do a man's work." Denis snorted with disgust. "It seems I have pushed you too far, and now you are useless to me." To one of the jailers, he said, "Take her down."

Two accomplices appeared at either side, and Rebecca collapsed.

"So, how does one dispatch a member of the peerage, and a female, at that?" Denis strolled to the table, lifted a thick volume, and flipped through page after page. "Ah, here is a method I have been saving for a special occasion such as this."

Free of her manacles, but re-cuffed with hands behind her back, Rebecca made no attempt to resist. Soon, there would be no more suffering, and she would rest in the arms of her beloved.

"Let me see, I shall require a neck restraint, a foot of heavy chain, and an iron pike. This will be my masterpiece. And, as you are to die, perhaps you would like to know the identity of your captor?" With a demonic cackle, Denis unlaced the hood, drew it from his head, and stood before her. "Lady Wainsbrough, meet your executioner."

Rebecca gazed on the familiar face and screamed.

THE JOURNEY to Portsmouth seemed never-ending, which provided Dirk ample opportunity to assess and reassess the situation. To make haste, he had elected to travel by horseback and change mounts in town. They could not have passed through the wrought-iron gates of the elegant seaside estate fast enough, and he urged his bay into a full gallop, with Sir Ross and the Brethren of the Coast in his wake. Before an impressive baroque doorway, he drew rein, slid from the saddle, and bounded up the entry stairs, where a very proper butler addressed him.

"I am sorry, sir. His lordship is for a ride, as is his routine, and he will return after sunset. You are, of course, welcome to wait. May I show you to the drawing room?"

"From where does he take his view?" asked Sir Ross. "Perhaps we could join him, as his lordship sent for me, and he will be displeased by the delay."

How smoothly the veteran secret agent dissembled, and Dirk was grateful for his assistance, as he could hardly muster rational thought.

"The southern coastline, sir." The butler stared down his nose. "I believe he favors the incoming tide."

"Excellent. And what of Lady Wainsbrough? Is she with his lordship?" inquired the head of the Counterintelligence Corps.

"I beg your pardon, sir?" The butler appeared genuinely surprised. "There is no such person in residence."

"Have you not seen her?" Dirk stepped forward, hands fisted at either side.

With a furrowed brow, the butler said, "The only women in abidance are servants in this household, your lordship."

At the end of his tether, Dirk intended to question the manservant, but Sir Ross stayed him with a telling glance.

"Thank you." Sir Ross nodded once. "You have been most helpful."

On the gravel drive, beyond the watchful gaze of the butler, Sir Ross quarried the men.

"Lord Wainsbrough, I believe Rebecca is here, though I cannot say why."

"The sun is below the yardarm, so we have not much daylight remaining." Dirk raked a hand through his hair. "What do you suggest?"

"Blake and Damian, head east. Lance, Trevor, and Dalton survey the grounds, and check all outbuildings. Dirk and I will ride west." Sir Ross regained his saddle. "Sharply men, we have little time."

With thoughts of his wife and child tucked deep in his heart, Dirk forced himself to focus on the task and heeled the bay's flanks. As they galloped through the fields, Dirk and Sir Ross caught a trail in the meadow, which disappeared into a copse of trees. Charging the verge, they veered left, then right, then left again, until they came to a fork in the path.

"Hold hard." Sir Ross reined in and arched a brow."

"What is it?"

"Shh." The secret agent pressed a finger to his lips. After a few seconds, he glanced at Dirk. "Do you hear that?"

"It is the surf."

"This way." Sir Ross set a blazing pace, until the foliage thinned and then opened to reveal a breathtaking vista.

In the distance, near the cliff's edge, Dirk spotted a lone figure sitting atop a grey stallion. He slowed to a canter and then halted. "Over there."

Sir Ross pulled a spyglass from his coat pocket and leveled it. "It is him."

"Is he alone?"

"Aye."

"What is he doing?"

"Apparently, just as his man claimed." Sir Ross leaned forward in the saddle. "He looks over the ocean."

For some reason Dirk could not fathom, he shuddered, and gooseflesh covered him from head to toe. "There is no sign of Rebecca?"

"No." Sir Ross frowned. "Let us dismount here, as I would take him unaware."

Every muscle tensed and ready to act, Dirk moved in concert with Sir Ross. As he neared his prey, he withdrew a pistol from his waistband, and his cohort slipped one from his coat pocket. A mere ten feet from the villain, Sir Ross stopped Dirk with an upraised hand, just as the stallion shifted and whinnied, and the blackguard turned in the saddle.

"Good evening, Lord Varringdale." Dirk cast him a lethal stare.

"*You*?" Eyes wide as saucers, Varringdale's jaw dropped. "But—you are supposed to be dead. You were hit, and you went down."

"It was a flesh wound. Sorry to disappoint you." Given the shock in the scoundrel's expression, Dirk knew with certainty that he addressed the traitor. "Now, if you do not mind, I have come to collect my wife."

For a moment, the turncoat gazed intermittently at Dirk and Sir Ross. When Varringdale lowered his chin and smiled, the hair stood on end at the nape of Dirk's neck. "I am afraid you are a tad late, as Lady Wainsbrough has departed."

"You set her free?" Not for a second had Dirk trusted the villain. Nothing made sense.

"More or less."

"How did you do it?" Sir Ross asked. "How could you betray your country?"

"Why does anyone do anything?" Varringdale shrugged. "Wealth beyond the dreams of avarice."

"And how much did Colin's head earn you?" Dirk inquired in disgust.

"That was an unfortunate occurrence. You see, he confided in me, and that was not the wisest decision." Lord Varringdale frowned. "After I trained him not to trust a soul."

"But he trusted you," Sir Ross stated flatly.

"More's the pity."

"With whom are you allied?" Legs planted wide, Sir Ross lowered his tone. "Have you partnered Denis?"

"Oh, it is much better than that." Varringdale laughed. "I am Denis. And I have the distinct honor of meeting my end having bested the great Sir Ross Logan."

"You will dance at Beilby's ball for your treachery." The head of the Corps stepped forward and took careful aim.

"I think not." Varringdale licked his lips. "I operated under your nose for years, and you never suspected me. And although I may not have discovered *L'araignee*, I beat you, and that is satisfaction enough."

"You beat no one, Varringdale," Sir Ross sneered. "You had *L'araignee* in your grasp, and you let her slip your grip."

"It cannot be." Varringdale tugged his cravat and studied Sir Ross and then Dirk. "*Her*?"

"Indeed." Sir Ross smiled. "Lady Wainsbrough is the operative known as *L'araignee*."

For a long while, Lord Varringdale simply stared at the ground, tapping a finger to his chin. When he lifted his head, the arrogant expression returned. "You mean Lady Wainsbrough was *L'araignee*."

Thunderous hoofbeats heralded the arrival of Dalton and Trevor. Seizing the opportunity, Varringdale drew a pistol and bore down.

"Watch out!" Dalton shouted the alarm.

Dirk and Sir Ross fired simultaneously. Struck in the chest and the belly, the traitor slumped and then fell from his horse.

Dirk knelt at Varringdale's side and clutched the lapels of his coat. "Where is Rebecca?"

"I win, Lord Wainsbrough." Varringdale choked, as blood trickled from the corner of his mouth. "She was quite the sport, that wife of yours, so difficult to break. Alas, she faltered, as do they all, and I buried her with your heir."

"Filthy, gotch-gutted bastard!" For the first time in his life, the urge to kill seared Dirk's consciousness, and inside him something fractured. Logic and reason, so long the hallmarks of his character, fled in an instant. Driven by rage unlike any he had ever known, he wound his hands about the murderer's neck and squeezed the life from him. The man of two names died with eyes open and an evil grin.

"Brother—no." Dalton grabbed Dirk's shoulder.

"Let him be," Sir Ross said softly. "The wound is mortal."

Gasping for air, and guarding against fast rising nausea, Dirk sat on his heels. "Please, tell me you located Rebecca."

It was a plea of raw desperation, not a question.

"We did not." Dalton glanced at Trevor.

"What is it?" Dirk stood upright. "What did you find?"

"A torture chamber. Never have I seen its equal." Trevor shuffled his feet. "And blood."

Clinging to the last vestiges of hope, and refusing to believe his wife and child were lost, Dirk shook his head. "But that does not—"

"There is one more thing." Dalton hesitated and then held up a mangled, dirty garment. "A lady's riding habit—red, as you described. Thrown in with the refuse."

"Oh, no." Dirk snatched the gown, hugged it to his

chest, and closed his eyes. In his mind, he envisioned Rebecca, smiling and happy, as they charged the fields of Lyvedon. He remembered the brave *L'araignee*, who strapped a dagger to her thigh and sacrificed herself for King and Country, with nary a second thought for her own safety. He revisited the honey lips of the enchanting seductress, who boldly claimed him in the study and later pronounced him the man of her choosing. There were countless memories they had yet to share, so when reality beckoned, the future Dirk had planned with such precision crumbled.

With a deep breath, he threw back his head and roared in soul-stealing agony. As the primitive cry echoed, he filled his lungs and again blared in heartrending misery. Tears welled as he stumbled and then dropped to all fours. Awash with grief, he crawled to the cliff's edge and slumped.

How would he live without Rebecca?

As he stared at the crystal blue waters of the Channel, he bemoaned the beauty. Sea gulls keened in the distance, and a light breeze kissed his damp cheeks. The setting sun cast golden light on the ocean, forming a shimmering mosaic.

But nature's splendor brought him no joy.

On the beach below, the tide receded, depositing bits of driftwood tangled with kelp, along with a curious figure he could not quite distinguish. He dragged his coat sleeve across his face, focused his vision, and froze.

"*Rebecca.*"

CHAPTER TWENTY-TWO

*L*eading his horse down a steep and rocky path at a reckless pace, Dirk never took his gaze off his wife. And although he called to her, Rebecca had not acknowledged his presence. Despite the soft sand, he urged the bay faster, jumping large dunes, until he gained the beach. The rising tide covered her briefly before retreating in preparation to repeat the nocturnal dance, and he prayed he was not too late. At water's edge, he jumped from the saddle and ran to her.

"Rebecca, I am here."

At her head, an iron pike protruded a mere foot above the surface of the sand. Attached to the pike was a wrought iron chain, which connected to a heavy manacle about her neck. As the tide encroached, she remained at anchor and unable to breathe. It was the ultimate ordeal of water torture.

"Oh, love. What did he do to you?"

Slumped on her side, Rebecca lay motionless and naked, with hands bound behind her. Matted hair shrouded her face, and bloody welts contrasted sharply with the milky white skin on her back. While her eyes were open, she made no response. As the tide rushed in, she listed gently, and he hugged her to his chest. When the water rose to her neck, he inhaled a deep breath, pinched her nose, covered her mouth with his, and braced for the deluge. Submerged, Dirk fought the current, until the ocean subsided.

"Bloody everlasting hell." Dalton kicked at the pike. "It will not budge."

"Shoot the chain." Dirk surmised he had seconds to spare. "Quickly, brother."

"I have it." Trevor drew his pistol, aimed, and fired.

The round barely nicked the thick link.

"All together." Sir Ross pulled a weapon from his coat and then paused. "There is no time. Watch out."

The sea stormed the beach with an unholy roar.

"Hell and the Reaper." Dirk gasped for air, held her nose, and set his lips to hers. The torrent assailed him with bits of driftwood, kelp, and all manner of shells dredged from the ocean floor, and he shielded his wife. When the flood ebbed, he cradled Rebecca's head and said, "Aim sharply, men."

"On my mark, take the link closest to the pike." Sir Ross leveled his pistol. "Three, two, one—*fire*."

The combined shot severed the chain, and Dirk swept Rebecca into his arms. When he reached the berm, he sat and nestled her in his lap. Kneeling before him, Dalton shrugged out of his coat and draped it over her shoulders. Trevor produced a knife and cut the twine at her wrists, revealing raw, bloody skin. Sir Ross pressed his fingers to her neck, and Dirk searched his expression.

Swallowing hard, he asked, "Is she—"

"Her pulse is strong." Sir Ross bowed his head. "She lives."

Dirk nuzzled her temple. "Thank God."

After a minute, he checked her condition. With a haunting visage, Rebecca seemed a shadow of her former self. Gone were the fire, the inimitable vitality, and the effervescence with which she greeted every day. Lips once lush and rosy manifested an unnaturally blue hue, and no charming blush colored her cheeks.

"I am here, Becca, my love." Resting his forehead to hers, he warmed her with his body and sighed. "We will survive this, I swear it."

A FORTNIGHT HAD PASSED since Dirk and Rebecca returned to Lyvedon Hall, and while the seasons changed, and the leaves turned, the atmosphere within the great house remained one of somber placidity. In the morning room, he studied his wife as she perched before a window, staring beyond the glass at a world she refused to rejoin. Locked in some imaginary prison, she sat motionless, and her despondence wrenched his heart.

No matter what Dirk tried, he could not free Rebecca from her invisible jail. Though he tempted his wife with her favorite foods, including the peach jam pudding she loved, she consumed only what he fed her by hand. After bathing her as he would a child, he brushed her hair and dressed her. As he resumed what he could of his daily routine, he kept her at his side, often carrying her from room to room or outside to sit in the garden. And yet she remained mute, with a forlorn expression investing her beautiful face.

At night, he often woke to her screams. In the wee

hours, and while all in the house were abed, her bloodcurdling wails left him reeling and shaken. Rocking gently, he hugged her to his chest until she quieted and slept. And though some might question his logic, he moved her belongings into his suite, as he could not rest without her presence. But what truly tore at his gut was the grudging admission that Rebecca was once again his spy with sad eyes, and it was no small surprise given what she had survived.

At Dirk's request, Dr. Handley journeyed from London to give her a thorough examination, and the physician confirmed Dirk's worst fears. Aside from being beaten, starved, and nearly drowned, Rebecca had indeed miscarried their child. Call him a lunatic, but he had clung to some small measure of hope that their babe lived. And yet all was not lost, as the good doctor assured Dirk that Rebecca could have more children, and her current state was merely a temporary response to the shock of her ordeal.

"I beg your pardon, my lord."

Dirk shifted his weight. "What is it, Hughes?"

The butler cast a sympathetic glance at Rebecca and softly said, "Lady Wainsbrough has a caller."

In the hall, Dirk closed the door behind him. "Who is it?"

"Lord Eddington is just arrived from London."

Like bloody hell would he allow Colin's father to rake Rebecca over the coals in her delicate condition. "Where did you put him?"

"In the drawing room, your lordship."

In a matter of seconds, Dirk descended the stone staircase of his ancestral home and in the foyer turned right. At a double-door entry, he paused. With a deep breath, he prepared for another heated confrontation and set wide the oak panels.

Lord Richard Eddington stood, hands clasped behind his back, gazing at the west lawn. As Dirk entered the room, Eddington turned and smiled. "Dirk, how fare you and your wife?"

The informal greeting caught him by surprise and spiked his guns. Dirk stopped in his tracks. "I am in good health."

"And Rebecca, if I may be so bold as to address her as such?"

"Physically, my wife recovers well." Bowing his head, Dirk frowned. "But I fear her spirit is mortally wounded."

"My dear boy, I have spoken with Sir Ross, and he relayed the events surrounding my son's death, as well as your misfortune. I am very sorry." Eddington rested a hand on Dirk's shoulder. "I counted Varringdale a friend and entrusted him with my son's life, much to my regret. And now I have only to be ashamed of my conduct toward your wife."

"You could not have known." Dirk sighed. "And, per orders, I could not reveal the truth. I hope you understand?"

"Of course, I do." The gray-haired gentleman wiped his brow. "Now, how may I help Rebecca?"

"I am not sure you can."

"As a father, I would speak with her. There must be something I can do to ease her suffering."

For a minute, Dirk pondered the offer. Desperate circumstances required desperate measures, and he was a desperate man. "All right, but be gentle with her. She is very fragile. And before I take you in, I must give you something."

Dirk tugged at the gold chain about his neck and then slipped it over his head. In his palm he held the gold pendant that once concealed the infamous code.

"Colin's shako," said Lord Eddington, with a wistful expression. "How he loved the infantry."

"He gave it to Rebecca the night he died." Dirk compressed his lips. "You should have it."

"Thank you, son." Colin's father wiped a stray tear, donned the necklace, and pressed the medallion to his heart. "This means the world to me. Now then, let us see what we can do for your wife."

Together they ascended the stairs, trading inconsequential but light-hearted banter that eased the tension twisting Dirk's insides. At the entrance to the morning room, Dirk paused. "Remember, Rebecca has had a terrible shock."

Lord Eddington nodded. "I understand."

Dirk opened the door and was not surprised to discover his wife remained much as he left her. Eddington crossed the floor, grabbed the back of a chair, and dragged it next to the one Rebecca occupied. After unfastening his coat, he sat. Ever so slowly, he took Rebecca's hand in his and mirrored her pose.

"My Colin adored the country. As a child, he spent hours roaming the meadows, and his mother was forever sending me to fetch him for dinner." Eddington shook his head and chuckled. "Did he tell you of the time he broke his arm in a fall from a large oak? I fretted horribly when he joined the infantry, but he wanted to follow in my footsteps, and I have never been prouder."

With nary a sound, Dirk eased to the *chaise*, pressed a fist to his mouth, and hoped for a miracle.

"All too soon, my good-natured son despaired the useless carnage on the battlefield, and the Corps presented

Colin an irresistible opportunity to make a difference." Lord Eddington stretched his booted feet. "When he informed me of his transfer, I tried to talk him out of it, but he would not be swayed."

With a pang of remorse, Dirk recalled that time and his own efforts to dissuade his friend.

"Now that Colin is gone, I fear I have lost part of myself I shall never recover, but I am so pleased with his achievements." Lord Eddington sniffed and dabbed a tear from his cheek. "And I am equally certain that your tenure with the Counterintelligence Corps does your parents great honor."

In that instant, Rebecca turned and peered at Eddington. Dirk jumped from the *chaise* but quickly checked himself.

"My dear, you cannot continue in this fashion." Lord Eddington cupped her chin. "Your mother and father would not want you to suffer and neither would Colin. My son lived to the fullest, and he would wish you the same."

"I did so love him." Tears welled in her eyes, and Rebecca whimpered. "He was a brother to me."

"I know, darling girl. Ours is a shared sacrifice, given that we have both lost children, and this tragedy binds us for eternity. But we will rally again, you and I." He whisked a wayward tendril from her face. "If I may call on you, from time to time, that we might further our acquaintance. Perhaps, when you feel up to it, you could share stories of your work with my son, as memories are all that remain of him."

"I should like that very much," she whispered. "He was the best of men."

"Praise, indeed." Lord Eddington smiled. "I suppose we shall accustom ourselves to his absence, but not too soon, I hope."

CHAPTER TWENTY-THREE

*I*n her bedchamber, Rebecca lit a candle and tiptoed into her dressing room. Quickly, she pulled on breeches and a lawn shirt. Just as fast, she grasped various items from the wall pegs and bundled them for travel. With her boots in one hand, and the balled clothing in the other, she turned—and shrieked.

Naked, Dirk stood in the doorway. "What are you doing?"

Trembling and ashamed, she dropped the items and retreated, unable to form a response.

He glanced at the floor and then pinned her with a narrow stare. "You are leaving me?"

The pain in his voice struck a lethal wound to her heart, and she desperately wanted to hold him, but she could only bring him misery and death. As Rebecca feared all along, the dark world of espionage presented a very real threat to those she loved, and the cost was no longer one she was willing to pay.

"If you care anything for me, you must let me go."

"Becca, you are not being rational." He reached for her, and she sidestepped him. "Come to bed."

"I cannot stay." Rebecca splayed her arms in supplication. "Can you not see that my presence endangers you?"

"What do you mean?" Dirk furrowed his brow. "Varringdale is dead."

"There could be others." Would that it were that easy. "I spied these five years."

"Let them come." He tightened his fists. "We will face them—together."

"No." She lifted her chin a fraction and vowed to be strong, even if it killed her. And it might. "I will not jeopardize your life, at least, no more than I have already. Is it not bad enough that I killed our child?"

"You killed no one, sweetheart." Dirk backed her into a corner. "It was not your fault. The responsibility lies solely with Lord Varringdale."

"The responsibility is mine." Rebecca pressed a palm to her chest and hugged the wall. "I never should have married you. What was I thinking? We cannot escape *L'araignee* or her enemies."

"Actually, we can." Planting a hand at either side of her head, he leaned close and softly said, "After Varringdale's demise, Sir Ross circulated a rumor in the halls of the Ministry of Defense that *L'araignee* died in the line duty while capturing the traitor. You are a hero."

"A hero?" She vented a snort of sarcasm. "I am a fool. I should have resigned the Corps before we married. If I had, perhaps Varringdale would not have come for me, and our child would still be alive."

"Darling, you are weaving unsustainable conclusions from whole cloth." He rubbed the back of his neck. "Varringdale was convinced you were in possession of

Napoleon's code, and he knew not of your alter ego. He would have come at you regardless."

"Then you must know I have to go." Tears welled, and Rebecca wrapped her arms about herself. "Else others will come for me."

"You do not know that," he argued.

"But what if someone does?" She closed her eyes and shook her head. Oh, why would her no-nonsense captain make no sense? "We cannot ignore the risk."

"So this is your answer—to run away? What of us? What of our vows? Till death do us part, do you not remember?" Dirk pulled her to him, crushing her to his muscular frame. "I will never let you go, Becca. I will hunt you to the ends of the earth if you leave me."

"Why can you not be logical about this?" she muttered.

"I have been logical all my life." Cradling her head beneath his chin, he rested his cheek to her hair. "My relationship with you defies reason, and I would have it no other way."

"You cannot stop me. I am determined." Though Rebecca was not, in truth. But if she could raise his ire, he might relinquish his rights. "Perhaps, while you are at sea, I shall flee."

"Then I will be hot on your tail." Dirk squeezed her bottom and chuckled. "And what a lovely tail you have, my lady."

His gentle teasing had done much to soothe her frazzled nerves, and she relaxed, as she realized resistance was futile. "You could marry again and build the family you have always wanted, safe in the knowledge they would not be hunted by some fiend seeking *L'araignee*."

"Let the whole damn French Army march on us. We will face the future, as husband and wife." Dirk remained firm and at the ready, despite her protests. "And should you choose to continue your work with the Corps, then so be it. If must needs, we can resurrect *L'araignee*. I will not stand in your way. I know it sounds crazy, but we will make it work, somehow. Whatever happens, we can survive —together."

Rebecca could not believe her ears. "You would do that for me?"

"I never thought I would say that or feel as I do now. When we first married, my main priority was to end your career, but I was wrong, Becca."

The man was a veritable saint and her savior. "How so?"

"My dear wife and *L'araignee*, the courageous secret agent, exist as two sides of the same coin." Dirk sighed. "I should not have insisted you forsake what was so much a part of your identity, an extension of yourself. That facet of you, the spy, is as relevant as our marriage. Knowing, understanding, and accepting that, do you really think I will allow you to simply walk out of our home—out of my life? I love you, Becca—all of you, my brave wife, and my lady, the spy. You are my world. I could never let you go."

That was it.

No embellishments.

No flowery language.

It was a no-nonsense declaration from a no-nonsense man.

If she wanted to put the past behind her, she had to make peace with the truth. And more importantly, she had to deal with her husband.

When she married Dirk, she had thought it possible to shed the sullied skin of a spy, like a soiled gown, and live as a conventional woman. She had dressed as a lady, acted as a lady, and spoke as a lady. But deep in her heart, where she was always honest with herself, the specter of doom loomed large.

At question was how much control over her life she would yield an imaginary adversary?

On life's center stage, sacrifice seemed an obvious solution—at least, until that moment. Running away, relinquishing the lead part of Lady Wainsbrough, and her subroles of wife, mother, sister, lover, and friend, was too easy. Assuredly the most painful option, it was, in the end, also the most cowardly.

Making it work—that was the challenge and the courageous choice. Given Dirk's declaration, she could not deny the future he laid at her feet. But she had to battle her demons, as had her husband. "I would have you know the whole of my captivity. And if you still want me, I will stay."

"Say what you will," he said without hesitation. "My feelings remain unchanged."

Slowly, she shrugged from his clutch, shed the fine lawn shirt, and then wiggled out of the breeches. Embracing her husband, skin to skin, she rested her head to his chest and found calming reassurance in his steady heartbeat. She had to lay herself bare, had to share her inner self, and have him accept her—all of her.

"It began while I slept. At first, there was immeasurable pain. As I had never been pregnant, I did not understand the significance. No one told me anything—until later. I would have endured countless lashings rather than lose our babe."

"I know, darling."

Rebecca shivered, and Dirk drew her closer still. "He asked of *L'araignee*, and I told him the truth." She sniffed. "He did not believe me. Is that not comical? He thought me insane."

When Dirk lifted her chin, bringing her gaze to his, she discovered his tears matched hers. In their shared sorrow, she fortified herself.

"As a harnessed mare Varringdale led me to the beach, and I neither protested nor fought. When he bolted the chain to my neck, and the other end to the pike, I welcomed my fate. As far as I knew, you and our baby were gone, and I wanted to die, too. Each successive wave brought me closer to you. If we could not be together in life, I had hoped we would reunite in the hereafter. So, you see, my lord, I am not brave, because I surrendered. I am a coward."

"Oh, my sweet girl." Dirk framed her cheeks and rubbed his nose to hers. "You are no coward, as it is not in your nature. Faced with similar circumstances, I would have done the same."

With no more to say, Rebecca buried her face to his chest and sobbed unashamedly.

She wept for her parents, who she never really knew. She wept for Colin, who would never marry and have a family of his own. She wept for their child, who never tasted the beauty of love or life without war. She bawled until her body shook, pouring forth enough misery for two lifetimes, and still she cried.

As the waters that nearly took her life, grief swelled, overtook, and consumed her. And like the tide that washes footprints from the sand, leaving behind a pristine surface, unmarred till trod upon anew, so the tears erased her pain and cleansed her soul.

$\sim$

DIRK SAT BEHIND HIS DESK, pouring over various ledgers and account books. Having long ago doffed his coat and cravat, he unfastened the hook at his throat and speared his fingers through his hair. In the hall, the long case clock signaled the hour, and birds beyond the windows serenaded him with a playful singsong. A faint click presented the first hint that someone had invaded his domain. When he glanced up, his jaw dropped.

Barefooted, wearing his favorite robe and a glowing smile, and no doubt little else, his wife stood before him. "Good afternoon, my lord."

The sultry voice that never failed to rouse his heartbeat, as well as a particularly potent six inches of his anatomy, had made a stunning and most unexpected return. "Becca, why are you not still abed? You need rest."

"I need you," quick as a wink, she replied.

"Where are your slippers?" Ignoring the stout salute from his mainmast, he managed to frown. "You will catch cold."

"Not if you keep me warm." Prowling, as a jungle cat, she favored him with a flirty pout. "Will you not warm me, my oh-so-resourceful Captain?"

His mouth watered. "And what of the servants? You cannot parade about the house in that state of undress."

"Do tell." She giggled, and how he had missed that charming sound. "I ran into Hughes in the hallway. Daresay the poor man is red as a tomato, and I fear the condition may be permanent."

"Rebecca, what are you about?" They had not made love since their first journey to Lyvedon, prior to the attack, and he had not wanted to rush her, given her fragile state. But he was near to exploding.

"I needed to speak with him, as I had a matter of utmost urgency and required his assistance," she said, with an air of whimsy.

"That is not what I mean, and you know it." He blinked. "Wait a minute. What is wrong?"

"Nothing is wrong." She sidled between him and the desk, canted her head, and cast him a heated stare he swore he felt in his toes. "I asked that Hughes have the cushioned two-seater bench brought from London."

All right, he was going to be hard until Christmas. Marshaling his wits, Dirk held tight to his reins, else he might unintentionally hurt his wife, and he would rather cut off his arm. But when Rebecca pressed her palms to his chest and splayed her fingers, he thought he might swoon.

"Would you not prefer to return to your chamber and—"

"I would prefer to stay here, with you." She skimmed his belly with questing hands and then moved lower, to caress his Jolly Roger, which was overly jolly and only too happy to cooperate. "My aggrieved husband, I have not performed my wifely duty by you, and I would rectify said deficiency, posthaste."

Lest he plunder Rebecca, Dirk gazed at the ceiling and sought refuge in an old standby, mentally replaying the words to "God Save the King." He licked his lips. "It is not your fault. You have been indisposed."

"Perhaps." She unhooked his breeches as she nipped his chin. "But not so, anymore."

"Becca, it has been some time, and I would be gentle—"

"And I would be rough." She touched him where he wanted it most, just as he grasped her wrist. "Do not be afraid, my love. I will not break."

Resting his forehead to hers, he sighed. "Here?"

"Now." She unbelted the robe, shimmied, and it dropped to the floor.

With a wide sweep of his arm, Dirk sent the ledger and various items flying in all directions. He grasped his wife at her waist and set her atop the blotter. Wrapping her legs about his flanks, she reclined. Moving swift and sure, he speared her and thrust once, and then twice, before violent spasms shook him to the core.

"Did you just—"

"Bloody everlasting hell." Cursed with a humiliating blush, Dirk buried his face in the elegant curve of her neck. "That has not occurred since I was a randy lad at Eton and had just discovered new use for a bar of soap and a wash rag. I am sorry, but I lost control."

"Darling Dirk, that is the sweetest compliment you have ever paid me." She giggled, and he groaned. "And we can always try again. Practice makes perfect, you know."

He lifted his head and grinned. "I missed you."

She arched a brow. "So I gather."

For a minute, they simply stared at each other. And then they burst into laughter. When he shifted his hips, she gasped and bit her lip.

"My lusty lord, it appears you are still primed for battle."

"So it seems." Dirk peered at the point of their joining. "Cannot recall that ever happening."

"Praise, indeed." With eyes glittering, Rebecca heeled his bottom. "Shall we commence the dance?"

As he gazed on his bride, he caught his breath. For as long he lived, he would never forget her inimitable effervescence, as his Becca was radiant with happiness. The unanticipated but prayed for return of her ebullient spirit worked on him in ways he could not have imagined and brought him well nigh to tears. Unable to resist her lure, not that he ever could, Dirk framed her face and kissed her with tenderness he had not known he possessed.

Moving over her, on her, and within her, he invested every endearment with a single refrain: *I love you.*

"Dirk?"

"Mmm hmm?"

"The things we discussed, our plans for the future—I want it all."

"Everything I have is yours."

"And if I only want you?"

"That goes without saying." Hugging her close, Dirk lifted his wife from the desk, stepped in reverse, and sat in his chair. As Rebecca resituated herself and grabbed the reins, taking his flesh deep within hers, he rested his head to the cushioned back. Then the shot fired, and she boldly charged the field. His last coherent thought before ecstasy claimed him was that, indeed, the spy with *sad* eyes was no more.

EPILOGUE

Seven months later, Rebecca stood on the docks at Deptford, awaiting Dirk's arrival from a six-week mission. Winter had long since yielded to spring, as birds chirped and flowers bloomed on that cool May morning. Huddled with Caroline, and bouncing with excitement, Rebecca craned her neck in search of the *Gawain*.

"So how do you intend to share the happy news?" inquired Trevor's wife.

"I have not given it thought." She shrugged. "I suppose the opportunity will present itself, and I will out with it."

"You must be joking." Caroline elbowed her ever so gently. "It is momentous, and such glad tidings require a suitable ceremony."

"Perhaps I will tell him at dinner." Rebecca tapped a finger to her chin and considered the possibility. "Cook prepares Dirk's favorite dish. No doubt he will toast the future addition to our family with his preferred brandy and a cigar."

"Is that all?" Caroline appeared horrified. "How can you be so calm?"

In truth, Rebecca was anything but calm. Ever since her miscarriage, and her husband rescued her from Varringdale's death trap, they had been desperately trying to conceive, and it was nice work. But with each passing day, her hopes waned, until the morning malaise set in with a vengeance. "Well, I am not sure Dirk will be surprised."

"May I impart a secret?"

"Of course."

"Upon Dr. Handley's confirmation, I orchestrated a lovely affair, but I could not wait, and I revealed my pregnancy in the carriage, on our way home." Caroline peered from left to right and then leaned close. "And Trevor wept."

"No." Rebecca was positive Dirk would never be so emotional.

Her eyes widened. "Oh, yes."

"Well, my no-nonsense captain is not given to dramatics."

"How can you be certain?" Caroline arched a brow.

"Remember, I married Dirk."

Caroline whistled in monotone. "Yes, you did."

"Might I ask a question?" She bit her lip.

"Indeed." Caroline nodded once.

"What was he like as a child?"

Trevor's wife gurgled. "Shorter."

Rebecca glanced at Caroline, and together they laughed.

"Men are such silly creatures—"

"There they are!" Caroline pointed to the silhouettes in the distance. "Soon we shall be in the arms of our beloved."

The *Hera* sailed into the harbor, and in her wake glided the *Gawain*. How Rebecca had begged Dirk to take her with him on his mission, but he steadfastly refused, arguing that he could not focus clearly on the task with his bride within reach, thus jeopardizing the safety of everyone aboard his ship. She had shed a river of tears, but he had not been swayed, promising that their reunion, after so many weeks apart, would be all the more sweet.

"By the by, how fares your belly?" Caroline asked with a sympathetic expression.

"Much better, thank you." Trembling with anticipation, she shuffled her feet. "The chamomile tea worked wonders."

"I have an extra tin, should you have need of it." Caroline perched on tiptoes. "And I found the burgundy cloak. It will see you through the birth."

"Are you sure you would part with it—the cloak, I mean? And I could use the tea, as my order has not yet arrived."

"My dear sister, I have a wardrobe filled with clothes, and the color will bring out your brown eyes." Caroline clucked her tongue and patted Rebecca's arm. "I will send it with the tea, posthaste."

"Thank you for everything." She smiled. "I do not know what I would have done without you these past weeks."

The decks of the *Gawain* were alive with the activity one would expect of a ship coming into port. At the helm, Dirk bellowed various assignments, and men danced amid the rigging.

"You are always welcome." Caroline clasped Rebecca's hand and squeezed. "So you still intend to wait until dinner?"

"Yes." The *Gawain* eased to its berth, and Rebecca wanted to prance a merry jig. "We dine alone tonight, so it will be a private affair."

Sailors tossed lines to dockworkers, and the anchor plunged into the water with a mighty splash. As soon as the gangplank hit the deck, Rebecca bolted. At the waist, she veered left and flew up the companion ladder.

Mr. Scott, the first mate, dipped his chin. "Captain, you have a visitor."

Dirk turned and caught her, midair. "Hello, beautiful. I was going to—"

Right there, in front of the crew, Rebecca kissed her husband with all she had and for all she was worth.

"Clear the deck, lads," said Mr. Scott.

When her husband lifted his head and grinned, she was breathless. And though he tried to look stern, he did not fool her for a minute. "My lovely wife, what are you about?"

"I am sorry, but I just had to see you. Ever since Dr. Handley—"

"What is it?" He set her on her feet and gave her a quick inspection. "What is wrong? Are you injured?"

"I am fine." Rebecca could only giggle. "In fact, I am better than fine. I am pregnant."

In a move Rebecca would never forget, her no-nonsense captain had done something completely out of character. With mouth agape and tears welling, Dirk dropped to his knees before her and pressed his face to her belly.

"Oh, no." She speared her fingers through his hair. "Darling Dirk, do not cry. This is joyous news."

All of a sudden, Dirk stood upright and whisked her into his arms. Whirling in circles, he gazed into her eyes. "My lady wife, this is bloody splendid news."

Together, they laughed in a remarkably lighthearted exultation hard won. And then he stopped and kissed her-- and kept kissing her, until catcalls and hoots brought them up short. Dirk carried her to the railing, rested his forehead to hers, and sighed in an achingly sweet sign of unutterable contentment.

"Mr. Scott, an extra boon for every man."

"Aye, sir," replied the first mate. "You hear that lads?"

A cheer erupted on the waist.

"And what would be the occasion, Cap'n?" asked Mr. Scott.

Slowly, Dirk smiled, nipped her nose, and then he addressed his crew.

"I am to be a father!"

ABOUT BARBARA DEVLIN

A proud Latina, USA Today bestselling author Barbara Devlin was born a storyteller, but it was a weeklong vacation to Bethany Beach, Delaware that forever changed her life. The little house her parents rented had a collection of books by Kathleen Woodiwiss, which exposed Barbara to the world of romance, and *Shanna* remains a personal favorite.

Barbara writes heartfelt historical romances that feature not so perfect heroes who may know how to seduce a woman but know nothing of marriage. And she prefers feisty but smart heroines who sometimes save the hero before they find their happily ever after.

Barbara is a disabled-in-the-line-of-duty retired police officer, and she earned an MA in English and continued a course of study for a Doctorate in Literature and Rhetoric. She happily considered herself an exceedingly eccentric English professor, until success in Indie publishing lured her into writing, full-time, featuring her fictional knighthood, the Brethren of the Coast.

Connect with Barbara Devlin at BarbaraDevlin.com, where you can sign up for her newsletter, The Knightly News.

ALSO BY BARBARA DEVLIN

BRETHREN OF THE COAST

Loving Lieutenant Douglas

Enter the Brethren

My Lady, the Spy

The Most Unlikely Lady

One-Knight Stand

Captain of Her Heart

The Lucky One

Love with an Improper Stranger

To Catch a Fallen Spy

Hold Me, Thrill Me, Kiss Me

The Duke Wears Nada

A Very Brethren Christmas

Owner of a Lonely Heart

BRETHREN ORIGINS

Arucard

Demetrius

Aristide

Morgan

Geoffrey

PIRATES OF THE COAST

The Black Morass

The Iron Corsair

The Buccaneer

The Stablemaster's Daughter

The Marooner

Once Upon a Christmas Knight

The Reaper

WORLD OF DE WOLFE PACK

Lone Wolfe

The Big Bad De Wolfe

Tall, Dark & De Wolfe

MAGICK TRILOGY

Magick, Straight Up

A Taste of Magick

Magick in the Air

PIRATES OF BRITANNIA

The Blood Reaver

THE MAD MATCHMAKING MEN OF WATERLOO

The Accidental Duke

The Accidental Groom